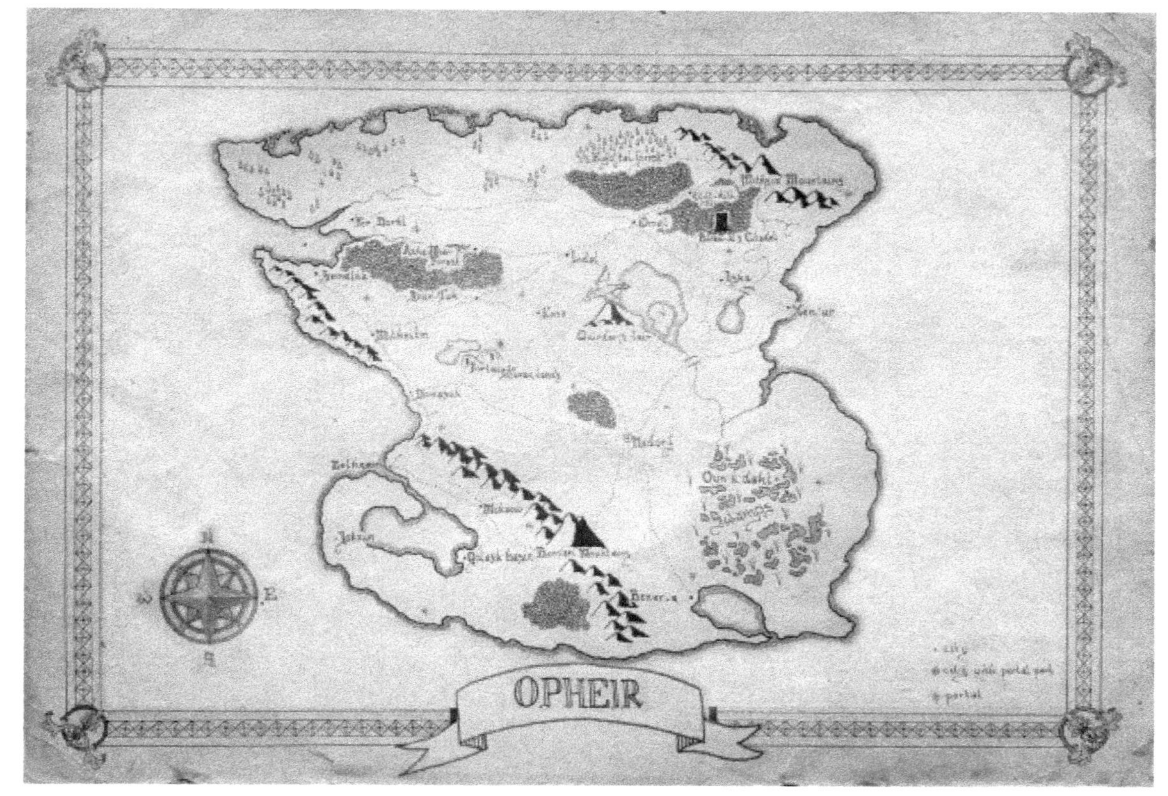

1

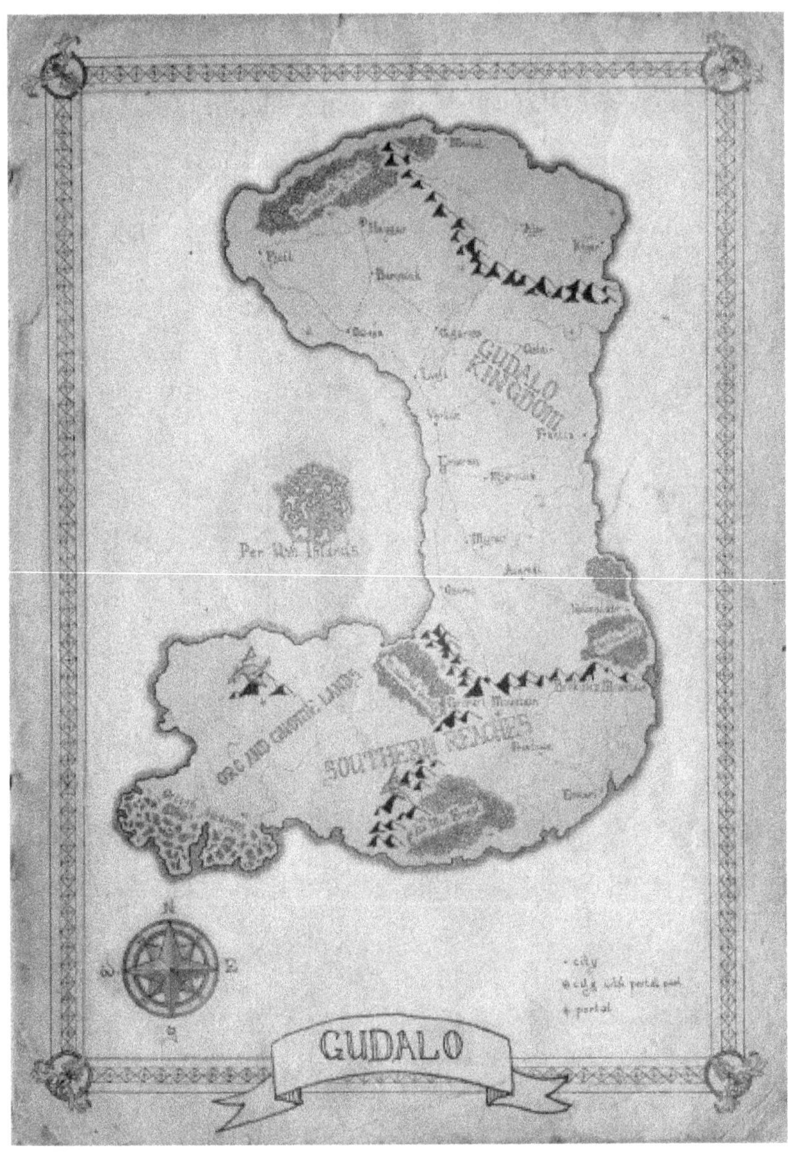
GUDALO KINGDOM
Per Noi Islands
ORC AND GNOLL LANDS
SOUTHERN REACHES
N
E
S
W
city
city with portal node
portal
GUDALO

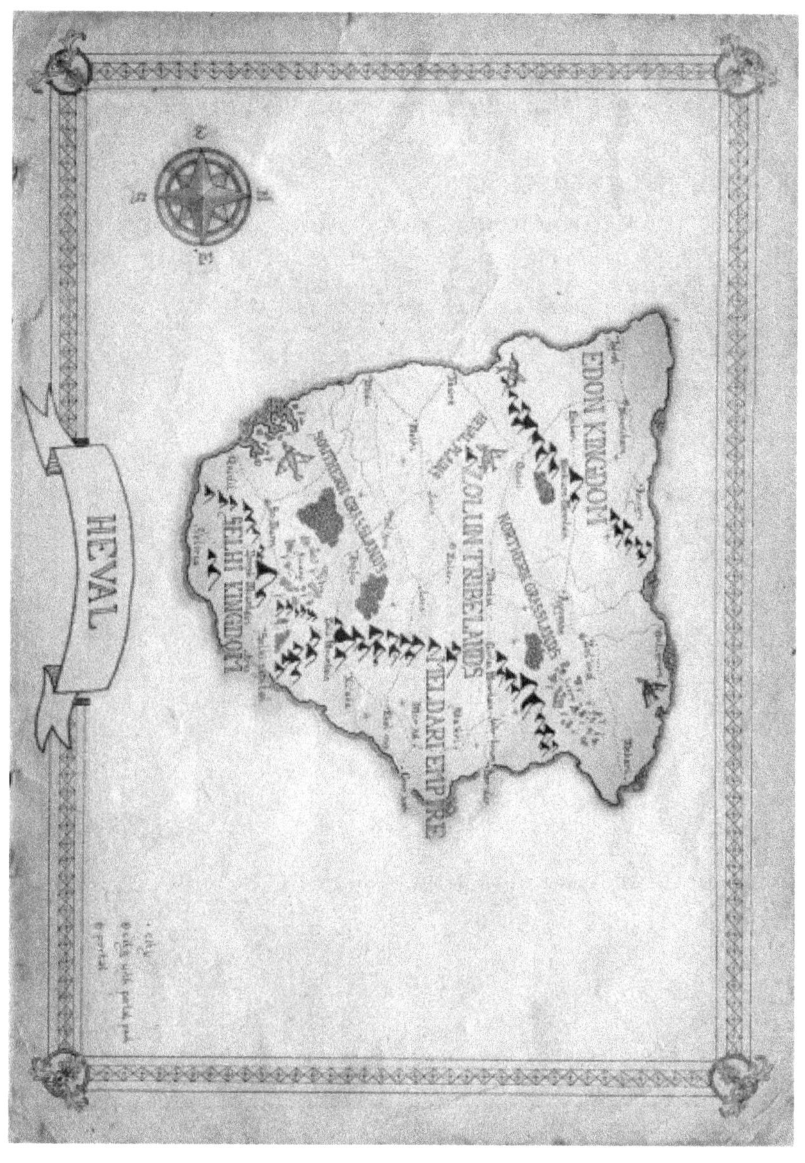

HEVAL
EDON KINGDOM
OLIN TRIBELANDS
NELDARI EMPIRE
ELHI KINGDOM

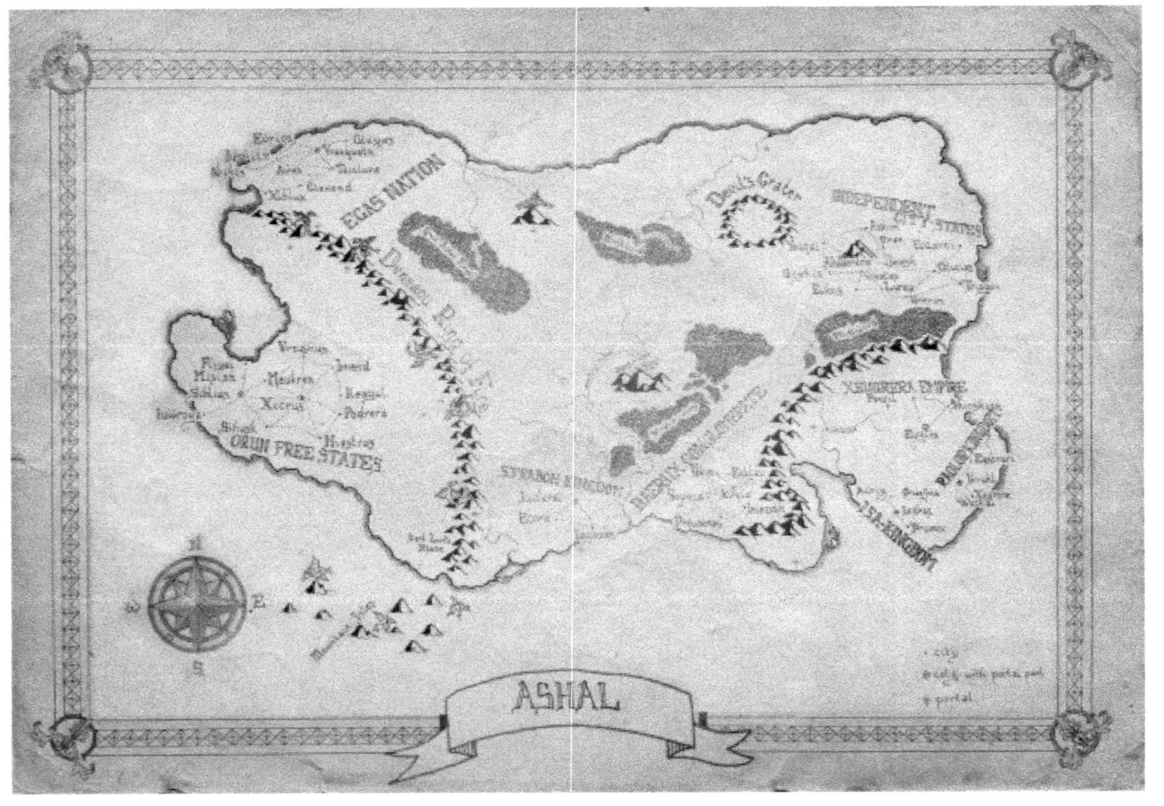
ASHAL
EGAS NATION
OKUN FREE STATES
INDEPENDENT CITY STATES
Devil's Crater
NEUGREIRA EMPIRE
STRABOR KINGDOM
PHOENIX CONFEDERATE

Want a bigger map of Emerilia and the continents? Check out
http://theeternalwriter.deviantart.com/
Character Sheet is located in the back of the book for reference.

Emerilia

For The Guild

Chapter 1: Inner Turmoil

All eyes were on the massive twenty-meter-thick beam that was being forced into the sky. Spell formations spread out over the entire Xelur citadel, redirecting the energy from expanding outward and killing everyone, and pushing it toward the heavens.

Multiple layers of spell formations contained and directed that rampaging magical energy. As some started to falter, other magical runes took over.

The sky of the Densaou Ring of Fire, normally dark from the ash and the volcano's discharge, now had a pillar of pure soul energy rushing up above the citadel, past the three flying citadels, through the heavens and tearing those clouds apart.

The ripples of energy made the clouds open, revealing the sky above as the energy stream finally lost energy and started to dissipate across the sky.

The ground below was bathed in harsh light that came from that massive pillar.

Esa's heart shook at the sight of that power. The very air screamed with the pillar's rise.

Just as the spell formations started to weaken, again a stronger force took over. Trails of air circled the pillar and created a spiral. These air streams were made from magical runes rising up to encircle the pillar of light. The spell formations around it became more solid, rotating slightly as they forced the energy up and away. The air currents solidified, a spiral encompassing the pillar of soul energy.

Esa's eyes moved to the kill log. Steve's name appeared, then Jekoni's.

She felt as if the world had stopped. Steve could come back as long as he'd backed himself up. Jekoni, however, was a spiritual imprint on Jung Lee's sword. If that imprint was destroyed, then there would be no way to recover him.

The last of the energy pillar was hurled upward. The world seemed to become dark as Esa's eyes adjusted to the new landscape in front of her.

Sunlight poured in from above through the hole in the clouds while ash that had covered the sky rained down.

None of the artillery cannons fired; none of the attack spells were released. The battle had stopped, all in a state of shock.

Esa's breath stopped in her chest. Her heart beat heavily as a new name was added to the kill log.

Anna Killed by Soul Energy Bomb.

Esa looked to the western citadel. The landscape showed signs of the heavy fighting over the last few months. The walls were broken and the castle was in pieces. Bodies lay across that desolate wasteland.

Pain turned to anger and hot tears that silently fell down Esa's face.

She didn't blame the Xelur. She hated them, but she didn't blame them for this. All of this—the fighting, the event, the portals opening, all of the death and destruction, the struggle for power and the twisted minds of those within Emerilia and the other aggressive species—all of it was all just a show to watch, a way to pass the time for the Jukal Empire.

They think of us as sport, of nothing more than an interesting side show. Esa's anger built hotter and hotter as she gritted her teeth and tightened her fists. *Fuck them and their empire!* Pain lanced through Esa as the faces of her friends she had lost flashed behind her eyes, people of Emerilia who had died for their families, to defend their homes. Those who had lived in oppression under the Jukal their entire lives, not knowing the truth. She thought of the players who had died in previous generations.

Their deaths, their dreams and hopes—all of them had been cut off by the empire.

I will not stop—not now, not ever—until the Jukal Empire falls. I swear it.

"Give the Xelur terms for surrender. If they don't take it, destroy them," Esa said over the commander's party chat.

***

Bob sat down heavily in a chair, his face slack and pale as if he had received a killing blow and was waiting for the end. In front of him, a screen floated.

Lady Air took a sharp intake of breath as she saw what was on the screen.

It showed a video loop of Anna stepping forward into a beam of soul energy. Around her, thick streams of runes that seemed to create air currents came from her body, swirling around her before expanding and wrapping around the pillar of light. Anna touched a necklace around her neck, a sad smile on her face. Power surged around her, as the rune-filled streams clamped onto the pillar of soul energy and constricted it, forcing it upward, not allowing any of it to escape and shoot outward.

Party Zero were all screaming out, but their words couldn't be heard.

Dave rose to his feet again and again, exerting any power he could to try to contain the beam, but he was clearly drained and pushing out much more energy than he could control.

Deia created a Mana barrier around Anna and Jekoni, pouring out her power and the power of her armor. Suzy, Malsour, Induca, and Jung Lee also poured their power into the spell formation.

Dave nearly bit off his finger writing out runes on the spell formation, pouring power from himself and the armor through to the Mana barrier.

Lox and Gurren left their armor, placing their hands down and pouring in any power they had.

All of them forced out every part of energy they had, the Mana barriers fighting against the soul energy.

Steve's body was being destroyed but still it stood there, runic lines on it assisting on shifting that tremendous power upward.

Jekoni's body shuddered. Even with the Mana barrier, the power of that soul energy even being close to his spiritual body was wearing him down faster and faster. His body started to become more and more faint before it was torn apart.

Anna's control over her restricting air currents became stronger as she was the only one left, besides Steve's body, directing that energy. She closed her eyes, gritting her teeth against that pain. All of that soul energy, even if it wasn't hitting her directly, still filled the air.

The Mana barrier shook and shivered. The rest of Party Zero were covered in sweat. The barrier could no longer hold up as power rushed back at Party Zero, sending them flying and receiving all manner of wounds. Smoke drifted up from them.

Anna yelled out as the power started to hammer against her Abscondita armor's Mana barrier. Still, she never lost control as her Mana barrier was worn away. Soul energy rushed through her body, making her cry out. It was not merely physical but took a toll on her mind and her own soul. It ripped and tore at her, causing great pain.

The pillar gradually came to a halt before the last of the energy shot off into the sky.

Anna stood there for a moment, looking at peace. A breeze came through the citadel. Like a statue of sand, Anna's body was reduced to dust. Her sword fell to the ground, sticking into it as the necklace she had been holding fell next to it.

"The backups!" Bob yelled out. Light filled his eyes as he disappeared from the laboratory in a teleportation spell.

Air looked blankly at where he had been sitting.

"Air, we're about to wake this one up," Venfik said, reading through her thoughts and her want to follow Bob to help and console him.

Air paused. All of the people in the room looked at her, not knowing what had happened to Bob or why he had left so quickly when he'd just finished one of the first stages to getting the players of Emerilia out of their simulation and gain their freedom.

"Very well. Shall we set up the conference room?" Air asked.

"Yes, Lady Air. Everything is ready for you." Venfik nodded.

"Good, then let's go talk to our first customer," Air said.

***

All of the Jakan commanders were looking to Fire with respect and awe on their faces. Water opened a book and started to read and make notes. He'd been pulled from the ice planet within the Nal system for this meeting in hopes that the Jakan would come to Emerilia's side and help to fight off the other invading races as well as the people within the event of Myths and Legends.

"We will need a bit of time to think over this," the Jakan commander said in a respectful tone, looking to the other commanders around the table, who nodded in agreement.

Fire was about to talk again when Josh's voice came over a private party chat. "Dozens of Light's legions have appeared in the sky over Emerilia. The angel generals are being dispatched across the planet to gather them together. We have reports of them converging on Markolm."

Fire and Water looked to each other. The shock in their eyes fell away to reveal a chilling gleam.

The longer Light had her angels near her, the stronger they could become.

Right now, they were too wrapped up in fighting off those coming from the portals, as well as the event's creatures and people. Emerilia was in a state of chaos and there was little that they could do.

"What's the plan?" Fire asked.

"All flying citadel groups are to move between all of the known portal locations and the ones that we can pick up with our sensing spells. They'll leave an Ono at each location as well as a shielding soul gem construct that will encompass the portal not allowing anything to enter or exit without our say so. We need to get this invasion contained before the Jukal have time to use it to their advantage.

"Any portal that still has fighting occurring around it, will be beaten into submission. We don't have time to mess around anymore.

"At the locations we've already gained victories and there are citadels around their location we're going to move engineers and mages in to start converting them into flying Citadels. Pandora's Initiative think that they can get another two groups of flying citadels operational in no more than six weeks. Suzy and Florence are currently dumping money through the Earth simulation to gain resources in Emerilia until the AI's fail. Then we'll only be able to rely on the resources that we can mine."

Water nodded silently. Clearly the fight had reached a new level; now was not the time to hold back anything.

Chapter 2: Loss and Purpose

Party Zero let out hisses and groans of pain as they rose from the ground to look at the melted shell that had been the citadel's castle.

With one of the stronger blasts, Induca's Mana barrier had failed. She and Malsour were thrown into the walls around the central castle; those of Party Zero who had been able to escape had crashed with them.

The castle had been destroyed. The ground where the soul array had been was now a crater with a soul energy fog dissipating around it. Anna's sword and half melted necklace lay next to each other.

Jekoni's body had been destroyed completely. There was not even a hint of his remains.

Steve's body was nothing but a few melted soul gem fragments and his axe. It, too, was smoking but it didn't seem to have any lasting damage.

Dave's armor was left, as was Suzy's, but there was no sign of them.

No one said anything as they looked upon the crater, all of them feeling different emotions.

"Suzy! Suzy!" Induca yelled in a panic, opening up a private channel to Suzy as Deia did the same to Dave, both of them calling out to their loved ones.

"Anna?" Dave's voice came through the private channel.

Deia fell to the ground, crying. Her tears were a catalyst for the others as their emotions got to them—some crying, some with blank faces, shock, anger, sadness.

Dave went silent on the other end, hearing Deia's relief. Even as she knew he was okay, it couldn't dull the pain of knowing Jekoni and Anna were unable to return.

The sounds of fighting were dying down outside, but Party Zero didn't react, their bodies and souls in turmoil from the loss of their friends.

"I'm okay," Steve said over the party chat as his replacement body was activated within Pandora's Box.

There was some relief from that, but even Steve's normally happy and carefree voice was heavy and somber.

A screen flashed before their eyes.

Castle Conquest

You have captured a contested castle!

Rewards:

2,000 Conquest points

Castle Conquest

You currently control (8/8) Castles

Earning: (8) conquest points per minute

Bonus: For controlling all of the Castles, you earn an additional (2) conquest points per minute.

Total points: 12,847

Rights: Administrative (Can spend conquest points to upgrade castle infrastructure and repair castles. Can also delete Castle infrastructure)

Western Castle 1

Status: Under Control by Terra Alliance

Earn: 1 conquest point per minute

Evolution: 1 (Second evolution 0%). Can increase evolution to Level 2 by paying (100,000) Conquest points.

Upgrades: Trebuchet, Siege Towers, Increased combat abilities for defenders (damaged), Soul Gem construct defenses (destroyed), Dwarven Artillery batteries (3/40), Aleph Repeater batteries (0/ 12)

Durability: 21,548/ 60,000

Castle Conquest

For controlling 4 conquest castles, you gain an extra conquest point (1) per minute

Castle Conquest

For controlling 8 conquest castles, you gain an extra conquest point (1) per minute

None of them cared as they grouped together, not needing to say words. They shared looks, a pat or a hug, their breathing shaky and disordered.

***

Dave looked at the screen in front of him.

You have died in Emerilia

You have been returned home.

You have 0:01 hours (game time) until you can respawn at (Nadorf, Opheir)

Or

0.01 hours in real life

Would you like to play a different game while you wait?

Respawn

You can now respawn.

Your new level:

196

You have lost 330 stat points. These stat points will be randomly removed from your attributes.

You have lost a class! (If you drop below a class gaining Level 50, 100, 200, 300, etc., you will lose 1 random class. It is possible to regain this class at a later time.)

You have lost the class:

Mine Manager

See Character Sheet to see the changes.

Dave didn't say anything. Instead, he felt a sourness in his gut, knowing that he would die a hundred more times and lose all of his classes and stat points in order to save Jekoni or Anna.

The loss of resources would be annoying, but with the Asteroid base and all of the mining going on there they were hauling in massive amounts of different resources.

A flash of light surrounded him. He felt weaker than he'd had in a long time. As he sat up on the Altar of Rebirth, Deia barreled into him, hugging him, in fear of him disappearing. Dave picked her up; she curled into his chest, crying like a little girl.

He moved to the side. He sat on the ground, Deia sitting in his lap for some time. Dave wished there was something he could do to stop the pain she was feeling. All he could do was move her hair away from her face, kissing her head, reassure her with whispers and hug her tight.

Suzy spawned in some time later. She and Induca hugged each other and cried as they, too, moved out of the way of other Stone Raiders who were spawning in Nadorf, which had become their linked spawn point.

It wasn't until a long time later, Deia raised her head from where she had been curled up on Dave's lap and crying into his chest.

"Yes, understood," Deia said slowly. She sniffed and tried to wipe away the tears, her eyes red and puffy from the crying.

Dave kissed her before his features hardened. "What happened while I was out?"

"The flying citadels are moving out. An order has been sent out to all of the portal locations, as well as the flying citadels. The angel legions under Light's command have returned. All forces are to focus on clearing out any remaining portal locations. We've got people moving to the portal here to seal it with a Mana shield and set up defensive runes to stop any more Xelur from coming through. All flying citadel forces will be lifted back up to the citadels and we will move to the next location. We'll be in support of the forces on the ground and move with the flying citadels."

Deia took a deep breath. "I know that we're all reeling right now and that we haven't had time to process what just happened. If anyone needs to, they can return to Terra."

The looks of sadness all hardened while the hidden anger was finally released. Powerful auras shook the very ground and air.

"Dave, what do you need to get my armor back up and running?" Lox asked.

"Mine too," Gurren said.

"We're going to need to charge them up again and tack on new armor plates if you want to be ready for the next fight." Dave stood, his face a cold mask. He hadn't recovered from the severe Mana fatigue yet but his fighting spirit had surged.

"I'll help out," Malsour said.

"Jekoni and Anna were people of Emerilia. If we just hide away from this, I wouldn't be able to hold my head up when thinking about them," Suzy said.

"Time we rid Emerilia of these creatures," Induca agreed.

"Jekoni saved our lives. He was not prone to violence but never shirked from his duty toward Emerilia and its people. I will carry out his wishes and pledge my blade to eradicating those who wish to harm the people of Emerilia. To kill a hundred to possibly save a thousand." Jung Lee's normally calm voice became harder and harsher as he talked. He gripped the handle of his sword and stared at the others, firm resolve in his eyes.

A weaker person might look away in fear and shock. The rest of Party Zero understood that look and shared in it with him. They might be tired and their strength was only just starting to recover, but together they would charge forward into what came.

Dave opened up his interface and went to his character sheet.

Character Sheet

Name:	David Grahslagg	Gender:	Male
Level:	196	Class:	Dwarven Master Smith, Friend of the Grey God, Bleeder, Librarian, Skill Creator, Aleph Engineer, Weapons Master, Champion Slayer, Master of Space and Time, Master of Gravitational Anomalies
Race:	Human/Dwarf	Alignment:	Chaotic Good

Unspent points: 0

Health:	4,550	Regen:	24.90 /s
Mana:	15,490	Regen:	61.70 /s
Stamina:	4,780	Regen:	52.65 /s
Vitality:	455	Endurance:	1,245
Intelligence:	1,549	Willpower:	1,234
Strength:	478	Agility:	1,053

The nervousness was gone, replaced by the numbness that came after combat and the loss of friends and comrades.

Dave closed his character sheet, a determined look in his eyes.

***

Frank Simmons sank into his couch. The springs had long since given way. His mind was dull and his eyes lifeless. His job at the local supermarket had long, boring hours, with not much to show for it in his paycheck. He felt drained from the physical work and the pressures on his meager income.

He grabbed his controller from under the couch and pressed the start button. His console booted up as the television turned on, showing the console's logo and the familiar sounds of it starting up.

A smile appeared on his face as he pulled on his headset.

He'd served with the United States Marines for ten years. He'd left without anything but a diploma. He'd moved back home to look after his parents. His useless sister had come in and got his mother with dementia to sign over everything to her.

She lived in some mansion in Texas while he lived in the middle of nowhere, looking after his parents until they passed away. His dad had gone first, lung cancer; his mother followed three years later when there was a mess-up with the medication she was on.

That was two years ago. Worn down by life, Frank retreated into video games. There he was not some guy who had been fucked over by life. He could be a thief, an outstanding paragon of virtue, or the devil incarnate. He didn't have to care about whether the new coupons were going out and when old lady Lucinda showed up with her fifteen stamps for *everything* she bought.

The main menu appeared in front of him. He moved over to boot up his game when he heard someone clear their throat.

Frank turned and jumped, pulling out his earbud.

Oh shit I hope I didn't break it!

Frank looked at the young woman who sat in the recliner to his side. "What the fuck are you doing here? Who are you?" Frank demanded, embarrassed by his reaction and pissed at the fact he might have broken his headset.

"Why is it all you gamers love swearing so much?" The woman sighed. She disappeared from Frank's seat and appeared in front of him.

He looked at her in shock. What she'd done was clearly impossible.

"Frank Simmons, age thirty-five within Earth simulation. Actual age, four and a half years," the woman said.

"What do you want? How is that possible? What did you do?" Frank's mind was already moving a hundred miles per second as he rushed through possibilities. His mind kept going back to the books and video games he'd read and played. There was no way that someone could simply teleport across a room in reality!

A chair appeared behind the lady as the room appeared brighter, as if someone had increased the brightness.

Frank rubbed his eyes, unable to understand the impossible things that were happening in front of his eyes.

"My name is the Lady of Air. I'm one of the figures within what we call the Affinities Pantheon. I know it sounds all rather strange, but soon everything will be revealed. Frank, it's time you found out what's really going on." Air gave Frank a deep look.

"What are you going to do to me?" Frank had lost his fighting trim from his time in the marines, but once someone was a marine, they were always a marine. He was readying himself to fight if he needed to.

"I'm going to do nothing to you. I'm going to show you a few things, let you make up your own mind and let you make a decision. There's a war going on, one for your survival. I'm simply asking if you want to help fight for your survival and the survival of the human race, or hide in this simulation," Air said, her voice neither forceful nor soft.

Frank frowned. "What do you want to show me?" Frank no longer felt tired and drained. His body and mind was alive as he unconsciously sat taller and his eyes carried a demanding light in them instead of the glazed-over defeat that usually registered in his eyes.

"Reality," Air said.

The room around them disappeared. They appeared within a room with a star map and people rushing around from console to console. People yelled to one another; a captain sat in his seat as explosions shook the ship.

Frank looked around at everything. The people looked so real but their talking was dimmed and one couldn't make out what they were saying.

Frank was still sitting on his couch at the back of the room.

"Do you know why your room disappeared?" Air stood up from her chair. It disappeared into nothing as she looked from Frank to the rest of the ship's bridge.

"What?" Frank was only starting to take in the sights of everything in the room when Air's words sunk in. He frowned, trying to figure out a way to answer her.

"Have you ever heard about the debate that we could be only brains in a vat in a massive game?" Air asked.

"Yeah, I've heard of it before." Frank nodded.

"Well, currently your brain is being destroyed and put into a real body. All of this, all that you know, is a simulation. The universe's biggest prison, eradication system, and entertainment center all rolled up into one. The human race stuck in the illusion of Earth being real. I'm going to tell you the history of Earth, its true history, and free you of this simulation." Air looked into Frank's eyes, piercing through him. "It's time to wake up from your dreams, Frank Simmons. A war is about to begin, the likes of which has never been seen before. It's up to you to decide if you're willing to help or not."

Frank's mind reeled from all that had happened in just the space of a few minutes. But with Air's words and the way that she looked at him, he felt as if he had woken up. He stood from his couch, a fierce look in his eyes. He didn't know what was going on, but he knew he wanted to see it through.

***

Frank Simmons opened his eyes for the first time, ever.

He was on a table, wearing a simple shirt and pants. He sat up, all manner of stickers on his body with runes covering them. The table underneath him was also covered in runic lines. There were people around him, all looking at him in shock. His eyes fell on Air, who stood off to the side.

It was if an explosion had gone off in his mind. He opened and closed his hand. It felt the same as if he had been on Earth. However, now with all Air had shown him—the things that they had done, racing across Earth, seeing different sights, her replaying different moments of his life that had been recorded—all of it only served to prove that Earth was a simulation.

He was still in a state of shock. But as he closed his hand again, it formed a fist. His lips thinned, anger building within him.

His entire life, he had been pushed and pulled by AI controllers. Air had given him a way out from that life and that prison. His life was his own once again and he had options. Not only that, but he had also gained purpose: to free others like him and win the ability to do what he wanted to.

His first step would be to become stronger, to help where he could to remove the Jukal Empire that had destroyed Sol and worked to kill off any remaining humans.

***

Alkao watched as his secretary left the room and closed the door behind her. Alkao could feel the pity, the way she wished to help relieve his pain more.

He could only give a slight smile and try to excuse himself.

The door closed and the magical coding around the room activated.

Alkao turned from his desk to the twin glass doors that looked out over Unity City located in the heart of Devil's Crater.

Images and scenes rolled through his mind. His first time meeting Anna and getting his ass kicked. How he had come to know her; his desire to see her smile; blooming in the joy he took as they became closer. When she'd "trained" with him and kicked his ass, but still he'd got back to his feet, honing his fighting skill with her just to spend more time with her. The small dates they'd gone on here and there. The times when she'd forgotten about her tail, which would wag behind her in happiness. Or when she smiled and the world seemed to be a better place.

Tears fell down his cheeks, but there was also a small but heartbreaking smile on his lips as he lived through those precious memories, savoring them all but knowing that the person who had made them special was gone.

There was a knock from his door. He let it go, not answering. A message appeared on his interface. He glanced to it; he wiped his eyes and checked his appearance. He hid his grief and pain deep. He was Alkao, king of Devil's Crater and leader of the Devil's Crater council and army.

He would mourn later. Right now he had to deal with the new threat that had emerged; the sworn enemies of the demons, the Lady of Light's angels.

His eyes flashed with a cold light thinking of them and the other creatures and people who had invaded Emerilia. He promised that their day would come; he would do his all to save as many Emerilians as possible.

Before he could press the button that would unlock his office, a gray light filled his room. Sitting there in a recliner, looking dejected, was an elderly gnome.

"Hello, Alkao. It's been some time." Bob looked at him.

"Bob?" Alkao said, stunned by his appearance.

"Since you were Anna's boyfriend, I felt like it would be best to tell you something." Bob took a deep breath and leaned forward in his chair somewhat. "There is a chance that I can bring her back."

"What? How? What do you need from me?" Alkao lurched forward from his seat, his hands on the desk as he looked at Bob.

"I don't need anything from you, but I have a warning. If I am to complete this, Anna will not be as you remember her," Bob said in a heavy voice.

"How?" Alkao braced himself but was unwilling to let this moment and possibility pass.

"Originally, Anna was meant to be an AI assistant to help me look after Emerilia and monitor its progress. But as time went on, she became more and more attached to the people of Emerilia and she asked for me to make her a body that would allow her to walk among the people of Emerilia.

"She stopped being an administrative AI and instead became a person of Emerilia. However, she was originally an AI at first. A part of her mind was connected to the *Datskun* at all times. This was meant as a way for me to look after her and in the event that I died or was removed that she would be able to take over my work and look after Emerilia. It was only a seed and a small connection at that. However, from it, I think that I can recover some of her memories. They might be buried in there and I'm not sure how much she would remember or not. It might be that she comes back fine; it might be that she can't remember anything but the days when she was first created. There is not much information there but I hope enough to return a part of her." Bob paused.

"Well, why are we talking? When can you begin?" Alkao asked.

"That is a problem. We can only start to pull her information and take it apart to once again code her so that she can assimilate a new body once all of the other AI controllers are taken offline.

"She is the center of the whole system. She controls nearly everything. However, if I was to remove her, she would disrupt the system. The AIs would look into it, the Jukal would look into it—and we would be exposed. We can only think of reviving her when we announce ourselves to the Jukal. However, I can wake up the part of her memory that was kept aboard the *Datskun*," Bob said.

"When can I see her? When will you know when it works?"

"I will need to try to wake her up. I don't know how long this will take and I can't guarantee you anything. I want her AI program to figure out what's going on on its own before I start introducing it to people she knew. If we go too fast, it could make her have a break and corrupt her drives and information banks. For this, I need to talk to Air to sort it out," Bob said.

"Okay, okay. Just please let me know if it works or not. Standing on the edge like this..." Alkao shook his head.

"As soon as I know something, I'll let you know," Bob promised. He paused, as if wondering to say what he was thinking. "Anna and I might be father and daughter but I wasn't able to see her much these past couple of years. She was one of the things that kept me going in the early years of Emerilia. I never saw her take a boyfriend before—she was always too scared to lose someone. With you, I think that she knew she might lose you, but it was worth that pain to know you and have you as her boyfriend for as long as possible."

Bob's words made Alkao clear his throat that seemed to have tightened up as his eyes once again itched with unshed tears. "Thank you," Alkao said.

Bob nodded and sniffed, finding it hard to hold back tears before he and his chair disappeared from Alkao's office.

Chapter 3: Flying Citadels' Advance

As soon as Josh heard about the Lady of Light's legions of angels returning to Emerilia, he felt as if a timer had run out for his Guild and the Terra Alliance.

Markolm had become a land of fanatics in the space of a few months. Those who believed in the Lady of Light flowed to the island, increasing the population by four times. Power continued to flow into the Lady of Light's divine well. Her power grew every day as more champions were picked among the people and an army was being raised.

All of this information had come from the spies the Stone Raiders' leader Lucy commanded with a high level of skill and efficiency.

All of the angel generals had also been converted from not only Creatures of Power but champions of Light, with their great Affinity and the fact that they were made through the power of Light. Thereby doubling their levels, making all of them Level 1500 powerhouses or stronger.

The angel legions were strong and their coordination was powerful. Seeing the images of them flying in formation was enough to make Josh's heart tighten in fear. If they were to all gain the Lady of Light's blessing and become champions, then the legion's power would be incredible.

"We're getting reports that there are a number of the Earth Lord's forces attacking the Lady of Light's legions. The Dark Lord seemed to have joined in on the fight as well," one of the people within the command center said.

"Good. If any of the flying citadels or the different locations under the Terra Alliances control see them, they're to attack with everything they have." Josh knew that he couldn't fight the legions now; his forces were spread out too thin. He was dealing with enemies across Emerilia, from portals and from the event.

"What is the status of our flying citadels?" Josh asked.

"The Goblin Mountain flying citadels have secured the portal. The two southern citadels and the western have been suppressed. The forces originally within the other citadels are moving to occupy them and rebuild their defenses. Esa reports that she is ready to move half of her strength back to Terra in order to rest them and make them ready for any further actions. The Goblin Mountain citadels are moving toward the second open portal inside the Densaou Ring of Fire lying to the south of the Xelur portal and east of the Orun Free States. The Nalheim, dragons, and Terra Alliance have kept the Alturarans suppressed at that location. The citadels will provide additional support to help in taking control of the area. The commander of the Goblin Mountain flying citadels requests to break down into wings and send his second group of citadels to assist the portal locations that are to the east of the Densaou Ring of Fire," one assistant called out.

"If he believes it is the best use of his group, then he has my permission. How is the second wing of the Gudalo flying citadels faring?" Josh asked.

"They are moving northwest near to the old location of Quindar's lair where the portal is located on the island within the nearby lake. The area is filled with Ooinfa. They will provide long-range fire support so as to not get caught within the illusion spells. They will move from the air, dropping their forces on the four Ooinfa-controlled citadels, concentrating their forces on one citadel at a time. With their suppression abilities, they should be able to counteract the illusion spells to a great extent, as well with the Band-Aid's ability to reduce the effect of magic cast at our people. They will be arriving within a few hours," another assistant said.

"Good. Have all of the reserve citadel forces on standby and ready to replace those active as soon as possible. I want those citadels moving throughout the day and night in order to defeat these portal groups," Josh said.

"Yes sir!" The two assistants turned back to their work as Josh looked toward the Jakan citadel.

A red and blue streak left the citadel and headed for the flying citadels.

"The Jakan will take nine days to think it over and consult with their people back home," Fire said in a private chat with Josh.

"Good. Dwayne, I want you to send forty percent of your people back to Terra for immediate reassignment. We're going to bolster our numbers at the different portal locations and clear as many of them as possible in nine days.

"After those nine days, we'll be back here. If the Jakan decide to ally themselves with us, we'll move them around to deal with the different threats we're facing. If they decide to not take our deal, we'll have to hammer them with everything we have and seal off that portal, even if it means we have to break it. Having a long, drawn out battle with the Jakan will only weaken us." Josh talked to Fire, Water, and Dwayne in the party chat.

If he could, he would grant mercy. But if the Jakan decided to fight, then a number of players would lose their hard-earned levels, making them a weaker force, and they would lose the people of Emerilia without the ability to replace them.

They had to draw a line, and be ready to enforce it with everything they had when the time came.

"Understood," Dwayne said.

"Agreed," Water said.

"I will lend my help with overcoming the other portal locations," Fire said.

Josh's eyebrows rose in surprise. "Then I thank you for your help," Josh said sincerely. He had yet to see what amounted to a god of Emerilia go all out. He'd seen Deia do it a few times and he was shocked at her awesome display of power. However, her mother was nearly twice her age and there was no true record of her fighting personally.

"I will not participate. I am needed for the Pandora's Box Initiative. Also, it would be good if we kept some trump cards hidden at this time," Water said.

"Gotcha." Josh wasn't privy to all the details about what the Pandora's Box Initiative was doing. However, the number of people who seemed to have disappeared into the program was tremendous. All of them were geniuses in their field. "I hope that we won't need them in the near future."

"You and me both," Water said.

The top of Josh's scalp tingled at Water's tone.

***

Party Zero looked down upon the Alturarans who controlled a few of the citadels at the portal located inside the Densaou Ring of Fire and east of the Orun Free States. The Alturarans were a race of sentients who had taken on inorganic bodies as their planet had died, trapped in these bodies for centuries, splicing their memories and minds from one generation to the next until they had lost their history and identity. Now, when they interacted with organic matter and creatures made of organic material, they wished to destroy them, to make the universe as dead as they were. They were largely formed from crystals and were great practitioners of using Dark Mana to change their own bodies to attack and create various poisons to kill off organics.

A shimmering mist of green hung over their portal, a poison that they were pumping into the air. They would make more and more of it as time went on, using it to kill off anything in the area around the Densaou Ring of Fire and then Emerilia as a whole.

The Nalheim had come over to Emerilia and moved to some territories around the Densaou Ring of Fire, pledging their allegiance to the dragons who lived in the desolate area within the ring of volcanoes. The Nalheim needed the warmth to survive and thrive, making the Densaou Ring of Fire an excellent place for them to live.

When they had first arrived, they had been fighting against the Terra Alliance. In a twist of fate, they were now on the same side as the alliance as they faced off against the Alturarans.

The Terra Alliance was using all manner of grand workings and different ranged spells and attacks on the Alturarans. However, the Nalheims' disrupting attacks that they cast with their spears or with their massive Nerhoun mounts were highly effective against the Alturarans.

The dragons had also come out to support the attacks against the portal near their home.

None of the Alturarans looked the same but they were placed into different classes. There were normals, heavies, tanks, ranged, mutated, and worms.

The normals were just normal, low-level Alturarans; they had not only close combat abilities but also ranged ones. Heavies were larger versions of the normals. Tanks were ones that were focused on defense; ranged those with more ranged attack focus. Worms were massive long creatures that could make it through a portal and then would eat their way through the natural vegetation, turning it into power. They could supply this power to the other Alturarans or use it themselves to create massive Dark magic spells. Mutated were Alturarans that might fall outside of these categories. They were unpredictable and the most dangerous, but they were the rarest.

The portal was located in the middle of the citadels. Originally it had been buried in a hill but now the hill had been blasted apart, revealing its hollow center.

Three of the worms gathered around the portal. Rot seemed to spread out from their bodies as they created a circle around the portal. Alturarans swarmed over them. Under the thunder of the guns and ranged attacks, they weren't able to make it very far but there was no break in the firing. If the guns stopped, then the tide would rush forth.

The Nalheim mounted on sky screams worked to pick off any of those that made it past the line of destruction that the Terra Alliance had carved into the ground.

Dave had a grim look on his face. "If I could use just one of the grand workings we've been working on with the Pandora's Box Initiative, we could wipe them clear of Emerilia," Dave said over the party chat with cold anger.

"There's nothing that you can do about it." Deia gripped his hand.

Dave took a deep breath. The air shifted around him as his Mana circulated. "Well, there is one thing I think we *can* do," Dave said, his eyes focused on the Alturarans.

He looked to Malsour, who was in his human form. "I'll need your help."

"What are we doing?" Malsour asked.

"Making a disrupting ray. Can you ask the Nalheim to come and see us? We're also going to need Shard's help with modulating everything."

"I'll contact them," Malsour said.

"Deia, give me two hours and I might have something to deal with the Alturarans," Dave said.

"Will it be something to get the Jukal AI's attention?" she asked, with a worried expression.

"Well, it might be, but I don't think that it'll trigger them coming after us and looking into our secrets—just taking what the Nalheim have and making it on a much larger scale."

"Okay." Deia nodded and squeezed his hand. "Good luck. And let me know if you need anything."

Dave gave her a smile and squeezed her hand too. He could see that she was blaming herself for the loss of Jekoni and Anna.

He turned and headed for one of the entrances into the soul gem island below the citadel. His eyes passed over Steve. His playful demeanor was dulled as he stood off to the side, looking out over the citadel and the landscape.

Dave wished that he could do something for Steve to help him through the pain he was suffering. However, he knew that if Steve needed his help, he'd come to him, and if he didn't in some time, then Dave would go and search him out.

Dave shared a look with Malsour. The two of them had solemn and hard faces. Dave opened up a private chat with Malsour. "After this, we've got to do everything in our power to speed up things with the Initiative. As soon as we can, we'll work on that battleship. I also want to work through the destroyers. We don't have many ships, so we need to make sure they're the strongest possible."

"Agreed. And if we can create these disintegrating rays, then maybe we can use it for the ships."

"It's not a question of if—just how much time it will take," Dave said as they walked through the citadel. People moved out of the way as a cold air made their cloaks rise behind them slightly.

Once getting Malsour's order, nearly fifty Nalheim arrived on the flying citadel within ten minutes. Dave and Malsour met them in one of the bays that were used for the drop platforms. Already people milled around, ready to board the platforms at any minute.

Dave and Malsour took a number of the Nalheim's weapons and watched them show how they used them. With Dave and Malsour's Intelligence, they had nearly perfect photographic memory. If they thought on it, then it would be like replaying a video.

Armed with a few dozen spears, Dave and Malsour each took a few of them and started to destroy them. The magical coding and runes filled Dave and Malsour's minds.

"Shard, I need you to translate some magical runes over," Dave said. In one hand he held a Mirror of Communication while his other hand flickered over his interface screens as he quickly put down the runes that he had perceived through destroying a number of the spears. Although he knew the runes that were being used, he didn't know how they functioned because of course, every runic language just had to be different.

"I can do that," Shard said as Dave started to send over the runes. There were a few hundred of them, so it took time. As he sent them, Shard was sending back a translated version of the runes that was in Dave's format of runes.

Dave and Malsour looked over the translated runes.

"Okay, so it uses vibrations but also has a light wavelength variation," Dave said.

"Everything has a resonate frequency. If it's possible to tune right in on the frequency of what you're hitting, then up the amplitude—you can shake it apart. The light wavelength is pretty similar—basically goes through all manner of different wavelengths until it finds one that is capable of destroying what it's hitting."

"The most complicated thing about these weapons is not the way that it uses vibrations or light to break things apart. It's the fact that it goes through all of these different possibilities in such a short time. Hell, I'm not even seeing all of the coding that would be needed to do this! If there isn't anything to regulate it, then how is it supposed to work?" Dave looked to Malsour.

"Well, there is one other variable when these weapons are being fired—the user."

"The Nalheim?" Dave stopped his walking and closed his eyes as he went through the different images that he remembered of the Nalheim using the weapons just moments ago.

"It must be." Malsour watched Dave, clearly hoping that he was right. Otherwise they would need to code nearly an AI-level intelligence to use these weapons.

In Dave's mind, he watched the arcane as it moved through the Nalheim.

It moved from both of their heads; when they shot their spear forward, it was like an electric shock. He'd thought it was just a blunt-force Mana burst that activated the spear. The sheer amount of Mana being tossed out made it look heavy-handed. Now that he studied it closer, he saw that from one of the heads came the changes for the vibration attack, while the other head sent down commands for the light vibration.

"When we asked them, they said that they were just attacking." Dave shook his head. "They're doing complicated light and audio vibration on the fly. That large discharge of Mana with their shots was them figuring out what kind of modulation they need to make. If we could get them working with the automated miners, then we could experience a thirty percent increase in how fast they mine, at least. They just keep on attacking with everything each time instead of refining it down. Also, all of the different sound and light wavelengths are timed differently. They all travel so fast that we don't really perceive that it's all these different attacks. If they were to combine them all together, there would be no change, but because they're just perfectly timed, so that they don't interfere with one another, they're able to hit a target in the space of microseconds with all of the different wavelengths."

"When I was looking at the conditions that they lived in, I kind of looked down on them, but it seems that I was the idiot," Malsour said, in awe of the speed at which they were able to cast the all-encompassing command spell that activated the spear fully. It allowed them to have extremely powerful weapons, without the need for massive magical arrays to control them.

"An impressive feat of them understanding their strengths and utilizing them to their fullest," Dave said in a praising tone. "Though it means that we're going to need them to use the disrupting ray. We simply don't have the time or resources right now to code an AI to control all of this on the fly."

"If we are able to set up a terminal or something that could record what they're doing, I can check all of the different wavelengths—see which ones are functioning and isolate them down. So, we would need them to fire the first few shots, then I can go from there, removing the extra wavelengths," Shard said.

"Perfect. Once this is all over, we're going to need to get them into a lab to have them shoot their spears, record it all, so that we can get down the information of how they time the different wavelengths. That, more than the fact that they're using different wavelengths, is hugely important. We can shoot all kinds of wavelengths of light and vibration at a target, but if they're not staggered then they'll cancel out each other. I'm not going to lie, I'm a bit in shock of it all," Dave admitted.

"I'll get a few of them to come down here, see how we can hook them up to the system to get them to control the beam," Malsour said.

"Okay. I'll look into the coding, try to get a better feel for it and code it into the flying citadel's weapon banks," Dave said.

"Meet you in the command center?" Malsour asked, backtracking toward the drop platform area once again.

"Sounds like a plan!" Dave continued on his way. There was no time to waste.

***

Dave looked over the coding in the main weapons' banks. The flying citadel was a lot different from more conventional weapon systems.

A weapons bank was a soul gem storage core. It held a number of different Magical Circuit plans. When one of them was selected, then the various "mounts" would change over to the new magical coding, altering the soul gem constructs throughout the flying citadel to bring down different spells on the enemy. This was how the citadels were able to suppress the Xelur's ability to gather up souls to increase their power. However, they hadn't used the mounts but instead the magical circuitry had spread through the citadel, giving it more power and a larger effect.

These banks held myriad different codings. Now Dave had input the coding that the Nalheim used for their spears. He didn't play around with the runes at all for fear that if he altered them now, they wouldn't work properly. He didn't have the time to troubleshoot it all and try to increase its power. It was too foreign to him right now.

Dave slid in the coded plate with the spear's attack engraved into it.

It lit up. The main weapons banks copied down the information as changes went through the magical coding throughout the soul gem island. Now it would only take someone activating the right weapon coding and they could bring up the disruption ray magical coding.

Dave moved to where Malsour was with five Nalheim. They were all around a single station that had magical inputs on either side. This would take their modulating spell, then run it through the main weapons banks, activating the disruption ray.

"Keep at it," Malsour said. A device the Nalheim used translated his words. They continued to press their hands against the input ports.

"Something wrong?" Dave asked through the party chat, seeing the expression on Malsour's face.

"They're not able to do it," Malsour said.

"Can they do it with the spear still?"

"I'm not sure." Malsour looked over to them and exited the party chat. "Could you use your spear and attack that wall?" Malsour asked one of the Nalheim, pointing to a wall of the room.

"Yes, King Malsour." The Nalheim summoned their spears from their bag of holding. They stabbed their spear out. A hole appeared in the soul gem wall.

Malsour and Dave looked at each other; Malsour rejoined the party chat.

"Okay, so that shows that they can still do it. Maybe it's not them but the interface? They've become used to using their spears so much that it's nothing more than a reaction at this time, but doing it by force sends them around the bend?" Dave asked.

"I think that's a good assumption, though how are we going to fire this thing?" Malsour asked.

"We make a firing range."

"Okay." Malsour frowned in question.

"We make a magical formation that takes the input from the spear, breaks it down and sends it to the main weapons bank. We're going to need to revert the effect of the spear. If we can reverse the coding of the spear then we remove the attacking part of it, funnel the input from the firing range right through." Dave opened the chat to Shard. "Hey Shard, looks like we need your help again."

"What do you need?" Shard asked, eager to help.

"We're going to need you to reverse code the Nalheim spear's runes," Dave said.

"Never with the simple jobs. All right, it might take me a few minutes. Do you want it in Nalheim runes?" Shard asked.

"I think that would be best—less possibility of a mess-up," Malsour said.

"Okay, I'll get back to you when I have it sorted out," Shard said.

"In the meantime, we need to shield up one of these walls and make an input formation to take everything and process it through," Dave said to Malsour.

"Why don't we try making a spear that looks and feels the same as the ones that they're using, but have input runes inside them?"

"Well, that would be a whole lot easier to do!" Dave tapped his finger on his leg as he held his chin. "Worth a try."

They left the room. Malsour pulled out a length of metal from his bag of holding. As it came out, he exerted his magic. The lump of metal stretched out into the shaft of a spear, with the same magical runes on the outside. However, these ones were merely decorative; the real coding was inside and was linked to the flying citadel.

The spearhead formed and the cap on the base of the spear was finished. Malsour even made the spear a bit weathered, making it look well used so that the Nalheim would be confused. It looked identical to the spear that the Nalheim were using.

They checked the coding and walked back into the room.

"Try using this spear." Malsour passed it to the person who had put a crater in the wall just a few moments ago.

They took the spear, checking the weight and, not seeing anything special with it, they stabbed outward at the wall. A new crater didn't appear. However, one of the interface screens linked to the disruption ray magical coded program showed that it had been activated.

Dave and Malsour looked at each other.

"Seems that I was overthinking things. Shard, there's no need to do the reverse spear coding," Dave said.

"Well, I was only about half done anyways," Shard said.

The corner of Dave's mouth twitched upward in a slight smile before he looked to the Nalheim who was looking at the spear in confusion.

"I think that there is something wrong with this spear, King Malsour," the Nalheim said.

"I've just taken the power source out from it. I'm just checking over your form with the spear." Malsour opened the party chat once again. "I'm thinking that we keep them in the dark about what they're doing. It seems that their attack is more instinctual than anything. If they know that we're testing them for that, they might get nervous and mess it up."

"Understandable. Also, with each of their attacks, I have a program recording it all. Maybe later we can work out a system that doesn't need them to activate the disruption ray by stabbing wildly into the air," Dave said.

"Well, we've never been a group that really goes by the more orthodox methods," Malsour said dryly.

"No, we're not," Dave agreed. "I'm looking forward to seeing how this ray will do."

***

Denur looked over the Alturaran portal. All of the aerial forces and those that moved in close to the portal had been recalled a little bit ago as four of the flying citadels were now moving between the citadels on the ground. As they got closer, magical formations started to form underneath their islands.

The Alturarans seemed to sense something was amiss. Their ranged attacks sparked off the Mana shield.

Lines made of light and compressed runic lines spread out from the magical formations underneath the four flying citadels. A diamond was created between the flying citadels with round magical formations appearing inside all of them, rotating in different directions lazily.

The Alturarans picked up their attacks as the air started to get hazy with the release of Mana between the massive flying citadels.

The citadels stopped moving. The Alturarans attacks were little more than annoyances to the flying citadels that were two kilometers up in the air.

The air suddenly erupted with myriad noises and a blinding flash that originated from the center of the magical formation that lay between the flying citadels.

Anything that lay in this blast's path was destroyed. The green poison that had been hovering in the air was wiped out by the blast that weakened slightly as it passed.

It smashed down against the Alturarans. It killed off hundreds of them in a single blast and severely weakened the various shield and Mana barriers of those remaining.

It was if watching a massive flaming hammer smashing down upon them all.

Again, that deep noise ignited the air, with light smacking against all that were below. All magical spells and ranged attacks had stopped as the blast from the combined flying citadels continued to rain down upon the Alturarans.

"It looks like...could it be those Nalheim's disrupting spear attacks?" Denur muttered to herself. She watched as that blast of light and noise continued to form below the spell formation, smashing into those below.

Her eyes moved to the flying citadels. She was the mother of dragons, one of the most powerful creatures in all of Emerilia. But here, looking upon those citadels, she felt a chill run through her body as she shook her head to free herself of that feeling.

These flying citadels had taken the Nalheim's already powerful attack, increased its power and area of effect, and used it to completely suppress the Alturarans.

As Denur watched, the Alturarans' fate had already been sealed.

There was nowhere that they could escape to as the attacks ate through their different protective shields and barriers. Once reaching their actual bodies, many of them seemed to make screeching noises before their bodies shattered and exploded outward.

The ground around the Alturarans was churned into dust. The portal shifted as the ground was wrecked around it.

Even its own protective measures took a pounding. For twenty minutes, it continued, the Alturarans unable to do anything about their fate.

A plume of dust spread up into the air, being pulled by the wind. The portal shifted and fell on its side.

The magical runes along the outside of the portal's ring shut off as the sand-covered plains on the other side of the portal disappeared.

In a flash of light, the portal was teleported away.

In the space of an hour and a half, the flying citadels had crushed the Alturaran forces. The solid runic lines made from Mana faded away as the flying citadels moved away from the portal's old location.

They moved into formation with the rest of the Goblin Mountain flying citadel group and set out toward the west, where four more portals waited for them.

The citadel commanders at the Alturaran portal called out different orders, calling for people to check their people and gear and be ready to move out to Terra.

Denur looked up from her perch on the edge of a volcano, watching those eight flying citadels continue on their path.

Chapter 4: The Tide

"Did you just see that?" The Jukal controllers all looked to one another as they watched the Alturarans get smashed into oblivion.

"That was so awesome! How the hell did Dave do that?" a green-furred Jukal controller asked the others.

"He somehow took it from the Nalheim, had some guy whipping around a spear—whenever they used the spear, then that disrupting ray would smash down on the Alturarans. That's so badass!" a purple-furred controller said.

"You better not be watching them having sex again," a Jukal wearing a thicker necklace than the other controllers said in a bored tone.

"Controller Commander, the flying citadels just crushed the Alturarans. They couldn't do anything!" the green-furred controller said.

The controller commander let out a bored nod as mist sprayed down on him. He rubbed his furred chest and stomach, lazily opening up the video recorded from the satellites above Emerilia. His scratching paused as he watched the flying citadels send blast after blast down on the Alturarans.

He let out a warbling chuckle, his frog-like body shaking in glee. "Looks like we'll be getting a nice bonus! That'll definitely bring in the ratings!" the controller commander said. His tastes were expensive, part of the reason that he had got his mother with her high status to get him on controller duty for Emerilia.

It was a military position but there was no threat of anything going wrong. As long as they garnered good ratings and viewership, they could get a bonus from the higher-ups. Also, if anything did go wrong, the AI were there to warn them and deal with the people of Emerilia. It made it an essentially brainless job that anyone could fulfil.

In over five centuries, nothing had gone wrong in Emerilia and there had been no need for the AI or the controllers to step in.

"The portal was removed and is now being looked over by our techs," the purple-furred controller said.

The controller commander frowned as an alert appeared on his screen. It showed a warning about the strength of the flying citadel's weapon. Another alert underneath showed the number of people who were logging into the Emerilia stream to watch everything. The controlling commander dismissed it and looked to his people. "Get some video chopped together of the Party Zero POE's dying—hack it together with the flying citadels and their attacks, something about the underdogs coming out on top, or about their revenge and reclaiming their land. That'll bring in the people."

Another alert came up about the forces used by the disrupting ray as the AI controllers were running calculations and firing it back to the Jukal controllers.

This one said that it was going to a higher authority.

The controller commander rolled his eyes and continued working.

***

"Brilliant, brilliant! Yes!" The Jukal emperor stood up from his bed, bowling over the slaves who looked after his every need.

They all flinched back slightly, afraid to incur the emperor's wrath as he watched the overwhelming power of the disrupting ray smash the Alturarans down again and again until they were destroyed.

"Did you see that!" he roared, a bloodthirsty look on his face as he ripped a mist bottle from one of the slaves and used it to spray his fur. He let out a satisfied noise as he slumped back onto his seat. His arms grasped the beauties around him and pulled them onto his lap. "This emperor is not yet satisfied."

Two of the slaves grabbed the newest female slave and pushed them onto the emperor, making sure to not block his view as a new scene appeared in front of him, showing the loss of Anna and Jekoni, as well as the destruction of Steve's body.

The emperor roared with laughter at the expressions on their faces. His beauties fed him, his every need seen to as the scene changed and the flying citadels charged forward in a valiant light, like war chariots advancing on the enemy.

Cut scenes showed the clashes of Xelur and the Terra Alliance drop forces; the atmosphere grew tense. The emperor was wrapped up in it all, as his excitement grew once again. Finally, the flying citadels defeated the Xelur; then, painted in a valiant light, they once again charged toward battle, music in the background bringing up the atmosphere. The scene was cut to show the flying citadels arriving and almost immediately crushing the Alturarans. It panned to those on the ground who looked up at the flying citadels as if they were watching the war gods descending to Emerilia.

It ended with the emperor cheering from his seat. The beauties held smiles on their faces, as they were shocked in their hearts. Usually their emperor was bored and morose, but with the death and destruction that was happening on Emerilia, it was as if the blood-thirsty beast within him had awoken.

The scene cut to the flying citadels now moving across Emerilia.

The emperor settled down. A voice came from behind him, waiting for the emperor to calm before talking.

"My Emperor, this humble one begs your forgiveness for interrupting." The underling's face scraped the floor.

"Speak." The emperor was in a good mood. The underling had thankfully talked after the video was finished; otherwise, he might find himself being thrown to the emperor's beasts for interrupting his fun.

"The AI controllers of Emerilia have expressed concerns with the level of destruction that this disruption ray has caused. Even the portal that the Alturarans were using was damaged," the underling said quickly.

The emperor snorted. Mist sprayed on his fur, the massive and heavy chain of the emperor shifting around his neck and chest. "Those AIs know nothing but numbers and stupid rules! Did we not change those rules to give this great display to the people! Ignore it!" the emperor bellowed. He wasn't about to have his entertainment destroyed by a few AIs calling out warnings.

"Do you wish for us to increase the level of damage that the Emerilians are allowed to use?" the underling asked.

"Those controllers seem to know what they're doing better than you! Did you see the video that they made or the way that they're already compiling a list of the best fighters on the Terra Alliance's and Xelur's side? Let them deal with it! They've not come to annoy me and they've shown that they know how to provide entertainment for their emperor!" the Jukal emperor yelled.

The underling pressed their face further into the ground. "This one understands. I will pass control over to the Jukal controllers at Emerilia."

"Leave." The emperor dismissed the underling as he moved to partake in the delicacies his beauties held out for him.

***

Party Zero once again stood atop the citadel. Aerial scout groups were out with dragons supporting them; the artillery cannons as well as repeater batteries were secured and ready for action at a moment's notice. Soul gems were being shipped in from Terra to keep the citadels fully charged. The various power-creating devices were all active to pull in power to the flying citadels.

People looked upward to see the massive soul gem islands brimming with guns, the drop tubes and bays visible as they cruised by. The Goblin Mountain group split; the second wing of four flying citadels headed to the dragon mountain in central Ashal, to deal with the portal before the mouth of Ashal River and the one between the mountain and the Strabon woods.

The first wing, which Party Zero was a part of, was headed more south. Their target was the portal at the southernmost point of Ashal, south of the Baerux Conglomerate. As they passed, the beasts and creatures of Emerilia, as well as those that had been released for the event of Myths and Legends, looked up with a sense of fear filling them; from the control room's vision displays, you could see them scatter in all directions.

The flying citadels were visible from the Strabon Kingdom the city, numbering some three hundred thousand all looked up at the powerful and dominating Citadels.

As they passed over the Baerux Conglomerate, the Terra Alliance members who had been defending the walls of the various villages and cities got a boost of morale, forcing the attacking forces backward.

"New targets! Support fire!" the commander of Goblin Mountain Wing One called out. The artillery cannons on the top of the citadel as well as those at the underside of the island rotated onto their new targets, the dwarven crews working with polished efficiency.

"Fire!" As the commander's words dropped, the flying citadels were covered in the Mana shock waves of the fired rounds.

The guns had barely finished moving when the dwarves changed targets and fired again. All of these cannons were the new soul gem-powered versions. They used a soul gem crystal at the base of their firing tubes that would power up the runes inside the cannon, creating an impressive and powerful artillery spell without needing the round.

These cannons were also made to dissipate heat quickly and efficiently, turning it into residual power to be used later. Their rate of fire was nearly four times of the normal dwarven artillery cannons. They could also fire grand working shells; that did require them to load and remove shells every time but then their destructive power couldn't be compared to that of the original dwarven cannons.

The ground was covered with all manner of creatures that wished to tear apart the different walled villages and cities. These creatures looked to the whistling noises that seemed to come from overhead. Explosions bloomed among their ranks, killing tens of them and leaving them in a state of shock as a rolling dwarven artillery barrage descended upon them from the passing flying citadels.

As they started to react, already the third volley was released from the dwarven artillery cannons.

While Deia, Induca, and Suzy watched those impacts across the different groups that were trying to attack the people of the Baerux Conglomerate, Dave, Malsour, Steve, Lox, and Gurren were in a workshop within Flying Citadel One. Lox and Gurren were cutting out different pieces of metal and passed them to Malsour, who used his abilities to refine the pieces down and combine them before passing them to Steve and Dave. Dave replaced the parts that had been broken in the armor while Steve helped him and made sure that he didn't forget anything and also added in the magical coding for each piece. There was so much magical coding in the Devastator armor that Dave took a moment to pull the complete plans from his memory. Thankfully, with Steve's memory storage, he could easily help Dave to carve out the necessary magical coding and runic lines.

Steve looked identical to the body that had been destroyed at the Xelur citadel. He had a number of copies made after seeing that it worked, practically making him like a player. But, unlike players, his body still had the exact same stats as it did before.

They paused in their work to look at the images on the interfaces around the workshop that showed the Baerux Conglomerate. They had been in heavy fighting but now with the flying citadels, the enemy was in confusion and shock, unable to do anything as they tried to escape the hail of powerful rounds coming down. As they did so, they ran into other groups from the event that they had bad blood with, adding to the confusion as battles ignited in the midst of their retreat.

The dwarven artillery was merciless as it continued to rain down hell upon the attackers.

"Alter flight path to move in closer to Baerux Conglomerate's southernmost city Ieiezoth. Maintain speed. We can't stop, but give them as much help as possible." The flying citadels' wing commander's voice passed through the flying citadels.

Dave once again turned to what he was doing, holding a piece of metal in one hand and a torch in the other. He used the torch to heat up where the piece was going, match up with the actual replacement part; then, using his soul smithing skill, he was able to place it within the Devastator armor he was working on.

"Steve, are you updating the runes used within the armor?" Dave asked.

"A few of them. As more runes have been added to the magical coding database, I've been able to find a few ways to modify the armor. It might give another five percent increase to power." Steve's voice was serious. Ever since Jekoni and Anna had died, he'd been professional and detached, none of his normal humor appearing as he seemed to have slipped into a sort of depression.

Dave spared Steve a glance as Steve worked on a new replacement sheet filled with runic lines. No person could create them but with Steve's body and abilities, it was simple for him. His hand raced down the sheet and the tip of the carver darted across the sheet of metal.

"Nice," Dave praised, continuing on with his work as he fused another piece into the armor. The soul gem construct that had been added into the armor moved through the different gaps in the coded metal sheet, using it as a housing as complex runic lining covered the soul gem construct.

Dave paused and looked at the armor. "You know what, Steve? You've given me an idea. We've got another what, ten or so hours until we get to the portal location? I think it's time that we upgraded a few things about the Devastator armor." Dave turned to where Lox and Gurren were covered in sweat and grime like the rest of them, working with a simple forge and some cutting tools.

They weren't master smiths by any stretch, but both of them were Journeymen in smithing and experts in maintaining, making it much easier for Malsour to work with the different materials that they gave him. None of them were too far off what he needed.

"What you thinking?" Gurren looked up and wiped his sweat-covered brow.

"I'm thinking you need some storage devices in your wrists so that you can hold or shoot out grenades—link it up with the Mana bolt and spear wristband. Then add in some orbs, like the ones I have, be able to set up a sort of domain where they will be able to limit their opponents Mana regeneration or be suppressed by gravity, or whatever. Also, they can be used to increase your flight speed, modify your shields and barriers so it's not only around your body but can propagate it ahead of you. Allowing you to move instead of having to fight off an attack directed at you. Also has a self-destruction ability that's much more powerful than your grenades if you need it. These things do need to get charged up every so often but I have a number of them extra right now."

Dave opened a party chat with them so that no one else could hear them. "Also, they will have the added ability to teleport you if you need it. However, this is something that can only be used after we've revealed some of our other trump cards."

The trust he was placing in them was powerful indeed and it showed that he cared for them deeply.

"We'll take anything that can increase our fighting ability." Lox stood a bit taller as he looked at Dave with clear and resolute eyes.

"Aye," Gurren agreed.

"Very well then." Dave turned back to the armor, opening his interface and sending Steve the magical coding that he had on his arm bracers to control the orbs.

Once we get back to the Pandora's Box Initiative, I'll get a few factories to work on these orbs. They could save a lot of lives in the upcoming fight against the angels as well as the other forces of the Pantheon.

The flying citadels' artillery fire slowed as they passed the Baerux Conglomerate. Those who had been finally given a break from the fighting let out ragged cheers as the flying citadels continued forward on their war path.

***

Gudalo Flying Citadel Wing One was moving from Opheir toward Heval to assist in the removal of the Xelur portal that was located there. Goblin Mountain Flying Citadel One had passed Baerux Conglomerate and headed for their portals.

The second wing of the Goblin Mountain flying citadels had reached their first location and was engaged in a ground battle with the Galis race. Reserve forces were being called up in order to assist them and finish off the battle quickly.

Meanwhile, everyone's eyes were on the main screens where Gudalo Flying Citadel Wing Two was advancing on the island located in the lake next to Quindar's lair. As soon as they got into range, ranged attacks started to rain down on the Ooinfa that controlled a number of the citadels.

The Ooinfa had the ability to deflect attacks and used this as well as Mana shields and barriers to try to remove some of the pressure coming down on them. It was as if they were trying to put out a raging forest fire with a garden hose.

The Ooinfa's combat abilities were highly effective against those they were fighting on the ground and when they had already gained a position within their enemy's lines. They had held the Terra Alliance at a stalemate, not because of their fighting abilities, but because every time the Terra Alliance tried to advance, they would end up tricked by the Ooinfa. After the incident where members of the Terra Alliance injured other members of the alliance, they'd stopped sending out attacks to try to control the Ooinfa's citadels. Instead, they created a no-man's land between the inner and outer citadels, cutting down the Ooinfa that tried to attack.

The only option was to fight them from long distance, and this was something the flying citadels excelled at.

A streak of red light took off from one of the flying citadels and rushed up into the air.

Josh's full attention was focused on the screen that was watching this single flame that seemed to be suspended in mid-air. This was actually Lady Fire. She had gone with the flying citadel group in order to speed up the process of removing the threat of the portals and take some of the pressure off the Terra Alliance.

At first, a red fog seemed to gather around Fire. It quickly turned into red streams, becoming thicker and thicker as they looked like ropes of flames that condensed around Fire. They spun faster and faster, creating a sphere of fire. It looked as if a new sun had been born in the mid-morning light.

The citadels had attacked with their ranged weaponry, driving the Ooinfa backward. It took five minutes for Fire to complete her spell, telling of its complexities and power.

The massive sphere changed its form creating several massive suns which further divided, creating smaller suns that orbited around the first, like electrons flying around an atom or moons around a planet.

Suddenly, the suns lined up with the four Ooinfa-occupied citadels. They shot outward, descending toward the ground like meteorites from the sky. The fireballs smashed against the defenses of the Ooinfa citadels, burning like Greek fire as they stuck to the defensive structures and melted Mana barriers and shields. It burned unceasingly, melting through any and all protective measures that the Ooinfa tried to throw up. The Ooinfa's cries were heard as their barriers broke, being cooked by those raging flames.

The citadels swiftly turned into nothing more than roiling magma, leaving no sign of the Ooinfa that had been commanding those citadels. The area around the portal turned into a magma pit. The Ooinfa that walked out were burned alive in mere seconds, unable to do anything.

Fire laid down a magical formation in the ground around the portal so that the magma wouldn't cool down.

Josh swallowed his spit. The sheer power of Fire's one attack and the spell formation she had burned into the ground was something that none of the Stone Raiders could compare to, not even Party Zero. She didn't even look slightly tired after it at all as she returned to her flying citadel. All of their guns and ranged weaponry were now silent as they looked over the destruction brought down on by a true war goddess.

Moments later, they received their new target and turned to the west and their new target—a portal located in the Medlari Empire on the Heval continent.

The second wing of the Goblin Mountain flying citadel had reached their first location and were engaged in a ground battle with the Galis there. Reserve forces were being called up in order to assist them and finish off the battle quickly.

Josh had a grim look on his face as he then turned to the reports of Light's fanatics as well as her angels rushing toward Markolm.

They had come under multiple attacks by the different groups and people dotted across Emerilia. The Earth and Dark Lord seemed to be showing their hands as well; forces that Lucy was watching had set ambushes, killing off as many of Light's angels as possible.

After finding out the fact that Creatures of Power, when awarded a championship by their creator, allowed them to double their levels, no one was willing to let Lady Light have the time to bring up her angels' power.

Though most of the angels have already made it to Markolm and there are signs of power being built up throughout the entire Markolm continent. Seems that she's not willing to just sit by idly.

***

The Lady of Light looked out from her hall. In every direction, there were men and women wearing golden armor and with the purest white wings on their backs. All of them knelt, their heads bowed in reverence, hundreds of meters below her great hall. At the front of the eight different formations were her generals who led these legions of angels. None of them dared to move an inch; they had been like this for a number of hours but they didn't complain in the least. Wind blew over them but it was as if they were all statues, not moving at all despite the breeze.

More and more formations appeared from the sky. All of them were as close to the ground as they could be, their bodies bent out of respect for their creator and god. They landed in their legion and fell to their knees, remaining like that, waiting.

The Lady of Light frowned as she saw a group come from Heval. It looked to be in worse condition than was first reported.

"Khanundra," Light said softly.

"My goddess." Khanundra moved forward so she was just a few steps back from the Lady of Light as she bowed from the waist.

"What happened?" Light waved at the incoming formation.

"It seems that the blasphemers of your name, the ones called the Dark Lord and the Earth Lord, worked in concert to lay down ambushes for our forces. With your orders, all of the legion rushed to Markolm instead of engaging in prolonged battle," Khanundra said.

A heated look ran through Light's eyes as she curled her fist. Golden light covered her hand. She looked at her fist and the corner of her mouth lifted into a sneer. "Soon they'll be able to taste the real power that I have saved up to wipe them from Emerilia once and for all." Light's words sounded like a vow to herself.

In the recent weeks, her power had only grown with the number of people who gave her devotions. Now, Khanundra and the angel generals had groomed an army from those who came to Markolm for the Lady of Light's protection and believed in her fully.

Daeundra rooted out any who opposed her and removed them quickly and quietly. She also had operatives who created propaganda against Light's enemies. This gave Light the perfect conditions for creating a holy land that was once again devoted to her.

Light opened her fist. Her anger fell away as her face smoothed out, with no trace of her emotions showing. She looked at another formation that slotted into the legions. "Is that the last one?"

"Yes, my lady," Khanundra said, still bent over in a bow, not daring to stand up until she was given the order. Even though she couldn't see them with her eyes, she could sense all of the other angels.

"Good." Light stepped forward so that she could look down upon them all. She was a picture of benevolence, even looking a bit heartbroken as her eyes misted slightly.

"Please rise," Light said softly, but her words carried to all of the angels arrayed below her. Her voice seemed to shake with emotion. Light took a moment, as if she needed to recover her state of mind as she looked at them. Her hand rested on her chest as she "worked" to reclaim her calm state of mind.

"When you were banished from Emerilia—no, when you were *taken* from me, I...I was in a state of shock and pain. I wished with all my being that there was a way for me to once again be in the company of you all again, my angels, my creations, my"—Light paused as a smile that seemed to mix sad and happy appeared on her face and tears made lines down her face—"children." The word came out breathlessly, as if she were finally admitting a secret that she had held in her heart for her life, fearing that to say it would break something important to her.

"While you were gone, I was lost. But with your return, it is possible for us to once again bring the light to Emerilia, to enlighten those who have been blinded by these other lords and ladies of the Affinities Pantheon. To remove the scourge of those races that believe in nothing but themselves. Thinking to be above the divine power of Light! To leave these people alive is to pollute this glorious and precious Emerilia. I only desire for a place where the believers can live and flourish, turning this place into a paradise. A place where you will no longer be needed to fight but can lay down your arms and live in the grace of light." Her words were filled with passion.

All of the angels showed passion in their normally complacent eyes. They had killed countless people without care. Hearing Light's words moved their minds and ignited a fire within their hearts.

"For that, I will do everything in my power to see that you are protected from the threats of the unbelievers and those who have lost their path into the Light." Light raised her hands. Golden pillars dropped from the sky, falling upon the strongest of the angels. Dozens of them were lifted up from the ground as Light's blessing fell over them. Afterward, they lowered to the ground, their aura incomparable to what it had been before.

Light dropped to a knee, coughing slightly as blood appeared on her lips.

Khanundra rushed forward, supporting Light.

"Thank you, daughter," Light said.

Khanundra's eyes misted up as she helped the feeble-looking Light to her feet.

"I am sorry that I was only able to raise up some of you. But in the coming weeks, I will be able to raise you all to be my champions through your merits and abilities." Light used Khanundra to support herself to standing.

An emotion hidden deep in her eyes flashed. She knew that her words would create competition between the angels to increase their power and carry out whatever deeds possible to be worthy of being Light's Champion. Also seeing that she had poured out all of her power and even inflicted an injury upon herself, all of them were deeply moved.

Not one of them would not sacrifice their lives without a care if she asked for it.

Light looked out over them once again, a happy expression on her face. "I will let you get settled in and come to know what has happened to Emerilia. The days ahead will be hard but I know that we will persevere."

"For Goddess Light!" the angels roared out as one.

Light looked moved to tears, barely holding them back. Finally, she moved from the outside of her hall to the interior.

Khanundra assisted her gently, as if she were some decrepit old lady. She took Light to her chambers before being dismissed.

As soon as the door was closed, Light's soft exterior disappeared and she stood upright, no sign of injury on her body or by her actions.

"Still as moldable as ever." Light snorted and rolled her eyes. "Didn't even need to use a tenth of my new divine pool's capacity. They should hurry up and go kill those who support the others in the Pantheon and those who don't even make devotions. Bah, children? Better to call them refined dogs that need an emotional plea from their 'mother' instead of treats to go and fight."

For a while, she stood at the windows into her room and looked out over Markolm. Angels were moving out from around her hall.

"The time I remove my brothers and sisters of the Pantheon from this planet is coming closer."

***

Boran-al looked up from his work as a shadow formed within his laboratory, quickly resolving into the robed figure of the Dark Lord.

"Master." Boran-al dropped to his knee.

"You have done well, Boran-al." The Dark Lord looked over the laboratory. Divine wells were in various states of assembly. The Dark Champions who were assembling these wells all dropped to a knee in front of their master.

There were also a number of mutated Alturarans who were kept in different enclosures and states of dissection.

"Thank you, master," Boran-al said, filled with pride.

"I will have someone send you your rewards. There have been a number of creatures that have returned through the event that might interest you." The Dark Lord looked at Boran-al.

A cold and sinister smile spread across Boran-al as a terrifying darkness filled his eyes. "I thank you, master. This lowly one does not deserve these extravagant gifts." Boran-al was excited to get his hands on these new subjects to conduct research on.

"I sent out orders to capture them alive. I would be interested to watch as you work with your live dissections," the Dark Lord said.

"It would be my honor to show off my art." Boran-al bowed deeply. Others called him sick and perverse, but here he was lauded and seen as an innovator of torture and making someone last for weeks in unimaginable pain.

"How are the preparations?"

"The Dark Champions are watching over the portal in the Per'ush islands. We have dozens of divine wells that are ready to be used whenever you need it. I have moved them all to the portal in Alturara that is connected to the portal in Opheir. There are forces loyal to us waiting at that location, ready to gather the divine wells when they come through. I have given them the teleportation scroll that you had given me so that as soon as they get the divine wells, they will be able to teleport them directly into your hall. I have kept all of the loyal Alturarans here as to not alert the others in the Pantheon," Boran-al said.

"Good. For now, they think me to be weak. If we were to have our own Alturaran force come through, they would sense my power gain from their devotions. For now, we will work with the Earth Lord to attack Light. Water and Fire seem to care about the people of Emerilia." The Dark Lord's voice made it clear that the people of Emerilia didn't matter to him. "They are being attacked on all sides. Maybe they will provide some entertainment after this is all done."

"I heard that they have flying citadels that are able to shoot down from the sky?" Boran-al asked.

"They do, merely a replication of Light's own island but with weapons and spell formations. They will fall just as Light's island did." The Dark Lord's voice was filled with confidence. "Then I will take my time tearing apart this so-called Terra Alliance and have those who are part of the Stone Raiders beg for death."

Boran-al gritted his teeth. An ugly expression appeared on his face at the mention of the Stone Raiders. They had destroyed his cult, killed off the demons he had created and assisted the demons who had rebelled against Boran-al and the Dark Lord. Boundless bloodlust passed through the depths of his eyes.

"Once Light and Earth have shown all of their cards, then we will move ahead with our plan." The Dark Lord's voice was heavy and filled with excitement at the coming slaughter he envisioned.

Chapter 5: Awake

The server banks of the *Datskun* looked like chaos as Bob, looking as though he hadn't slept in weeks and smelling like it, tried to connect a cord into the servers and then to a tablet he was holding.

He had kept the kernel of Anna's consciousness only on the servers, never connecting to her with his interface, so as to give the Jukal and the other AIs no chance to discover her. He had already made sure that there were no records of him being in the servers and cut off any ability for the Jukal to see what he was doing.

He had compiled and shifted files. These seemed like simple things but it was in fact a code that brought all of Anna's different information files together and into the kernel. She was distributed over the network, making it so that it was nearly impossible to track her down. If one part of her coding was destroyed, then there were still thousands of other backups and parts of her distributed through Emerilia's network.

Bob held onto the tablet with unblinking eyes.

A screen popped up; lines of complicated code rushed past before being compiled and completed.

The screen went blank for a few moments.

"Dad, what happened?" Anna's voice came through, distorted and confused.

"Anna." Bob fell to the ground, holding the tablet as if it were some heavenly treasure as tears fell down his face.

"Dad, what happened? I can sense memory loss. I think I've lost a lot of my backup." Anna sounded confused and scared.

An alert appeared on the tablet that pulled at Bob's heart.

"It's okay, honey. There was just a corrupted bit of information—you've lost a bit of it." Bob bit his lip.

"I see that from all the records of you sneaking in here to watch over me." Her voice was soft and filled with emotion. "Something big must've happened for you to wake me."

Bob's heart twisted in his chest as Anna said the same words that she had when he'd woken her up from cold storage.

"Yes, something did happen, but it's okay now that you're back," Bob said. "No matter what, I'll always be here for you."

"Dad, why do you sound so sad?" Anna asked.

"You..." Bob's lower lip quivered and a look of pain flashed across his face before disappearing without a trace. "It's nothing. Just happy to have you back with me again."

"Big softie," Anna teased.

A soft smile appeared on Bob's lips. His eyes looked to the tablet on his lap.

Memory files corrupted

Memory files corrupted from last start-up. Memory fragments detected and integrated.

All of her memories since she had last woken up were nothing but fragments. Bob didn't know what this would mean and right now he didn't want to aggravate these memories. Waking them up might cause unknown problems.

Right at this moment, merilia needed Anna where she was. There was no way to upload her to a new body without the other AI or Jukal finding out.

For now, he would need to keep her largely isolated. Once this was all done, then maybe he could start trying to recover her memories and seeing what she remembered. It made him feel as if he were lying to her as he maintained his silence.

I have my daughter back, though how much of her was lost from the last three years, I don't know.

***

Frank Simmons looked at the flame in his hand. With a thought, it changed shapes, growing taller and smaller. He waved his hand; the flame disappeared and a wind vortex swirled in his hand now.

He looked up to Air with a shocked expression.

"Seems that you're getting a good handle on magic." Air smiled.

"I just can't really believe that this is all real." Frank had come to understand what was going on. But there was still a part of his mind that expected him to wake up on his couch and he'd have to go back to work at the local supermarket, all of this being nothing more than a dream.

He looked around the room and then back to Air. He had been inside this room and a few others since he had woken up.

"Want to see a bit more than just this room?" Air asked.

"Wouldn't say no to a little road trip." Frank smiled.

Air seemed to think for a few minutes before she nodded. "I don't see that being a problem. You should get to know what we're doing here." Air rose from her seat. "Come with me."

She stepped out of the room, Frank right behind her with an eager expression on his face. As Bob had been making the different bodies for the players, he had increased their base stats to that of a Level 300 right when they woke up. This took some time for them to get used to it, but afterward they were able to do all manner of different activities.

He followed Air through the halls until they reached a large glass window that ran the length of the corridor they were in. Frank moved to the glass, a look of awe on his face as he looked over Ice City. Carts moved through the air in every direction, coming from the mining areas, refineries, factories, as well as transitioning through the portals to Pandora's Box and the asteroid base.

As they watched, a soul gem building was being made. Mages circled the building; their hands moved, while some chanted as spell formations appeared around different materials. The materials came together and seemed to transform into a living being. They sunk deep into the ice planet's ground, connecting to a massive metal plate that had been created to secure all of the buildings within the city. Then they started to grow upward, interconnecting and merging together to make the superstructure of the building. As they rose, a soul gem construct grew with it, covering the superstructure and forming the rooms and interior of the tower.

"Welcome to Ice City. Most of the people from the Pandora's Box Initiative live here with their families. We've got a number of research and development areas here. We've also got the biggest refinery within the Initiative, though it seems that will be quickly changing with the dwarves working on the refinery asteroid. Here we mine out the ice in the surrounding areas to grow the city and to also supply us with a number of chemicals and materials we can use for various products."

Frank was shocked by what he saw. A sense of excitement built within him as he looked at this magical scene.

For a while, they were silent. Frank's face turned thoughtful as he glanced at Air.

"Something on your mind?" Air asked.

"I know that my body is a lot more powerful than it was and I can see that while you've got all of this, there's not too many people walking around. Even this facility is nearly completely empty. I know that you feel a sense of duty in waking up all of us players who are stuck in the Earth simulation, but what do you want to gain from this?"

Air tapped her lips with a finger. "Most will say that we're doing it because you are humans and in a way, you're the brothers and sisters of the other players on Emerilia. Dave, the leader of this all, is a player who was able to get past the simulation and find out the reality of Emerilia. He would want to be woken up to know what was really going on and be allowed to make his own decisions. Now, while we are doing it for that reason, we're also doing it for another that you've touched on." Air looked out over the city and rested her hands on the banister of the corridor.

"Emerilia is in the midst of a massive war. The people and players of Emerilia are all wrapped up in that—there's little that they can do to help us. All of this would take a lot more explaining than we're able to do right now. Also, revealing it to others leads to a greater chance of the Jukal finding out that we know what's going on and we're taking steps to gain our freedom back again.

"What we need is people, people who are motivated to work with the Pandora's Box Initiative. We've got automatons all over the place but we've only got a few hundred researchers and helpers. A few hundred people to run all of this and push us forward. With waking up the players, we hope that you can help to push the Initiative forward. We know not everyone will be willing, but there are millions of you. If even only a small percentage helps out, then maybe we can be ready for the Jukal and whatever they send at us."

Air's words resounded in Frank's soul. He wasn't a mean man nor was he easily driven to anger, but when someone did incite his fury, he would hunt them down. He wasn't able to do this within Earth's simulation and had always been frustrated within the military when they didn't seem to be doing anything but getting into constant fights over the same piece of land over and over again. The only thing that seemed to come from it was losing those he cared for, deepening his depression.

He thought of the people he had lost, the AI programs that had run the world to make him feel helpless, to feel as if he couldn't control anything in his life. But when he stepped into the world of video games, he could. When he was gaming, then there was nothing that could stand in his way. If someone wanted to try to kill him for his loot, then he'd gain more strength than them or better allies to tear them apart.

Those who crossed him quickly regretted their actions.

Here, within reality, he had once again regained the ability for him to act, to push his life forward in a meaningful way. Right now, that meaningful way was driving him toward tearing down the Jukal Empire.

He took a breath and stood straighter. The excitement and wonder in his eyes were still there but now there was determination. His fighting spirit filled him, much like how it had done when he had been first called a marine and passed his basic training. He felt a kinship with the people of Emerilia, seeing them much as he did his fellow marines.

"I might not be that good with the research stuff, but I can fight," Frank said, his voice deeper and stronger.

A smile spread across Air's face. "Well, then seems that we best get you started on training with magic."

***

Within a large laboratory, there were nearly fifty different beds; on all of these there were different runic lines carved into them and different machines hooked up to the people's bodies.

They looked like corpses, completely lifeless and no sense of movement coming from them.

One of the tables' runes flashed. The person on the table took massive gulps of air, as if they were surfacing from the depths of the ocean, as they sat up, a look of shock and panic on their face. They looked at the person at the end of the bed.

"Hello, Diana. Welcome to reality," the person wearing neutral clothing said with a smile.

Other people sucked in air as they awoke on their tables.

Diana looked around as she stared at the others on tables like hers.

"They're…" Diana's words trailed off as she saw the same mix of emotions in the others' eyes: shock, fear, confusion, excitement.

"Players. Just like you, they were stuck in the Earth simulation." The woman at the end of her bed checked different items on screens that appeared in front of her. "You're going to feel a bit different from how you were in the simulation. All of your stats have been greatly increased. You'll be stronger, faster, need less sleep and food. This is normal," the woman reassured Diana.

"I just—this is real?" Diana moved her eyes to the woman at the end of the table. The others on the tables all looked to one another and asked the same questions. Even though Diana hadn't talked to them before, she felt a sort of relationship with them due to their circumstances and similar situation.

The woman dismissed her screens and looked to Diana. "I will never lie to you in this orientation and yes, all of this is real—as shocking as that is." The woman smiled. "I didn't even know that this was possible until a few days ago."

Diana didn't sense any signs that the woman was trying to deceive her. Her head started to spin as she thought things over. Connections that she had never made before started to be made, her higher Intelligence at work as she thought through it all.

"Wow," Diana said. The wealth of information was like a puzzle where she had picked up the first piece and the others had just started to fall into place with ease.

She looked over her body. Her weight gain had disappeared and she looked like she had when she was in her mid-twenties. "Not bad. Looks like this upgrade came with some good features." Diana glanced underneath her shirt and nodded with appreciation.

The woman at the end of her table laughed at Diana's actions.

Diana paused and then laughed as well.

After a few moments, it calmed down.

"Interface," Diana said. A frame of different icons appeared around her vision. "All right, well, seems that I'm about thirty years late, mentally, to this game. Time that I started to run through the tutorial and figure out how it works." With a determined expression on her face, she started to work through the interface.

"How did you get those screens?" one of the other players asked.

"Just say interface and it should work," Diana said.

"Ah crap!" Someone getting off the bed flew five feet before coming to rest on the ground. The minders at the end of the tables moved to help them.

"Well, tell you what—the control interface is a bit touchy!" the player on the ground complained.

The other players grinned at their words.

"Hey, looks like we can create party chats, nice," one player said.

"Found stat sheets! You can just call out character sheet, or go to your profile on the left side and find it in there," another said.

"I found forums with information on Emerilia. Got a whole bunch of videos on the basics of fighting, magic and stuff like that." Diana frowned.

"The hell is magical coding?" another asked.

"I don't know—check the forums?" another player said.

All of them were on their interfaces. In just a few minutes, they were all discussing what they knew, sharing tips and tricks they'd already figured out.

The minders all looked at one another, a confused and shocked look passing between them before they looked back to the players.

Their initial shock had dissipated. All of them were treating this just as they would when starting up a new game, working through the basics and helping one another out. They laughed and joked together, drawing attention to different things that they had found out.

"So how do I access my inventory?" one asked.

"From what I'm reading, you need some kind of bag of holding to gain an inventory. It'll be added to your profile sheet. Check out the equip tab so that you can see what's on your body—just got standard clothing right now," Diana said as she read through the forums.

And so it went: the players tried moving, talking to one another and figuring out the best way to get used to their new bodies together; then they grouped together, discussing what they had found out when the minders led them to a shared living area.

A few of the minders remained, getting bombarded with questions from the players grouped together in the main living area, lounging in chairs, on tables or even on the floor.

The shock was still coming in but right now they were wrapped up in a dream and quickly using what they knew as gamers to get to know the new reality that they had been thrust into.

Chapter 6: Reclaim

"As you all know, the race that is coming through the portal are called Uoue. They're melee-based types with high Agility and speed that allows them to hit targets and then run away. Right now, the DCA and a number of elven forces have been holding them down, using all of their tricks to try to stop the Uoue from escaping the citadel's containment. They only hold one citadel but they are masters of disguise. There are an estimated two to three times their numbers within the citadel and hiding in the area around it. We're being sent in to clear the Uoue out. With the sensing abilities of the citadels, we will be able to find and push them back. The forces on the ground are already advancing from their citadels. We will be dropping down behind them to provide support. We don't expect that we will have many long-ranged attacks by the Uoue on landing. However, the Uoue and their abilities are not well known so don't take anything for granted." The commander of the Goblin Mountain's flying citadel's first wing's voice was broadcasted to all of those within the flying citadels under his command.

Party Zero looked to one another. They were once again waiting next to a drop chute. Everyone was seated as the citadels advanced on the portal location and moved between the Terra Alliance-controlled citadels.

"Prepare for drop!"

The two seated groups stood and turned, forming a line that faced the drop chute and its red light.

"Check drop packs!"

They checked the person in front of them, making sure that the drop pack was secured. There were no mistakes or issues.

"Ready!" the drop master said, listening to their party chat where the different drop masters were talking.

The chute opened and wind pulled at those waiting to drop inside. The light beside the chute snapped over to green.

"Drop, drop, drop!" Before they had said the second drop, the first person jumped down the chute, crossing their arms as the chute guided them out of the flying citadel and toward the ground below.

The line moved forward swiftly. Soon it was Dave's turn. He jumped down the chute. An overlay showed him different way points he needed to hit in order to make it down to the ground with Party Zero.

He looked around him. Hundreds of people with drop packs rained out from the citadel as drop pads rushed past. Streamers of air currents that were broken in their passing lit their trail as they rushed toward the ground. The magical coding lit up as soon as they came close to the ground in order to reduce the impact of the fall.

Dave concentrated on his flight path, increasing his speed as he shot through the various way points ahead of him. He could see the forces that had already moved out of the citadels and were now lined up in formations, ready to clear out the Uoue that they faced.

Dave flipped, his speed greatly reducing as he touched down on the ground. Steve, Gurren, and Lox smashed into the ground. Dirt exploded out from around them. Malsour and Induca, in their dragon form, remained in the sky, banking over the formations. Aerial forces moved around them, operating as one unit in direct support of the dragons.

The weapons on the leading edge of the flying citadels scanned the ground. Here and there, they fired at the ground, exploding before the gathered forces of the Terra Alliance, announcing the death of some Uoue that had been discovered by the flying citadel groups' sensors.

Deia, Induca, and Jung Lee landed easily; their heads on a swivel and searching the battlefield ahead of them.

The different forces that had dropped from the flying citadels were getting organized. Different drums, horns, and the sound of leaders yelling at their soldiers rang through the air as formations were pulled together and then moved up to the line or moved into supporting positions behind the front lines.

It was a complicated manoeuvre but they pulled it off seamlessly.

Dave looked to Deia, noticing the hidden look of pride in her eyes. After all, she had been in charge of training all of the men and women who made up the drop forces of the flying citadels. As the first group made it down, the drop pads were already returning to the flying citadels for the reserve forces that were being brought up from Terra in support. There were three onos in the surrounding citadels. Even now there was a great shortage of onos throughout all of Emerilia, resulting in them not being able to meet all the needs of the various citadels that were around the portals. It also meant that they were unable to link all of Emerilia.

"One day I'll get that class upgrade for linking all of Emerilia together," Dave muttered to himself.

"Prepare to move out! Detection mages and scouts to the front! Protect them and follow their commands!" the leader of the assault forces said.

Already the DCA mages with powerful detection spells, as well as the elven rangers and those with the best detection abilities, had been littered throughout the formations to make sure that none of the Uoue would make it past their lines.

Dave pulled up a picture of the Uoue. Their skin looked like bark; it had the ability to change form slightly and it could change color. They had an innate ability to make them nearly undetectable by magic and hard to see with an untrained eye. Most people wouldn't know that there were Uoue around until they stepped on one and were killed.

They had a central body and four limbs. They splayed out on the ground, waiting for when their prey would come past and then snap together, impaling their prey. Not only were their ambushing abilities great, their physical strength was enough to get through most S-classed armors.

They were able to extend thorn-like protrusions from their hands that they used to pierce their enemies or fight them. Fighting them was like fighting a buzz saw that had intelligence; every move was done with the force to pulverize and the accuracy to kill in one hit. They were not an enemy to be underestimated those that did, would not live to underestimate them again.

The area they were in was inhospitable, a mix of gray sand and slate rocks that could easily make anyone lose their footing. Among this, the Uoue waited. It could be considered a perfect hunting ground for them.

As soon as the force was all assembled, they moved forward, taking it slowly so that they wouldn't be surprised by the Uoue and their tricks.

Whenever one of the scouts or detection mages noticed something, they would get an attack mage to drop destructive spells on the location. This happened more and more as they moved closer to the portal. A number of times, there was nothing there but no one complained about wasting a bit of Mana instead of getting torn apart by the Uoue.

The citadels hovered above, with the aerial forces seeing if they could spot anything from above. The citadels fired down a few times, throwing up the dust and bits of the slate into the sky and obscuring the ground. This reduced as time went on for fear of giving the Uoue an advantage with all the dust and debris.

The aerial forces also stopped dropping their larger scale weapons of destruction or spells, moving to use their bows, repeaters, and other weapons that wouldn't cause the battlefield to be covered in dust and debris.

Dave frowned. Unseen, he released two orbs from his left hand hidden underneath his cloak. The orbs disappeared as soon as they made contact with the air and shot out from Dave. There was no sign of their passing as Dave showed no signs of doing anything out of the ordinary.

However, on his mini-map, red dots started to appear, telling of the Uoue waiting for the advancing assault force.

Dave moved a series of bracelets on his armband, connecting to the flying citadels and sending them commands, unlocking part of the abilities that they weren't supposed to have. They wouldn't be as accurate as they would be when fully active; however, they would give those in the flying citadels and those on the ground a better idea of where the Uoue were hiding.

Spells started to fly as more and more Uoue pockets were wiped out.

The dust increased and a distorting feeling seemed to fall over Dave's senses as he used his Touch of the Land spell. Dave shook his head, slightly dizzy. His mind cleared as he looked up and down the lines of people. They also seemed to be in a sort of stupor, moving mechanically while the scouts looked confused and shook their heads.

They were walking in the fog created by the explosions from earlier, though the effects from this dust shouldn't have been anything to make Dave feel confused.

"Deia, send out a wave of flame—see if you burn anything," Dave said in a hurried voice.

Deia didn't ask and did as he said. A wave of fire extended from her hand. As it passed through the sky, flames were left burning different areas. The sky filled with slowly moving flames that turned green instead of the red from Deia's hands.

"What the hell is that?" the assault forces commander demanded.

"The Uoue put something in the air. I felt that there was something funny going on with my head. The Uoue don't use magic, so they must be using some sort of poison or organic. I had someone shoot out fire—seems that they're sending out some kind of compound to reduce our sensitivity to Mana while also making us more sluggish," Dave said quickly.

There was a sound of scraping and rapid footsteps as slate broke ahead of the assault formation.

"Everyone, take your positions!" the commander said.

From the dust and debris, the Uoue charged forth. Their bodies looked like the gray sand and slate that the assault formation was walking through. They didn't make any noise other than their footsteps as they broke through the slate. Their razor-sharp appendages stuck out, ready to carve anyone in front of them apart.

The aerial forces came in without having to be told, laying down their attacks into the charging Uoue. Formation commanders called out orders as dwarven shield walls slammed into place. Ranged attackers unleashed their attacks together; the waves of Uoue were met with spells that tore them apart, with the power of Mana bolts, lightning that descended from the sky, or any of the other attacks that the Terra Alliance forces knew.

The charging Uoue fell under these attacks but they were still advancing. They didn't make any noise as they died.

The ranged beasts that had been contracted to the dwarven warclans and also the other members of the Terra Alliance unleashed their attacks.

The Uoue took heavy losses, but with their unnatural speed and agility, they continued to advance bloody meter by bloody meter. Without the aid of shields or barriers, they were unable to defend against the oncoming attacks, only dodging if they were given the chance.

A half dozen orbs appeared above Party Zero. Lox, Gurren, and Dave used their orbs to target the Uoue, sending Mana bolt after Mana bolt into their formations. Under these destructive attacks, the air continued to be filled with more and more debris, making it harder for the Terra Alliance forces to see the Uoue that continued their charge.

The first Uoue met the dwarven lines that stood at the front of the alliance's assault formation. A Uoue made a massive leap, covering fifteen meters in one go, and landed on the dwarves. Its appendages dug through the shields, hitting those below. Pained cries rang out as the Uoue pierced the dwarves below and dropped into the dwarven shield formation.

It spun and moved in impossible ways. With each and every movement, armor was pierced and blood let out into the sky. As it was attacking, the dwarves were also fighting back, their swords hacking at the Uoue.

"Use Mana shields!" a dwarven warclan leader yelled out. With the Mana barriers, the Uoue weren't moving fast enough to trigger the Mana barrier, nor were they using magical attacks.

With the Mana shields, more of them weren't making it into the dwarven formations and after hitting the Mana shields over the dwarves, they shot forward toward those behind the dwarves. A number of them were cut down in this desperate dash; a few got through here and there. The players stepped up, clashing with the Uoue. They were incredibly fast, needing multiple tanks to fight them to deal with the damage while others wore them down or landed a killing blow. The dwarves finally defeated the last Uoue in their formations and started to push their wounded to the rear. The front lines could do nothing in the Mana shield, unable to attack but completely safe. They were merely an annoying obstacle that the Uoue had to climb over to get at those behind them.

With every step the Uoue took, their pointed appendages stabbed into the Mana shield that the dwarves were using. Combined with the power in their bodies and their weight, they were doing heavy damage to the protections that the warclans had laid down.

The mounted forces worked to move people from the battlefield and reacted to the areas where the Uoue were the thickest. Overhead, the flying citadels fired at the area ahead of the assault force. Still more of the Uoue seemed to appear from out of the fog created by the impacts, slamming into the assault force.

"Go back to whence you came!" Steve barked. His axe smashed forward and hit an Uoue in mid-air. Steve, who had jumped up to head them off, was also thrown back by the impact of his weapon. He used his feet and free hand to slow his momentum; as soon as he had come to a stop, he rushed forward again. "What insane bastard came up with killer trees with sword feet and arms!? I'd like to hit him over the head with Alex!"

Dave cracked a smile, hearing some life come back into Steve's words.

The dragons came in low and dangerous, unleashing their attacks that destroyed swathes of the Uoue with every pass.

Deia was using her bow, hitting Uoue that came into her range. Her hands were a blur as red streaks tore through the Uoue.

Lox and Gurren were on either side of Dave, using all of the orbs as well as their hands to unleash Mana bolts on the Uoue, providing support to those fighting at the front.

Stone Raiders and players led the charge against the Uoue, figuring out how to fight them as they crossed the dwarven formations.

Jung Lee flashed through the sky. The Uoue were no different than chickens in front of him. He could easily kill them, but their numbers were vast and the area that they were spread over was too large for him to be everywhere at once.

Suzy's creations engaged with the Uoue, holding them down and suppressing them to give the reacting forces the time they needed to get to the scene.

Dave felt the loss of Anna and Jekoni. The balance of the party felt off. Instead of wallowing in his pain, he fought harder.

Howling noises came from above as spears conjured miles upward dropped down toward the battlefield. They smashed into the ground. A shock wave shot out from the impact craters, the Uoue nearby torn apart by the kinetic force while the air was temporarily cleared of dust and debris.

"Move into war parties! Staggered!" the warclan leader called out across the assault force.

The dwarven formations pulled apart and moved into their five shield bearer war parties, allowing them greater mobility and to focus on themselves instead of working with the entire dwarven formation.

"Players and those with Weapons of Power, move to support the frontline formations!" the assault force commander called out.

Party Zero stood at the extreme rear of the dwarves. They were still covered by the Mana shield, making it impossible for them to enter the dwarven formations as shields came apart and the dwarves moved as one, leaving large gaps between each of the war parties.

"Mana shield coming down!" the dwarven warclan leader yelled out.

The thick and substantial Mana shield disappeared. The Uoue that had been on top of the shield fell down to the ground.

The dwarves yelled out as they attacked the Uoue, working in their war parties. Players and those with Weapons of Power let out yells as they charged forward into the melee.

Party Zero was part of this force. Dave activated his flying runes and floated into the sky. From his hands, Mana bolts tore through the sky, each with enough force to melt through a foot of tempered steel, any less force wouldn't kill a Uoue.

The Uoue liked to lead with jumping attacks and fall on their enemies, stunning them and slaughtering those within range of their limbs. The Uoue were like a surging tide smashing against the dwarven warclans.

The ranged members of the Terra Alliance unleashed their abilities filling the skies with colourful but deadly attacks.

Dave didn't need to directly act as Uoue came into his sphere of influence with his high Intelligence attribute he could command a few dozen orbs without any strain as they acted as floating Mana bolt throwers.

This, combined with the other sensor orbs he had released secretly, allowed him to clearly see all of the battlefield, much clearer than anyone else.

Lox and Gurren were just starting to test out the new floating orbs. They weren't as good with them as Dave but the added Mana bolts were no less deadly as they raked the Uoue's front lines.

With the dust and debris, a number of the attacks weren't hitting the Uoue and instead were wasted into the ground. The Uoue seemed to have gone all out as they turned the dwarven formations into a sea of chaos. The sounds of close combat rang out over the lines.

"Players, form up at the front!" a new voice yelled out.

Dave's head whipped around in recognition of it. Josh had been the one speaking. From the Terra-controlled citadels, players from the Stone Raiders and other allied guilds charged forward.

At this time, there were nearly forty percent of the players on Emerilia fighting as part of the Terra Alliance, with nearly sixty percent of them having a relationship with the Stone Raiders Guild.

The Stone Raiders led the charge through the assault formations, hoping to draw the attention onto themselves and away from the POEs.

"Move with them—we'll push back the Uoue!" Deia yelled out.

Party Zero was swept up in the wave of players. The Uoue that had been leaping to attack the dwarven war parties were now ruthlessly cut down as the players, filled with fighting spirit, collided with the Uoue that were in close combat with the dwarves. Riled up with the excitement of the battle, the players were a powerful force, showing off fighting skills and abilities that left the POEs stunned.

Dave moved the different sliders on his arms as he tapped out things on his interface, unlocking different things within the flying citadels and creating some magical coding that could help out the forces on the ground. He sent it to the commander of the Goblin Mountain's flying citadel second wing leader.

He grabbed his two conjuration rods. "Time for a special brew!" Gray smoke appeared around the two of them as he held them out like a T in front of himself, flicking the different bands on the conjuration rods.

The smoke formed what looked to be two crossbows that had been stuck together bottom to bottom. There were intricate runic lines on either side. Gray smoke wafted out from the runes. Dave raised the crossbow. He took a breath; the runic lines of his Lux armor and the attached cloak grew brighter as the runic lines on his hood and across his body lit up.

Dave put the Mana bolt orbs on automatic, allowing them to fire at the targets that the sensing orbs found. His mind linked to the sensing orbs.

His eyes opened in a flash. His crossbow moved; he fired and turned, firing again. With each pull of the crossbow's trigger, a bolt was released. A new string and bolt was conjured in their place as soon as they had left the crossbow, allowing Dave to shoot as fast as he could pull the trigger.

Dave's movements were nimble and fluid. By the time the third bolt had been fired, the first hit its target. The bolt hit the Uoue, damaging them and pushing them back slightly. It started to recover when the crossbow bolt's conjuration spell changed; all of the Mana within it lost the containment of the spell formation.

The resulting free Mana exploded, opening a fist-sized hole through the Uoue and destroying its internals.

"Show-off! Look at me, I'm Dave—got a cool new weird crossbow thingy!" Steve complained, cutting through a Uoue's leg and then burying the pick at the back end of his axe into the Uoue's body. He slammed them to the ground with so much force that a crater appeared around them.

"Just need a way to compete with the wife!" Dave said.

He saw the corner of Deia's mouth rise as her eyes sharpened. The rate at which she shot out arrows only increased. She used the environment around her to move, cutting down Uoue from across the assault formation, smacking another's limb away from her with the tip of her bow. Flames surged out from her body to burn the Uoue to a crisp. She pulled back on her bowstring again; an arrow was conjured between her fingers and released to hit another Uoue as the one that she'd set aflame fell to the ground.

Around Suzy, her six Affinity creations were even more stable and powerful, each of them on a strength comparable to the Uoue.

However, they could use limited Affinity spells, giving them an advantage.

Jung Lee landed in front of the formation in a pillar of dust. Only the noises of his sword moving filled the air.

Dave could see that he was fighting Uoue that were now converging on his position. He met them all. Combined with his six Affinities, he left only traces of gray smoke behind him. His sword flashed as he moved with a deadly grace that Dave felt incapable of replicating.

After a few minutes, the assault force got into a rhythm of dealing with the Uoue, greatly reducing their casualties.

The Uoue stopped attacking and started to flee back into the dust and debris that covered the area around their portal.

"Do not chase them!" Josh yelled out. But his words weren't enough to stop some as they rushed out into that black and gray dust-filled hell.

Screams could be heard as names were added to the kill log along everyone's screens.

"Hold your positions and get the wounded to the rear. The flying citadels have a magical formation they want to try. It should at least get rid of this dust," Josh said.

The assault formation, their blood cooled down from hearing the deaths of those who had chased the Uoue, quickly followed Josh's orders.

Runic lines along the flying citadels' soul gem island and the bodies of the citadels atop started to light up. The air filled with humming as complicated spell formations appeared around the flying citadels. Thick lines of power shot out from the four citadels, meeting between them, right over the Uoue portal.

From the different lines, spell formations grew out in a clockwise manner and connected to the other lines from the citadels. The lines were not as thick in the center but the powerful spell formation was thick with runes. Smaller spell formations grew along the lines between the massive one in the center and the citadels.

They were various sizes and carried different runes.

A buzzing sound filled the air as the runes lit up and the spell formations activated. The air seemed to become heavy as clouds appeared in the sky, further darkening the area around the gray and black dust that filled the visions of the assault force.

Thick, rolling clouds converged above that spell formation. There was a booming sound of thunder; lightning arced through those black clouds.

Suddenly, all at once, it was as if a sheet of rain had fallen. The dust over the assault force was forced back as the dust and debris in the air in front of them and under the rain clouds was pushed to the ground. The assault forces looked upon the torrential downpour that was happening just a meter or so away from the front line.

With the rain, all of the dust was suppressed. However, the Uoue were sneaky and a number of them looked to stealth their ways to the front lines. People found the Uoue once again emerging right in front of their front lines.

"Pull your heads out of your asses—this fight isn't over yet!" Josh yelled as a few people succumbed to the Uoue's attacks.

Here and there, fighting broke out but none of the Uoue were able to get too close to the assault formation.

The magical formation above the portal dissipated, allowing the rain to come to a stop.

"Nice, a sauna," Dave said. The air was now humid with the mixture of heat and rain; however, they could now all see through the gray sand and slate plains to the abandoned-looking city that the portal rested in the center of.

"I have a feeling that this is not going to be a fun battle," Lox said.

New magical lines ran from the flying citadels as a spell formation appeared.

"Well, it might not be all that bad," Dave said, recognizing the spell formation.

The spell formation was completed in the sky. A few moments later, a disrupting attack rained down from it. The blast of distorted light smashed against the abandoned city.

"Looked like it needed a remodeling anyway." Steve raised his axe to his shoulder.

The buildings were eaten away by the disruption ray.

"Did you fix the firing mechanism?" Gurren asked Dave.

"Nope. Still got a Nalheim up there stabbing away with a spear to use this," Dave said, understanding just how ridiculous that was.

"Well, as long as it works," Deia said.

Dave nodded and watched as the disruption ray fell from the sky, flattening the city, eating through the ground, making the buildings that looked as if a giant had eaten them teeter and fall over.

"While it will be easier to see and fight the Uoue, we're still going to need to get in there and clear them out." Suzy frowned.

"Nothing for it—it's the job that we signed up for," Steve said. "Well, I guess I was technically contracted into it at the first."

Steve struck a thoughtful pose as Dave let out a slight laugh. The dark atmosphere that had been following them ever since the deaths of Jekoni and Anna had eased slightly.

It hadn't gone, but with all things, time was starting to heal them.

There was much for them to do and it helped for them to get through their inner pain. Dave could see that a number of them blamed themselves for what had happened. However, they were coming to know that Anna and Jekoni had done it for them, knowing full well what would happen to them. They had died to give them and the others within that Xelur citadel the ability to fight on, to be able to continue on. Still, the members of Party Zero couldn't help be selfish and hope that there was a way that they could have saved them both.

Dave looked around. His eyebrows pinched together.

He wanted to be here, to look after the people he cared about, but that was his emotions speaking.

He didn't want to admit it, but right now he was here fighting for his own gain.

Sure, I can help out a bit here, but I'm needed to help with the Pandora's Box Initiative. Already the more isolated players in the Earth simulation have been woken up and soon Sato's people will be starting to build their outpost. There's also the fact that the test portal is nearing completion and I want to work on the battleship and destroyer, and possibly make them from scratch just to look over all of the magical coding with everyone working together. Only then can we get the best results from our warships.

Dave's mind turned back to the issues that he had found when Ela-Dorn, Malsour, and he had confronted one of Sato's stealth ships, the *Sprite*. He wasn't pleased with the results, sure he could go through and troubleshoot it all. But by building it together with the others in the Initiative, then they could get to know the ins and outs of the ship and pick apart any small issues, making it stronger and more powerful. They didn't have endless resources or time, so they needed everything they were building to be in working condition as soon as it was built.

He also hadn't seen Koi in too long. It felt like with everything going on, he was letting his daughter down. Deia and he had already talked about how much they wanted to spend time with their daughter but it seemed they weren't able to step away from their duties for even a moment.

Dave took a deep breath as the last disruption ray landed. All of the buildings around the portal had been reduced to nothing but dust. With the humidity, this dust fell to the ground instead of being tossed up into the air.

The portal stood in the middle of the crater, tilted slightly at an odd angle.

The spell formation changed once again between the flying citadels, solidifying and then dropping toward the ground. This spell formation was a shield spell. If anyone stepped out of the portal, they would slam into the shield, then become torn apart by the power of the portal's event horizon. This would stop any more Uoue from rushing through the portal to help those already in Emerilia.

"Prepare to move—scouts and detection mages out front! Check your mini-maps for anything that the flying citadels are able to find!" Josh called out.

The player-led forces moved forward. They had the best detection abilities and were backed up by the POEs who called out as soon as they found a disturbance, calling down fire from the ranged attackers on the ground or from the flying citadels.

A sand dune flew up in the air. A Uoue stabbed out at a player; they looked down at their chest that had one of the Uoue's limbs stabbed through them.

Dave and Deia fired at the same time; their bolt and arrow tore the Uoue apart as the other ranged members in the force added in their own attacks.

The Uoue didn't have time to get a second victim.

Uoue that had been buried underneath the sands and evaded detection exploded upward across the formation at random times, usually claiming at least one victim before they were put down ruthlessly.

Everyone was tense as they continued forward. Everyone on the front scanned the ground, looking for any trace of the Uoue.

Sometimes the Uoue would charge out in packs but without the cover of the dust cloud, all of the assault force could see them. All of their ranged weapons bore down on them as soon as they appeared, mercilessly cutting them down.

Under that hot sun, the Terra Alliance continued forward, gritting their teeth and tightening their hands around their weapons. The atmosphere tensed as no one wished to talk, as if doing so would alert the Uoue and bring them down upon them.

It wasn't pleasant and it took nearly three hours before they finally reached the edge of the crater that led to the portal that allowed access to Emerilia. There were no cheers of victory, only weary relief as the assault force finally started to release the high state of alert that they had maintained throughout the advance.

Scouts continued to move over the area, making sure that none of the Uoue had escaped while mages used their more powerful detection spells. These took time and Mana that wasn't convenient to use when they were moving or fighting. These groups were heavily protected as they worked to clear up the remaining Uoue.

Party Zero looked over this all as a familiar face with a group of high-leveled Stone Raiders moved closer to them.

"Hey, Josh," Dave called out in greeting, waving to them.

"Hey." Josh looked as if he had aged decades in the last couple of months. They had dropped the truth of Emerilia on him, then he'd been engaged in fighting the creatures of the event as well as whatever decided to come through the portals.

He was the official head of the Terra Alliance, which meant managing all of the different guilds, kingdoms, and groups that had come to join the alliance. It was a lot of pressure and he knew if he didn't do his best then people would die.

They all stood there in companionable silence. It had been some time since they'd had a minute for them to just be with their own thoughts.

Malsour opened up a party chat with them all so that no one might be able to hear them. "I've decided that I'm going to return to the Initiative," he said, his voice firm even as it contained a thread of guilt.

"I will be doing the same," Dave said in a heavy voice. He didn't want to leave his friends to face the dangers that lay ahead alone, but he was needed by the Initiative much more than Party Zero needed him.

Josh looked to them both and nodded. "I know it's a hard decision to make but, even though you're great fighters, if you can make a few more things like the flying citadels, it will increase our fighting abilities a hundredfold. Which is much more aid than just your fighting can offer." Josh let out a sigh. He didn't want to say the words but they needed to be said.

Deia and Dave shared a look. He didn't want to leave her but he needed to, for now. She smiled at him, sensing his inner turmoil, her eyes telling him that she would be fine.

Dave nodded slightly to her. The corners of his mouth lifted slightly.

Chapter 7: Show and Tell

Ela-Dorn was pouring over the plans for the portals as well as the wealth of information that Dave had supplied her on his various theories and the documents that detailed plans on portals, teleport pads and Onos. All of it had served as fuel to further her research.

She was now working toward her next class-changing level so that she could add in having the gravitational anomalies and master of space and time classes. With all that she now knew, by just getting those two classes she would gain a wealth of stat points.

People all through the Initiative were also changing their classes, building up skills that they didn't know existed and opening their horizons further than ever. These people who had thought of themselves being on top of Emerilia in all of its knowledge were now learning that they had been deluded. As they came to know more, the more they found questions. Most of them were submerged in research and experimentation, spending every waking moment working on different experiments and projects.

There was a serious atmosphere to Ice City and the various bases. But under it, there was excitement. Here they were on the leading edge of discoveries and making leaps that people on Emerilia would think them crazy for even mentioning.

They had adapted a similar outlook to what Dave had introduced: they were seeing just how far they could push the boundaries. If they thought it might work, they would put in all their effort to figure out how to bring about the changes that they wanted. There were people from all over now putting forward theories that were being proved or dismissed every day. These theories had turned the different bases into a wealth of furious activity, each and every day it seemed some new connection was made, or a theory proved or disproved. To them it was researching bliss.

Then the players who had been woken up had added in their efforts.

They came without the ability to help out at first, but they were quick learners and their imagination hadn't dulled in the slightest. They came up with some incredible ideas, some of them were even insane, but still it got the others thinking and they worked to see whether they could make these ideas a reality.

The population of Ice City had been scared and tense when they had heard about the players being woken up from their slumber. There was truly no way of knowing how they would react. However, now there were already players who had not only been introduced to the community but had taken up jobs within it. The number of them who wished to help out was incredible. Much like how players on Emerilia were, if they were given a quest they would do everything in their power to complete it.

They shared all that they learned with one another in their own slang and language, easily getting the point across. What might take Ela-Dorn and her colleagues hours, only took them a few minutes.

There was a knock from Ela-Dorn's doorway. She turned from the interface she was reading to find Dave in the doorway to her laboratory.

"Seems like you're always looking over some project or stuck in some book," Dave said with a small smile.

"Well, it seems that I'm always finding myself behind you and the rest of the people in this Initiative!" Ela-Dorn retorted. "So, what are you coming looking for me for?"

"Well, I was thinking that it might be a good idea to have someone who knows a few things about portals with me when I fire up our first prototype."

"You're going to start it up?" Ela-Dorn asked. "Wait—the ship one or the smaller one?"

"The smaller one. Don't want to have the big one just start melting down. Any changes that need to be made with the smaller one we can just make and apply them to the bigger version." Dave paused and looked thoughtful. His mouth opened and closed as he frowned; his finger rested against his lip. "Maybe that would work—well, it should anyway."

"What are you muttering about?" Ela-Dorn's eyebrow arched in question to Dave's sudden look of discovery. She'd seen it before. Either he'd come up with an incredibly good idea, or an incredibly stupid one. There was no real knowing of what would come out from his mind.

"Well, I've been thinking on the battleship. There were a number of issues I found with it when we used it that one time. I wasn't sure how we could fix them. I was thinking that if we got everyone together, we'd build a ship section by section until it's all complete. That would take a bunch of time, resources, and manpower, but then we could take that design, replicate it again and again for functioning warships as soon as they're complete. I was thinking too big. We can already make the different components and as long as we're not running a ton of power through it, then we can make everything smaller. We don't need to make a full battleship—we just need to make a model, see how it works, fix the issues and then copy it over to the other battleships. I'm thinking that we make a model of the battleship, but at a thousandth the size. It will be easy to detect any issues and changing them out would be easy and not require nearly as much Mana.

"We sort everything out. Then when it's complete, we feed it power and resources, then it uses them to just expand the systems that already make it up. Think of those sponges in the pill caps—you add water and they expand a hundred times their original size!" Dave snapped his fingers, a look of relief on his face as well as excitement.

Ela-Dorn didn't know what the sponge-like things were but she understood what Dave was talking about. It was her turn to look thoughtful. After a few moments, she started to nod, becoming more and more confident. "I don't see any problems with it," she agreed.

"It'll be a bit slower than building it in one go, and take a lot more energy but with all the fusion reactors and Mana wells we've got around, power is not a problem. What it will also do is take some strain off the automatons that are running around. We could have one of these for every two battleships we make normally—we'd actually be able to increase production. Well, I'm getting a bit ahead of myself and I would need Jeeves to look over that—"

"I will begin simulations for viability," Jeeves said from overhead, interrupting Dave.

"Thanks, dude," Dave said

"In the meantime, portal?" Ela-Dorn stood up from her seat. A look of excitement filled her eyes.

"Onward!" Dave waved for her to take the lead. They talked about different things. Ela-Dorn was more than willing to pick his brain for all it was worth, so that she might advance her own research.

Dave's shock at how much had changed in the short time he had been gone was written all over his face.

Under Water and his colleagues' work, they had been able to increase the rate at which Ice City could expand. They had also increased the rate at which they could mine from the ice planet and refine it. They now had an abundance of different elements that were being used throughout the Initiative. All of the various vessels that were held and controlled by the Pandora's Box Initiative weren't fully fueled but it was believed that in no more than one month they would all have full fuel tanks and be completely charged. At this state, they would be able to move at a moment's notice.

However, weapons and their armaments that had been lagging behind had now increased in production speed.

Dave had a somber look on his face as he heard of Jekoni's breakthroughs and what he had passed on to the rest of the Ice City researchers that had greatly accelerated their production times. New factories were being stepped up all the time and the first asteroid refinery was being worked on.

"Jesal is running the project but a number of the dwarven master smiths are throwing their weight behind it. They've picked out an asteroid heavy in various metals that we need. The mining is already underway the automated drills are opening up an entrance for the newly built excavator. Once it's inside, it will start clearing out the interior of the asteroid. An ono will be placed inside the asteroid and connected to the asteroid base to allow quick transition. The refinery will be built first. We've got a large number of resources building up and nowhere to push them through. It's one of the biggest reasons why we're behind on the ship production," Ela-Dorn said.

"How many ships do we have?" Dave asked.

"At this time, we have twenty-four arks, sixty-four missile boats, three complete destroyers, two more under construction and two battleships under construction. The rest are shuttles and smaller craft to move resources, automatons, and other items for short distances," Ela-Dorn reported.

"We really need to speed up production on those ships," Dave said, clearly not happy with the production speed.

"We'll be able to do it," Ela-Dorn said with confidence.

"Why are you so sure?" Dave asked, a bit stunned by how confident she was.

"The players." Ela-Dorn looked to the large apartment buildings and storage facilities that were governed by Bob and Air, with their staffs looking after the creation of the players' bodies as well as their awakening and integration into reality.

It was one hell of a job but Dave had continued to hear good things about it.

"I know that they've been seen as good to have around and having a few laborers around is good, but I don't know how useful they're going to be overall," Dave said, revealing his own thoughts toward the players' abilities and the effect of them being awake.

Ela-Dorn's footsteps paused. "As much as I want to see this portal—active or not—I think you need to see something first."

"Okay," Dave said, curious.

She turned and guided him toward a MOC— Mirror of Communication—store. These were hubs that had popped up all over Emerilia as well as throughout the Pandora's Box Initiative. With the riskiest of experiments and even trying to gain more knowledge, the best place to start was with the Mirror of Communication school that had been set up by Dave. They could test out ideas there, then take it to the real world and make sure that their experiments wouldn't blow up in their faces. This ability of trial and error without having to worry too much about the loss of resources or one's life was invaluable.

The information that was available and passing through the school was also impressive, possibly only second to the mage's college in certain areas.

Dave and Ela-Dorn sat in a seat and connected to the Mirror of Communication, passing through lobbies, meeting up and heading into the private school that they had set up. This allowed them to be part of the Mirror of Communication school but no one could see what they looked like and they could pass through different classes without anyone seeing them if they wanted to.

They were in a class that was talking about advanced magical theories. The teacher seemed to be in a thrall as they discussed the ways to change spells to maximize their power.

Ela-Dorn added a filter to the class. Nearly a hundred different people were highlighted, either in anonymous mode or blurred out and attending class.

"All of these people are players who have been woken up. Their higher stats allow them to pass quickly through different knowledge-based classes. They all have the ability to pick classes and have been holding out on it. A number of them are running simulations on the best builds, using data collected on your own player forums for the generation of players on Emerilia.

"They're taking all of the information that is on Emerilia, using the basics that they learn here, combining it together and they're quickly becoming more than just practitioners of the different skills they're trying out. Here in Ice City and for the Initiative, we've got the best people in all different areas—the players have been making use of them to gain more knowledge. A number of them are actually providing ideas to us that we didn't even think of." Ela-Dorn made some adjustments with her interface that was linked to the Mirror of Communication.

The scene in front of them changed to one of a training area where people were sparring with one another. Again, a filter fell over everyone; there were a few hundred players in this area.

"All of them have gained a basic understanding of the various magics and of how to fight. A good amount of them have expressed interest in working with us to defeat the Jukal. They want to be on the front lines and fighting." Ela-Dorn shook her head as she, too, couldn't understand the mindset that these people had.

"I don't think that normal gamers would be like this, but after their lives that have forced them to become gamers—the AIs used more ruthless means than necessary—this has oppressed them.

Now they're given a way to fight and they're instilled with the confidence of their gaming talents and knowledge. I never thought that this would happen." Dave looked at his fellow players, at a loss for words. But deep down he felt a sense of pride.

A smile touched his face. *These are my people—these are gamers!* he cried out in his heart.

"Air's people had decided at first to only wake a few people at a time, to take care of them and to personally guide them through their new lives. They were not expecting for this to happen. Instead of having a few people being woken a week, it's happening by the hour. The players network with one another and they have started to work together and form groups aiming toward different sectors," Ela-Dorn said. Dave frowned at this but Ela-Dorn didn't notice as she continued. "With them asking the people of the Initiative questions, it has decreased the speed at which we are to advance our plans but in the future, I think that it will greatly increase the speed at which we can accomplish our plans."

"They're making guilds," Dave said.

"From the look on your face, it doesn't seem as if you're too happy with that," Ela-Dorn said.

"It's not that I am or not; it's just that as guilds are made, each of them want to be at the top. If we have that, then it's going to create conflict and issues. What to do, what to do?"

Ela-Dorn watched Dave. It was some time before he started talking again.

"Okay, well, the first thing, we need to start making quests. All gamers are going to get bored if they don't have quests. With this, the quests should be to assist the different researchers or various areas. Say, for completing a quest, they are able to gain tokens. These can be used to gain tutoring from the people within the Initiative, if they're willing to give the lessons. Also, it can allow them to exchange it into gold to get different things that they can buy through the trading hubs and the branch from the Exdar's that we've roped in to supply us with various materials."

The Pandora's Box Initiative needed a number of different resources and Emerilia was still the richest place for the majority of these items. A special group from the Exdar's Traders had been checked over by Lucy, Air, Suzy, Josh, as well as Dave. Their job was to acquire the materials and items that the Initiative needed. They didn't know what it was for and thought that they were just supplying the Aleph College.

Through them, the players in Ice City would be able to get all manner of different items. If anything was a great lure to players, well, nothing spoke of excitement quite like loot!

"I think it might also be beneficial to bring over the different leaders of the Stone Raiders at one time or another, so that they can meet these players, rope them into the Stone Raiders Guild or at least get them thinking that we're pretty good to work with. With the rewards, visits from other players and the purpose to fight against the Jukal—oh, and throw in the feeds to Emerilia—they need to know what's going on and get up to date," Dave said, his face grim.

Even though they were now clearing out the different portal locations, there was a vast sea of creatures and people that had arrived with the event. A number of them had been invited to join the ranks of the different members in the Affinities Pantheon, which made Dave unsure of the future that lay ahead.

Ela-Dorn also knew that one of the biggest reasons Dave was pushing everything ahead as fast as possible was because there was a very real possibility that with the Affinities Pantheon coming to blows, there would be no option but for the Pandora's Box Initiative to activate in order to save the people of Emerilia and drive back these overpowered individuals who had been molded into gods by the Jukal Empire.

Ela-Dorn and Dave lapsed into silence for a bit, each of them within their own thoughts.

"How is Bob?" Dave asked, his voice quiet.

"When he heard the news, he disappeared. Someone who went to the *Datskun* said that there were signs of someone being there. The carrier was too large for them to find Bob in it all."

Dave had a complicated look on his face as he took a deep breath and let it out slowly. His eyes shook with emotions hidden within.

Ela-Dorn looked away, feeling as if she was seeing something she shouldn't.

After a few minutes, Dave turned to Ela-Dorn. "Okay, let's go and see this portal."

"Let's," Ela-Dorn said, excitedly, happy to be able to do something to distract him from his internal pain.

They left the Mirror of Communication and headed through the portal to the asteroid base.

"Every time I come here, it's changed a bit," Dave said in wonder as they used party chat to talk. Both of them used Mana barriers in order to capture air around them before they left Ice City.

"Well, it's the look of progress," Ela-Dorn said as they walked through the laboratories. Soul gem walls and flooring met their eyes; runic lines lit their way while others carried commands, information, and power throughout the base. Carts with heavy loads of resources passed through the portal to the ice planet as refined resources and machined items from the factories and the refinery were sent back.

"Have we been able to step up the factories within the asteroid base?" Dave asked.

"We're working on it right now. We've got two factories that are partially online, one for building the structural members of the ships and another working on the armor. We hope to have weapons and ammunition factories up and working within the month," Ela-Dorn said. "If we didn't have those soul gem constructs, it would take years to get all of this done."

Dave paused at one of the workshops. The interior was filled with different kinds of automatons and there were different passageways for them to enter and exit the workshop. A number of people moved around, checking out the automatons, fixing them up in different places and replacing broken or busted parts.

"One second—I think I see a familiar face." Dave moved into the workshop. Ela-Dorn stood at the entrance to the workshop, passing through the Mana barrier that lay at the door, keeping the atmosphere inside the workshop so the people could work without having to worry about having their Mana barrier up all the time.

Sparks came off from different places and the sounds of wrenches being used and the banging of heavy machinery at work filled the air.

Dave moved past the different workstations, reaching one where a dwarf was using a terminal to move a crane holding a new limb for the large automaton in front of him.

The arm moved into place; two others on either side of the arm moved in with their tools, securing it in place.

"So, whose time did you steal to get out here this time?" Dave asked the dwarf with the console.

"You ever tried walking quietly through my workshop?" Kol turned around, a mock annoyed look on his face.

Dave barked out a laugh as Kol broke into a smile.

"It's good to see you back and in one piece, boy." Kol widened his arms.

Dave and Kol hugged, patting each other on the back. A look of genuine affection passed between the two of them as they smiled at each other.

"So, I see that the automaton program is going ahead well." Dave looked at the different automatons moving through the area. A number of them were just being checked over by the different techs before being allowed to leave and take on jobs.

"Yeah, we're hoping to get a factory to do all of this. However, right now we're in a bit of a pinch. Should have it ready within about a week or so. Then we can really start increasing the production time of these ships and large projects you have on the go," Kol said.

Dave nodded and clapped Kol on the shoulder. "Well, I just came to say hi. If I keep making detours then Ela-Dorn is going to start to get annoyed." Dave grinned. "Want to do dinner with me and Koi tonight? I can probably rope in Mal as well."

"I'd love that," Kol said, practically beaming. Ela-Dorn knew that Kol saw Koi as much as he would see his own great-granddaughter. While he'd been in Ice City, he'd taken time to go to the Dracul day care to meet up with Oson'Mal, his son Desmond, as well as Deia and Dave's daughter Koi. If he wasn't in the automaton workshop, then he was there.

Dave turned back to Ela-Dorn. "No more side trips, I swear!"

"I'll believe it when I see it." Ela-Dorn snorted as they left the workshop and continued on their way.

They passed areas that were under construction as well as those that were packed with storage crates of resources ready to be shipped to the refinery in Ice City.

Areas that had been carved out had mages and engineers working together to make superstructures for new construction as soul gem constructs grew, forming factories, power plants and any other necessary areas for the asteroid base.

"These are new," Dave said as they reached a massive armored blast door. It closed behind them. As soon as it was closed, the next one started to open, their speed and timing fast enough so that Ela-Dorn and Dave didn't even need to pause their steps.

"We've been fitting air locks throughout the asteroid base. In case we come under attack, we want to be able to secure different sections of the base off. We've been adding the same features to Ice City," Ela-Dorn said.

The main thoroughfare within the asteroid base had increased in size drastically. Along the walls, there were multiple racks and more doorways.

Soul gem tethers reached out from the walls and the slips where the ships were being built, feeding them power and relaying information to the different people working on their design from those in the asteroid base to those in Ice City.

The destroyers that had been simple superstructures with armor here and there and soul gem constructs growing inside had undergone a radical change. Many of them had most of their armor in place; some of them even had their guns and missile tubes mounted in their hulls. Runic lining made of soul gem ran through the armor plates, creating spells to increase the strength of the armor as well as creating Mana barriers and shields around the vessels.

There were raised areas on the ships that glowed with magical formations. These were the Mana barrier modules, the drop coding that could pick up and drop people and items off on the ground below the destroyers.

Runic lines ran down the different cannons along the ship, sectioning off the barrel of the gun as they glowed with a cold light.

The thoroughfare was busier than ever with cargo shuttles coming in and dropping off their containers, picking up empty ones and heading out to the different mining sites. Automated excavators were still digging out the interior of the massive asteroid, the light flickering in front of them as they worked.

Smaller automated mining drills cleared up the area left behind, cutting out the different slips as well as corridors, work spaces, and hatches. All of this happened in a process with the different layers of automated machines peeling back a layer of the asteroid to reveal the base that was growing underneath.

Ela-Dorn's eyes moved to the massive portal that was pulled behind the mining machines. It was the size of the thoroughfare. A dozen different crafts had to move with it as soul gem tethers continued to pump energy and resources into the portal. It was truly massive. It could fit two of the battleships, if they were flying next to each other.

The basic structure of the portal had been finished off. It was still pretty transparent and the inner sections were being built up. It was a massive power draw, but as they had stepped up their latest fusion plant, all of its energy had been dedicated to getting this portal functioning and completed.

Her eyes moved to a slip not far away. Instead of a ship or other large item, there was a portal resting on the walkway that would have extended out to a ship.

Dave and Ela-Dorn walked forward toward this portal. Nerves fluttered through Ela-Dorn's stomach as she looked upon the portal prototype. She had seen many of them in her life, but this would be the first time she knew of anyone attempting to make one by themselves. If this worked, then it would mean that they were no longer restrained by the number of portals that Dave still had within the seeder under Cliff-Hill.

Ela-Dorn used her senses to reach out to the portal and looked it over. It seemed to work with the plans in her mind and matched up with what she understood from the knowledge she had gained and also learned from Dave, his notes, or other Aleph who worked with teleporters and onos.

Dave walked up to the portal, putting his hand on it as he closed his eyes. Ela-Dorn watched it all, forgetting to even blink lest she might miss something.

Dave took some time before he took his hand from the portal and nodded. "Okay, well, it looks like everything should be good. All of the internal structure is laid out. Nearly all of it is made from magical coding and the compressed runic lining instead of the overly complex Magical Circuits that had been coded into the massive metal plates," Dave said. "Well, let's fire it up and see what happens!"

"Ready when you are," Ela-Dorn said.

They moved back from the portal. Dave sent out orbs that erected a Mana shield around the portal. That way, if something did go terribly wrong and it was destroyed, then it wouldn't hurt anyone else.

Dave raised his arm and moved the different bracelets that were there. He wasn't wearing his full armor but he kept the bracers on, allowing him greater control whenever he might need it. He moved the final slider into place as power started to move through the portal. Being made out of soul gem, it was able to use its own power to start itself up.

The portal's runic lines started to glow and change colors. Ela-Dorn's eyes focused on it as the light increased on the portal, becoming brighter and brighter. Then the lights started to blink in and out; the lights dimmed and then burst into myriad colors.

"Shit." Dave's hands moved, his eyes closed.

Ela-Dorn pushed out her arcane senses, watching as Dave fixed the portal's weaknesses as it started up, creating more robust magical coding contained within the runic lines.

The portal's faltering lights became stronger, and the shuddering lights of failures started to calm down. The portal seemed to gather itself together. The lights swirled and then settled down.

Ela-Dorn looked at the portal, her eyes wide as she looked into the seeder at Cliff-Hill. "It worked!" Ela-Dorn practically screamed out.

She had been nervous before, knowing that the chance of connecting was low. Then, with all of the different things they had to work on and the repairs he had made, she was sure that it was going to fail. Instead, it was holding a wormhole open with Cliff-Hill—star systems away.

The wormhole collapsed as the lights dimmed around the portal. A few of them flashed here and there; some sections looked as if they had been melted under the strain of opening the wormhole. But they had done it!

"Going to need some tweaking, but I think from that we'll be able to figure out what works and what doesn't." Dave sounded a little tired as he wiped sweat from his face. Doing such complicated changes in such a short time had put a strain on his mind as well as his magical abilities.

"I never thought that it might work out with the first try! With this, we can truly start to make a network across everything! We can start to connect the different bases to Emerilia, not just the moon, shipyard one and Ice City, but the asteroid refineries, the asteroid, Cliff-Hill. We can even start to put portals inside of the different ships that we have so we can move personnel from one ship to another without worries," Ela-Dorn said.

"We'll get there eventually." Dave smiled. "Now, I was having a lot of problems with the location data down to the ten-kilometer range. Variations in that were messing up the calculations between the different portals and their location data. I think that's something we need to look into."

"If it's just the one thing that's causing the issues, maybe there's a hidden variable we haven't accounted for. If the meters, centimeters, light-years, months, minutes and all of that is working, then we've got one weird issue going on," Ela-Dorn said.

Their initial excitement was there but now it was tempered by the issues that they had encountered and the ways they were figuring out to improve upon their prototype and turn it into a working model.

Ela-Dorn and Dave talked to each other, moving toward the portal. They used different sensing spells and tools to take readings from the portal. Once that was done, they headed back toward Ice City. There was still more work to be done before they were able to mass-produce their own portals.

Chapter 8: Purpose

Frank looked around at the different people in the room with him. All of them were players and all of them were interested in fighting the Jukal.

They could help out with different manual labor jobs, maybe even stretch their minds to help out the different people who were building the amazing machines that they had seen.

What ignited their passion was not bending and breaking magic to their will; it was paying back those who had imprisoned them within their own minds and within a simulation of Earth.

A thickly built man with scruff on his face and a deep tan stood at the front of them all, looking over them.

Frank could see by the way this man held himself that he had been part of a military unit. Frank didn't flinch from those cold eyes that scanned the room.

"Welcome to reality, brains! My name is Dwayne. Like you, I'm a player. Unlike you, I'm a player from this generation." Dwayne's voice echoed through the room. A number of people started to talk as soon as his words sunk in.

"That's right!" Dwayne's voice cut through them all, once again returning their attention to him. "Right now, I am fighting on Emerilia with other players and people of Emerilia against the creatures and people of the events, the aggressive species that are connected to Emerilia via portals. And, according to our intelligence, it seems the Pantheon is going to have an all-out brawl as well!"

Everyone in the room was focused on Dwayne. They wanted to get into the fight to be able to help out; just watching it all was driving them insane.

"I'm not here to welcome you to reality, nor am I here to tell you what to do. Instead, I come with an option: join the fighting force of the Pandora's Box Initiative, or go and do something else.

You have one minute to make your decision." Dwayne sat down on a seat behind him and started to move through his interface screens.

Frank looked over Dwayne. He had heard about Dwayne from the different Emerilians. He was one of the leaders in the Stone Raiders Guild. He fought on the front lines with his people, leading players and POEs alike. It also seemed that he was one of the few players on Emerilia who knew the truth.

Frank had not only heard of him, he'd seen him in action as he'd checked out the different battles the Stone Raiders had been in. It was clear that all of this was being run mostly by the Stone Raiders Guild, which had led to a number of people looking over their battles and information. It was stunning the things that they had gone through. When thinking of it as a game, it was an impressive list of achievements.

When finding out that the list of fights and tribulations that they had gone through were not part of a video game but were instead part of real life, it led to the newly awakened players to feel deep respect and awe toward this guild that had essentially made it possible for them to wake up to reality.

A few people left the room, but the majority stayed there. They were now a few thousands of the players who had been woken up. Every hour, more of them were joining. These were all of the players from rural areas that could be covered over by the AI bots that Jeeves had inserted into the Earth simulation.

Dwayne closed his interfaces at the one-minute mark, stood and looked at them all. "Good. Well, seeing as this is the first time I've even been in this place, I'm learning everything the same time as you. However, Malsour Dracul will be our guide today!"

From a side door, a nondescript man stepped through. "Follow me and listen to all of my commands. You'll get a party invite in a minute—accept it," Malsour said.

Almos as soon as he thought about it, a party chat invite appeared in front of Frank. He clicked on it and opened it up.

"Good, seems that all of you are now connected. Follow me. We're going to head to the asteroid base. Stay in an orderly line and make sure that you aren't separated." Malsour turned for the door.

The players moved to follow him. With their speed and reaction times, it didn't take them long until they were all following after him.

"As you know, Emerilia is a world based off fantasies that the human race came up with. Dragons, elves, dwarves, human sub-races, magic spells and the rest. This was made possible through the changing of the planet now called Emerilia as well as growing humans, inserting powerful energy-based conductors, material synthesizers, nanites, and a number of complex different systems that come together to make Emerilia seem as if it is a video game. The Jukal Empire does not live on worlds that are like a fantasy video game. They are a multi-system spacefaring empire made up of a total of thirty-nine different races. Thirty-eight of which are under the command of the Jukal Empire. The Jukal were the first spacefaring race and the most powerful. They had the fastest ships, portal technology, and weapons. Using these, they were able to expand rapidly, taking over multiple different systems. Expanding their empire and making those they ruled over members of the empire. The Jukal Empire is a powerful and dominating creation. Each and every race is constrained to making limited things and live at the empire's pleasure. If they are to disagree with the empire, the empire can quickly dispatch a carrier group to remove them or destroy them. Rebellions happen but they are rare and not one of them has succeeded." Malsour led them out of where they had gathered and into Ice City, headed for the portal that was connected to the asteroid base.

"Emerilia was made to make up for the loss of their military power. Humanity hit them a heavy blow and they needed to keep the aggressive species, or at least the groups that they didn't agree with, at bay. Using humans to soak this up was a risky plan, but it worked and has done so for five hundred years. The Jukal Empire was able to recover a lot of their power. However, the empire was on the decline. With the Jukal only trusting their race, there is no new blood coming in. They can't trust the other races because they're all suppressed, too. If they were to gain freedom, there's no telling what might happen. Now you're probably all wondering what this means. What this means is that the Jukal don't fight on the ground that much; they don't like to risk their people. It's much easier for them to use ships. So, there's not much use in training you all in hand-to-hand combat or even how to use spells if you're not in a place where you can use them. So, we've adapted a few things that you can use in order to fight the Jukal. Everyone grab a necklace from over on that wall and turn the dial until the letters turn blue." Malsour pointed to a wall filled with necklaces.

Everyone quickly grabbed one and pulled it on. A humming noise filled the air.

"These are simple Mana barriers. Stronger versions can be used to protect yourselves—these ones have been made so that you have enough oxygen that you don't pass out and die in the asteroid base," Malsour said. "Come with me!"

Malsour walked through a few more armored doors and past armed automatons that protected the portals.

Frank swore he could feel them scanning him as he passed.

They made it into the center of the armored building, finding a portal with carts moving back and forth at a terrifying speed.

Malsour stepped forward without a care. The carts paused as he stepped up to the portal. On the other side, there seemed to be a room identical to the one they were in. A number of people hesitated. Frank pushed forward. Others, seeing him, also stepped up, passing through the portal and onto the other side.

They quickly passed through the portal, Malsour not slowing in the slightest as he walked ahead of them. They moved quickly to catch up with him. They exited the portal's armored location and entered the asteroid base.

It was illuminated by the soul gem constructs. But instead of the blue glow of Ice City, this was instead darker, making Frank think that he was tens of miles beneath the ground.

"We are now in space, people. That means no atmosphere. If you deactivate your necklace, then your Mana barrier will give way and you will be exposed to vacuum!" Malsour warned, not stopping his steps.

Carts moved at an even faster pace within the asteroid base. People here were all using Mana barriers that shimmered as they moved around in groups. One couldn't hear them talking even if they were beside one another. They studied the players but they were all hurrying to and from jobs; they didn't have the time to look over them closely.

They passed shops with automatons, others with missiles, more with cannons.

Frank kept looking into these rooms but he didn't slow his pace for fear of losing Malsour.

Dwayne and Malsour were walking ahead of the group, talking to each other. Malsour seemed to be explaining things to Dwayne, who had a look of surprise on his face. It looked as if it was his first time being in the asteroid base as well.

Quickly, they passed all of these different workshops and secondary areas, and reached a massive armored door.

"What we need are not people who know how to simply wield a sword and use their magic in close combat roles. We have hundreds of thousands of people—more powerful than you can truly comprehend—we can use. What your mission will be is to get them to their battlefields," Malsour said to the group.

They passed through the armored door, finding another behind it. The armored door closed behind them and the one ahead of them opened, revealing a massive open space.

Frank's eyes were drawn to the spaceships in front of him.

"What we need you to do is learn how to crew and fight in these ships, to get people where they need to go, gather information about the Jukal and fight them in space," Malsour said.

All of the players looked to the massive warships with stars in their eyes. It was impossible to look away from these machines. Their runic lines, the way that they seemed to dominate the area—they pressured the players.

"As time goes on, we will be able to move more people to assist you, like the dwarven artillery crews, who will be able to look after and maintain the weapons on these vessels. While Emerilia is a planet of fantasy, we have found allies in a group of humans who have spacefaring abilities. With their help and training, we hope to bring you up to fighting standards. These ships are not made from pure technology like the ones you know on Earth. These ships are a hybrid of Earth ideas and technology, matched with Emerilia's magical constructs and practices. These ships will be faster than the Jukal's; they will hit harder and have stealth capabilities that the Jukal could only wish for. To be able to crew these vessels, you must be worthy. We will be running simulations again and again. Only those who do the best will be allowed to crew them. This does not mean that you must have the best reaction times; you must be the best at everything that is in the realm of your activities. While you are not training, you will be building more of these ships, their weapons, and their ammunition. You will build their reactors, their armor plating, come to understand magical coding. These will be the beasts you ride into war with. Do not slack on your training or your work. If you slack, then your mistake could kill your friends. There is no respawn ability for you folks. We've taken you out of the simulation and off Emerilia. One mistake and you are dead!" Malsour looked over them all, his dark eyes solemn.

Many looked away from him at his words.

"The Jukal feared humanity not for their technology, but for their tenacity and training. We never give up and we train to be the best. We will be using simulations and Mirrors of Communication to train with. We have the luxury of time, so we will train against simulations of Jukal groups of all kinds in all different types of systems. You will fight one another to sharpen each other's skills. In the simulation, you can blow one another up in a hundred different ways and come back again. From each of these turns, you will learn! If you do not learn, then you will die."

Malsour's last sentence was not loud nor was it quiet but it shook those in front of him, hitting home that everything they had seen and gone through wasn't a game; it wasn't a simulation—if they messed up, they wouldn't be coming back.

A few looked nervous as this hit in; for some, it didn't. But others like Frank nodded, understanding that this was it: do or die—it was all on the line.

I'd live here for an hour with the possibility of dying instead of eternity in my old life, Frank thought.

"When going into battle, we will do our best to see that you are prepared for it and we will be standing right beside you, ready to face the dangers that you do together," Malsour said.

Dwayne, beside him, nodded.

"This is something that you will all need to think on. There are plenty of other positions that need people. Not everyone is meant to be a fighter, but we are willing to help you find your place to see where you fit in and what you can do," Malsour said, his voice reassuring.

***

Sato watched the plot where multiple stealth ships were moving from the Deq'ual system through various other systems. Their path looked random and they went in random directions at times. However, all of them that had left the Deq'ual system were all headed to the Nal system. They carried the materials and people who would be setting up the outpost within the system. It had been a massive undertaking to get everything sorted out and organized. Sato had a number of sleepless nights as he planned out everything to the last detail.

He smiled to himself as he watched those ships as they continued on their journey. The first one would arrive in as little as a week, the longest taking a month and a half to reach them.

It wouldn't take them too long to set up the outpost. Most of the time, Sato wished for his people to work with those from Emerilia to try to understand more about the technology they were using to grow their own abilities. He also hoped that they would be able to create better relations with them and help them in their efforts. The council had essentially tied his hands but he hoped that through the outpost, his people would be able to help out the humans from Emerilia.

Edwards stepped into the conference room, where Sato was staring at the screen with the plans for the different ships.

"You're looking pretty morose today," Edwards said, eloquent as ever as he slumped into a seat. He looked like crap.

While Sato and Adams had been sorting out the security over in the Nal system as well as flight paths and administrative details, Edwards had been the man who should have been sent to aid in creating this outpost. However, with politics, he'd had to remain behind.

This was no simple undertaking as he had to design the outpost, figure out how to build it and what would be needed, all within the space of a few short days.

Sato shook his head as the screen changed to show Admiral Adams inside the third asteroid shipyard, in her personal quarters.

"Fellas." Adams saluted them both with a bulb of coffee, a plastic squeeze bottle that one could use with and without gravity and atmosphere, her hair out of her regulation ponytail and her clothes in a state of disarray as she'd gotten off work.

"What I called you here for is to discuss the real purpose of the outpost. It is meant to be a place for people to be stationed, but its biggest goal is to assist the people of Emerilia in being ready for the coming conflict they will have with the Jukal. This means helping with building various weapons of war and the like. I want to sound out Dave and the others a bit more but I think we all agree that they're trustworthy." Sato looked to them both.

Even in their tired states, they agreed completely with Sato's words.

"The council is getting all scared at where this might go. We're doing things that most of them didn't think would be possible. Dave and the others have a plan to deal with the Jukal. I want to see that we help them as much as possible. The best way to do this is through the outpost. We can funnel them resources, information, help train up their people to fight in space," Sato said.

"So, help them establish a proper space navy without the council finding out?" Adams asked.

"Yes." Sato nodded.

"Give them access to technology that is normally restricted and offer the services of our people to assist in building their different ships and systems?" Edwards asked.

"Yes," Sato repeated once again.

"Well, they might as well learn from the best. We were born and raised in space, after all." Adams's serious demeanor evaporated with a smile.

"I don't know how much we can help them, but if we can give them laborers and also help supply them with resources, that'd be the best," Edwards said.

Sato nodded. He trusted the both of them completely, but this—it wasn't going against the council or their orders but it was seriously pushing them. If the council were to ever find out, they would probably strip Sato of his position and also stop the outpost from being established in the first place.

"I just hope that whatever plan they come up with to destroy the Jukal Empire is a damn good one," Adams said.

***

Dave, Oson'Mal, and Kol were all sitting around, eating dinner. Koi and Desmond were both in their cribs. They'd been fed first and put down for a nap. The men finished off their food and started to sip on the fire whisky that Kol had supplied.

"How long do you think it will be before we need to start using the machines from the Initiative?" Kol asked after some time. He was unwilling to ask the question but he was driven to do it.

"I'm not sure. We're currently clearing out the last locations where the portals were taken over. However, it's clear that Earth, Light, and Dark are all gearing up for a fight." Dave sighed and shook his head before taking a sip from his drink.

"With the flying citadels, it's clear that there's little chance of the portals staying around for long. Also, with the Jakan being hired on as mercenaries, it's become a lot easier to deal with the various difficult groups, both the ones coming through the portal and the ones that arrived here through the event." Oson'Mal had been keeping abreast of the war. Both his son-in-law and daughter—not to mention his wife—were heavily involved in it; there was no way that he wouldn't keep an eye on it all.

"When we have to reveal them, we're going to need to pull out everything," Kol said.

"I know," Dave breathed, reluctant to think on this. "In the meantime, I want to step up a factory capable of making the orbs that I use, give the people of the Terra Alliance a simpler version, one that's automatic, can give them extra shields, also can allow them to have gravity and retain air so that when they do get on a ship after this all, they don't die immediately or trip over themselves."

"When are you thinking of telling the other leaders of the alliance?" Kol asked. Both he and Mal looked at Dave with expectant eyes.

"Soon. They need to get their people ready for the coming fight. Not the one that will be waged on Emerilia, but the one that will be waged across the Jukal Empire."

Mal and Kol took heavy breaths and sipped on their drinks. Dave's tired eyes looked across the room to where Desmond and Koi were sleeping peacefully, not knowing what was going on in the world around them.

He had his purpose for doing this and he would do anything to see it through. He took a long draw from the whisky, savoring the burn as it went down.

Chapter 9: Craft

"Well, this doesn't look complicated at all." Dave looked around the special room. There were seats all in a circle, looking at the center of the room. In the armrest of each of these chairs, there was a Mirror of Communication and a thick bundle of runic lines that ran from the chairs to larger runic lines that met underneath a magical circle in the middle of the room. Above the circle, there was a set of manipulative arms of all different sizes.

The others in the room, people from all manner of races across Emerilia, smiled at Dave's words, taking up a seat and reclining in it. Many of them closed their eyes as they were submerged into the Mirror of Communication conference room.

Dave looked to Malsour as the two of them moved to their seats. "So, how were the players yesterday?" Dave asked as they moved to two seats next to each other.

"They were a little stunned—kind of a big thing to know that we want to train them to be warship pilots. A number of them were excited. Others really want to just fight on the ground. I think we should give them that opportunity but train them up with everything we have and try to temper them through the battles on Emerilia. We need veterans, not just people with good training," Malsour said, as always the voice of cold reason.

"I heard that some people who weren't interested before caught wind of the spaceships and started to join up the fighting force," Dave said.

"Well, it takes different kinds of people to fight on a spacefaring warship and in a fantasy setting. Some can do both—some find it really odd."

"Well, this whole thing is out of whack." Dave shook his head.

"How is this supposed to work?" Malsour said, indicating what was around them.

"I'm not sure." Dave shrugged. "Ela-Dorn had been all mysterious after talking about the smaller version of the portal and the battleship. Saying that she had an idea that she had to check with some people."

Malsour shrugged and sat in his seat, connecting to the Mirror of Communication in his armrest.

They all appeared within what looked like an auditorium. Standing up at the front there was Ela-Dorn and a small but cute-looking elven boy who played with his hands nervously as he glanced up at the nearly two hundred people in the room and then quickly averted his gaze.

Dave chuckled slightly. His face filled with warmth. The boy's reactions made him remember the boys and girls of the Dracul day care. *I wonder what Koi will be like at his age?*

Dave's smile gained a hint of melancholy as Ela-Dorn cleared her throat, returning him to reality.

"As you all know, the battleships that we have been working on have multiple issues going on with the ship's systems." Ela-Dorn's words brought frowns and unhappy looks to the faces of the people in the room. They hated not having something that worked perfectly and they knew the monumental task ahead of them with making the battleship functional would not be an easy one. "Now, in a discussion with Dave, we were talking about a possible way of fixing the issues within the battleship, without making one totally from scratch, or going through the ones we have, finding the issues and fixing them all. We make a scaled-down version of it!"

"The conversion of different items from the scaled-down version to the real version would all be skewed," one person said. A few others nodded.

"They might, so I've been looking into it and I found out about Olue-Jacques's project." Ela-Dorn waved to the boy near her, who anxiously scratched his head and gave them a weak smile.

His clear awkwardness made those in the room relax their expressions. Ela-Dorn turned to the boy with a gentle smile on her face. "Olue-Jacques, could you please tell us about your project?"

"Ermm, okay, well, it was really an idea. Where I used to live, we all work together at what strengths we have and then combine them together to make our homes and different places. Someone might be good at making a tree reinforce its roots, another might be good at creating an overhead canopy, another the interior and all that. We use it when doing spells, too, which makes them stronger!" Olue-Jacques said, getting excited. By his appearance, it looked as if he was part of the wood-elf race that lived in trees that they had used their magic to alter and grow. "When people work together, then it's a lot easier to make harder things. Like how we need all kinds of people in order to get the automated miners to where they are! So, umm, I wanted to make something where people could work together to make something. My dad said it wasn't safe for me to use a lab or work space, but then, in the college in the Mirror of Communication, you can make all kinds of things and they can't hurt you," Olue-Jacques said with a pleased expression.

"In here, we can create and work without worries of causing any damage. We will be working at full scale. Everything can be recorded so we can check through our steps. Also, all of our actions, once confirmed, will be replicated by Jeeves—who is connected to this conference room—taking our input to create a fully functional model. Allowing us to create everything in here easily, instead of having us all crammed around one model we're working on," Ela-Dorn said, clearing up Olue-Jacques's words.

There were quite a few people with wide eyes and impressed expressions on their faces.

At seeing the expression on their faces, Olue-Jacques smiled happily, most of his nervousness falling away.

"Thank you, Olue-Jacques," Ela-Dorn said.

"No problem, Miss Ela-Dorn." Olue-Jacques smiled. "Can I log off now?"

"Yes, you can. Go and play," Ela-Dorn said, her voice almost musical as she stopped herself from laughing at the boy's childish manners.

"See you later, Dad!" Olue-Jacques waved to his dad, who was with the others in the room, before he logged off.

His father chuckled. A few people who knew him and were near him teased him and also praised his son's abilities. Even though he'd been slightly embarrassed, there was a large smile on his face as he heard them talking about his son.

"Okay, so the idea is that we'll review the different blueprints for the various systems in here, then we'll move to make them. We'll go section by section, building from the inside out and fixing any issues we find along the way." Ela-Dorn clapped her hands together. Information packets were sent out to them, detailing which issues they would be working on.

Different people moved into groups centered around their issue and started to converse with one another. Dave and Malsour both opened up their interfaces and looked over the various blueprints that they were familiar with and had designed. Dave was looking at the teleportation system within the battleships, which would allow them to teleport within a system as well as between systems.

Dave lost himself in the theories and ideas that had come together to make up these different systems. Different groups disappeared off into various areas, leaving smaller groups and single people who were all reviewing their own systems in peace, focusing their mind on the project ahead.

This is good for moving within a few hundred light-years, but the power usage is too much. Instead of covering over the ship and moving it along space, wrapping it in a wormhole, it would be better to project it and allow the ship to travel through. However, this is only at a distance between star systems; the straight teleportation within star systems would work fine and give us an advantage.

With these thoughts, Dave moved to alter the different coding that he had created. It was a small change but its impact would be great. They had first made these plans for the battleship months ago; now they had all gained a greater insight and the number of people who could help them develop the battleship and its capabilities had only grown. With these increased resources, their improvements were vast.

Once Dave finished with his alterations, he disappeared from the room where they had gathered. In front of him there was a slip; there was nothing around him but white space.

Floating around this space there were already different people who were talking to one another. Ela-Dorn was there with them, discussing how to use the tools of the facility. Off to the side, there was an array of resources that could be pulled down into the slip and be used, or one might take them off to the side to create something.

"Well, our facilities are pretty impressive." Malsour moved forward.

Dave joined him as they floated toward the slip in the middle of the area. "I'm just hoping it will be good enough to sort out the issues we've found with the battleship."

"We will," Malsour said.

They knew that the fate of Emerilia, whether they survived or not, lay on their shoulders and with these projects. They would do all in their power to make sure that they succeeded.

Dark mages and engineers talked to one another. After a few minutes, the Dark mages started to move their hands, their bodies being covered in the Dark Mana.

Threads of metal floated from the walls where they were stored. Dwarves moved in with those who knew metallurgy; as the metals twisted and moved, they called out instructions to the Dark mages. The metal that they were working with was combined with a number of different items, changing the composition of the metal. A few used furnaces to add in different elements, taking the pure metals and turning them into composites.

As these were finished, they were once again put under the control of the Dark mages. Several of them created lines through the middle of the slip, forming a rough cylinder.

As they did, other metals moved in from the sides, creating lines that bisected this cylinder while others curled around, attaching to the bisecting lines and the metal struts and supports that made up the cylinder.

As these metals connected to one another to create the all-important superstructure of the battleship and what was to be its backbone, the ends of the cylinder started to come together. The cylinder's ends closed off with metal from these end pieces, banding the ends and creating nose cones.

The bisecting metal that created levels inside the battleship extruded out smaller pieces of metal that attached to the metal supports on the same level as it, connecting the rough supports for each level together. In some places, they grew up and downward, connecting these different levels.

The metal moved organically, as if it were a living creature. Every movement was smooth and sure.

In here, the power needed to mold metal was minimal, allowing each of the Dark mages to control it down to a finite detail, checking the densities of the metals and making sure that they were all uniform.

Other mages, engineers, and techs moved soul gem constructs from the wall and to different sections of the ship. They touched down on the metal supports that had been finished, creating a rough superstructure for the entire battleship.

The soul gems touched down on the supports and then seemed to explode outward. The soul gem constructs raced through the levels that they were placed on. Between the supports, they created the floor and raced up the walls to create rooms and spread out across the entirety of the battleship. As each of the soul gem constructs touched down, the growth of the soul gem would only increase in speed.

People who were working on specific systems moved into the battleship that was growing around them.

The last piece of metal for the superstructure had finished growing. The soul gem construct moved to eat it up, the battleship's interior becoming more and more substantial.

The speed started to decrease as power techs moved in with Mana wells. Consulting the plans, they placed them in key locations, maximizing their output coverage and protection from battle damage.

As they made contact with the ground, runic lines spread outward. The soul gems' speed increased once again as they became thicker and more substantial. Inside, there were only lighting strips to allow the different techs to see.

The Dark mages moved their attention to the metals on the walls once again, moving it and manipulating it with the metallurgy. People made sheets and sheets of reinforced armor that would be the plates for the battleship's hull.

Dave sunk his consciousness into the battleship. As he closed his eyes, he was able to see everything that was going on within the ship.

From the soul gem construct, multiple machines started to take form, growing from the walls, floors, and ceilings; air ducts were created, runic lines to carry power.

Dave added in his gravitational runes along the floors and ceilings of the ship. These would make it so that the gravity inside the ship always remained the same.

Everywhere he looked, the different groups were creating the machines that would keep the ship functioning and make it battle ready.

Dave's consciousness passed through these as he moved to raised sections of the soul gem construct in different areas. He ran control lines through the soul gem construct from the command center in the middle of the battleship to these modules. Runic lines started to form on these nodes, swirling together in a complex pattern and revealing powerful gravity runes that would allow the ship to maneuver in any direction.

Dave moved from node to node, checking out the connected systems. There were issues here and there but with a quick talk to those making these systems, they were able to work out the issues.

Dave and Ela-Dorn worked together, breaking up the job of creating the teleport coding. Time had no meaning in this place as they were all stuck in the excitement of building and seeing the results in front of their eyes.

All across the ship, different parts and sections were growing. The bland walls and simple areas were built up. Metal plates came together in one room, the different sections already created by a Dark mage, coming together as if they were part of a three-dimensional puzzle. Runic lines spread out and connected to the fusion plant, racing through the ship to connect to other systems.

Sections grew out from the soul gem construct, making complicated plates filled with runic lines. Storage areas were coded with holding runes, making them larger on the inside to store items. Power runic lines met up with completed machines and different parts of the ship, powering them on and bringing them to life.

Air filtration centers were created. They were based off the growing towers in Terra, and modified to increase their ability to clean air. Magical coding was laid in the different growing beds, to increase the rate of growth for the altered plants to unheard of speeds. They were capable of keeping the air within the battleship clean and breathable instead of using purely chemical means like the human ships that fought the Jukal did.

Heating and cooling were adjusted with heat and cold exchangers based off the much larger prototypes that were in the flying citadels on Emerilia. They could manage the temperature of the ship, while also creating power.

Modified fusion power plants based off the information from the Jukal, as well as the versions that Dave had made, were created. Dave's fusion plant looked rudimentary compared to these newer versions. He had been making them simply to create more power in a shorter time; these new techs and researchers delved into the fusion plants, updating them, increasing their power output and decreasing the fuel consumption.

Beds had runes that would increase one's Endurance, allowing them to get more rest in less time.

Teleporters, updated with magical coding instead of Magical Circuits and runes, were added in, as were onos, which allowed one to move throughout the ship at greater speed, or even between ships. A mix of gravity runes and Fire runes were created in order to move the ship. Although the gravity runes were extremely powerful, they were complicated. If they were damaged, repairing them would take a long time.

The Fire runes were pulled from destruction staffs, refined down to create the most thrust possible in the direction the coded runes were pointing. This gave them essentially thrusters to move the ship in every direction, without needing the thruster housing to direct the blast.

In the medical bay, there were beds covered in runes that would promote healing and recovery. They were similar to the ones Jules had in Terra but were heavily updated.

All of these items and many more were being built concurrently, using the best magical coding and current tech.

As issues came to light, machines that had been completed were destroyed and rebuilt again and again until they were perfected.

Missile tubes that had been formed outside the ship were all slotted in; attaching to the different structural members of the ship.

, attaching to the different structural members of the ship. The soul gem construct wrapped around them as power and control runic lines appeared, connecting to the opposite points on these tubes.

The different parts of the massive cannons came together in mid-air as they approached the battleship. The different structural members reached out, fusing to these cannons and securing them in place. The soul gem construct connected to them as well.

Dave stopped moving through the ship as he saw the interceptor modules come together. The different parts connected to one another—the disruptor spell formation and the twin runic line-covered barrels that fired Mana bolts, before they, too, were placed at different locations around the battleship.

The last of the weapon systems were completed. The soul gem construct grew once again, covering the exterior of the ship's superstructure. Here and there, runic lining pushed out from the soul gem construct, creating lines down the length of the battleship.

The soul gem construct inside started to change colors as the floor turned black and became rough to have grip; the walls and ceilings became gray.

Inside the walls, there was thick runic lining that passed through the entirety of the ship. Along the ceilings, the runic lining that provided light stayed on, illuminating all of the different parts of the ship that were still under the process of being altered or created.

Beds grew from the walls; lockers were created; touchpads to turn on and off lights. Water lines were added; air locks and armored doors formed. Handrails grew from the walls in case the gravity runes failed; the crew and those aboard the ship could use these handles to move from place to place.

Dave appeared within the command center. The flat ground changed as runic lines like a swarm of snakes came in from across the walls, ceiling, and floor. They came together, reaching certain places; consoles grew out from these runic lines.

Others appeared in the room, working on these consoles, checking their functionality and doing tests. As failures were found, other groups would move through the ship, altering and changing things until everything was functional.

Seats were grown out from the ground as the forward area of the command center displayed screens that connected into runic lines running from the different consoles in the command center. There was a weapons fire control, a navigation, power management, shields and barriers, communication, sensors, and then the command staff.

All of these areas were separated by area of responsibility and setup to maximize efficiency and flow.

Looking upon the growing details of the command center, Dave felt a shift outside the battleship, turning his attention to that area, scouring it with sensing spells.

The layered armor and soul gem constructs all landed on the battleship's sides, fusing with the superstructure of the battleship, and both metal and the soul gem construct that had grown throughout the ship.

Layer after layer fit perfectly together as they compressed and collapsed down onto the battleship. Each of them fit around the different weapon mounts and the holes in their side, allowing the raised sections from the soul gem construct to peek through.

Dave looked at it from the outside. Alterations were made here and there as the layered armor was pulled off and then re-applied. Dave moved to the different runes and control runes he had laid down, altering and changing them so that they worked perfectly.

The frantic building of earlier had died down as fewer and fewer items needed to be changed. It was like a wave as things were completed and left as they were.

The last air converter came together and lit up the runic lines connected to it.

Everyone looked through the battleship. Here and there, changes were made as they passed through a few times. From the drives, to the weapon systems and the structural supports—everything was reviewed and looked over.

They all left the battleship. None of them had anything to say as they studied its hull and the dangerous lines that shaped it.

The battleships in the slips at the asteroid base had an imposing aura, but to those who had made the systems of it, they had always felt that it was hollow. A good-looking toy with no functionality.

Now, as they looked upon this battleship, their hearts beat with pride.

Their demons about how the battleships would function in battle were pushed away. They knew that this battleship they had created was the best that they could have done.

It was an impressive piece of engineering, combining the magical abilities of Emerilia with the technology of Earth, the Jukal, and the vision of the players. It spoke of power, the cutting edge of magical technology possible.

The battleships before were all paper boats compared to this.

The aura that came from the completed battleship was of a powerful tool, craving to be used. It exuded power and strength, as if it would sweep away all who stood in its way.

Even being around it, all of those who had come together to make it; felt as if they could charge through the lines of anything they faced, destroying all who tried to stop them.

For a while, they studied it. All of the systems were running perfectly, ready and waiting for what was to come.

"Time we got some food." Ela-Dorn's words pulled them all out of the construction fugue that they had been in for an unknown time.

Thankfully, all of them had high Endurance from focusing on their projects so long.

Dave was shocked to see that a week had gone by as they had been working. The different problems that they had run into were not simple ones; it had taken them time and effort in order to break past them. Taking a week to create everything was still shocking.

Dave opened up his interface and logged off the Mirror of Communication.

He opened his eyes and looked at the ceiling. The seat he was in started to raise itself from its reclined position. His body felt tense and sore from sitting so long. He started to stretch, pausing midway as he looked into the middle of the room. Floating there, in the center of everything, was a scaled-down model of the battleship they had created within the Mirror of Communication conference room.

Dave had forgotten about the model. All of their efforts inside the conference room had been replicated and applied to this physical model once it was completed. Here and there, sections were being finalized as the model was only now updating everything had been confirmed.

"Looks like it's time for us to start testing it," Dave said.

With the scaled-down model, they could get Jeeves to put it through every test they could think of—see what the limits would be for a scaled-up version, spot any problems they had missed.

Dave opened up his interface. Using his administrator rights, he took the completed files and plans for the ships that they had created and Jeeves recorded, updating the battleships that were in the shipyard.

With his simple commands, automatons pulled apart armored panels while the soul gem constructs inside started to melt apart before reforming to meet the specifications that the design team had put together.

There were still going to be mistakes and things that needed to be fixed—Dave didn't doubt that. However, now they had a ship that was functional and without the major issues he had found with the first versions of the battleships.

"Looks like we've got some visitors." Malsour sent Dave a report on multiple stealth ships appearing from the peripheral of the Nal system, moving to where the *Sprite* was located and they had begun work on an asteroid that they were going to build their outpost on.

These ships dropped off gear and personnel who got to work hollowing out the asteroid.

"There have also been requests by Captain Xue and Councilmember Lisdel to meet with you and discuss the future of working together," Malsour said.

"A council member?" Dave frowned, feeling uncomfortable. "Why do I have a feeling that things have become a little bit more complicated?"

"Well, whatever the case, we run this side of things—it doesn't matter what they try to do," Malsour reminded Dave.

"True, but I don't want to isolate the people who might be able to help train our people how to fight and work in space better," Dave said. "Which reminds me—Jeeves!"

"Yes, Dave?" Jeeves's voice came through the ceiling.

"Take the plans for the battleship version two and upload them to the Mirror of Communication training simulators. See if the trainees can find any issues with the new version and get used to it so that they're not all messed up when it comes time to fight in them," Dave said.

"I will give them an overview and update the ships when they are waiting between battles," Jeeves said.

"Good. And what were the results of the simulation for the portals with the new upgrades?" Dave asked.

"They were all positive, but they will need verification due to unknown factors that I cannot simulate within the Mirror of Communication," Jeeves said.

This was why they made prototypes. The Mirror of Communication was really good for testing out different things, but it wasn't perfect. There were always extra things to consider when they were being used in real life, which was why everything they did was so rigorously tested to try to find out what those flaws would be before they were needed.

It was also why a number of the different people who had worked to create battleship version two were now around the scaled-down model, running tests on it to make sure that their fixes had worked.

Dave let out a sigh as a sense of satisfaction filled him. They were that much closer to having not only a battleship but a fully functional one.

"So, what next?" Malsour asked.

"Next we ramp up our production as much as possible, issue out quests for the different players to speed things up. I want to have that new aerosol healing potion ready for Emerilia as well as those healing beds to Terra. I want to manufacture enough personal orbs for everyone to help them out with the coming battle between the Pantheon.

"I want to bring the other leaders of the Terra Alliance in on this and get their people ready for the fight that's to come and I want to have a fleet that is capable of going up against the Jukal and can ensure the safety of Emerilia," Dave said.

"Well, then I guess we should lend a hand to the refinery being built first," Malsour said.

Dave sighed and nodded.

"Dave, Malsour!" Ela-Dorn said as she saw the two of them making to leave.

"What's up?" Dave asked.

"The council member and Captain Xue still need to see you," she reminded them.

"That's all you." Malsour moved away.

"Ah, but aren't we good friends who love to support each other?" Dave wrapped his arm around Malsour's shoulders.

Malsour let out a heavy sigh before he rolled his eyes. "Well, let's get this done with sooner rather than later."

"That's the spirit!" Dave said with enthusiasm and teleported the two of them out of the room.

***

Captain Xue looked at the work that was going on at what was to be the Deq'ual system's outpost.

Councilmember Lisdel had retired to his quarters. People hadn't complained about him yet, but the man was overbearing and it was clear that he came from the group that believed the Emerilians to be some sort of half-breed.

Every sentence he talked about the Emerilians was derisive and confrontational. He talked over those who were even voicing neutral opinions, saying that the Emerilians were "hiding their true intentions," or "not true humans who are worthy of our trust."

Xue's hand tightened in anger before he let out a cold breath. Of course, the politician had not been without his extras. He was "reporting" back to the people of the Deq'ual system every day, boasting of the work that the Deq'ual military were doing, making the Emerilians' achievements look as if they were nothing important.

Xue had been apprehensive of the Emerilians at first. But as they had come to work together, searching for an asteroid and the Emerilians even sending over a few of their automated miners to start the building, he'd come to realize that the Emerilians were helping them more than they were helping them. Once he realized this and all of the things that the Emerilians were effectively giving them, he had made sure that no matter what the small things that they asked for; were on time and done to the highest standard.

As soon as Lisdel showed up, he'd had Xue get rid of the automated miners by the Emerilians. Then he'd had the gall to take a picture after they had left, telling about the great and impressive work that the Deq'ual military were doing.

It grated on the nerves of most of the military members there.

Taking credit for someone else's work didn't make them feel good; it made them feel cheap. They wanted their own accomplishments to show through.

Xue's eyes moved to the growing asteroid base. There were now three ships from the Deq'ual system. Two of them were filled with supplies and personnel to help turn the asteroid into a base.

The work was much slower without the Emerilians' help, who were ready and willing to help. Xue looked up from the asteroid base. The screen in front of him showed outlines around several different asteroids. These ranged from ones that were simply being hollowed out for resources, and the ones that were being made into bases.

Their production speed was something that even the home Deq'ual system couldn't match, no less the outpost that they were building in the Nal system.

He pulled his eyes from the screen in front of him and checked his armored plates, breathing apparatus, and sidearm. As he moved through the checks, his brows were knitted in thought. He had watched the different battles that were happening on Emerilia. Flying citadels moved between different locations; everywhere they went, they used everything they had to pummel the races that had made it through the portal locations. The Emerilians in the towns and cities were also pushing back, while different forces were regrouping. Even though the Emerilians were getting some semblance of peace back and security, even Xue sensed that a storm was brewing. Simply too many people and beasts had stopped fighting and seemed to disappear overnight.

Xue finished his checks and checked his communications.

"Chief, how are we looking?" Xue turned and moved for the door in his office.

"Running final checks on the shuttle. Boys and girls are arming up—they're all a little bit excited about visiting Ice City," the chief said in an excited voice.

"Looking forward to having a real meal." The corners of Xue's mouth rose into a smile. "I'll be there in five."

"Yes, sir. I've been trying to contact Councilmember Lisdel. Both he and his secretary are not responding." The chief's voice was filled with hidden meaning.

Xue sighed and shook his head. The council member was married, but on a ship as small as the *Sprite,* everyone knew what everyone was doing—and the walls weren't exactly thin. It seemed that he had not only hired his secretary for his acute managing of his timetable.

"Call them on internal comms. I don't want to be late. We're going to be meeting with Dave and he's a busy guy," Xue said.

"Yes, sir, I'll see to that," the chief said.

"See that you do." Xue cut the channel as he walked through the *Sprite*. He made a detour to the bridge, checking in and making sure everything was fine. Showing his face to show that he had confidence in them helped to calm any of the nerves they might have not having the captain on the bridge. They were a well-trained team at this point, so, he truly had no fear in leaving his command under their care.

Xue made it to the shuttle bay, which was barely big enough to fit the two standard combat shuttles of the *Sprite*.

The doors were open on the craft, with the security detail checking their gear and weapons.

"Officer on deck!" the chief yelled out, saluting Xue as all the others came to attention.

"At ease." Xue returned the chief's salute.

A few nodded in greeting to Xue; the rest continued their conversations and went back to what they were doing. They had all come to know Xue in their travels from Deq'ual space and were comfortable with all of their officers.

Most of them were excited as they talked about going to see the asteroid base, talking about different things that they had seen, enlightening those who were going on their first trip.

"All right, we leave in five. Load up!" the chief called out.

The security detail pulled on their helmets, which sealed to their suits. The clear front of the helmets turned black and hid their faces. They pointed their weapons to the ground, organizing into two lines as they rushed up the ramp of the shuttle.

Xue pulled on his helmet and opened up a private channel to the chief. "Any word from Lisdel?"

"Wasn't too happy about me interrupting him and his secretary." From his voice, Xue could tell that the chief didn't hold the council member in much regard. "He also demanded that a position be made for his secretary for the trip."

Xue shook his head as he and the chief made their way up the ramp and to their seats in the shuttle. "Guess it's time we played the waiting game."

The chief let out a tired grunt, accepting his fate.

The excited atmosphere in the shuttle slowly faded away as they passed their launch time, waiting for Councilmember Lisdel and his secretary. The security detail undid the tint on their helmets. Xue could see the annoyance on their faces. The council member had an easy timing to meet but instead he'd wrapped himself up in his secretary.

After a half hour, there was a message from the bridge.

"Captain, we have a message from Dave Grahslagg, asking if we're all right. If you want, he is willing to come meet you on the *Sprite*," Xue's second-in-command said.

Xue and the chief shared a look before Xue responded. "Tell Dave that we're running a bit behind but we will be there shortly." Xue could only hope that he was right.

Nearly forty-five minutes after their supposed lift time, Lisdel and his secretary, wearing their high-quality space suits with armor plates over top, showed up.

Lisdel's helmet was made so that people could see his head at all times. His hair was coiffed and he wore makeup to emphasize his charm. He was bit thicker around his stomach, something that was rare in the Deq'ual system and pointed to someone eating—regularly—much more than their normal food ration.

His secretary was a flamboyant-looking character; he moved ahead, getting the security detail people to move so that the council member could sit between them.

"Well, let's get this shuttle moving already." Lisdel smiled, as if he were waiting on the shuttle crew to get flying for the last twenty minutes. Lisdel sat in the shuttle and the secretary snapped photos of the council member "among the soldiers."

"Sir, you should take a seat," the chief said to the secretary, who was in the middle of the shuttle, looking to get the best angle for the photo.

The secretary gave the chief a look of disdain and tilted his head as if questioning the chief's credentials before he rolled his eyes and got back to the important job of taking photos.

The shuttle sealed and the air was evacuated from the shuttle bay.

The shuttle rose, not so gently, knocking the secretary over as the shuttle then accelerated out of the shuttle bay. The secretary hit the rear ramp of the shuttle, in disarray.

Xue's eyebrow rose as he looked at the chief, who had a look of pure innocence on his face even as his eyes had some hints of pride. Xue saw that the security team's chatter was filled with noise. He listened in to it, hearing the chuckles of the team.

The secretary was flustered as he ambled back to his seat, looking at them all as if it was their fault for letting him make an ass of himself.

Xue sat back in his seat as they traveled toward the asteroid base.

Lisdel tried to contact him a few times but Xue made it look as though he were sleeping.

Lisdel had a cold light in his eyes before it was quickly hidden and he started trying to talk to the security detail around him. They gave him one-word answers and felt obliged to answer him even if they didn't want to.

It didn't take long for them to reach the asteroid base. The same hidden entrance greeted them as they passed through.

Xue used the sensor feed of the shuttle to look out at the main thoroughfare. It was larger than before. He could see the asteroid base's interior growing with the visible eye as an army of automated miners and machines worked to carve out the slips, offices, and different parts of the asteroid base as they went.

Xue's eyes moved to the main attractions in the thoroughfare. In the slips, there were shuttles, the massive automated mining excavators, and their smaller automated mining drills, though two massive battleships and now eight destroyers in various stages of completion dominated the space.

Automatons moved all around. The battleships were having some panels removed from their armor. Xue could see them with his eyes but the sensors of the shuttle were unable to even perceive the battleship and the destroyers.

If it was not for Xue looking at them, he wouldn't have thought that they were there in the first place. He was once again struck by just how advanced the machines and items the Emerilians used were. Even though it was magic, and it sounded unstable and confusing, they had melded it with scientific methods to increase their understanding of it to the point where it was more potent and powerful than any technology the Deq'ual had.

Xue looked upon the different ships and machines. The activity had increased by a massive margin. The speed at which the destroyers were coming along was impressive. There was even another superstructure that seemed to be laid down for a new battleship.

The shuttle moved into a landing area, where shuttles were moving cargo crates to and from.

The doors opened up as Dave and his entourage appeared at the end of the ramp, using teleportation. There was just Dave and Suzy. Dave had called her back from the front lines in order to help handle the different needs of the Initiative and manage it all. She was also there to help sort out a way to help gain the Deq'ual system's trust.

Lisdel pushed past the different soldiers and moved to the front of the line, a brilliant smile on his face as he moved down after Captain Xue.

Xue saw Dave frowning. Suzy's expression didn't change but he saw something flash behind her eyes.

"Captain Xue, good to see you," Dave said as soon as Xue entered his Mana barrier, the atmosphere inside allowing them to talk. Dave shook Xue's hand and then indicated to Suzy. "This is Suzy, my right-hand woman and the one who keeps all of this and everything else under control." Dave laughed and waved at the asteroid base.

"My job is hell," Suzy confirmed with a straight face before she let out a short laugh and shook Xue's hand.

"Well, I know I wouldn't be able to manage all of this. I'm still in shock with how fast you've been able to do everything!" Xue admitted.

"Councilmember Lisdel." Lisdel put his hand forward.

"Dave," the man replied, shaking Lisdel's hand.

"It's so good to meet you. I'm very interested in seeing how we can benefit one another in the future. For the good of the human race, the council and the people I represent are very interested in the plans and trade you have," Lisdel said forcefully.

Xue hid his displeasure while Dave's smile became a bit more forced. There was no trace of changes on Suzy's face as she hid her emotions deep.

"Now let's have a pose of the first meeting between the Emerilians and humans." The secretary moved among them, not caring about propriety as he tried to arrange Suzy and Dave for the photo shoot.

"Sorry, we don't have much time on the schedule for photos," Suzy said with a smile that actually looked disappointed. "We've got a lunch set up to discuss our future endeavors together. Need to keep Dave on track or else he would be all over the place."

Dave laughed good-naturedly, showing their skills in working together as a team.

Xue was impressed with their skills. It was as if they had experienced situations like this multiple times.

Quickly they got everyone organized and walked through the asteroid base.

Suzy informed the secretary of the upcoming schedule. The secretary tried to exercise power over what was to happen, but Suzy's skills were not to be underestimated. As even the secretary felt as if he had won, Suzy had maneuvered them expertly.

Dave, in turn, talked to Xue—citing military secrets—on a private channel. Lisdel was not very pleased to be left out of it all and instead walked with the poor security detail.

Xue's face turned ugly as he heard Lisdel's comments on the different people they passed. He called them half-breeds, pests, and a stain on humanity's purity.

The security detail had all experienced meeting these people before and although a few of them might have some similar viewpoints, the majority didn't and they tried to hammer reality in to those who had similar ideas to the council member.

However, Xue was happy that he wasn't dealing with the council member. He made sure all of the recording devices were off as he cleared his throat.

"Dave, could you make sure that our conversation is private?" Xue looked at the secretary and Lisdel, who were caught up in their own worlds.

There was a change in the air that the sensors in Xue's armor barely registered.

"Done," Dave said in a serious tone, obviously feeling that this conversation had a bit more weight to it.

"The council of my system are dragging their feet on helping you. They want resources, technology, and all of that but they want to stay hidden and give limited to no benefits. They've even passed orders for us to secretly gather all information on your technology as well as your facilities," Xue said, his tone dark.

Dave didn't say anything but his eyes became cold as his expression dimmed from smiling to apathy.

Xue continued on, his own anger building. He trained to fight, not to go around stabbing their allies in the back and then hiding within their own system, doing nothing against the forces that put them there. "I have been given another set of orders from Commander Sato, Admiral Adams, and Edwards. Lisdel is supposed to leave within a month. When he does so, I hope that we can work together completely. Whatever you need and we can help you with, we would be happy to do so."

Dave seemed to be scanning Xue before he nodded. By his look, it seemed he understood what kind of pressure this would put Xue under and how going against the council wouldn't be a good thing, but they felt it was their duty to help out the Emerilians.

"Well, if that is the case, then I indeed do have something that I need your help with," Dave said. "We've started to wake up the players who were stuck in the Earth simulation. We have a number of them who want to help and fight the Jukal, but they are green. They're quick at learning from their mistakes and they take to the simulations in the Mirror of Communication like fish to water. However, only very few of them have a background in the military or other related areas. I hope that you and your people might be able to aid in their training. I want them to get down the basics, come to understand space, the dangers that they face as well as the issues they will have when fighting in a spacecraft." Dave watched Xue for his reaction.

"We can certainly do our best," Xue said.

"That's all I ask," Dave said.

"I didn't know that you were able to wake them up," Xue said.

"Well, it's not simple. We only just got the capability to do it and we're walking on a tightrope. We're currently disconnecting and waking up only the players who don't have many other players around them. The players will easily recognize when another is acting strangely. However, we can trick the AI easy enough—Bob knows how they were coded, after all. We're pulling out more and more of them every day. However, it's only a small number when compared to them all."

"If you don't mind my asking, how many of them are there and how many are awake?" Xue asked.

"There are around five million in the simulation—two point five million for the next two generations who have been ramped up. However, some of them are at different stages of their life. We've been speeding up the simulations slightly so that all of the people who come out will have the mental age and experience of an eighteen-year-old at least. Right now, we've got maybe fifty thousand moving around. It's a lot of resources being burned through by having them awake. However, we're starting to see results from it already as they're helping out with the various facilities and helping us in growing the different bases, driving production to new heights and allowing us to build up a core group that will be able to man the different ships that we have." Dave looked to Xue, who felt an unseen pressure on him as he felt the trust that Dave had put in him was no small matter.

Xue was lost in his own thoughts as he considered the numbers Dave mentioned. There were nearly three million people in the Deq'ual system. With all of the players awake, then the Pandora's Box Initiative by itself would have nearly two times the amount of people they had. That wasn't even starting to consider the forces that were on Emerilia.

Dave guided them through the asteroid base. Since they had last come, there were more armored doors, people, and automatons. Even in just a few short weeks, it was clear that the Pandora's Box Initiative was not some small entity and they were only just starting.

They passed through a portal. Lisdel inspected the different Aleph automatons that stood watching the portal like statues. "Well, they look good, but all statues do. Waste of resources that can't move." Lisdel let out a barking laugh, calling the defenses of the Initiative simple statues.

Xue remembered how one of the battleships had appeared above his own *Sprite*, with its missile tubes and cannons runes glowing as Mana surged through them. He didn't deem to make a comment as they exited the facility holding the portal and looked at Ice City.

Xue smiled. The buildings of Ice City now had more green areas, where parks had been allowed to grow. These parks were filled with different plants that would create food and air. Xue approved; living in Deq'ual, there was nothing that was done for just simple decoration. People needed a place to relax and get away from their worries like the park; they wouldn't fill it with useless items, but items that could help support the station and the people within it.

There were more people moving around. The city seemed pretty full, with people talking and chatting everywhere. Most of them wore casual clothes that seemed a bit more modern than the simple hemp clothing. Others wore close-fitting clothes covered in runic lines.

Xue's eyes fell on these people. They had a familiar atmosphere about them—he felt a connection with them. He looked to Dave, who smiled as he created a dome around them that wouldn't allow noise out.

"They're your new trainees," Dave said.

"What are they wearing?" Xue asked.

"They're wearing the best in magical coding protection. The clothing has a Mana barrier built in that they can activate at will or will activate when it senses an incoming threat. In the soles and the clothing, there are slight gravity runes that will allow them to stick to anything they step on and walk on it without the nauseous feeling of null gravity. There's heat and cold exchangers so that they don't freeze or burn up no matter where they are. Also, we've added in some slight enhancements to increase their stats. If you look on their arms, they have armbands. We code different armbands with these enhancements. They usually only have one or two active at a time; having them all going is a huge power draw and it's likely that after five minutes of use that they'll burn out. It's the newest design—switch and change your enhancements on the fly. We're going to add support orbs that will be able to help them in their jobs but the factory is only just coming online and the people in Emerilia will be getting them first. For the time being, they will just have to get used to them while they're in the Mirrors of Communication training," Dave said.

Xue looked at their armor with interest. As with most things that he had seen from the Initiative, there was more to it than met the eye.

The different groups looked them over, with people using their private chats to talk to one another.

When Xue had first come to Ice City, he felt as if they were finding their feet; they had great ambition and they were moving toward it but it would take time. Now, seeing the speed at which they were advancing and the attitudes of the people around them, it seemed that they were already comfortable with their roles and sure in what they were doing. They were pushing their advancement further and faster.

Why do I have the feeling that we're just simply going to fall further and further behind them? Right now we have more ships and production, but their ships have many unknowns, and their building is on a scale that is set to eclipse all of the efforts in the Deq'ual system.

Xue looked back at Lisdel.

"If we built this city, it would be greater and better. The true humanity of Earth doesn't need half-breeds and these bastard children to prop us up," Lisdel said with a note of disgust, even as he smiled outwardly at the people they passed. "Look at the two leading us—some large mutated being and one with extended ears and height. They're good for looking different but when it comes down to it, they can't be as good compared to Deq'ual." Lisdel's words were filled with disdain.

Xue frowned and looked away. He knew a number of people referred to Deq'ual as the true humans of Earth. That the Emerilians were just abominations created by the Jukal. Making them closer to the Jukal than to humanity. Calling into question their heritage, alliances, abilities, and even their intelligence.

They were accustomed to being at the top of everything. Now that there was a slight change showing that the Emerilians were actually quite able, they felt threatened and were lashing out. Many of them talked about the achievements that the Deq'ual system had made over the last couple of years, none of them saying that these advancements would not have been possible without the help of the Emerilians.

The blind and power-greedy leading the stupid and weak-willed. Xue shook his head. He knew that the council as a whole didn't think this way, but the xenophobic groups were vocal in their arguments and retaliations. Right now, the Emerilians were helping them and requested nothing. They had only been given slight favors by the Deq'ual system, like helping with their stabilization issues on their ships, or finding out where they could find fuel from the ice planet. Their latest request to have their help in training their fighting force was only their third request.

"We showed them where to drill, practically made this place ourselves—we should be demanding that they pay rent to us!" Lisdel continued.

Xue hoped more level heads would prevail. *If they don't, then I don't want to be part of the Deq'ual system any more.*

Xue's footsteps faltered for a moment as that thought caught him off guard. It was not the words; it was the fact that he actually believed in those words. If the place he was supporting decided to go so against his values he couldn't reconcile them, then there was little reason for him to stay and support something he didn't believe in. Captain Xue was wrapped up in his own thoughts as they entered one of the many towers. They passed a number of growing areas before they reached a conference room overlooking Ice City.

Most of the security detail waited outside. A few people brought them food and drink, while three of them came into the conference room with Xue, Lisdel, and his secretary.

"So, to the trade agreements between the Initiative and the group that you represent, we were wondering what your thoughts were on it." Suzy looked to Lisdel and Xue.

"We ag—"

"The terms that you have given us are a bit too harsh. You're asking for a lot of resources that we ourselves need and the technology that you are willing to sell us is something that we will arrive at in a few years. I think it would be best for relations if a gift was made to show the commitment between our groups. We have already created an outpost that will give you piece of mind with our *capable* men and women in uniform nearby and also highly *effective* ships nearby. I think this is only fair," Lisdel said with a winning smile, as if what he was proposing was only natural.

Suzy and Dave looked to each other. They used a private chat to talk to each other, the rest of the room unable to hear what they were seeing or read their lips.

Xue had been stopped from accepting the generous terms of the trade agreement as the military side of the Deq'ual complex had understood them.

Lisdel gave Xue a look that seemed to dismiss him.

Xue kept his anger hidden. The terms were generous; the technology was impressive but the Initiative needed different resources and items. They could make them themselves but it would take them time. Whereas the Deq'ual system could make most of the things without too much extra effort. It truly was a win for Deq'ual. However, Lisdel had said that their people weren't as useful as those from Deq'ual; he had also gone on to say that they were providing security for the Initiative, and also threatening them at the same time.

Xue had a sour feeling in his mouth from it all.

"We had negotiated with Sato and his people and he had agreed to our terms. This was to complete the acceptance of this business agreement as well as sort out trade between our two groups," Dave finally said. Dave didn't seem threatened at all by Lisdel and sounded rather bored with it all.

Suzy crossed her arms and sat back.

Xue, who had been pushed to the side, saw Suzy's displeasure for a split second as she watched Lisdel, gauging him while Dave sounded him out.

"These terms—I can't accept them. They're not what the people of my system want and it will put them at a disadvantage," Lisdel said, as if reasoning with an idiot.

"You seem to think that we're a democracy over here, Mister Lisdel..."

"*Councilor* or *council member*, please," Lisdel said with a bright smile, talking over Dave.

"This is a business, a subsidiary of the joint efforts of the Stone Raiders Guild, Terra Alliance, and the Grahslagg Corporation. We are building up a military organization but it is run like a business to support that. We cannot start giving away our products for free without any compensation." Dave ignored Lisdel's words.

"It is but a token, to show your appreciation of the *protection* of my system. You should be aware of the protection you should make sure that you don't do anything wrong, lest that protection is lost. Who knows what you might lose? Lisdel said, his voice light an arrogant smile on his lips as he looked to the exterior of the office with a meaningful look in his eyes. "A city like this is a beautiful refuge, but under new management, it could truly flourish." Lisdel sighed, as if saddened by the state of affairs.

Dave's open and calm face changed, turning dark and cold.

Xue's scalp tingled as a pressure seemed to fill the room.

Dave let out a cold laugh.

"Is that right? You think you can come in here, make your idle threats against this city,"

"Dave," Lisdel said, his tone dismissive. The gravity in the room spiked as Lisdel's raised hand slammed into the desk, a look of panic in his eyes as he was forced into his seat.

Xue found it hard to breath and he was on the outside of Dave's focus.

"This is my city, the home of my wife, of my *daughter*. You threaten me with taking away your protection, fuck you, fuck your protection. You come for me, I'll be fucking waiting. You even *think* about threatening my daughter again," The pressure in the room doubled again.

Lisdel's face was a picture of pain.

Suzy placed her hand on Dave's arm pulling him back to reality.

The pressure stopped as Dave looked to them all, Xue's guts twisted seeing that expression on Dave's face, feeling guilty for Lisdel's words.

"Get the fuck out of my city. This agreement is done." Dave raised his hand. Lisdel, his secretary, and the security detail were forcefully transported back to the building with the portal in it.

"That guy is a fucking waste of oxygen. I'm sorry, Dave. What I wanted to say is that we accept your terms. He's just a politician who has ruled over my system for so long that he thinks he's some kind of god. He's looking to get a gift to show off to the people at home, to improve his standing. Sato and the military complex agree with your terms," Xue said quickly, feeling shame and guilt.

"He threatens Ice City and my daughter again I'll fucking turn him into paste." The look in Dave's eyes and the violent fluctuations in the air had cold sweat fall down Xue's back. "I'm not in a good mood. Make sure he never steps onto another one of my bases."

Suzy put her hand on Dave's shoulder. He looked to her and nodded before he disappeared from the room.

"Koi and the rest of Party Zero are his bottom line, and Lisdel touched it. From now on, we will only deal with you, Adams, Edwards, and Sato. We want this to be a partnership, but it seems that it will be more of a business relationship than anything. Your council is not behind you," Suzy said.

"We know, it's an issue," Xue said. "The politicians were not thinking of the military forces—they didn't listen to our input. They think of us as a political toy to be used."

"We want allies, not people we're going to butt heads with. If you can't deliver, we won't either. We're doing this to survive—it seems your system is in this to gain more strength." Suzy shrugged.

"I'm truly sorry about today. Here is the information on when we hope different shipments of materials and items will be coming in." Xue passed her a tablet. "I'll take my leave."

"We'll see you later," Suzy said. Clearly, she was not happy with how the meeting ended but she understood why it had, knowing that the blame was neither on Xue nor Dave.

Xue left the room and headed for the portal and back to his shuttle, gnashing his teeth as his hands curled into fists at his side. As soon as he crossed the portal's threshold and entered the asteroid base, he opened up his Mirror of Communication, connecting to the Deq'ual system.

"Get me Commander Sato," Captain Xue said as an operator was connected.

Moments later, Sato was connected.

"Captain Xue, how did the meeting go?" Sato sounded excited.

"Badly." Xue went on to send a recording of the events to Commander Sato. All of the armor that they wore recorded the goings-on around them.

"That fucking idiot," Sato said, sounding not one bit less angry than Dave, especially when Xue highlighted the fact that his daughter was actually living in Ice City.

"I'll take this to the council and get him removed as soon as possible. We don't need him fucking up everything we've got thus far," Sato said.

"Yes, sir," Xue said.

Chapter 10: Consolidate

The leaders of the Terra Alliance were all looking a lot better than they had over the last couple of weeks.

Josh sat at the top of the table with the Stone Raiders leadership around him. Representatives from various guilds, nations, and city states were also around the large table.

Josh cleared his throat as the rest of the members of the alliance quickly became silent. "I know that this meeting was on short notice, but it seems that in the last couple of weeks everything that we've done has been on short notice. I have a big announcement to make that I'll leave to the end. Right now, I want to talk about the situation on Emerilia."

In front of them all, Shard created a map that showed Emerilia, marking the different portal locations that were contested. A number of them were green, showing that they were under the alliance's control. Others in red or yellow showed the forces at the portal location had a foothold there, or that they were in battle.

"The flying citadels have proved to be highly effective. It is taking time to move them from location to location but we have already dealt with over half of the contested portals. We have pulled back the forces from the portals that are under our control in order to get them rested, rearmed, and ready for the battle to come. While it should take us no longer than a few months to take all of the portals, it is unknown if we will have this amount of time before the citadels are needed for other reasons. The Jakan have taken on a mercenary role and have moved to fight over two portal locations. They are engaged in a pitched battle at a Heval-based portal right now and are preparing their offensive against another portal in Gudalo. It seems thus far the Jakan have upheld their side of the bargain. We've got people watching them and ready to fight them if they turn on the agreement, but it is a risk that we must take in the face of the fight that is to come." Josh looked around the room.

No one looked away. They all knew what he was saying and what he was going to say.

Air, who watched the meeting, smiled to herself. *Well, it seems that all of my maneuvering turned out well. Seems that they have good heads on their shoulders,* she thought proudly, looking at the various leaders who sat at the table for the Terra Alliance.

"Water and Fire have already shown their support for the Terra Alliance, as have the merpeople and the dragons. The merpeople are, however, fighting against the various creatures in the seas and other than a sharing of resources, are unable to do much to aid us. We all know that Dark, Light, and Earth have been building up their forces in order to fight one another and try to dominate the Affinities Pantheon. The Dark Lord and Earth Lord are working together; both of them have assembled armies of creatures and people who they could rope into their service. The Lady of Light has turned Markolm into a land of fanatics and her angel legions have returned to her. From our reports, she is working to change all of the angels to her champions. Their training and abilities have greatly improved all of them, fighting to get her power first.

"She has also raised a much larger army from Emerilians who were moved by her words and her people's teachings. This army is not to be underrated. They are trained by the angels; they are the cannon fodder of Light's fighting strength; they are many and they are decently powerful, making them a large threat. Every day, all three of them gain more power from their believers, channeling it into their divine wells. Earth's forces have moved to the south of Opheir, in the forest located near the coast. The Dark Lord has moved his forces to Heval, between Zolu Mountain and the coast. Both of them are ready to hit the Lady of Light. We know a fight is going to happen; however, we do not know when it will happen.

The flying citadels will continue to fight off the forces coming from the portals but they are to be stocked and ready to fight at a moment's notice, to shift away from their targets and move to whatever battlefield the Pantheon decides on.

"To this end, I want all of the people under the command of this alliance to be ready to act at a moment's notice. Training and skill improvements are at the peak. If there is a need for any resources to increase a person's combat strength, then they are to be given it. We are going to be fighting the gods of Emerilia—it's not going to be so simple." Josh looked to Florence, who looked as though she wished to say something.

"We will also be receiving new technology that Dave has been working on. It's a type of defensive artifact. It's called an orb. If you've seen Dave and Party Zero fighting, then you've probably seen these orbs. They are usually hidden but can create shields, fire Mana bolts, as well as give those fighting with them an advantage within a certain area when fighting others. Production is low but we're hoping to move some of that to the Aleph to increase speed." Florence looked to Koza, who was the representative for the Aleph at this council meeting.

"I will pass the information to Frenik. I know that we will be able to free up some space," Koza vowed. Such an item was invaluable on the battlefield. They had long ago stopped caring about the resources that they were paying out, only caring about how effective they could produce and push them through the industrial complexes of those in the Terra Alliance.

"Good. I want you to put that all in your minds, but the second part, I'll get someone else to talk about it." Josh looked to where Air waited off to the side.

"Thanks, Joshie!" Air stood up like an eager little girl.

The people in the room looked at Air, confused looks on their face. She grinned as her illusion disappeared. Looks of shock appeared on people's faces. None of them had been able to see through her magic, which meant that she was incredibly powerful or that her level of understanding over the illusions had reached such a high degree that it surpassed magical power levels.

Others, upon seeing her face, looked around as if trying to find someone; their eyes fell on a simple-looking elf who smiled and returned their looks.

"Lady Air." A dwarf from the war council nodded in greeting.

"Hey, Bobbins." Air greeted the rough-looking dwarf who had seen multiple battles with a clear "pet" name.

So-called "Bobbins" let out a cough. The part of his cheeks not covered by beard turned red as he shot a look to Venfik.

"Air," Venfik said, a gentle reminder.

"Fine, okay, meeting blagh, information blargh." Air shook her head as she moved to the front of the table. Josh and Kim moved apart to allow her room to stand.

There were looks of shock, others of reverence, others of fear. She was one of the people in the Pantheon; if she decided to, she could easily kill them all. She could also report their plans to her brothers and sisters.

Her playful attitude fell away as a serious expression fell on her face. She looked at the people and aides in the room. A powerful blast of air was emitted from her body. The walls, floor, and ceiling became white. The room brightened a bit as they were separated off from the rest of the world.

"As you have all gained positions highest in your land, I know that the words I'm about to say will have a great meaning to you. After all, throughout your history, I have been moving among the various different lines and groups, making sure that this message and this knowledge was passed down. It was one of the things that I agreed with Bob about, that stuffy old gnome." Air had a soft smile on her lips instead of a frown, speaking to the position Bob held in her heart as a sort of father figure.

Her expression turned severe once again. "You should all know about the Jukal."

This one word sent ripples through the people in the meeting. If anyone else had said it, they might think of it as a slip of the tongue. But with everything that Air had said and done, it was clear that this was not a simple slip. All of their faces became dark—some with anger, others with fear. This told of the power this word wielded. These were people who were going up against the gods of Emerilia, but one word from Air was capable of making them go into a cold sweat.

"This battle we're fighting, in order to win it, we might need to use means that the Jukal will pay attention to. Whether this is the different magical spells we've added to the flying citadels, the new grand working rounds, or even the overall power that our forces can display in one attack. Your people don't need to just prepare for the coming war against the Pantheon—they need to be ready for the coming Jukal." Air threw out her hand. White crystals as clear as glass appeared in front of all those in the room.

"Hold it in your hand and focus on it with your eyes and you will learn all about our preparations," Air said.

Some people who had met Air before took the crystals and looked into the depths, their faces going slack after a few moments.

The others in the room followed after them.

It took about five minutes before the first blinked and started to shake their heads, rubbing their temples slightly. Their faces were pale, not from the information now flooding their minds but because of the depth of that information and the preparations made.

The only one who wasn't so pale was the dwarven war council leader. He simply pursed his lips and looked back to Air.

It seemed as if the Council of Anvil and Fire had told the war council already.

"These resources are impressive, but the information on the Jukal—how is it possible to defeat something like this?" one of the people around the table asked.

Included in the memory crystal, that was similar to a spell book but had been refined and simplified by Air because she hated explaining things, she'd included up-to-date information on the Jukal Empire.

"In stages." Air looked to Lucy, who sat at the table.

"There are three main stages." Lucy looked to the others in the room. "The first is that we need to secure Emerilia. There is a Jukal military base in one of our moons as well as multiple methods they have of destroying Emerilia. We will need to defeat all of those as well as the three ships that are currently hiding behind that same moon that they've made a base of. Once we secure Emerilia, we can begin the second part of the campaign. Air and her people will start to use the information networks that are set up in Emerilia to hopefully ignite the anger of the people within the Jukal Empire.

"The portals are all controlled by the Jukal and they have placed them outside of the different domains they control. If these regions are to rebel, they can mobilize their empire's military and ruthlessly snuff it out. Each of these portals need the right coordinates as well as proper security codes to move from one to the other. All of these codes are random and are held by special code computers within Jukal ships. We happen to have access to a carrier, as well as its code box. Using this and our knowledge of portals, we will be able to get into the portal network and turn them over for our use. We will move between different systems and hit different places that emphasize the control of the empire. We get them to spread their forces out, to try to get to these different locations. They use the portals, spread themselves out. We shut down the portals, isolate them and defeat them, piece by piece. As this is going on, we send down factories that will give those in the Jukal Empire weapons, power, food. We break the hold that the Jukal Empire has on them. We don't need to destroy the Jukal straight up. By undermining their hold over others, then they will not have the supplies to maintain themselves." Lucy looked to them all.

They all understood the plan. Before the onos and the teleports, if they were under siege, there was no way for them to bring in new supplies from other places unless they lifted the siege. If their military in the field was already defeated, then they could only wait for a slow and painful death of starvation.

Air nodded, knowing that this had been Dave's plan when he had started to work things out. He hadn't passed it on to Sato and his people, as, like Sato, he trusted them, but he didn't truly know them. Things like this plan were too important to trust to someone he had never met before.

The fear that had broken out in the room was now tempered as the men and women of the Terra Alliance looked to one another. These were powerful and ruthless people. Air had picked them for their ethics and their ability. They all knew what their orders would bring about: the loss of life. Many of them had been adventurers or people in the military they were now sending forth.

By the way they moved, even without their actions, Air knew she had them.

"What do you need from us to complete this plan?" one of them asked.

Air didn't smile, knowing that this meeting right now would not only decide what happened in the fight with the Pantheon, it would decide the fate of Emerilia and all of those who called it home. Player and POE alike.

***

Party Zero marched with the flying citadel force. They had been going nearly nonstop for an entire week now, moving from one location to the next, subduing portals and the creatures that came from them and helping those they passed.

It had taken a direct order from the top people in the Terra Alliance to get them to stop, and they needed it.

As they exited the teleport pad, another group was entering the teleport pad, exiting the ono that was located on Goblin Mountain's Flying Citadel One.

Deia looked to the rest of Party Zero. Dave, Malsour, and Suzy had already been called away with other work to do. None of them had the time to actually take in the losses of Jekoni and Anna.

They'd driven themselves to exhaustion, trying to make it so that less people would die on their side, but now all of them looked as if they were soulless from the heavy fatigue they were suffering from.

As they stepped into Terra, it was a vastly different city than from when they had left it.

People were everywhere: Terra had taken in as many as possible to try to relieve some of the pressure on the other places that were dealing with a massive influx of refugees.

The Aleph had helped out and accepted a bunch of new citizens into their cities but still Terra was the staging point for most of the massive operations happening across Emerilia.

Deia raised her eyes, looking to where the next section of the city was nearing completion. The Blood Kin had worked tirelessly to expand Terra, as well as the flying citadels. They were seen as heroes and many people were freely giving them the lifeblood of the animals that they killed in thanks for all they had done. The Blood Kin had become a powerful group within Terra but they worked hard to help their fellow Terra residents.

Party Zero moved away from the marching lines of soldiers who were coming back from the flying citadels. People noticed their badges and a number of people recognized the famous Party Zero as they headed for another teleport pad.

Deia looked to the others as all of them continued to follow. She passed through the teleport pad and entered the power station. They quickly entered Pandora's Box and then passed through a portal into Ice City.

It was half the size of Terra but it was growing even faster with the aid of the massive machinery at work. There were more people here but it wasn't as packed as it was in Terra. As they exited the armored building holding the portal, Dave appeared in front of them.

He smiled to them all before he moved to Deia.

She wrapped her arms around him, finally feeling safe and home after all she had seen in the last couple of days. She just wanted to hold onto him forever like that.

"Let's get you all off to your rooms—can smell you clean across Ice City," Dave said with a joking smile, his humor subdued as the recent losses made it hard to joke.

They disappeared from the portal and reappeared in an apartment building.

Dave led them to different rooms. They were numb as they listened to his instructions. Malsour also appeared, greeting them but letting them get much-needed rest.

Dave guided Deia into their room. Dave helped to take off her boots.

Deia saw Dave, his rugged looks and the strength of his muscles. The heat of her body climbed as she looked over him.

Dave, sensing her gaze, looked up at her.

She lurched forward, toppling Dave over on the floor. Her hands gripped his hair as she roughly kissed him.

Dave grabbed her hair slightly as he kissed her back; his other hand pulled her to him. They forgot the world as they tore at each other's clothes, letting their instincts take over.

***

After their hurried lovemaking, they took a shower together, some of the tension that had built up being released.

Dave felt a whole lot better than he had in days.

They lay on their bed, the two of them entwined in one another's embrace.

"We can go see Koi right now," Dave said.

"I know, it's just, I'm fresh off of fighting. I want some time before I see her," Deia said in a small voice, her face troubled.

Dave pulled her closer and kissed the top of her head.

After a few minutes, she looked up at Dave, her face serious. "Am I a bad mother?"

"What?" Dave asked, stunned by the question.

"Am I a bad mother?" Deia repeated, her voice firmer.

"No, not at all. Why would you think that?" Dave's brows pulled together in concern as he put both his arms around her.

"I went into battle with her while I was carrying her. Now she's been born and I've spent more time training people than I've seen her! I've been fighting for weeks straight and instead of wanting to see her, I jumped you and hid in here." Deia's emotions came out as she started to cry, her whole body shaking.

"Come here." Dave sat up and wrapped her up in his arms.

She cried on his shoulder as he hugged her.

"You're a great mother. Yes, you were near battle when you were pregnant, but you were in the rear, fighting at a distance and you had the speed to be able to escape at any time. And I had teleportation orbs around you so nothing could happen to either of you. Was it a good idea? No. But you wouldn't be you if you simply just stayed at home and let us do all the fighting. You've been fighting and training people for the last couple of months, but all of these people, without your training they might not be making it home to their loved ones. I know you—you worry over her all the time. Look at you right now. You're in a state because you care so much for her. How could a mother who cares for her this much be a bad mother?" Dave asked, his voice gentle and reassuring.

Deia cried for a little while longer but finally she started to calm down. Not many would think of the leader of the Stone Raiders' famous Party Zero crying on her husband's shoulder as if she were nothing but a little girl.

Past the legends and the stories, they were truly just people underneath. People who had been thrown into an impossible situation, but strove to make their own path, their own future. That was what made them powerful. Not their magic, their weapons, or their gear—but the drive to push forward, no matter the obstacles.

Chapter 11: War Forges

Denur looked across the battlefield. She banked sideways, leading a wing of aerial forces and her own family members. Spells and ranged attacks all tried to hit them as they came down out of the cloud cover created by the explosions that ringed the citadel.

The Terra Alliance's attacks smashed upon the Mana barrier of the citadel. From the flying citadels in the air to those on the ground, their attacks made the barrier turn a darker color, showing it was close to failure.

"Break it!" Denur's voice carried as she unleashed her dragon breath. Blue flames shot from her mouth, creating a new light in the day. The others following her added in their attacks. The barrier shivered and shook under the impact of their powerful attacks. The aerial forces dropped bombs and hit with their own ranged attacks.

"Break!" Denur called out. Their aerial formation broke apart as they passed over the citadel. The ranged attacks flew by, illuminating the sky as the defenders tried to take down the dragons and their protection in the air.

Denur arced and weaved through the incoming fire. As she left, thunder seemed to erupt from the heavens. She looked to the flying citadels. Mana halos along the banks of cannons fired right down the line, all of their fire focused into the weaknesses of the defenders' barrier.

It collapsed under the fire of the flying citadels.

When the barrier went down, the artillery cannons' rate of fire increased. Runes running down their cannons lit up as they fired, their regular artillery spells fueled by the soul gem they were connected to. It allowed them a higher rate of fire but they were much less destructive than the grand working artillery rounds.

The cannons didn't stop firing at a rate of one artillery spell per second. They recoiled and returned to their original positions just as they fired again.

It was an impressive display of firepower that hammered the citadel on the ground.

Denur gained altitude, picking a different flight path and moving for the citadel she was based on. She came in to land; her size decreased so that she was only half of her normal size.

People waiting off to the side brought over Mana, Stamina, and Health potions; healers checked her over.

She downed the potions. Energy filled her once again as she moved toward one of the exits. She jumped off the catwalk and into the jet stream. Her wings snapped out as her speed shot up and she returned to her normal size, looking at the battlefield below.

The citadel on the ground was being torn apart. As the artillery spells and other ranged attacks hit, walls exploded, shooting out rocks and metal that made them up.

The castle and tower in the center was being torn apart, the interior of the castle being revealed as artillery crews blew out sections of the tower.

A round exploded inside the tower. The already weakened structure gave way. The entire building became unstable as it shook and then started to fall down, crushing what was below before it toppled over, landing on the castle and inner area below.

Even as it fell, more rounds smashed into it, tearing it apart.

It was a scene of pure destruction.

The drop forces were all in defensive positions outside the range of the citadel, watching and ready to move in once the bombardment was finished.

Denur looked for the aerial forces that had been assigned as her protectors. She banked and dove, flapping her wings as she cut through the smoke and dust that had been thrown up by the fighting below. She used her wings and tail to slow her speed as she entered the flying formation.

The DCA aerial forces nodded to her. Some poured more power into their armor to alter their course while others flapped their large wings as they circled the citadel, ready to move in and support as needed.

If they were to head lower, they were at risk of getting hit by their own artillery. The aerial battlefield was complex and hard to fight in, but Deia and her training staff had stressed safety again and again, working to minimize the risk of friendly fire.

Denur and the aerial forces didn't talk as they watched the destruction below. They had seen too many scenes like this in the last couple of days, becoming their new norm.

By the time that the other citadels had stopped releasing their ranged attacks, the dust cleared over the citadel on the ground. The once proud citadel was now nothing but a pile of rubble.

"Keep an eye out for anything left down there," the wing commander said, banking and taking them toward the citadel.

They stretched out their senses as much as possible, watching the citadel.

Other aerial groups beat them to the citadel, racing over it. They unleashed a few attacks here and there to kill off anything that looked as if it might be able to resist.

Denur and her group went past. Not sensing any threats, they didn't use any attacks and returned to the sky.

After the citadel had been checked from the sky, the drop forces started to march forward.

"We're being moved to the portal," the wing commander called up as they altered their flight path, leading them away from the citadel and toward the portal that was in the midst of rubble.

There were still creatures coming out of the portal but they were simply stepping into their own deaths. All around the portal, there were trap grand workings.

They were similar to grand workings in that they had a massive amount of power behind them to replicate spells; however, the trap grand workings didn't exhaust all of that power in one go. If they were triggered, they would let off a burst of power, saving the rest for any others that entered their area of effect. There was also a cold heat exchanger that pulled out the cold energy from within the Mana shield that encapsulated the portal and its traps.

Anything that passed the portal was cooked alive, or they made it to the grand working traps to be torn apart. There was no escaping anymore.

Techs were on the ground with mounted forces, watching the portal, ready to pull them back at a moment's notice.

Denur let out a sad sigh as she looked at the different items that had been created for the purpose of extinguishing life.

Every day it seemed that there was a new, more powerful weapon being introduced. She understood it and she accepted it: the stronger the weapon, the less people who needed to die on the Terra Alliance's side. This was the progress of war and she was scared to see what would happen with it in the future.

She looked toward Markolm. Her eyebrows came together as she let out a breath. Flames illuminated her mouth and nose in anger.

She had watched the Affinities Pantheon, been privy to their actions through Fire's explanations and teachings. She had no mercy in her heart for Light, Earth, or Dark. All of them used people simply to gain more power. Air used people too but it was mostly to entertain herself, and she had brought peace and alliances to fruition. Fire looked to strengthen the people through learning magic. Water kept the seas safe with his merpeople.

As she flew over that battlefield, watching the advancing drop forces like an impossible juggernaut as the last vestiges of the aggressive species were being wiped out and the portal essentially blocked off, Denur knew that this was only the beginning. She hoped that these battles were enough to raise the levels and temper those of the Terra Alliance for what was to come.

"We've secured this portal. We're being ordered to move to the Densaou Ring of Fire," the aerial wing commander called out. "The rest of the portals will be dealt with by the Jakan."

Denur and the others didn't say anything as they moved slowly over the portal location.

The drop forces had made it to the citadel. There was sporadic fighting here and there but they hadn't used any of their Stamina or Mana, while the defenders had been fighting for nearly a full day now.

They quickly swept over the citadel. Scouts and those with detection abilities made sure that there was no one left.

"Citadel is secured. Let's go home," the wing leader called out, flapping their wings and leading them toward the flying citadel they were based out of.

***

Kol walked past an armored door. Waves of heat pressed against his body, making him start sweating right away. He stepped forward and looked upon the massive factory complex. He was in the ark shipyard on Emerilia. With all of the arks now complete, the factories that had been making the different parts and materials for them had been retooled and were now working on making supplies needed by the frontline forces.

Here they were making orbs based off the designs Dave had given them, as well as swords, shields, the wristbands and breastplates that the DCA were issued and that were now being issued to all manner of forces. Here, different parts of the weapon systems that were installed on the missile ships, arks, battleships, and destroyers were all being created.

Kol looked to an artillery cannon assembly line surrounded by automatons.

Different parts that had been machined and created in the different factories came together. The inner coded lining of the barrel matched up with the outer barrel, followed by the firing system, sensing system, and control runes. All of these parts were interconnected and slotted into place, the simple barrel becoming a cannon over the space of just a few minutes.

On another belt, the different spheres that made up the orbs were being put together and fused. As they were finished, they were pulled off, put into crates and then stored in holding cargo containers, ready to be shipped out to Terra.

Swords were sent down a conveyor belt; carvers on either side engraved runes into the weapons as they passed.

There were bows, shields, armor, wristbands. All of it was passed down the line. The metal formed into the different items, engravers going to work and then the finished product placed into crates.

They weren't the highest quality, but hundreds of them could be produced in a day. These weapons were not simply for the fighting forces of the Terra Alliance but also the people who were learning combat training in the different cities and towns.

Weapons were expensive items and smiths were dealing with repairs instead of making new weapons and armor. These weapons and armor were awarded to one once they passed apprentice level in their fighting skills.

This strengthened these different areas, so that the Terra Alliance wouldn't need to stretch their forces to these areas.

Kol's eyes fell on one of the larger assembly lines—the missile assembly line.

A missile was made in three sections. In the rear, there was the drive, which was coded with runes, as well as a soul gem power source. The middle section contained the grand working modified payload. The forward section had a soul gem construct that recognized targets and used sensing spells to find them.

The internals of the missile were connected together by soul gem strands. The rear drive was attached, the soul gem construct fusing with it and intertwining with the areas for the drive runic lines. The middle section was added, secured to the soul gem internals and the rear drive plate.

Finally, the forward section was attached, hiding the soul gem internals. It looked like a cigar that had been cut at one end where the drive was.

The dark-gray metal had black runic lines up and down its surface. These were the different sensing spells and stealth codings, as well as drive spells, for the missiles. They were black to make it harder to see the missile. If it was giving off light constantly, then it would be easier for the Jukal's sensors to read them.

Kol's steps came to a halt as he looked at it all. There was the constant noise of machines working, as well as crates and weapons being readied as carts took on the payloads and rushed off to deliver the weapons to where they needed to go while other carts brought in refined materials for the factories to assemble more weapons.

The grand working shells that were used with the artillery cannons were not assembled here but in the asteroid base with the different shield modules, missile tubes, drive plates, and interceptor weapon systems. All the parts that were needed for the growing fleet were assembled and readied before being added to the different ship platforms.

Kol checked on the different factories, looking over the production numbers.

Another facility within the ark shipyard tested all of these systems and readied them for use.

Kol arrived in front of a massive armored door. As he approached, the sounds of mechanisms unlocking could be heard. Magical seals that were floating over the door submerged into it, the different protections being unlocked before the door opened.

Inside, multiple factories and assembly lines were at work. Lines where metal plates were passing, being engraved by carvers that darted down from overhead.

Soul gem constructs that were coded, growing into different parts as they went down assembly lines, connected to power runic lines that were part of the machines moving them.

Armored plates were fused together, being sent to different lines where they were formed into breastplates, shoulders, upper and lower arms, legs, kneecaps, ankles and feet.

A complicated assembly made the different knuckles, fingers and other parts, all of them being connected together to create hands.

Humanoid-looking forms made up of multiple engraved sheets and runic line-covered items moved down the lines, being assembled piece by piece before finally their interior was complete.

The shoulders were put on first, and then the back plate was added. A flurry of sparks appeared as they were tack-welded on, fusing arms, working to complete the seal between the two parts. The arms started to take form, coming in from the sides, tack-welded and fused. On one mannequin, the back sections of the armor were added; on the mannequin beside it, the front section was formed.

Arms came from above, attaching in the soul gem constructs and the different carved-out metal pieces. They were clamped into place and fused as rack after rack of back and front armor moved forward.

A helmet appeared from above. Different small pieces came together, being fused into the two sections of the helmet. As the helmet's components came together, the front and rear sections of armor were picked up and put together. As the helmet descended, a soul gem construct reached out from the helmet and neck section into the armor, attaching the two. The armor came together as the neck section and helmet were fused on top of them.

The final fusing was completed between the different parts of the armor. Power ran through it. The soul gem construct that had been embedded into the lines carved in the armor started to glow with power as the armor seemed to come alive. It was carried off the rack, a complete set of armor, before being set down in a formation.

To the side of the factory, there was a massive open area. Standing in that area were row upon row of the identical armors. Kol looked at it all.

Just looking at them, Kol was filled with a sense of power as well as respect.

Every ten minutes, three sets of Devastator armor were completed. These sets weren't as powerful as the ones that Gurren and Lox used. However, instead of needing Dave to spend weeks and his own Willpower to complete one of them, these could be mass-produced.

Kol moved his eyes from the ready ranks and looked over the console that was managing the factories and assembly lines for the armor.

A cart appeared in front of Kol. On the back of it, there were a half dozen crates that had come from the missile factory line. Kol finished checking the factory's reports and stepped up onto the cart.

It took off, taking him through the portal to Pandora's Box. He entered the now empty work space.

The hub with all of the portals that connected to different parts of the Pandora's Box Initiative was filled with activity.

The fusion power plant was still going and the smaller factories were producing things like the Mana wells and modifying the onos received from the Aleph.

The teleportation array was still there, now with a crane to drop things through the teleportation array as needed. The teleportation array started to glow. The different parts of the room moved and changed before suddenly stopping. A surge of power blasted through the room as a dark area was revealed on the other side of the teleport array's wormhole that now appeared in the center.

Kol took command of the cart. It floated forward, entering the wormhole and appearing on the other side.

Waiting there was a member of the war council, as well as a number of the dwarven protectors who were usually hidden from the outside world. Now with the fighting going on, a number of them had once again returned to the battlefield, shaking those who believed them to have been dead or traveling across Emerilia.

"Kol," the war council leader said with a nod.

"Feli, good to see you again." Kol stopped the cart.

"Go, grab one." The war council leader waved the dwarven protectors forward.

They grabbed one of the large crates that was nearly two meters long. With a grunt, they picked up the crate and moved it to a cart that they had ready off to the side.

The war council member worked a station in front of him. The teleport pad that Kol had just come through closed its wormhole and started to move, changing the runes around and connecting to a different teleport pad.

"I'll see to them personally," Feli assured Kol.

"Do that, and they will work with our large-calibre mountain artillery," Kol said.

"We'll be ready when it's needed," Feli pledged.

Kol nodded, his face solemn as he turned his cart around and headed through the teleport pad.

He found another two dwarven protectors and a war council member, and repeated the process he had done at the first dwarven mountain he had just left.

***

Frank Simmons sat up from his chair. He had been in the Mirror of Communication, working with the different techs and people who had created the different warships in the asteroid base.

This was to get them familiar with the different ships, so if anything was broken they would know how to fix it, and they could use the systems.

Frank was aiming to be a weapons controller, so it wasn't as in-depth as those who were on the engineering crews who would service the different ships and look after them. Nor the damage control personnel whose second role was to assess and deal with any damage that happened to the ship that they were on.

He opened up his interface, looking at the quest board that had been set up for everyone. He was on an extended quest for the battleship building slips.

He checked that his gear was all sorted out and turned on his Mana barrier. He passed those who were waiting outside to go to class, exiting the Mirror of Communication room. He passed through an airlock and out into the asteroid base.

He grabbed a ride with a cart that took him over the thoroughfare and toward the battleship slips. Now there were not just two battleships being worked on. There were five scaled-down models that were constantly being fed resources, growing in different slips while another ten superstructures were in various stages of development. The destroyers were coming along at an even faster rate: ten were already sealed up—five of them combat ready and good to go—and another twenty superstructures were being built just for the planned warships.

All across the different slips, machines and people were working to bring them online as fast as possible.

Their pace was enough to leave Frank shocked.

Frank jumped off his cart as soon as he arrived at the way point of where everyone was supposed to meet before going on a shift.

With their higher Endurance, they only needed about four hours of sleep a night. It wasn't as impressive as some of the people who needed to only sleep every few days but it allowed them more time to work on the different quests they had and work on leveling up their skills and attributes.

The orc leading their group wore what looked like a blacksmith's apron, with tools in a belt around his waist. It looked at odds with the spaceships that were next to them. Around his neck, there was a necklace that showed his Mana barrier was active.

"All right, I know how much you all want to work on the battleship, but we're needed over at the asteroid factory—all hands on deck. Since this is going to take a while, I called in a few favors and we'll be taking a shuttle over." The orc turned and led them toward a shuttle bay nestled in the side of the asteroid's walls.

All of them moved a little faster, shooting excited looks to one another. They hadn't been outside of the asteroid base yet; this would be their first trip between the different asteroid bases. Normally all transport was done by portal, teleport pad, or ono. Getting a shuttle free was a rare occurrence.

All of them quickly followed their foreman, smiling as he led them to a shuttle that opened in front of them. They climbed aboard, finding that there were no pilots but there was a connection with the shuttle. They quickly accessed it and were able to use their interfaces to look outside of the shuttle.

"Everyone in?" the orc asked.

"Yes!" Frank said after a quick check.

"Good." The orc opened a private chat to talk to someone. The door to the shuttle closed and sealed before pushing up off the ground and heading out of its slip. It moved out along the large open area between the walls of the asteroid base and the slips. Materials, automatons, and people were everywhere, moving and working on different projects.

The shuttle passed them, carts going in the other direction.

It turned, going out into the main thoroughfare of the asteroid base, diving and turning toward a heavily armored area of the asteroid base.

Here there were different weapon systems protecting the large hatches that were opening and closing with the movement of shuttles.

The shuttle came to a halt with a few dozen others. They waited together before the armored doors opened and they rushed forward in formation. Another group entered the asteroid base at the same time, with plenty of room between the two large groups.

They kept a certain pace, speeding up or slowing down, to meet all of the armored doors as they opened.

Finally, the last armored door opened and they were looking out upon a star-filled sky.

The shuttle turned; increasing its speed and heading towards the refinery that they would be working on.

People talked in excited voices, able to hear one another in the atmosphere-filled cabin of the shuttle.

Frank looked upon the asteroid base as they left it. From the outside, it looked like a simple pitted rock that was gently rotating in different directions. His eyes moved to the spectacular star-filled void all around him.

As he looked upon those stars, it was a sight that he would never forget for the rest of his life. He felt truly insignificant, as complicated emotions rose up within his chest. He held his silence, taking it all in. His mind shook from the things that he was able to see.

They passed asteroids that were a few meters big to thousands of kilometers.

"We're heading into an asteroid-rich area, better for the refinery," the orc said as the shuttle started to move erratically. However, there was no gravity inside the shuttle, only the gravity that their clothes were exerting.

A few people had to close their eyes, unable to look at the screens as they moved around wildly. Others gained a new sense of excitement from the screens' movement.

Soon they cleared most of the asteroids and they headed toward a large asteroid.

Other shuttles were visible and on their sensors, they were able to identify mining drills that were opening up paths into different asteroids. They were too far away to be seen without zooming in their interfaces.

They finally reached the refinery asteroid, being greeted by more armored doors. There weren't as many as in the main asteroid base, so they quickly found themselves inside.

The calm of the exterior was at complete odds with the development inside.

There were mining drills and excavators working to expand out in every direction. The whole area had been cleared out, hollowed out and the mined material removed so it looked like a huge windowless warehouse on steroids.

Excavators spread out in every direction. The light of their laser drills illuminated the asteroid walls as they ate through everything in their path.

Massive metal pillars stretched out from the surrounding asteroid and met in the center, where a misshaped construction was being created.

Shuttles moved in close to this central area. Automatons and carts moved to meet them, grabbing the materials stored in the storage containers they were hauling. They were full of parts and refined metals to finish construction of the refinery.

The superstructure was growing at an incredible rate. The metal grew outward and automatons added in struts, braces, and supports, creating a structure of interconnecting lines.

The automatons could build the entire refinery by themselves. However, it could take months. With the aid of the people in the Pandora's Box Initiative, they could speed this process up dramatically, moving it from a few months to having the first section of the refinery online in just two days. But only if everyone pulled together.

Right now they needed more refineries. They had the raw materials taking up storage room but Pandora's refineries weren't fast enough to process all of the materials. They were sending out a trickle of resources to the people on Emerilia but it was nowhere close to meeting up with their demand.

The bottleneck was slowing down their timelines dramatically relying on these different refineries.

"All right, everyone check your Mana barriers and air!" the orc said.

A pressure filled the shuttle as people activated their Mana barriers and checked their air supply in their modified pouches of holding that acted as air tanks. Their Mana barriers covered their faces while their clothes, gloves, and boots sealed to one another. The air tank regulated the air that was contained around their head.

The shuttle settled down in a shuttle bay. Automatons rushed from the sides, opening up the cargo container it was carrying and hauling items out to be taken deeper into the refinery.

Their foreman led them off the shuttle and toward a way point.

"All right, welcome to Asteroid Refinery One. All of you are to assist with laying down supports. I know, not glamorous work, but the faster you get it done, the faster the soul gem construct can grow," a Beast Kin said, adding them to different work party chats.

New way points and goals appeared on Frank's quest screen.

The orc foreman accepted the changes and they headed off for an area filled with crates.

Their strength was great and the coding on the crates was the best. Each of the players could easily carry two of the one-meter-long crates, one on each shoulder.

They loaded one another up and headed out.

Frank passed through sections of growing soul gem construct, coming to the skeleton-like section of superstructure that was growing out from the center of the refinery.

All around him, people and automatons lay down the structural supports and braces from the crates he was carrying. It was like an army of ants, each building their own thing but it all coming together in one complex creation.

Frank's view showed where his braces and supports were supposed to be laid. The crates had no weight unless he activated the magical coding that would stick them to a surface. He felt as if gravity were pushing down on him but in reality there wasn't any.

He got down on his hands and knees, wrapping his legs around the structural member he was going to work on. Now it seemed as if it was growing upward instead or outward to his perspective.

He shimmied up the strut and opened the crate. He pulled out the structural brace and placed it where a hologram appeared of it. It fused with the metal beam that Frank had his legs wrapped around.

Runic lines ran from the metal beam he was on, through the other beam. When he saw that, a sign that they were properly fused, he moved upward, connecting the other beams. Sometimes they would go upward; sometimes they would go sideways.

He paused after a while to grab a canteen from his pouch of holding, holding it to his lips and squeezing some in. He watched the other people working around him.

Not all of them were simply adding in the superstructure.

Dark mages had their bags of holding open. Metal moved as if it were an intelligent creature, creating a path ahead of them; as they passed the metal, it looked no different from the other structural members. Their speed was a great improvement over the automatons; they could do it quickly but the Dark mages could to it at a walking pace.

Frank's eyes went wide as he saw one of the dragons shoot forward as if they were flying. Their legs were on two metal beams. All around them, dozens of structural members formed with smooth and exact precision. It made what Frank was doing look like child's play. In a moment, they had done more than Frank had in an entire hour.

He was left in a state of shock as he looked at all the different methods people were using to create the superstructure. One person ran from beam to beam, tossing down the beams they held. Frank swore that their lips were pursed, as if they were whistling as they showed off their acrobatic display.

Another stood on the top of a beam, shooting for the sky. More beams shot out from the beam underneath them at times, reaching out to connect to other beams nearby or waiting for others to catch up.

Frank had heard of the power of magic—he had seen it in the feeds of Emerilia—but this was his first time seeing it on such a large scale. All of the battleships were mostly made by the different automated machines as well as engineers and those trained in magical coding and Dark magic. He had thought that their estimate of taking just a few days to make the battleships if they had the materials and the power to be a vast understatement. Now, seeing their speed in just making this superstructure, he was stunned.

A look of determination crossed his face. "They've worked on their skills, so it's only fair that I work on mine." With that, Frank started to climb faster and faster, holding the crates with the structural beams in one hand as he raced forward and using the other hand and his feet to keep going. He'd grab a beam from the crates as he reached the end of the beam he was on, jumping up higher and continuing forward.

As more time went on, he got faster and faster, pushing his body past the limits he had set on himself and aiming to reach the ones of his body.

He was a Level 300; there were hidden depths to his strength. It had taken him seeing others and the incredible things that they could do to push past the ideas of what he thought he was capable of. In just a few hours, he was jumping from section to section, looking more monkey than man as he ambled through the superstructure, connecting beams together.

He looked behind him. The soul gem construct was growing faster and faster, spreading over the beams. He could sense the power coming off that soul gem construct through the metal he was working on. Machines and the innards of the refinery were taking shape at a speed that could be seen with Frank's eyes. An excited grin appeared on his face as he worked harder, pushing to be faster.

He was not as fast as some of the impressive Dark mages who had come out. However, he was among the fastest of the players. He only stopped to eat and drink to return his Stamina before taking off again. It was six hours later before his quest reappeared and told him that he was done for the day.

He looked back at the refinery, faint shock in his eyes as he saw that already one of the main separation areas had been created.

The refinery was growing outward along six different metal pillars that grew out from the asteroid.

The refinery looked like a square. However, at each face, there were openings. Shuttles would go in here, dropping off their storage crates filled with metal and debris along the walls of the tunnel and dumped into massive machines that would separate them out into their different metals. They would go through different refineries outside of the tunnel, being refined down and pushed further toward the outside of the square-looking refinery. This way, the raw materials would be processed out from the center.

They would be pushed through the different onos and teleport pads to the asteroid base to be used, or they could be further processed and combined to create different compound materials or basic shaped items. As the refinery progressed, then more and more shops would be added onto the outside of the refinery. These wouldn't just temper and refine the metal, but create large-scale items like armor or structural supports that could be used for a vast array of projects.

They could even have factories later on that would combine these different products to be used elsewhere.

Frank felt a sense of pride, knowing that he had been part of this massive project. He smiled and made his way to the way point, getting up and running along the beams. As he went, he threw down beams here and there as he saw them missing in places.

People watched his speed in shock as he passed and entered the refinery. There was an open ono connected to another ono in the asteroid base.

He caught sight of the different ships that were underway, a smile on his face. Knowing that they were about to become a whole lot busier, he checked out the forums and found people posting about the refinery already. As more people were being woken up, they were taking on different quests.

They might be simple quests but it allowed them to come to understand the world they were in, much like simple fetch and carry missions one might find starting out in games.

*****

Malsour looked over the refinery. The soul gem construction was still ongoing; a dozen fusion plants had been connected up and were pumping out power continuously. Another thirty Mana wells acted as backups.

The pillars that created the framework for the refinery were similar to trees: the metal spread out, reaching through the asteroid to secure the refinery in place and increase the durability of the asteroid.

The excavators had a lot of work to do before they hollowed out the inside of the asteroid but in the meantime, they would supply raw materials to the refinery.

Malsour looked over the inside of the facility. Catwalks crisscrossed the facility but the area was dominated by massive machinery.

"First load!" Jesal, the dwarven master smith who had trained Dave and the mastermind behind this project called out.

The first cargo container was backed in by the shuttle to a docking station; clamps reached out and grabbed the container. The hatch opened between the cargo container and the intake. Runic lines that created a gravity field activated and pulled materials from the cargo container into the refinery.

The rocks passed through different machines that crushed everything down and then various systems that sorted out the different metals and materials, sending them off to be smelted. They passed through a specially coded smelting area, quickly being refined down.

Jesal and a group of those running the refinery project looked over the different red-hot metals that were coming out after being smelted. "Looks like we're good to go! Bring in the rest of it!" Jesal yelled.

Doors that had been closed now snapped open along the intake tunnel. Gravity runes pulled in the materials held by the cargo container, being reduced down and then sorted out. Thousands of tons of materials were being dumped in as the basic facilities of the refinery went to work. The more advanced systems to make specialized materials weren't online yet, needing those materials to be transported to smiths and other specialized refineries and factories.

Malsour smiled at the different groups that were racing to place down the superstructure as the soul gem construct seemed to eat it up, forming the different sections of the refinery while automatons added in essential systems and parts.

Their production speed would have a sharp increase with the supply of materials from the refinery. It would also take pressure off the Ice City refinery, which could focus on refining down the materials hollowed out for the city instead of having its power divided between refining metals and frozen elemental compounds.

Malsour had a satisfied look on his face as some of the tension between his shoulders was able to relax.

***

Dave and Deia walked through the day care that was being run in Ice City.

People smiled and greeted them as they wandered through. Dave and Deia quickly moved to where Koi was being kept. One of the people who looked after the day care smiled as they entered; Koi was bawling her eyes out in her arms.

"I'm guessing you want to see her." The lady shifted Koi to pass her over. Dave smiled at the look of relief on her face as he pushed Deia forward so she had to take Koi.

Deia reached out her arms with hesitation, as if Koi would turn away from her.

The lady put Koi in Deia's arms. Koi continued crying, her eyes scrunched up from being closed so tight.

Deia adjusted her grip, no longer acting foreign to Koi as she rested in the crook of Deia's arm. "Oh, it's all right, Koi. Mommy's here. Everything is going to be fine," Deia said in a soothing tone as she moved Koi back and forth in her arms, looking to comfort her.

After a few minutes, Koi's cries did start to calm down as Deia's face bloomed into a massive smile, filled with joy at being able to comfort Koi in some small way. Deia shifted her shirt so that Koi could get underneath. Koi stopped her crying as she started feeding.

Dave leaned against the doorway frame, smiling as he watched Deia quietly talking to Koi, checking to make sure that she was okay and wiping away her tears. Koi looked up at Deia with eyes that looked like pools of water. Instead of the fiery red that hid in the depths of Deia's eyes, they seemed to be tempered with the gray of Dave's eyes. Dave moved from the doorway, putting his arm on Deia's back as he stood over her shoulder and looked at them both.

Deia leaned back into his embrace, none of the tension or fear plaguing her as they both just put the world away for a moment and lived as parents with a new little baby girl.

"You're the best mother I know and the only woman I want to marry," Dave whispered, kissing the side of Deia's head.

She blushed, raising the hand that was curled around Koi, showing off her engagement ring that she played with. "Good," Deia said, that one word filled with satisfaction as she looked up to Dave.

Dave kissed her. The two of them looked at each other, their thoughts and emotions deep as they both took deep breaths, working to capture that moment forever.

Chapter 12: A Push for the Future

Josh, Dwayne, Kim, Florence, Cassie, and Lucy were all in the main tower of the Stone Raiders Guild in Terra. They had spent a lot of time in this room, coming up with plans and looking over developments. However, now they were all quiet as they looked at the map in front of them.

"All of the people who are near the southern coast of Opheir as well as the southeastern coast of Heval have been pulled back. We've got different groups running scouting missions on the Earth and Dark Lord groups. Mostly we're using player alt accounts to do it," Lucy said.

Alt accounts or payable accounts were accounts that someone made to die. They didn't have high stats but they could do things like courier items from one place to another, go and scout out an area that they would likely die in and take on jobs that would make most people lose levels. These people got paid to sacrifice their avatars in order to gain more information for those contracting them.

In this case, it was scouting out the forces of the Pantheon. Many of them were killed, but they were such low levels that it was nearly useless to those who killed them and in turn, they found out more of the positioning and actions of both the Dark and Earth Lord.

Other interfaces showed the different videos that people had collected on their scouting trips. It showed Earth's forces moving around in the forest to the south of Opheir. Trees and dirt were bending to their will, extending out into the ocean, creating a raft. However, the size of it was closer to a small island than a raft.

There were also creatures in the ocean that Earth had been able to bring under his command that were helping to move these different plots of land from the shores and attach them to this floating island.

"I'm impressed by the Earth Lord's rallying abilities," Josh admitted. "He was able to rope in creatures and people from all kinds of Affinities under his command."

"They've all been hiding their true abilities." Cassie's eyebrows pinched together.

"Very true. We still don't know the realm of their full strength. They have been on Emerilia for close to four and a half centuries. Their strength is high and their abilities are truly unknown. We only need to look at how Fire defeated four citadels and a portal within less than a half hour to see this," Lucy said.

"Can we confirm that Earth and Dark are working together?" Florence asked.

"I think it's pretty much set in stone. If they don't work together here, then Light will bring her legions down upon them like nothing else." Dwayne looked at the Dark Lord's preparations. A massive platform of metal and stone was being formed above the ground. All around it, the vegetation and life had been killed; a black miasma and fog covered the growing platform. Dark mages and those with abilities to build worked to improve and strengthen the massive platform that was no smaller than the Earth Lord's island.

"This is going to be a battle that will shake Emerilia. Their true strengths are unknown. Their methods we can sort out, but what kind of magic and skills have these three people passed down to their followers?" Kim asked.

"Making guesses now won't help us. All we can do is prepare and give our people the best shot possible in coming through this and tearing these three down from their places on top of Emerilia." Josh gave Lucy a meaningful look.

"Right now, we have three of the flying citadel wings within the Densaou Ring of Fire. Their rally point is between the cities Iuwroya and Sihush," Lucy said. The screens changed, showing an aerial and ground view of the rally point.

Twelve flying citadels floated in the air proudly, the sun shining off them. A haze appeared around them as the heat and cold exchangers were working their hardest in order to charge the flying citadels.

In the distance, the cities Iuwroya and Sihush could be seen. They were only two times the size of the powerful and domineering flying citadels that brimmed with different magical weapons and systems to support their ground forces and tear down their enemies.

The citadels had a number of people moving around them and aerial patrols were out watching over the area.

"The Goblin flying citadel group will undergo their upgrade in a few days, with the Gudalo flying citadel group changing over in a week or two. We are unsure what these upgrades will bring, so seven of the Goblin Mountain flying citadels will be grounded as the upgrades happen. Seeing the results, we will either ground or keep the other citadels in the air," Lucy said.

"All of them are fully stocked and ready for action," Florence added. Her Exdar's Traders had taken over the supply chain for the Terra Alliance, using the other forces within it and making sure that those on the front lines had everything that they needed.

"What about the new items that the Initiative has been working on?" Josh asked.

"We have shipments of orbs coming in daily. We are pushing them out to the citadels and there are training modules within the Mirror of Communication that the drop forces and fighting forces that are in Terra are undergoing," Florence reported. "Also, the ono network is nearing completion. In just five days, we should have onos or teleport pads in every single city across Emerilia, as well as different locations of interest."

"Be good to have that defensive network in place," Dwayne said.

"Will they have enough power?" Kim asked.

"Someone in the Initiative worried about the same thing, so they will be sending out automatons with charged soul gems to charge up the different onos. The ones in the cities are actually holding a massive charge since we changed the cost of using the ono from money to soul gems. All of that power has been absorbed and used, increasing the soul gem capacity under the ono. Once the network is complete within the population centers, regional onos will be put down to provide complete coverage for all of Emerilia. These regional ones will be the focus of the automatons and charged soul gems. They're hidden away from the population centers so they won't be able to see how much power is being placed into the ono," Florence said.

"We need to play for time as much as possible," Cassie said.

"It's a hard balance: we want to have enough time for all of our preparations to be laid down, for us to have a fleet that is capable of defending Emerilia, but we don't want to give the leaders of the Pantheon time to build up their own strength," Dwayne said.

"More and more of the players are being woken up every day. With their numbers and the resources that they're pulling in, and the fact that Suzy has been opening up Austin Zane's accounts more and more, fueling both ours and the Grahslagg Corporation's needs for resources, we have all the parts except for time," Lucy said.

They looked at the different screens. The flying citadels hovered in the air. The Dark Lord's people built their massive metal platform and the Earth Lord's forces grew an island piece by piece.

"Lucy, I think it's time that we started to tell our own people," Josh said.

The room was quiet as they all seemed to hold their breath at Josh's words. The Stone Raiders Guild was one of the biggest powers in all of Emerilia. Their guild had nearly five thousand members at the time and was growing constantly. They didn't take many people in at once, so that they wouldn't lose the core of what the Stone Raiders were.

However, each and every person, once they joined, had been tempered by multiple battles, trained by some of the greatest experts and had earned their powerful gear. When they went on the battlefield, they dominated. Whether they were POE or player, they all had the same status and their power exceeded that of their overall level multiple times. They were wholly loyal to one another and instead of lording over other people, they had taken on the stance of working with others. Those who were filled with arrogance and pride that blinded them to the plights of others were quickly dealt with and removed from the Stone Raiders. It was rare but it did happen.

It had come to make a guild that was incredibly hard to gain entry to, but all of the people who were a part of it were highly respected by all of the different forces on Emerilia.

"I think that you're right," Dwayne agreed.

"I wonder what impact it will have, but I believe it is for the best," Kim agreed.

"I believe it's time," Cassie agreed.

"Hopefully they can help us in dealing with this oncoming war," Florence said.

"I will contact Air. She will have a good idea of what to do with them to show them the truth," Lucy said.

The air in the room felt heavy with the decisions they had just made.

The decisions we made here today—I hope they were the right ones, Josh thought.

***

Dave, Malsour, and Suzy were all in the asteroid base, overlooking the different slips. Along each of them, superstructures were expanding at an alarming rate. Soul gem constructs and the different parts of the ship being built were slotted into place by automatons.

This was not the only slip that was filled with activity, either.

Many of the slips that hadn't been used before now had people swarming all over them, creating the structure for the warships.

The refinery was going full blast and the materials were coming in from "Austin's" donation to the Stone Raiders and the money he'd put in Dave's account. Suzy also had siphoned off money into her account as well. Most of the Stone Raiders leadership were also pitching in money from the Earth simulation.

The resources draw was incredible but it was only with all of this that they were able to keep up with the demands of the Terra Alliance as well as the Pandora's Box Initiative.

The refinery was expanding faster and faster, directly using thirty percent of the materials that it produced to grow. They had a massive stockpile of unrefined materials that would take weeks for them to complete, so all of it was being stuffed into the refinery as fast as possible.

Fifty percent of the materials that came from the refinery were then used directly for the different warships. The twenty destroyers were supposed to be finished in just three weeks.

They would have four complete battleships by that time as well.

Another ten destroyers had already been started, with another two battleships.

Resources were flowing to the moonbase as well, speeding up their ongoing projects. The nearly sixty missile boats were coming together quickly; all of the systems and parts had been laid out a long time ago. In just the space of a few weeks, with the power and the resources, they would gain four fleets.

There would be one battleship, five missile boats, five destroyers, and two arks per fleet. The battleships and missile boats wouldn't be able to enter atmosphere, but they could cross truly massive distances. The destroyer would be able to enter atmosphere and jump long distances as they had been upgraded. However, they didn't have the pure destructive power of the missile boats, nor the armor of the battleships. The ark would have a teleportation ability to move in and assist after a battle, acting as a resupply and repair ship. However, moving system to system, it would need to make many smaller jumps or pass through a portal.

"We're up to nearly four hundred thousand players awake." Dave looked at the people below.

"We've slowed down the number that we're waking up so as to not alert the AI running the Earth simulation. But based on our simulations, we can get nearly three million people out of the simulation in two to three weeks. That will leave only two, nearly three million people in the simulation," Suzy said.

"Councilmember Lisdel is returning to wherever they come from and Sato has started up a training center over the Mirrors of Communication. It should be enough to cover the basics for the players in just a few days. We're going to be using the compression and insertion technology that Air has developed to take the information from those in the first trainees and then pass it onto the second group; they add in their own learnings and they pass the information around until they all understand what is going on. We take an imprint of that and in just a few hours, we can take a player with no prior knowledge and familiarize them with the different systems of the ships they will be fighting on. We're also going to be doing the same with the different techs, so that the people who are on the ships will know how to deal with everything on the ship. We should actually be getting the first imprint crystals ready this afternoon. Once we have them, then we will probably see an increase in production speed," Malsour said.

"We need to be careful, though. Even with all of this information, they haven't done anything with it before so we will have to make sure that they have all the correct skills, test them and make sure that they will be okay," Dave said.

The ability to push information into other people's minds like how it was done with spell books and other learning scrolls was an invaluable ability. However, Dave wanted to make sure that no matter whether they had the information he needed to make sure that their skill was up to his standards. It didn't matter whether they had all the plans for the battleship in their head when they didn't know how to make a single rune or control a soul gem construct.

"Don't worry—they'll be properly tested ahead of time," Suzy reassured Dave.

They watched over the complex goings-on in front of them. It looked like utter chaos around the different ships. However, even under that chaos, the ships were taking shape, the different parts being added together.

Everything that looked to be chaos added to the growth of the ships.

"We've come pretty far," Dave said as they watched their fleet grow before their eyes.

A notification appeared in Dave's vision. He opened it up. A relieved look on his face quickly turned to shock as he started to scroll down the notifications.

Quest: Friend of the Grey God Level 7

Distribute Band-Aid across Emerilia

Rewards: Unlock Level 8 Quest

+10 to stats (stacks with previous class levels)

+700,000 EXP

Quest: Friend of the Grey God Level 8

End the: Of Myths and Legends Event

Rewards: Unlock Level 9 Quest

Increase to stats

Class: Friend of the Grey God

Status: Level 7

          +70 to all stats

Effects: Access to hidden quests.

          Access to the Imperial Carrier *Datskun*

Quest Completed: Bleeder Level 5

Create transportation network across Emerilia

Rewards: Unlock Level 6 Quest

+10 increase to stats (stacks with previous class levels)

+500,000 EXP

Your understanding of the Jukal Link has greatly increased. You can not only cut the Jukal Link but now use it. Now what you going to do? Make unicorns?

Dave snorted to himself. It had been some time since he had heard from the snarky AI that wrote the skill descriptions and updated the skill boxes.

Class: Bleeder

Status: Level 5

Effects: +10 to all stats
Ability to use Jukal Link

Quest: Bleeder Level 6

End the: Of Myths and Legends Event

Rewards: Unlock Level 7 Quest

Increase to stats

Level 241

You have reached Level **243**; you have **15** stat points to use.

Dave looked at the level. He had seen it after Anna and Jekoni died; he'd become Level 204. At the time, he'd closed the notifications and tried to deal with his grief.

Now he thought back on Anna and Jekoni—his friends. He thought of the good times, when he'd first met them, when he'd gifted Anna her sword, or when Jekoni and he had worked late into the night on projects together. The way he could make complex ideas simple and they had been able to talk Magical Circuits and running all day and night long. As he reminisced, his smile grew brighter, knowing that he was a better person for knowing them.

"There is no way to go backwards, only forwards," Dave sighed.

He looked through the Classes, reading them as he went. If he got back the mine manager class then he would need to spend an astronomical amount of gold on it once again to earn back it's levels and the material output.

He paused over the class The Few the Mighty.

Class: The Few the Mighty

Fight against a numerically superior force and win time and time again. The larger the force you are fighting, the stronger your allies become.

Required: Master Leadership skill.

Master one weapon skill.

Fight 200 battles where your force is numerically weaker.

Effects: 5% increase to allies stats when facing a numerically superior force.

Well the mining drills are pulling out a lot of materials, sure its easier to have the materials just show up in my bank, but we're expanding a lot. If I was to get this class, then the party even the fighting force I'm with could get a boost. Dave thought to himself.

He paused for a few moments before clicking on the class.

You have gained a Class: The Few the Mighty

You again! Alright, well here's another class! Seems you lot are always fighting off waves of enemies so this should at least help out a bit. Don't get blood on my dammed carpet! I foresee rivers of experience for you and your fellows in the future. Mysterious and profound, that's me!

Status: Level 1

Effects: +5% to base stats to you and your allies when fighting a numerically superior force.

Dave rolled his eyes after reading the description. He opened up his character sheet and dumped all of the stat points he'd earned into intelligence and looked over it, accepting the changes.

Character Sheet

Name:	David Grahslagg	Gender:	Male
Level:	204	Class:	Dwarven Master Smith, Friend of the Grey God, Bleeder, Librarian, Skill Creator, Aleph Engineer, Weapons Master, Champion Slayer, Master of Space and Time, Master of Gravitational Anomalies, The Few the Mighty
Race:	Human/ Dwarf	Alignment:	Chaotic Neutral

Unspent points: 0

Health:	4,550	Regen:	24.62 /s
Mana:	16,280	Regen:	59.45 /s
Stamina:	5,620	Regen:	51.90 /s
Vitality:	455	Endurance:	1,231
Intelligence:	1,628	Willpower:	1,189
Strength:	562	Agility:	1,038

"It happened again guys," Dave said in an almost depressed tone, all around him mana fluctuated wildly, showing that he was growing stronger.

"Oh, you've got to be kidding me." Suzy waved her arms in the air.

"I think we need to get you a training bib, the kind that stops you from dumping points into your stats." Malsour sighed heavily as he moved to Dave, grabbing him and moving toward the portal that was connected to Ice City.

"Whoops?" Dave said with a sheepish smile, not moving for fear that his new stats would be more of a pain than a help and he would hurl himself out into the middle of the thoroughfare.

***

Frank listened to the man called Commander Sato, who stood in front of the classroom. With every sentence, he opened up the minds of those listening. He ran through scenarios, getting the people who wanted to man the ships of the Initiative to open their eyes wider.

He accepted questions, using them to create new scenarios.

He didn't simply lecture at them, telling them more about terms they didn't need to know; he dealt with the basic actions of each of the people in front of him, talking through their roles, how they would affect the ship, what they were needed to do, what they needed to focus on to make sure that the ship was running in optimal condition. It sounded as though it should have been boring but as he talked, it became clear how on a ship, every single person was needed. Only together could they tame the beast that was a warship in space. And going from that to how they would fight in space—all of those things were vastly more complicated.

When the lecture ended, he didn't let them go free. Instead, he started them out on training and test scenarios. These didn't deal with the specifics of their job but it was a general overview.

Their ships and the ones that Sato was working with were totally different. Sato worked with ships that were based off technology being assisted by the magical tech that they had been given and shared. However, the ships and systems that the players were working with were a fusion of magic and technology.

The people who had built the different systems were their testers. They would watch over them, doing every operation while Sato would watch their actions. He would listen to their communication and watch an interface that showed that the different areas were working.

The testers who had built the components reported to Sato, his questions pulling out and exacting information on each of the trainees' abilities and strengths.

After every single working run, they would again reappear in front of Sato. He would work through the different sections, talking to the people in there. They would talk about their own actions and the actions of others. This created some tension but with a few words from Sato, this tension fell away. Instead of people challenging one another, saying that the other was worse, they looked to improve their ability individually and as a team. This pulled them all together and made them much stronger as a team.

He would go through the mistakes he heard in communication; he would go through the information that he had been told by the testers. He would pull apart the issues that he saw in the command structure, the ways that the running of the ship had fallen apart. Then he would put this on them to correct.

Afterward, it would be time for more training.

This was to get them familiar with their stations. They were not only thinking of their station; they were working to keep the entire ship as effective as possible.

Sato reviewed working on communication throughout departments, as well as medical care and getting used to being in vacuum. He walked them through damage control; the weapon training they had already worked on through the Mirrors of Communication, so they had a good grasp on it.

He made them decide their rank structure and different warship crews started to form. These people worked together closer and closer, becoming one organism that was part of the ships they crewed.

Once they were finished with Sato's lectures and information, they were passed to the trainers.

They grilled them again and again, working to get the best out of them. Within their job, they became gods, knowing all and coming to understand everything that was connected to it.

Frank was a weapons officer but he knew how all of the missile tubes worked, the speed that the rounds left his canons, the different rounds and their effect. He knew their rate of fire, how to fix them, optimal firing parameters. He knew as much as the gun crews that kept his cannons operational and the missile techs who looked after the missile firing systems and their payloads.

He came to understand the Mana barriers and shields of the ship as well as the optimum angles to bring his batteries to bear. He used this information to create plots for the ship to move to increase their effectiveness against any enemy forces they might run into.

He looked over the weaknesses in the Jukal shields and armor, their interiors to plan out shots that would have the greatest effect. He worked with the different people under his command to come up with different strategies to fight the Jukal and deal with a variety of possibilities.

This allowed him to get closer to his team and also become an expert in his field.

Their higher levels of Intelligence made it easier for them to memorize the things that they saw. Their high Endurance allowed them to surpass their normal limits, being able to train for twenty hours of the day. Over the space of a week and a half, they were written off on by their testers, confirming that they knew the skills that were needed for their positions. Now some of the trainees were actually pointing out ways to work their stations better.

With their testers signing off on them, they weren't done. Instead, they had just entered the examination phase.

"Ready the sim," the captain of the battleship *BloodHawk* said. Before, they had been doing the simulations with the testers; now they would be operating like a normal ship just on patrol, with the testers watching over them to see how they performed in different environments from a normal day to fighting the enemy. This would look over their practices as they performed maintenance and looked after their ship. This went on for a day and a half, with people sleeping in the simulation in their designated racks.

Frank could have been the captain. He had a certain position, being the first of the players to be woken up. However, he didn't wish to take on that responsibility. It was clear that the captain trusted him and would come to him with a number of issues. All of the officers worked together to make it as easy as possible on one another.

If something went wrong, they didn't care about feelings and would tell one another exactly how they'd fucked up. It was harsh, but it made it so that people didn't mess up a second time. No one wanted to be the ship's noob.

They had started to get into a rhythm by the second day and were easily dealing with the issues that the different testers were throwing their way.

Still, this time they didn't spend fighting. Instead, they learned how to better communicate through a standard fleet and fleet groups, which comprised of two or more fleets of ships moving together.

They moved across star systems. The arks and destroyers did atmospheric drops, entering a planet's atmosphere, landing and coming back up. The battleships worked on establishing portal networks, laying down portals and connecting to them, going through them, actions when entering and leaving them. The missile boats went through transitions in space as well as working through different ways to use their weapons. The ark crews worked to understand the army of automatons they had, resupplying the other ships and fixing their issues.

At first, they were all nervous; their movements were sudden and unsure, leading to a number of problems and issues. However, as time went on, they became smoother. They came to grips with everything; their speed picked up as they moved as a fleet easily, different ships breaking off and joining up seamlessly.

They practiced exiting wormholes into enemy territory and built up methods of what to do when they were going through portals—operation procedures to be tested out.

So it went on. As Emerilia prepared for the war between the Pantheon, the Pandora's Box Initiative prepared for the war against the Jukal by waking more and more players and building more and more ships.

Frank was told that the portal technology had finally been perfected. A massive assembly line was made within an asteroid, which started to create portals from soul gem constructs. These portals were broken down into sections. They could be deployed by battleships, attaching as they spread outward and creating a portal. They were also stored within the arks in case they needed more upon their travels.

More hulls were laid down to make up the fifth and sixth fleet.

The refinery was growing faster and faster and the materials being pumped out were higher quality than they had predicted.

Now that there were none of the council members looking over the shoulders of Captain Xue and their people, they had asked for the help of the Emerilians to make their base as they lent out their experts and people to work with them to assist on their different projects. They offered different premade items that allowed the Emerilians the ability to work on the more complex systems.

Together, they were a building powerhouse.

The Pandora's Box Initiative was undergoing a massive expansion.

Frank and the rest of the players going through the Mirror of Communication training only left their ships when it was time for food, logging off and getting food from a cafeteria laid out like the ones on their ships.

They'd eat, return to the Mirrors of Communication and go about their life as if they were already living on their warships.

Late at night, one of the alarms started to go off all over the ship.

"Two Jukal destroyers and one carrier! Battle stations!" the captain called out.

Frank hadn't changed out of his clothes; he jumped out of his bed and ran toward the command center. He rushed through armored doors, jumping into his seat as he read the information updates scrolling down the side of his interface.

"They've spotted us!" Sensors confirmed.

"Ready for actions," the captain yelled.

Frank pressed a few buttons that brought all weapons online. The different batteries and missile tubes warmed up. Mana surged through their runic lining.

"Target destroyer one first, then the second and then we'll go for the carrier," the captain said, using the classic theory of destroying the smaller ships in order to leave the bigger ship without mobile defenses. This way, they poured all of their fire into one craft, not allowing them time to regain their shields. The other ships could use this time to attack them but they were confident in their shields and defenses in the tests that they had before. They had been shown how strong the battleship's shields and armor truly were.

"They're leaping!" Sensors called out.

The Jukal used different drive systems from what humans might. Instead of just having drives that applied constant thrust, mounting higher and higher, they had a two-stage thrust system. One system would mount up speed like the human method of thrust; the other was a system that stored up energy and then shot it all out in one massive push, making the ships surge ahead. To a human, this would have been hell with the changing pressures. The Jukal were used to it and it allowed them to gain incredible speed quickly.

As soon as they had seen the Pandora forces, they had started to leap forward, to try to pin them down. The carrier had started to flush out the Jukal fighters that were even faster and more mobile than the massive ships that made up the Jukal fleet.

The Jukal cannons mounted on the sides, underbelly, and spine of the ship opened fire as they could. Missiles shot out from their different launch points, spreading out in every direction before turning and aiming directly for the Pandora fleet.

Frank didn't even wait for the orders but activated the defensive measures and opened weapon locks on the weapons.

The captain paused, eyes wide at what was happening.

"Sir!" Frank barked. His voice carried across the command deck.

The captain was stuck up in just how "cool" everything was. With Frank's words, he snapped back. A red tinge crept up his features as he felt shame at his actions that had lost them precious seconds as the missiles were starting to come into range.

The interceptor modules opened fire and unleashed their rounds. There were no spells to speak of for them to defeat but their weapon systems shredded a number of the incoming missiles.

Here and there, the missile boats were responding, though it was all over the place.

"Concentrate fire! Raise shields! All weapons fire as they come to bear on the targets!" the captain called out. His words passed out to the rest of the fleet as they started to get their shit together.

However, it wasn't fast enough. The first barrage of missiles landed like a sea of destruction.

They smashed against the ships; their attacks served to make it hard for the sensor modules to see. The second barrage came in as the first cleared, then the third. By that time, the rounds from the Jukal ships were coming down, hitting those in front of the formation that had not yet changed, blocking those that were following behind.

The rounds and the missiles landed in waves. They tried launching different weapons but they were caught up in the destruction of the weapons coming down over them.

Then the Jukal fighters arrived. They were quick and their payloads were strong. They launched missiles in close that wrecked barriers until they started to fail. Different ships lost their shields altogether. The fighters fell on them before they passed the formation of ships. Their speeds were too great to counteract the inertia that threw them forward. They turned to face the fleet, using their leaping ability and their drives; however, it only slowed them slightly as they continued past the fleet.

The Jukal timed it well: their missiles and weapons fell upon the different ships that had been wounded or their shields had been taken down by the fighters.

They were massive, two to three times larger than the ships of the Pandora forces, and they had the weapons and missile tubes to prove it. As they entered the Pandora's formation, the true fight started.

Frank could finally hit back, slugging it out with the Jukal. Their weapons were powerful but their shields and barriers were weak. Their barriers failed and their armor took a pounding, getting torn apart. Still, Frank called out orders as his crews worked the different guns and missile tubes.

The fight was progressing way too fast for them. As fast as the Jukal were among them, they had passed. Two-thirds of the Pandora fleet had been destroyed or were useless; the rest barely had shields or were deeply damaged but still functional.

The fighting stopped and the area Frank was in turned into a white room with a prompt appearing in his vision.

Quest: Defeat the Jukal Fleet

Failure: Your fleet was destroyed

Simulation End

You have earned: 321,543 EXP

Leave simulation for debriefing lobby?

He accepted the prompt with a heavy expression. He knew they had messed up. They should have been able to defeat the Jukal; instead, they had been thrashed thoroughly.

With it being a simulation, the AI would still give them experience and as they were not dying, they would keep it. However, he and all of the players were at Level 300 already; they needed a truly massive amount of experience in order to increase level.

Thankfully, in space combat using such powerful machines and also working with new technology, the AI was giving them experience boosts. However, these would quickly fall as they got better. This meant they would need to fight in different situations and against harder enemies in order to keep up their experience gain.

The conference room disappeared and he reappeared in a lecture room where a human-looking hologram was waiting. Its body was made from different runes and runic lines. There was a cold, calculating look in its eyes as everyone took their seats.

"You might know me. My name is Jeeves. I am also your instructor over the next little bit. Right now, we will go through your combat footage, look over your issues, the ways that you might improve and then once we are finished, you will return to duty and training." Jeeves looked to them all. There was no argument in his voice nor did he seem to care.

Frank knew of Jeeves. He was the AI that ran everything for the Pandora's Box Initiative. He controlled the automatons and he was able to make a number of the runic lines and magical coding that was used in the different machines of the Initiative. He was a power that people knew of but few interacted with. At least that Frank knew. Those who were interested in dealing with research or developing technologies came into contact with Jeeves or a subroutine of his all the time. He was a constant presence that pushed the advancement of the entire Initiative.

"Good. Then we shall begin," Jeeves said. The lights disappeared from the room and a hologram appeared, showing the Jukal fleet and their own fleet. "We will begin from the start," Jeeves said as the hologram started, with the Jukal exiting jump space.

***

All of Party Zero were gathered together in Cliff-Hill at Dave and Deia's home. They had taken a rare moment to get away from their lives and watch what was happening to the flying citadels.

The flying citadels that had come from Goblin Mountain had reached their time for an upgrade.

All but one of the citadels had moved to the ground. Earth and Dark mages had worked to clear out a place for them to land. They were seated into the ground, only the citadel showing as the soul gem island was hidden underneath.

The timer finally hit zero and the air around the flying citadel in the air started to become distorted.

The citadels on the ground shook as well.

At the same time, walls started to emerge around the citadels. The one that was flying in the air, an impressive metal foundation grew out from the outer walls, extending out through the air before shooting upward and forming into the new outer walls. The now two inner walls became stronger and taller, completely formed from metal and smooth as glass.

The entire citadel grew in size and pushed outward. The castle rose higher and the towers that were at the four different compass points grew thicker. The tower in the center of the castle shot upward; sections pushed out from it, creating two levels and walkways pushing the roof at the top of the tower.

There were now five different towers and heavy walls that stood to make the first wall around the castle and large tower that stood at the peak of the citadel. The second wall had ten towers; there were a total of twenty in the new outer wall that had just formed.

The outer walls and towers were made from stone and metal supports. The middle walls were made from metal and much thicker and robust than before; the same went for the inner walls that had changed from steel to a stronger composite metal.

Across seven of the citadels, except for the one that the Nal had captured for a short while, the different citadels underwent the same changes.

The soul gem construct underneath the floating citadel grew outward, to encompass the new walls that had been created. Dark mages rooted the new walls into the soul gem island.

Even as Dave and Malsour felt the pull to help them, they saw that the magical coding people as well as the mages and engineers had everything under control.

"Looks like we'll have another advantage when fighting the Pantheon," Jung Lee said with approval.

They all showed signs of agreement. However, seeing it all, they were stuck thinking about the coming battle.

"Now, who's ready for dinner?" Dave closed the interface screen showing the flying citadels and picked up a rack of boar ribs while he moved toward the large table.

Food was doled out and drinks flowed.

Deia stopped the proceedings with a tap of her glass.

The noise around the table calmed down as they all looked to Deia.

"In these times, it's hard to find a minute to get away from it all. Thank you for all coming to share a meal with us and put the world's worries at the door. Today, while we have this meal, our table is two people shorter." Deia looked to the two places that had been set at the table but there was no one there.

"Anna and Jekoni gave their lives for the people of Emerilia. They gave their lives for us. A number of us have heavy hearts and minds thinking that we might have been able to save them in some way or, if we had done something different, that they would be with us here today. I understand these thoughts as I've had them myself." Deia found Dave's hand holding hers. She looked to him with a smile on her face before she continued.

"Whatever we think, here are the facts: Jekoni and Anna loved us to lose their own lives, so that we might live, so that we could continue on Emerilia. Many of the people at this table are alive because of their actions. Today we grieve for them, but tomorrow let us fight and live in memory of them. As they have left, we will forge ahead to live, to take this life that they have given us and do something with it!"

Deia raised her glass into the air in toast. "To those who were lost, may they never be forgotten and may we meet them in our next adventure! To Anna and Jekoni!"

"To Anna and Jekoni!" The others raised their glasses in salute before tapping them on the table and drinking from them.

After Deia's speech, it was as if a weight had lifted from the group. Here they didn't have to care about being the strongest or the most powerful; they could share their emotions and their feelings. They smiled, joked, and laughed; talked about memories they had of Jekoni and Anna—shared the people they knew with one another. There were tears but there were also smiles.

They ate and drank together late into the night and to the next morning, putting to rest their memories of Anna and Jekoni.

Through it all, Alkao had a strange light in his eyes as he remembered what Bob had told him after Anna died. He didn't tell anyone else, not wanting to raise hopes for something that might or might not work.

***

The Dark Lord and the Earth Lord looked to each other through seeing ponds. They were both overlooking the different launch points for their invasion into Markolm. Neither of them had actually gone onto the battlefield and were instead watching what was going on from their own halls. They wanted to defeat Light and they were working together, but they wouldn't be so close to each other in the midst of a massive battle. It would only make it too easy for the other to kill them in the confusion.

"It is time," the Earth Lord said, talking in his deep and gravelly voice.

"It is." The Dark Lord looked to one of his aides, an undead skeleton, at his side. "Forward!" the Dark Lord shouted.

The Earth Lord sent his own order through a sprite to his side.

On the Heval coast, an army of undead appeared from the ground. The ground fell apart as if it were corroding underneath the descending darkness of night. These creatures that were weak to the sunlight now emerged from where they had been resting and waiting. They moved upward and landed on the platform that rose just a few feet from the ground—one edge in the forest that was slowly dying, the other reaching the water's edge. Dark smoke moved over the platform, becoming stronger as night came. Looking upon it, one might instantly think of poison.

However, abominations, champions, creatures, and people who served the Dark Lord all came from the different places that they had been resting and mounted the platform.

As soon as they had finished, the platform shook. Metal and stone legs extended from the platform, reaching out into the sea. The platform rose up and moved forward. Other legs tore through the Heval land as they, too, stepped forward. Hundreds of legs moved like a slow caterpillar; the platform moved forward, passing over the waves of the sea and headed for Markolm.

At Opheir, a similar scene was taking place. Creatures seemed to emerge from the ground of the island that had been formed over the last two weeks. The trees and different plants seemed to come alive, showing off the different creatures that waited there. Other people and creatures from other Affinities stepped off the land around the island, onto it, or moved in the water to grab a hold of the different roots that extended down and made harnesses.

Once everyone was on the island, it moved forward, slow at first but then faster, creating waves with its passage as the monsters from the deep pulled the islands as if they were nothing but venerated beasts of labor.

In different locations overlooking these rally points that the two Pantheon lords had been waiting at, players and POEs emerged quickly and sent back word to the Terra Alliance. The Pantheon's battle seemed to have started.

Chapter 13: First Movements of the Pantheon

Dave looked at the portal in front of him. A well of emotions filled him.

Word had come down from the various scouts who had been watching the Dark and Earth Lord—both of them had started to move. Within Light's Markolm, the different legions that she had trained were arming themselves and preparing for the coming battle.

It would be a day before the island and platform reached Markolm but the Terra Alliance was already moving to their different positions. The forces that had been on break were now activated. The flying citadels were all in the sky. The teleport pads in Terra had all been closed down, ready and linked to the onos that were inside the citadels, ready to move the reserve forces to the flying citadels in a moment.

The fighting dragon force had left the safety of their Densaou Ring of Fire. A massive formation of nearly one hundred dragons met up with the citadels and rested in their towers.

The merpeople had left the safety of their cities. Their war shoals, or groups of mer-warriors, moved to rally points between Markolm and the Densaou Ring of Fire. Forces were being moved around, till they were ready and waiting in Terra.

All eyes were looking at the progress of the Dark and Earth Lord's forces as they traversed the sea between their staging points.

Dave steeled himself and stepped through the portal. He left the stone of Pandora's Box behind and stepped out onto the rubberized flooring of the Jukal carrier *Datskun*. He cast his Touch of the Land spell that ran through the entire ship. He didn't find Bob anywhere but he did find a number of areas that had been blocked off by stealth runes.

The areas that had held the living quarters were blocked from his vision; there were also entire sections of the fighter bays. However, the living quarters were closer so he headed toward them.

With the magical runes across the ship, teleporting within it was a bad idea so he was stuck with walking. Thankfully the power systems had recovered enough so that he could use the elevators and different conveyor belts to move through the massive carrier.

It still took him some time before he was able to reach the area that he thought Bob was hiding. He moved to the living quarters and opened up a door.

Inside, there were banks and banks of powerful servers that were working constantly; the flickering lights told him that they were online and working. Once inside, he was able to cast his spell again. He quickly found Bob, who was sleeping on a couch near a workstation.

Dave moved through the room, sensing Bob waking up.

"Who is it?" Bob sat up on his couch.

"Hey, Bob." Dave came around some servers and looked at Bob. He looked like hell, but he doubted anyone who had lost their child would look any better. Dave knew that he would be barely holding himself together if he lost Koi or Deia.

"Dave, oh, umm, sorry. I've been a bit busy with things." Bob got up from the couch. There were ration packs all around and there was a massive console with a rolling seat in front of it.

Dave remembered the seat; Bob had taken it a number of months ago, never to be seen again.

Dave looked at the complex lines of code as well as the information overlays on the old-fashioned screens. "What have you been working on?"

"Bit of a complicated question there. There's two real parts. It's more who and why." Bob moved to his seat and sat on it.

Dave stepped up behind him and looked over his shoulder, trying to understand some of what he was seeing. All of it was written in Jukal code, making it hard for him to understand.

Bob input a line of code. One of the screens changed from an update screen to a very familiar face.

"Hello, you must be Dave. My father has told me a lot about you," the head said with a smile.

Dave felt himself go into shock as he looked at Anna's face and heard her voice. "W...what?" Dave stuttered out, looking to Bob with wide eyes.

"As you might know, Anna was an AI at first. She was then transplanted into a Beast Kin body. However, I needed someone I could trust in the AI network of Emerilia." Bob waved to Anna. "Anna is the basis of the AI controllers. She has admin rights to everything, backdoors into all the systems that are attached to Emerilia. She isn't connected to the defensive networks, but with her we can shut down communication and the different broadcasts that are going on. She was distributed throughout the different networks, barely conscious—instead just a system running multiple processes. This was done to make it nearly impossible to wipe her out or for the Jukal to discover her. The other AIs have already been altered so that they will never recognize Anna being in the system, but they can have their programming changed by her. After Anna's body died at the Xelur citadel, I was in pretty bad shape. But I knew that Anna had backed up herself into the AI so that she was always consistent. Anna can tell you the rest."

Dave looked to Anna's face, which had a wry expression.

"Come on, Dave. AIs—we're pretty hard to destroy." The corners of her mouth lifted into a smile at Dave's stunned expression. "My physical body was destroyed and so were a number of my memories. I have faint recollections of Party Zero. Dad has been bringing me up to speed. I've been using the recorded information to compile what I can of my actions. My memory was fragmented and is all messed up with the destruction of my main body. However, over time I am coming to remember more. I do not remember anything from the time that I was woken up on Emerilia and that I started to fight alongside Party Zero—the power of that Xelur soul array was too powerful. Though with time and using the different records I have and interactions with people I met between that time to now, I can use them as reference points to help defragment my memories. Right now, I know of Party Zero and others, but it will take time for me to remember you all," Anna said.

"Now, if you're going to ask why is she in the server instead of in her body, that's because if I was to put her into a new body, then the Jukal would notice it. After all, I would be pulling out the center of the monitoring program. Also, with the servers, Anna will be able to recover a lot of her base memories faster here," Bob said.

"Just—" Dave was at a loss for words as he sat on the couch.

"She won't be the same Anna that you knew, but at her core she will be," Bob said.

Tears fell down Dave's face as he laughed, filled with happiness.

Bob had tears at the corners of his eyes, touched by the clear and true feelings that Dave showed toward Anna.

After a bit, Dave calmed down and was able to get a hold of himself.

"Now, I don't want this shared too much. After all, Anna might not be able to leave here for weeks or months and we don't know what state she'll be in when we transfer her over to her new body," Bob said seriously.

"I can do that. I don't think they need anything to distract them from what they're doing," Dave said, reassuring Bob.

"What's happening?" Bob frowned, catching onto the tone that Dave was using.

"Earth and Dark are getting ready to attack Light."

Lines filled Bob's face as his expression became serious and dark. "Tell me everything that has been going on."

Dave pulled out a memory crystal and held it to his head; his memories flowed into the crystal, hitting the high points before he tossed it over to Bob.

Bob took it and put it against his head, closing his eyes. They snapped open as the crystal turned to dust.

"Well, it seems that you've been busy!" Bob said with a slight smile before he looked to the screens in front of him. He let out a long sigh before he got to his feet. "Well, if the kids have finally decided to go to war, then it's time the Pantheon stopped existing. They've brought enough pain and suffering to Emerilia already."

Dave's scalp tingled with the cold anger that was held in Bob's words.

Bob's body expanded; his weak frame became more powerful and stronger. Hair appeared on his head and a thick tail extended from his spine. His hands grew into claws as his ears became pointed and moved to the top of his head. His thin body changed, powerful muscles covering his body as runic lines ran down his body.

Dave watched as Bob the gnome turned into Bob the wolfkin. He stood there, a proud alpha wolfkin. His body radiated power. Dave could see clear similarities between Bob and Anna.

Dave looked at him, his face stuck between shock and a frown. Bob in his wolfkin form was actually taller and bigger than Alkao.

Runic lines looking like tattoos covered his body, much like they did Dave's when he activated his conjuration powers.

Bob's body had fine gray hair over it with black and white lines. Anna didn't have fur on her face but Bob's face was more wolf-shaped than hers. Runic lines ran up his neck and onto his cheeks, giving him a fierce look. The lines emitted a gray smoke as the air around him seemed charged with Mana, as if he were ready to jump into battle at any moment.

Bob chuckled, revealing sharp teeth and a deep and powerful voice. "You should see your face." Bob reached to his pouch of holding and pulled out a cloak. It was covered in runic lines nearly identical to Dave's own cloak on his Lux armor. Bob twirled it around, putting his arms through the sleeves and flipping the hood up to cover his features and face. He didn't wear a shirt, revealing his strong upper body; he had on simple cloth pants with multiple pouches of holding and shoes. Only the edge of his snout was visible as silver eyes looked out at Dave.

"What?" Dave asked. The aura around Bob was similar to Fire, Water, and Air's—there was an unfathomable depth to it. However, he felt that the power Bob had was even deeper than the other lords and ladies he had met in the Pantheon. Standing next to him as he unleashed his full aura, Dave felt as if he were in the presence of a true god, as if kneeling was the right thing to do.

"Well, Anna got her good looks from somewhere." Bob laughed and clapped Dave on the back. The force nearly launched Dave across the room of servers as Bob started to walk toward the doorway into the server room.

"I have not always been in a gnome body. I took that body because gnomes are usually underrated. People see them as weak and useless while in actuality they have sharp minds and fast fingers. Never cross a gnome," Bob warned Dave. "In gnome form, I was small—looked weak. This was something that was imprinted on the different people in the Pantheon.

"However, it was not my first form. The first form I took was this. I used this form to move through Emerilia, watching over my people. Away from others, I would train in magic with this body. I came to understand this body more than the others. I might practice or make up spells in other bodies, but I was the most familiar with this. With this body, I can fully unleash my powers and strengths. I'm not simply someone who was going to sit on the sidelines if my Emerilia was attacked. I held back my power, hoping that the Pantheon would pull their heads out of their asses. Even though they might be my children, the time has come to show them why I was neutral." Bob's eyes flashed with cold light as he passed through the door to the server. "If I was to take a side, then anyone facing us would be destroyed."

A chill ran down Dave's spine as he saw a small hologram on a bracelet on Bob's wrist.

Anna flashed into existence before fading into the bracelet.

"You're bringing Anna?" Dave asked.

"Well, she does control my divine wells. Easier to have her use them than to try to do it all myself."

"You have divine wells?" Dave asked, stunned.

"Of course. I *did* make the Pantheon. You think I would give them all things that I don't have?"

"But you've never used them!" Dave said.

"Well, I used them sometimes for teleporting, but yes, otherwise I've been saving up for a rainy day, you could say," Bob said with an amused smile.

"Saving for a rainy day? That's five hundred years of saved up power," Dave said. "But wait—you don't have any followers."

"I don't, but I've got a fusion power plant as well as ley lines and whatever I can pour into them. Just like how Fire charges her own divine wells with her power instead of through her people's devotions," Bob said.

Dave went silent, unable to understand the power that Bob had been hiding. "Poor Alkao. His girlfriend's dad is scary as shit," Dave muttered.

Bob snorted and shook his head as they walked through *Datskun* toward the portal.

***

Light looked at the approaching forces of Dark and Earth.

"Seems that Earth had more rallying power than I gave him credit for. He's brought over a number of creatures from Water and Fire Affinities that neither Water nor Fire would have helped out," Light said casually. Her eyes thinned as she looked to the Dark Lord's platform. Although the other forces were more powerful in different areas, their attacks weren't as powerful as when Light and Dark clashed; their naturally opposite powers had a greater effect against each other.

"Seal Markolm and prepare our defenses. Let's see how devoted the people of Emerilia who have come to my banner are," Light said to Daeundra, who stood in the shadows of Light's personal apartments.

"Yes, mistress." Daeundra faded away from Light's sight to carry out her orders.

She looked coldly at the different viewing wells that were dotted around her. The normally clear liquids, now floating spheres in the air and pools on the ground, allowed her to see the different scenes over Markolm as well as Dark and Earth's platform and island.

"They will arrive just as night is coming in. Seems that the Dark Lord is not willing to lose any advantage," Light said coldly as she walked through the forest of floating viewing spheres.

She looked to another sphere that showed divine wells brimming with golden power. She smiled to herself as she let out a sigh, closing her eyes as she felt power rush through her body. The feeling was intoxicating.

These divine wells were connected to a complex series of Magical Circuits and circles that covered an area kilometers wide.

Light could sense everything on Markolm. It was as if the entire continent were her hall, her domain.

She looked to one of the spheres, watching as the fanatical army of Light that had been groomed for months marched toward the areas that Dark and Earth would land.

They moved, golden row after golden row. They were separated into different groups that came from all over Emerilia.

Her angel legions who lived around her hall, who had rested in the sky, assembled themselves, ready and waiting to carry out their goddess's commands. Light, seeing them, waved her hand. Rays of light descended from above, angels being raised up into the air as her power filled them. Their strength increased rapidly.

Light laughed to herself. It was a cold and cruel thing to hear.

"Since you've come first, oh brothers of mine, let me see you off. Then I will pull Fire, Water, and Air from the holes they hide in. The age of the Pantheon is done! The age of Light has begun!"

Her laughter filled the room as the different armies advanced to their inevitable confrontation.

Chapter 14: The Gods' Pawns

All eyes across Emerilia were watching interfaces of alt player accounts and spies who were looking at the northern edge of Markolm.

As the sun set, the Dark Lord's platform could be seen with its myriad legs cruising through the sea with massive strides.

Earth's island was making waves as it shot across the sea.

Facing them on the shores of Markolm there were ranks upon ranks of Light's soldiers. Their banners with golden runes that shone in the sunset's red light snapped back and forth with the winds that passed over their ranks. Light cannons were moved up on their carriages. They were covered in bands of golden runes on the hills behind the army, ready for what was to come.

Earth's island started to show different colors as Mana was circulated.

Clouds of black smoke curled around Dark's island. Any creatures living in the ocean around them were killed by the dark Mana that distorted the red color of the sunset, turning it into a black abyss.

The soldiers of Light's army tightened their grip on their weapons. Their anger mounted as they stared at the forces of the Dark Lord that dared to profane their lady's land and go against her teachings of Light. An officer called out an order to the Light cannons; rays of golden light made the dusk turn into day once again. The rays shot out. They weakened as they reached out to the oncoming attackers, but the power that they had unleashed was no small amount.

They collided with Mana barriers that covered the Earth and Dark Lord's forces.

Enraged by the army of Light's attack, the forces of Earth and Dark unleashed their own spells.

Mana bolts of every color tore across that sea, leaving deep grooves in the water in their wake. The waters were stirred up, crashing against the rocks of Markolm as a golden shield took the impacts of the bolts. Curses, hexes, Fire storms, cutting blades of Air, Water cannon spells and powerful spears of wood colored the sea between the two forces.

The green, black, and gold Mana barriers took impact after impact. Spells were traded faster and faster as the range decreased. The sea between the three groups turned into a raging storm, the power crossing over top tearing apart the balance that had been created by nature.

Pillars of light descended from the heavens and landed on the island's and platform's Mana barriers. But still they didn't go down under the powerful impacts. Their advance slowed under the constant attacks by Light's army but it wasn't enough to stop them.

Earth's island reached Markolm first.

Plants grew from the island, extending into the ground of Markolm. These thin weeds turned into plants that looked like living snakes and were three meters wide. They secured the island to Markolm, creating a ramp between the two islands.

The Water creatures that had come under Earth's commands moved around the island, unleashing their attacks upon the golden Mana barrier as Earth's forces charged off the island. Many of them were cut down by the different Light attacks, as they tried to close with Light's army.

Light's army charged forward to meet them, their yells audible between the earth shaking and ocean, splitting ranged attacks that were hurled between the two groups.

On one side, there was the golden army of Light. On the other was a mishmash of all different kinds of powerful creatures, from sprites and tree demons to flame atronachs and lightning stallions.

The Earth forces, now that they were on ground, greatly increased their combat power. The ground turned into traps and quagmires; plants came together to create Earth golems or were sucked of their power in order to strengthen the different Earth creatures.

Light's army might have been made up with fanatics, but it doesn't matter how much you believe in something when your enemy is that much stronger.

They waded through the enemy, their spells and attacks tearing into the ranks of Light's army.

It was a crazed and wild melee. Spells were used at close range for massive damage. Here and there, people from Earth's force were destroyed, but his people had established a beachhead and waded forward through the destruction. As people left the island, it transformed; the sections turned from island into massive creatures.

They stood fifteen foot tall and were made from Earth materials. Green Mana could be seen between the cracks of their bodies. As they entered the battle, their hands made up of vines twirled together, creating clubs and swords that cut through tens of Light's soldiers with each swipe.

The platform arrived. Different members of Dark's forces jumped from the platform as it started to walk up the shore of Markolm. Metal and stone pillars rose to meet them, lowering them toward the battle; they came off their pillars, dark smoke covering a number of them.

The Light soldiers screamed out in agony under this black smoke that seemed to be killing them from the inside out.

Dark clouds and hexes appeared in the sky. Area of effect spells came down; screams that would make the hardiest of veterans shiver tore through the battlefield.

The Dark Lord's forces laughed and cheered, enjoying the noises of battle.

The platform advanced, the ranged forces staying on it.

Necromancers chanted together, chaining their spells as the dead soldiers of Light's army started to rise from their slumber. Their bodies filled with life, now rotting and gray, as they turned and started to fight against their comrades.

Light's forces fought with everything they had, cutting down their comrades who had been turned into the necromancers' minions without pause. Their anger had no bounds, willing to take grievous wounds just to slow or wound those who profaned their goddess's name and stepped onto her holy ground.

Even as the Dark Lord's and Earth Lord's forces were clearly winning, their progress was slow, being hampered by Light's army.

The fighting was chaotic and brutal. There was no sign of order or lines, just a free-for-all melee as people fought all over the beaches and the hills that lay behind them.

A clarion call came from behind Light's army as the sound of marching shook the ground.

The views changed as they looked upon the two other armies that Light had created from her most fanatic of believers. Above them, three angel legions flew in formation, led by their generals. The light from these creatures drove back the darkness that had now settled over Markolm with the setting of the sun.

The angels didn't even pause as they started to rain attack after attack down on the Earth Lord's and Dark Lord's forces. They didn't care about hitting their own or the number of people they killed. In their eyes, everyone who died, so that they might eliminate the forces that went against their master and lady, were sacrifices who had given their lives to their lady.

Golden pillars descended from the sky, burning the ground below and tearing through the ranks of the advancing armies.

The Dark Lord's and Earth Lord's forces fired back with their own spells but they were unable to break the defenses of the angels.

Their Mana barriers shone in the night's sky, stronger than that of Light's army.

Even as Light's forces seemed to be throwing back the Dark Lord's and Earth Lord's fighting force, the plants and different growths of Markolm started to shoot up and attack Light's army and the angel legions. The undead within the ranks of Light's army were breaking it apart from the inside.

Light might have had forces coming in but her first army had been torn apart.

Earth's and Dark's forces made it to the other sides of Light's first army and tore apart those who had stood in their way.

Light's second army tried to attack but their attacks were now landing on the first army's Mana barrier that had not failed yet.

The two forces held their advance. Cultists and different groups got together and started to chant out spells or write down spell formations in the ground as they called upon their inner power.

The air was charged with power as different-colored Mana became a physical object and started to stream in toward the spell formations taking shape.

The ground shivered as hands and limbs made from stone and metal broke through the ground; magma turned into beasts from the deep that had come to Earth's command.

The wind howled as the sounds of tortured spirits came from the sky, tearing through all in their path, entering the defenses of Light's armies and legions.

Light's advancing forces were met with creatures that called every power their own, coming from the ground, the sky and every direction, attacking them and disrupting their fire so they could no longer concentrate their attacks on the Dark Lord's or Earth Lord's forces that had never stopped charging their own lines.

As night had set, the Dark Lord's forces gained an advantage over the forces of Light, which allowed them to increase the power of their spells. Some of their forces that would be harmed if they were out in the daylight could now show off their strength, not needing to create different wards in order to fight the power of the sun.

A little-known fact was that Light's forces, like the forces of Dark, were affected when they were not in sunlight. As the night fell, a number of them found that their skills and spells were not as powerful as before. The angels, a dominating force in the day-time, were now weakened, and a curse that was placed upon them came into effect. Much like how vampires were weakened in the day, the angels were weaker at night. However, for this weakness, when fighting in the day, the angels of Light gained a combat boost.

They had already cast different wards in order to not be affect-ed by the coming night; however, this was a drain on their Mana.

With Light's blessing and turning them into her champions and being her Creatures of Power, their strength had gone through a massive increase. When looking at the two forces, Light's angels and her armies still had a slight advantage even in the night, show-ing just how powerful turning Creatures of Power into champions was.

Earth's forces unleashed their full power at the same time that the Dark Lord's did. There were a few Creatures of Power among their ranks that the Earth Lord and Dark Lord had turned into champions.

The first army of Light were torn apart between the incoming reinforcements by Light and the invading forces.

Angels shot down attacks at the invaders; the second and third army of Light let out a yell and charged forward. Their boots on the ground sounded like rolling thunder.

The invaders freed themselves from the last remaining vestiges of the first army of Light and rushed forward to meet them. It was as if a wave had met a cliff: the golden lines of the second and third army were torn apart by the stronger invading forces.

Magic tore through the ranks of the golden armored angels. The second and third armies lost their momentum as the Earth Lord's and Dark Lord's forces carved through them.

The angels spread out and attacked from a distance. Impacts rang out around them as the Dark Lord's platform, still covered in his forces, advanced over the corpses of the first army and the invaders.

Dark spells appearing to be made from smoke and shadows hit the angels' defenses. They used all of their most powerful spells to make the angels' golden barrier shake under the strengthened impacts of the ranged attacks.

The angels switched their attacks from those on the ground to the ranged forces that either hovered in the air or attacked from the Dark Lord's platform. Golden light transformed into spears and arrows that were shot forward from the angels.

Waves of pressure, and the ear-shattering impacts of the two ranged forces fighting it out, slammed down upon those on the ground. Many of the Earth and Dark forces were staggered by the shock waves of the impacts. However, Light's armies were in a worse condition. One for one, they were not as strong as those that Earth or Dark had rallied. They were tossed back and some bled from their ears as their eardrums were broken by the noises from above.

The undead didn't care about eardrums as they moved forward like a plague, cutting down the wounded and distracted, adding more members to their ranks. Necromancers walked behind the army, waving their hands and raising the dead from the slaughter that lay behind the front lines.

Summoners laid down summoning circles to call forth creatures from the other realms that rushed forward to meet Light's forces. Golems and atronachs of every Affinity except Light were created and conjured, all of them adding their own attacks into the fray.

As time went on, the invading forces were able to call up more and more strength to aid them.

The armies of Light were only some decently leveled people of Emerilia and a few players; they weren't able to stop the invaders. The legions of angels were stronger than the invaders; however, with their attacks, they were hurting their own forces more than the invaders, giving the invaders the cover, resources, and time they needed to increase their strength.

Wraiths and tortured souls screamed out into the night sky. Summoning circles glowed with power as cultists pulled creatures from the darker realms. They shot into the sky, screaming in pain as they got closer to the angels, who were covered in armor that increased their power of Light. Their pain only seemed to drive them wilder as they met the angels' lines, attacking anything and anyone who came into their range.

The nearly two hundred thousand invaders clashed with the four hundred thousand defenders under Light's command.

The Dark and Earth invaders pushed the defenders back again and again, slaughtering those who made up the armies as the angels fought with those on the platform.

The Dark Mana barrier continued to take hit after hit while the golden barrier of the legion started to look weaker and weaker.

Neither side showed any sign of retreat as they clashed and fought, using everything they had to win the battle.

One of the legion generals raised their blade in anger, and rushed forward while yelling out a war cry. He turned into a golden ray of light as he shot forward. The rest of the legion followed on his heels.

They were without the Mana barrier, but with their own strength they were able to deflect most of the attacks. Still, here and there, a number of them were hit and tumbled to the ground, their bodies broken upon impact. The angels didn't even pause their attack, a fanatical gleam in their eyes as they were finally unleashed upon the enemy.

They reached the platform and dove through the Mana barrier. Their strength was weakened in the presence of so much Dark Mana. As they charged, the ranged mages' creatures rose from the depths of the platforms and defensive spells were activated.

Creatures of pain and suffering lashed out at the legion. Tentacled beasts and creatures of the shadows all attacked the angels of Light, their formations coming apart in the fighting.

***

Josh looked to the leaders of the Terra Alliance. They were talking to one another, pointing out different things that they saw going on in the epic battle between Earth, Light and Dark. Trying to find their advantages and weaknesses to predict what would happen and their possible response.

"What do you think the outcome will be?" Josh asked Dwayne, who was beside him.

"I think that Earth and Dark will get a foothold in Markolm. Their forces are powerful and they chose to hit at night, giving them a greater advantage. I'm not sure why Light is holding most of her angel legions in reserve while throwing out her armies to deal with the threat of Dark and Earth," Dwayne said.

"Probably for propaganda," Lucy interjected. "With the armies taking massive casualties, the people of Markolm will be in a state of fear. Fear can easily be turned into anger. If Light can do this right, then she'll be able to pull her supporters to her even more. This isn't just a war for Markolm. This is the Lady Light's bid toward becoming *the* god of Emerilia."

"If she can pull all of them over to her side and get them to believe in her even more, then they will give her more devotions. Hell, if they're just scared and hoping to be saved and give her more power hoping that they're going to be saved, she starts racking up a whole lot of energy she can use directly against the Earth Lord and the Dark Lord," Josh said.

"It's just a matter of when and how she wants to push Earth and Dark's forces off her island. If she waits, she gets more power, but she will lose more soldiers and she will be seen as their savior in the hour that they needed her the most. If she acts now, then she might not win. She will keep more of her angels and her soldiers, but she will be seen as a defender, not a savior, meaning she doesn't get as many panicked and fearful devotions." Kim shook her head.

"She is one smart and brutal bitch." Cassie said what they were all thinking.

"Putting it mildly." Josh sighed. The battle between the two groups was only just starting.

The army of Light used bugles, calling back their force, reforming them and readying them for another attack. Many weren't able to get free from the fighting in order to get back into formation.

Spells lit up the night sky or descended it into darkness. The contrasting lights illuminated a brutal battlefield in the sky and on the ground.

"Kol says that the first warclan worth of Devastator armor is ready," Dwayne said.

"How effective were they?" Josh asked. The Devastator armor had been awarded to the dwarven protectors who had been hiding away from the world. When in the armor, their abilities had a sharp increase, making them incredibly powerful. Also, as all dwarves, they had trained to be in warclans, so they had been organized once again as shield bearers.

Josh had seen some of the training. There was nothing quite as terrifying as three-meter-tall armors using massive dwarven shields and blades advancing on the enemy as their contracted beasts flew over top of them, lending support.

"Scary effective. We've got three more warclans' worth training up now. They're going to be used as drop forces for the Pandora's Box Initiative. There aren't many of them but they can shift the flow of a battle," Dwayne said.

"I want them on standby, ready to deploy with our Terra forces if we need it. Those angels are some bad news." Josh looked at the holy warriors that floated in the sky and were stuck in close combat with the Dark forces on the platform.

Even with the powerful spells, and their advantage at night and around Dark Mana, the people on the platform were barely able to defend themselves.

The angels were tearing through the creatures and creations that lay in their way, batting away or destroying the spells shot at them. Their power was impressive and scary, their soldiers able to fight against mages who had not only range, but the time to cast multiple spells.

Josh ground his teeth in frustration and fear of what might happen when the Terra Alliance clashed with them.

***

Light looked over the different interfaces and screens in front of her with little interest, luxuriating in a large bath that was filled with sweet-smelling soap and bubbles. She sipped from a goblet, drinking a golden wine that smelled refreshing and made one feel relaxed just being able to smell it. Light sipped on it as if it were no different from water.

She was "recuperating" from her last efforts to create champions from the angels under her command. To the angels who were on the battlefield, she had made a display of pouring her power out, raising them to be her champions in their greatest time of need.

They looked to save the armies of Light but it was a losing battle.

Still, the sacrifices and the ways that the Lady of Light had severely injured and worked herself to the point of exhaustion were a great rallying cry to her followers.

A number of people had fled Markolm under the cover of war. These people were those who had been suppressed by Light and Daeundra's fallen angels, but had never really been supporters of Light's.

Daeundra and her people looked out for these people, killing them silently, not allowing word on the conditions people were living in to get out. Some spies might report back to their leaders, but that was different from them having someone who had been there—a regular person of Emerilia.

People were pouring in their devotions, wanting their Lady of Light to win the battle, for her to support their loved ones on the battlefield. Even those who died on the battlefield sent their final vestiges of power to the Lady of Light in the shape of devotions as the end came for them.

A cold and hungry look spread across Light's face as the corners of her mouth raised into an ugly smile. She sipped on her wine and relaxed in her massive bath, attendants quietly standing in all corners of the room.

"Daeundra, have them do a fighting retreat. Pull them in the direction of one of the farming communities. Have the Light army try to pull the citizens out but in the midst of the fighting so that a few of them die and the army of Light tries to defend them but falls. It will be a heroic moment—shows the way that the Dark

Lord and Earth Lord don't care about the people. Maybe get a few images and videos of people who are being sacrificed or used by the invading forces, incite anger and fury in the people's hearts." Light coordinated a massive loss of life, only caring about the impact of it on her own devotions.

"Yes, mistress," Daeundra said.

"When that is going on, I'll drop a pillar of light, destroying everything. Then I'll do a speech about fighting them back and all of this. Something to inspire them all." Light waved her cup slightly, already seeing the scene of her people bowing before her, as she stirred the coals of rage within their hearts.

"Yes, mistress," Daeundra repeated, in her same monotone voice.

"Good pet." Light relaxed into her bath, her alluring figure at odds with her cold expression.

****

The Dark Lord raised his hand; a pillar of metal rose from the seabed. Water rolled off it as it breached the waves, spreading out and growing into a new semicircle island. The Earth Lord flashed into existence near him; he tossed out seeds that hit the sea below.

The churned water revealed different plants that interwove with one another, piercing the seabed, and created a second island that rested beside the one the Dark Lord had made.

The Earth Lord and Dark Lord nodded to each other as they arrived at the neutral ground they had created in the middle of the sea between Opheir, Heval, Ashal, and Markolm. The Earth Lord and Dark Lord both descended to the island. From the ground, seats rose with a thought. Different viewing pools and orbs floated around them, showing the battle between their two forces and Light's.

"Seems she is trying to build up the power held in her divine well," Earth said.

Dark sneered at Earth's words; under the hood, Earth couldn't see the expression on his face. "She can try, but it is a losing plan."

"Her angels are incredibly powerful now that she has started to raise many of them to champion status," Earth said.

"We have also raised any Creatures of Power that we have to the status of champions. Our forces together are much stronger than any of the armies that she can send against us. Fighting the legions will be difficult but we will only need to show a bit of our power in order to help them break through the angels' legions." The Dark Lord, too, didn't like how strong the legions of angels had become but even if he lost all of his forces here, his true plan hadn't been revealed.

He cast a hidden look at Earth, who was concentrating on the screens.

They had fought in the Pantheon constantly, but this was one of the first times it had been so blatant. They were aiming not only for the forces of another member of the Pantheon, but their hall and seat of power. Markolm was Light's continent and island. Stepping onto it was a declaration of war. If any of the other members of the Pantheon even thought of stepping onto Markolm, let alone trying to invade it, Light, with her narcissistic ways, would not stop until she destroyed those who profaned her island.

Earth was rightfully nervous. Light had home ground advantage and she had been growing her power rapidly over the last couple of weeks. If they lost this fight, then Earth would have little power to hold onto what he had left.

It was a big bet, but if it paid off, then Light, one of Dark's and Earth's biggest threats to power, would be removed.

They descended into silence on their perfectly split island. Waves rippled out from the island as they watched the progress of their forces and wondered what Light's actions would be. Neither of them gave the people of Emerilia nor the rest of the Pantheon any thought.

They worked with the weakest of people; in their minds, there was no way that they could even offer a resistance once they had defeated Light. They only needed to look at Light's armies made up of the people of Emerilia who were getting slaughtered under the attacks of Earth's and Dark's advancing forces.

Chapter 15: Use Every Moment

Lox and Gurren looked over the ranks of Devastator armor in front of them; a feeling of pride welled up in their chests.

They looked to the warclan leader Redal. He was a figure of legend, a dwarf who had led his warband into the depths of the Aldamire Mountain to rescue a group of children who had been captured by creatures of the Dark. They had come back barely alive but they did come back; carrying every child that was taken by the Dark.

When the dwarves went down to see where the creatures were hiding, they had found a bloodbath. All of the dwarves in Redal's warband had fought with their all, pushing past their limits and defeating these powerful creatures. Redal grew in fame from that first legendary fight, becoming a figure that demanded respect and an impressive tactician. He was a part of the war council at one time. He had been retired due to his advanced age. Now, with some of Jung Lee's revitalizing potions and some of the anti-aging treatments that the Terra healers could use, he had once again risen out of retirement and taken command of this Devastator warclan, the first of its kind.

Each and every dwarf was a powerful person with a storied past; with the armor they were even more terrifying.

In just a few weeks, they were able to not only adapt to the armor but take the teachings of Lox and Gurren and make it their own. On their shoulders, their summoned beasts rested; their eyes looked for the next target as Mana circulated their bodies, ready for combat at any moment.

"Well, you're certainly a sight to scare the shit out of some god's minions." Gurren laughed.

Redal chuckled as well. "They are an ugly-looking bunch, aren't they?" Redal looked to the other dwarves lined up in ranks.

Lox chuckled as the sets of armor let out amused laughs. Redal had pushed them to their limits but he had been right there with them, working two times harder than them and working to make them the best. He had earned their respect and undying loyalty.

"We wouldn't have become as strong as we are without your help, brothers," Redal said in a moment of seriousness, looking between the two of them.

Working with the armor, they had learned how to figure out what others were thinking by their actions and words.

Lox felt embarrassed and proud at Redal's words. "If it wasn't for the warclan's work and each and every shield bearer coming together, I don't think that another clan would have been able to train so fast," Lox said.

"Damn, you are a flatterer. Want to get me a beer before ya try to jump in my pants!" Redal stepped backward slightly. Those who heard started to laugh as Lox shook his head.

Even Gurren laughed at Lox, who was struck speechless by their words.

"Me and my clan appreciate everything you two have done—knowing the truth of Emerilia, the Jukal and all of it. It's not going to be an easy path, but hopefully we can do our part to get our freedom back and kick these bastards off our planet." Redal's light tone and joking manner faded away, his words biting and hard.

Lox nodded and looked at those in front of him.

There were two more warclans of five thousand that were also training with the Devastator armor. A few of the people from the first training group had been picked to teach them, as well as Lox and Gurren helping out as they could.

From their armor, Dave had made the armor that they now saw in front of them. Their numbers were low but the armor allowed these experts to become even more tyrannical.

Lox's thoughts soured as he remembered the images and videos he had seen of the war happening in Markolm. The news of the Jukal had broken through the ranks of the Terra Alliance leadership.

With it, a large number of people had been moved to the Pandora's Box Initiative.

They were getting closer and closer to wakening day—the day when they would pull all of the players from their simulation and wake them up. More and more facilities to wake players up had been created with that single goal in mind. Players now made up the vast majority of those within the Pandora's Box Initiative. Some of them couldn't wrap their heads around what was happening, getting a place to live and doing as they wanted. They were watched closely by Jeeves to make sure they didn't do anything that might put the Initiative into jeopardy.

A number of them helped with research and development, building and training to use the equipment that was coming online.

Every minute that the Pantheon was fighting was another minute that they could get their people ready for the coming fight with the Jukal.

Hopefully they could hold back their strength and defeat the Pantheon. Even if they deployed the Devastator warclans, it shouldn't be too big of a deal. But if they started to teleport or use some of their more powerful weapons, then the Jukal might be alerted to the fact that Emerilia was preparing to break free of their imprisonment.

***

Frank and all of the players who were training to man the different ships of the Emerilian fleet were excited. The first group had finally finished what was being called basic training. They had memory crystals taken and added into the minds of the second round of players who would be joining their ranks.

Afterward, the three different fleet groups had been pitched against one another in massive battles. They had commanded Jukal ships as well as Emerilian vessels. For days, they would simulate battle after battle and fighting engagements, sometimes not coming out of the simulation until their force was wholly destroyed or they made it to a checkpoint with vessels hitting them along the way.

It was as realistic as they could get without being in actual combat.

After a week of that, their leaderships had given them three days off. Frank and his fire control teams were in Ice City, having beers and food when notifications started to come in.

Frank opened up the notification and saw a video. The remaining legions of angels had finally taken to the sky and were moving on the forces of the Earth Lord and Dark Lord.

They had been fighting for three weeks now, with the Dark Lord's and Earth Lord's forces committing atrocities on the people of Markolm, inciting the rage of the entire continent as the armies of Light did their best to destroy those who attacked their homes and families.

The angels continued to slow them, just barely holding the lines it seemed. They flew up from all over Maphrol, the capital of Markolm, and where Light had placed her hall above the tallest tower.

The golden armor of the angels shone in the morning light as they moved. Their white wings extended as they moved into flying legions and filled the sky. It was a powerful sight to see as they advanced toward the battlefield.

It took them just a few minutes to reach where the fighting was happening. As they arrived, pillars of light fell from the sky, falling upon the angels who were fighting. All of them were blessed by the Lady of Light, becoming her champions.

The Earth Lord's and Dark Lord's forces separated themselves from the battles they were in, regrouping as the angels moved into the legion formations. The armies of Light looked up at their saviors, struck by the beauty and power of the angels.

With these guardians above, there was no way that they could fail now.

A light appeared in the air, showing the Lady of Light in front of the legions of angels. "You have gone too far, Dark and Earth. For your bloodied hands and cold souls, you will feel my judgement!" Light yelled out.

Powerful golden streams shot out from her hand. Those who weren't under the protection of a Mana barrier were torn apart under the power of her attack. It smashed against the Mana barrier that covered the platform and the ground below it, making it shake as the Dark Mana barrier started to become lighter.

"For the true goddess!" Khanundra yelled.

The angels' war cries filled the air, their wings flapping as they shot forward into battle.

The Mana barrier failed, Light's attack cracking it and breaking through.

The twin pillars of light tore through the black smoke that covered the platform, punching a hole through the platform itself and a half dozen of the legs underneath, and making it shudder and shake.

The Dark forces jumped from the platform. Pillars shot up from the ground, catching them and pushing them up to meet the angels of Light.

Those on the ground shot upward. Roots and plants sprouted under their feet; flames covered their bodies; air tunnels shot them upward and water streams coiled underneath their feet.

The invaders rose up, the creatures of hell meeting the creatures of heaven.

Fights broke out throughout the angels' legions. In the sky, fighting happened in every direction.

The angels' strength was incredible. With their training and Light doubling their strength by making them champions against the Dark's and Earth's invaders, they were unstoppable.

Creatures and people who were part of the Myths and Legends of Emerilia clashed: Massive beasts of the sky, creatures from the depths of the Earth and stone. Angels who had struck fear into Emerilia and a goddess who was talked about in lore.

Light wielded a sword of gold. With every wave of it, a swathe of her enemies would be felled.

The Pantheon's forces clashed, the shock waves enough to disturb the clouds above and tear the ground below. Each of the attacks unleashed a shock wave, the two sides having to block those impacts or dodge.

It was not something that a normal person could take easily.

The people of Emerilia had become a lot stronger with the help of the Mirror of Communication but even the trained and armored soldiers in the army of Light had to hide underneath their Mana barriers so that they weren't left with serious injuries or even killed by the forces that were secondary to the fight that now took up the sky.

There was no way a normal person would be able to help or hinder those who were fighting. All they could do was watch the display of power in awe and fear.

Even though there were more of the creatures that had rallied to Dark's and Earth's call, the angels were much stronger. They weren't without casualties—here and there, golden-clad warriors fell from the sky—but they were only a small portion of those who died in the battles.

With every one of Light's people who fell, there was one more person to increase the necromancer's strength. The creatures that struck fear into the hearts of the people of Emerilia—the ones that they had been told tales of as children—were torn apart by the angels' golden weapons and their powerful spells.

The angels took on a demonic appearance, covered in the blood of their enemies. They sliced through their larger opponents, not even sparing them a glance as they continued to throw themselves into fight after fight.

Those on the ground cheered and celebrated while fear grew within the invaders and those watching.

The angels didn't look anything like the righteous warriors they were supposed to be. They were nothing more than brutal and bloodthirsty soldiers who had been rallied to a cause. They cared nothing of their enemy, thinking of them as beneath their concern and lower life-forms not worth living. That showed in their fighting: they brutally cut down the different creatures, staining the ground with blood as they turned the sky into a slaughter.

This was the belief, the unwavering knowledge that the Lady of Light was their true goddess. She was the rightful leader of Emerilia; the rest of the Pantheon were nothing but pretenders. Whoever didn't believe in that and went against what they believed in didn't deserve to live in the paradise that their lady had created.

Thousands died in minutes. The brutal slaughter showed no signs of slowing down as the angel generals left only broken bodies behind them, leading their legions forth.

Nothing escaped Khanundra as she cut down legendary beasts and people from myth. Light was untouched. With a casual raise of her hand, she slaughtered tens of people.

There was nothing holy about the scene: it was pure, unadulterated slaughter. The air above Markolm had become a warzone.

Some of the people, seeing that Light had the upper hand, tried to flee. They were cut down before they were able to get more than a few hundred meters.

More and more of the invaders started to panic.

Light waved her sword; a beam of light cut through the platform. With a groan, the platform lost its strength, coming apart as it tumbled toward the ground.

Seeing the platform smash into the ground seemed to trigger something within the minds of the invaders.

Many of the survivors turned and shot out in different directions.

"You want to leave? Who said you could leave?" Light demanded. She opened up her arms. From the heavens, pillars of light crashed down from the heavens, hitting Earth's island and hitting the water that boiled away under the impact of the pillars. The water creatures that had come to Earth's side and moved the island into position didn't have time to react as the pillars of light cut through them.

The legions of angels surged outward, hurling spears of light. They had no mercy as they hunted down those trying to flee.

Here and there, battles broke out as the ones trying to flee fought with all they had, to try to get away from Light and her forces.

Those on the ground cheered the victory of Light and her angels.

Frank felt cold as those trying to escape were cut down. He closed his interface, his face pale, as a shiver ran down his spine. His hands clenched into fists as white-hot anger filled him.

It didn't take the Jukal doing much to get us to kill one another, as if we held nothing in common. He shook his head. It was something that he had seen all too often in the Earth simulation. Humanity was one big family; out of the entirety of the universe, they were the closest to one another. All it took was a good performance, the right words, and they would be willing to turn on those they were more alike in the entire known universe.

It was a situation that the Jukal had created and made but there was no hiding the fact that these were the very people they hoped to save. They were so filled with bloodlust and anger, looking to kill others and gain more power; all of it was nothing but a lie, an illusion that they had tricked themselves into believing.

***

The Dark Lord frowned as he looked at the viewing pools that showed him Light as her people cut down his own forces that were looking to flee.

He sent a quick message to people he had waiting in Opheir. *Seems that her forces were stronger than I had thought. Well, we've weakened her some—it doesn't matter. With my power and the Alturarans under my control, I will be able to kill her off and make them my loyal followers of Emerilia. What use are the people of Emerilia if I constantly have to try to make them follow me?*

"How did her angels get so powerful? We need to retreat." Earth stood up from his seat.

A flash of light blinded both Earth and Dark.

Dark grunted, highly affected by light as the dark smoke around him was burned away a bit.

It went from a slight covering to a raging torrent, like a flame raging in the night, as it pushed back the light coming near.

Light made a displeased sound as she looked down on Dark and Earth. *Seems that they want to kill me. I'll teach these useless creations who is the true god of Emerilia soon enough.* Light descended from above.

Around her there were the angel generals and Khanundra. All of the angels shot daggers at the two lords of the Pantheon who their lady had been in conflict with for hundreds of years.

Dark remained seated in his throne of stone and metal and looked at Light.

"Dear brothers, neither of you will be getting away today. Today, it seems that the Pantheon will become two people smaller." Light's smile showed the pleasure she took from their conflicted looks.

Earth's fists were balled together, fury on his face at losing all of the forces he had built up over the last few months.

However, no one could see the sardonic smile on Dark's face.

"Don't force me, sister," Earth said.

Dark looked at Earth in interest. He was regarded as the simplest person in the Pantheon; when he said that he would do something, then he would.

"Oh, I won't force you to do anything. All you need to do is hand over control of your divine wells and I will let you go." Light's voice was sweet but her eyes held killing intent.

Even if they were to give up their divine wells, no one knew Light better than Dark and Earth. They had been fighting for much too long for them to know how other battles had gone between them. Light's offer might be honorable up front, but the fact was that although she promised things, she would always find a loophole to allow her to do what she wanted without breaking the promise.

It was something that the Dark Lord praised Light for.

Earth didn't say anything but the sound of stone grinding on stone as he flexed his fists could be clearly heard.

Light looked over to Dark with a bored look in her eyes. "What? Not going to say anything, brother?" Light's eyes flashed with happiness. Dark could practically see her thought process as she looked over Dark, as if she were already cutting him apart piece by piece.

"Words are useless." Dark waved his hand.

"That they are. I have been wondering what is really under that robe of yours. I wonder how you would react if you were bathed in the holy flames of purification." Light sounded interested as Dark didn't do anything.

A flash of confusion was quickly hidden as she unconsciously moved, ready to advance or retreat.

"Why are you acting this way, sister dearest?" Dark floated out of his chair until he stood.

"There is no way to escape. I have made it impossible for you to teleport away. Anything that you say is just an excuse to prolong your life," Light said.

A message appeared in Dark's vision but he didn't need to even read it as a stream of power filled his body. The shadows around him started to shake and fluctuate, growing stronger for a moment before dying down.

"Trying to show off?" Light sneered, looking down on him.

"Nothing of the sort, sister dearest." Dark disappeared from where he was; a blade made from shadows appeared in his hands as sounds of pain filled the air.

Light and her angels' heads whipped over to see Dark as he stood behind Earth. A blade went through Earth's back and out of his chest.

Light's eyes went wide, confusion clear as Dark pulled his blade from Earth's body.

"It was about time I was rid of your useless talking and planning," Dark said.

Earth's mouth moved as if he were trying to form words. The plants, dirt, vines, and the stone trapped in it all fell away, Earth's power dissipating.

There was a twenty-year-old man who had similar features as the rest of the Pantheon. He was thin and wiry instead of the thick and larger being that had stood in front of them just moments ago. There was a look of pain and loss on his face before he collapsed, dying just like any person of Emerilia might.

"Kill him!" Light yelled.

Her angels reacted instantaneously, unleashing their own attacks. A Mana barrier as dark as the abyss absorbed the hits from the generals and Khanundra without the slightest fluctuation.

"Die!" Dark cast out a ray of darkness that landed on three of the generals and hit Khanundra. They screamed out in pain as the ray of darkness corroded their armor and their bodies.

Khanundra looked half dead but she survived. Dark was a black streak as he reached Khanundra. She didn't have the strength to escape. Even at her high level, she was unable to combat a member of the Pantheon's power. Especially one who had just received a massive power boost as Dark had.

She was pierced by Dark's sword; from her wound, her body started to decompose.

Dark looked from Khanundra on his sword to Light, who was in a state of shock having the odds turned on her.

Dark raised a fist. Another ray of darkness appeared.

"No!" Khanundra said. The ray shot out as Khanundra ignited all of her power, turning into a miniature sun.

Not even Dark was able to shrug it off. His Mana shield took a massive impact as he felt slightly burned from it all.

Light cried out in pain.

Dark looked at Light, who was holding her face, golden light fighting the corrupting flames on her face. Half of her face looked melted and horrific. Her hair burned away. She had always taken great pride in her beauty. Now that it was being burned away in front of his eyes, Dark felt a deep sense of satisfaction. "Next time,

I will take your life and mount your head on my walls to forever show off your disfigured face to all Emerilians!"

Light unleashed attacks at him, firing blindly.

Dark laughed. A few of the attacks hit the Mana barrier around him but fizzled into nothing. The portion of his mouth that was revealed was formed into an amused arc. Smoke crawled all up his body, making it impossible to see him within.

It dissipated as one of Light's bolts hit it, showing Dark had teleported away already.

Dark appeared in his hall, pleased with himself. He waved to one of the undead in his hall. "Notify Boran-al. I want the Alturarans ready to move in two days," Dark said lazily.

He wanted to kill Light, but he knew how smart and conniving she was. Even if he killed her, there was no guarantee that he wouldn't be severely wounded or killed because of the direct confrontation.

Chapter 16: Great Change

Air and Fire were both looking at the interface that showed Dark killing Earth then ignoring Light's attacks as if they were nothing more than a child's temper tantrum. They looked to each other with troubled eyes.

"He must have got some power from somewhere unknown," Fire said.

"I've had reports of him doing something that involved portals. Actually, a few people even said that they saw his most trusted champions moving items through the Alturaran portal in Opheir," Air said.

"Something from Alturara? What did they find?" Fire asked.

"I'm not sure." Air had a troubled look on her face. She didn't like having unanswered questions.

"I think they might be divine wells," a powerful voice said from behind them.

The people in the room glanced at the large character who had entered the command center. His face and features were covered by a hood and cloak but the outline of a wolf-like head and the tufts of fur that stuck out allowed Fire and Air to figure out that he was some kind of Beast Kin, probably a wolfkin.

"Who are you?" Fire asked. Divine wells were not something that people in the general population knew about.

"What—you don't recognize your own dad?" The man lowered his hood; indeed, he was from the wolfkin race.

Fire was about to say something back when she noticed his eyes. "Bob?"

"Hah! I knew that the gnome wasn't your only form!" Air said. "You owe me a gold coin!" Air pointed at Venfik.

Bob shook his head at Air's antics, a father who had given up on trying to shape her into a responsible adult. The corner of his lips slightly rose into a smile as his eyes softened.

Dave opened up a private chat and invited them into it so that they wouldn't have to worry about others overhearing what they had to say.

Seeing how Dark, Light, and Earth were simply moving their forces about, Dave and Bob had spent the time working on increasing the strength of the Terra Alliance and working on the different projects of the Pandora's Box Initiative.

"So, why do you think that they're divine wells?" Fire asked, a little shocked by Bob's new appearance but quickly moving past it. After all, she and her children all changed their appearance in different ways. A bit of shape shifting was an hourly thing.

"The power increase was at the same time that the wells came through. Also, with the new ono network, we're able to get really good readings on everything that is happening across Emerilia. It's not perfect but when something is out in the open, like the divine wells, it's not too hard to get a few good readings." Bob shrugged. "Dave knows more about it."

"We used the information we had to watch the carts. They moved from the portal to a remote location, where a teleportation scroll made from Dark Mana was used and the carts disappeared. All of the drivers were Dark Champions. The signatures from the divine wells weren't that clear. However, we looked at how the Mana energy levels of the area reacted. The light was adversely affected in the area around the carts—the others limited while there was a slight rise in Dark Mana density," Dave said.

"So, he's got new divine wells. Where the hell did he get them, or the power, from?" Fire asked.

"Well, it's probably one of Boran-al's projects. He's on Alturara right now. Looks like I finally know what he's been up to. We were even thinking that he was dead, he's been gone for so long. As for power—well, they could have made all kinds of different systems to charge up their divine wells. However, Dark isn't the type to just quietly increase his power with charging and this is much more power than he can create with any of the tech on Emerilia." Air let out a heavy breath, her brows pinched together in thought. She quickly glanced at Venfik before she looked to the others, a grave expression on her face. "I think that the Dark Lord has the support of the Alturarans."

Fire's scalp tingled as silence descended.

"It would make sense. They are inanimate creatures. They want to destroy all organics. With the Dark Lord, they are working with a master of their element and also someone who wants to destroy all life or rule it. It wouldn't take him much to convince them to be on his side," Venfik said.

"We need to move forces to all Alturaran portals to make sure that they don't break through. Even if we have to fight the angels and Light all by ourselves, we can't have Alturarans marching all across Emerilia. Wherever they go, they'll destroy life without care," Dave said.

"Agreed," Bob said.

"Even with this, I'm a bit more scared of Light," Air said.

Dave had a questioning look while the others showed signs of agreement.

"Light is highly narcissistic. There were mage's guilds on Markolm and she would do everything in her power to make their lives hell. The college and guild gained the support of the people, making it harder for Light to act, but we only sent some of our stronger people there for their own safety. This was when she didn't even control the continent. She loves to be this giving person and adored by the masses while in reality it's all a fantasy that she has created in order to make it easier to control the people of Emerilia that she's lying to," Fire said.

"And part of this fantasy she has created is about her holy image. How she is one of the most beautiful women in existence. She's killed more than one lady who has been even faintly compared to her level of beauty from the shadows. Nothing was connected but there is a reason that people don't compare ladies to the Lady of Light unless they want to have them killed. Doing so in some places is signing your own death warrant.

"Dark's Mana is a complete opposite from Light's; it will make it hard to remove and he used a spell that not only harms but corrodes. Light will be fighting off the corroding and the effect of the spell. As Dark actually has more power than her, it will probably take her a lot of power and time in order to stop the spell from corroding her face and then even more time to heal it and cleanse her body of Dark Mana impurities," Air said.

Fire nodded while Dave's face became a little paler, hearing about the personality behind Light's actions.

"Seems that things are going to be getting a little harder to deal with," Bob said.

"We need to have everything prepared. If we start to get a whole group of Alturarans coming through a portal, we're going to need to close it off somehow. If we can't hold the tide, then we're going to have to use some tools from the Initiative," Dave said.

Fire looked at the others. They didn't want to be forced into that position; however, these things had been made to be used. If their fears were realized, then they would be forced to advance their plans.

"We are agreed," Bob said, reading the room.

"Then the Initiative is going to need every person we can wake or recruit to help us," Dave said.

The word had been passed out, but with this they were not only alerting people to what was going on around Emerilia—they were actively looking to pull people into the different projects and bases to teach, train, and ready them for what was to come. It would take units from the battlefield but it would make them units ready to fight on multiple planets, on starships and moonbases.

They would take the forces of the Terra Alliance and turn them into the ground forces of the Pandora Fleet.

What was fighting against a Jukal in powered armor compared to fighting Xelur Grand Demon Lords?

***

Admiral Adams, Commander Sato, and Edwards were all in Sato's office with depressed looks on their faces.

After the expansion of the Deq'ual military, the different politicians started to become more aggressive, looking to put more funding toward public works, expanding out different areas and making the various stations more comfortable to live in.

This was at the expense of the military projects that were underway.

The refined materials by the military were being used as a public resource and delegated out to new builds instead of the ships, weapons, and platforms that the military complex needed if they were going to have a chance to deal with the Jukal.

"Seems we got too big too fast. Now the politicians are looking to do what they can now to leave a good impression so that they get re-elected. There's no care for what's going to happen in a year, or what we might need to get there." Adams took a deep drink from her glass, the burning alcohol soothing her nerves.

Sato let out a sigh. His space suit uniform was open. These were two of the few people he could relax with, go over plans and drive forward Deq'ual.

"What I find the most ridiculous is that those xenophobes and righteous humans are saying how we're coming up with such great stuff, and not even adding in the fact that most of the items we've created has not come from our own research but rather research that we've compiled and developed with the aid of the Emerilians." Edwards shook his head, anger in his eyes. As a researcher, scientist, and engineer, he liked to be accredited for what he had done. The fact that people were applauding him and his people for what they'd done and it was actually through their work, it was making quite a number of researchers and others annoyed.

"I saw that there were a few more people taking credit for what they hadn't done," Sato said.

"Interesting how they're apparently these brilliant people but when you ask about what they've made, they can't give you a straight answer and they're really good friends with the people who are applauding them for their 'great work.'" Edwards let out a frustrated huff of air before he, too, drank from his glass.

"The whole incident with Lisdel didn't go too well." Adams looked to them with an expression of disbelief.

"It's interesting how much they can twist words and accounts to what they want," Sato said. "Actually saying that Dave verbally assaulted them and used overpowering methods in order to falsely imprison them with a flagrant disregard for human rights and care for the people in the Deq'ual system. Made it sound as if Dave held him hostage, demanded all of these things from him while Lisdel stood up for the rights of the Deq'ual system and survived an interrogation. When in reality, Lisdel threatened thousands of people's deaths in order to get a better deal from Dave so that he could look better to the people in the Deq'ual system.

"There's little talk of the fact that the deal went through because Dave trusts us and not the council. Seems as soon as they've got more power and we're not just simply surviving here, they're all about keeping that power and increasing it." Sato ground his teeth in anger.

"Well, it might not be going on for long," Edwards said.

Adams and Sato, who had been making to drink from their glasses, put them down as they stared at Edwards, who had a fake smile on his face.

"So, the council—which, in all of its infinite wisdom, loves all of the great stuff we're doing, taking all the money and resources they can from us because we can create miracles out of nothing but farts and fairy dust—is putting forward bills to reduce production on the items that we are trading with the Emerilians. Effectively, we will have a third less of our production, with the materials instead being funneled to other projects to have windows in more places, different smelling rooms, more chairs in hallways and projects that are a good idea, but don't make a bit of sense when we can't support the military that we need in order to make sure that we're safe from the Jukal in the future. They're tying our damn arms."

"If we lose that production, then our agreement with Emerilia is over," Adams said. "And you know what, I don't blame the Emerilians at all if they cut the deal. This is just getting fucking stupid."

"How is the training going otherwise?" Sato asked, trying to find at least one good thing for them to talk about in this entire meeting.

"I don't know the complete numbers but I think that close to ninety thousand people are either in or have completed the military training program between our people and Emerilia. We still don't know the capabilities of the Emerilian ships or their fleets, but any crossover to see the inside of the asteroid base has been greatly restricted. Also, their refinery is hidden within an asteroid and we can't pick up anything inside it. They seem to be using different ways to keep their shuttles from moving between bases," Adams said.

"They must've got the portals working or they've got onos and teleport pads that are allowing them to ship materials from base to base. That refinery is going to be massive, from what we've been able to piece together. I'm thinking that it's probably already beating our own refining numbers, and they've got another massive refining complex in Ice City, and across Emerilia, they're hooked into multiple refineries probably," Edwards said.

Sato let out an amused snort as he saw the look on their faces. There was envy as well as respect and relief. Envy because they wished that they were free to do as the Emerilians were, not having their hands tied. But the relief was knowing that the Emerilians were able to do so much with the little they had and that they had a chance of surviving the battle with the Jukal.

The respect was similarly from their ability to push forward with so little.

"Convincing the people of Deq'ual will become harder and harder over time. I just hope that when the history books look back on this, we won't be the ones standing by the side as we watched the Emerilians push for victory," Sato said.

"You seem pretty confident," Adams said.

"Well, that would be because of this." Sato unlocked a part of his desk and pulled out a file made of actual paper. He handed it to Adams.

She put down her glass and looked over the pages. "This—it's their plan." Adams read through it. "How were they able to get this information on the different worlds and systems?" She looked up to Sato.

"I gave them the information I could, allowing them to refine their plan. Dave has also hinted at the fact that there might be a fleet leaving the Nal system in the near future to verify their own information on the Jukal Empire," Sato said.

None of them were too shocked at the speed with which the Emerilians were moving. Things on Emerilia were becoming heated and from the fighting, it was becoming clear that the advanced weaponry that they had could be put to good use, ending the loss of life and conflicts.

It was a hard decision to make, for they weighed the loss and benefits of life on Emerilia.

It took Adams some time to finish reading over the plan, sharing it with Edwards.

"If they could do this," Adams looked at it all, "they'd tear the different supply routes out, take out the military power aspect, disrupt the economy and make the people reliant on the different items they drop. They would need to use the items in order to survive. If they did, then they would be removing the need for supplies across the empire. Planets and races wouldn't produce one item; they'd be making them all. Allowing them to rely on themselves instead of the empire for their needs. Also, if they do use it, and they will in order to survive, then they've already gone against the empire. Are they going to fight for an empire that will be pissed at them for trying to survive, or the people who gave them options and broke the empire's rule over them and can fight the Jukal military?"

Sato nodded slowly.

"With this, they could win." Edwards held up the pages in his hand.

"I think so, and so does Councilwoman Wong," Sato said.

"I sense a but." Edwards's voice turned somber.

"It has become clear that this will be political ammunition. So, we will prepare to assist but we will not make this public or give it to all of the council members—only those we can trust. When the time comes, Deq'ual will be in a state of war." Sato's voice was heavy as he looked to them both.

They knew what that would mean for them.

"In a state of war, then the control of the Deq'ual system, its resources and its people, will all come under the military complex," Adams said, as if reciting from the Deq'ual's military rules and regulations.

"Yes, and at that time, we will move to support Emerilia and our fellow humans. So while these politicians mess about, let them—fight them, but let them. When the time comes, we will be free to fight this war," Sato said.

"Well, that is a relief," Adams said.

"We're going to need to focus on building more than development, and ramp up ammunition and fuel production, as well as work on the cargo ships to carry our necessary supplies," Edwards said, his mind moving ahead.

"We're also going to need to increase our monitoring of the different systems, and push out to the inner systems of the Jukal Empire. The more information the better," Adams said.

"It needs to be done in a way to draw little attention from the council. If they find out what we have planned, they'll try to pull control away from us and make it into a mess," Sato said.

"And if it was, then it won't cost votes—it'll cost lives." Adams had a fierce and grim look on her face.

They drank their drinks. There was no celebration as the weight of the air in the room seemed to increase with the thoughts that moved through their minds.

***

Frank and the crews of the different fleets looked over the different groups that were marching into Ice City.

These were some of the strongest and powerful military units on Emerilia. Yet even their training and their experiences as veterans did not prepare them for what they were seeing today.

As they stepped through a portal, they were greeted by another planet. But instead of it being filled with aggressive species, it instead held a number of scientists, engineers, mages, and geniuses from the Terra Alliance, as well as a complete city within a world of ice.

The different crews looked at them, studying the people who would be their drop forces and security details.

It would be Frank and the others' job to get them to where they needed to go and support them, while these people of Emerilia, who had never been players and lived their days in Emerilia, would face the forces of the Jukal Empire face-to-face, bringing victory on the ground.

The different groups came to a stop in front of five thousand dwarves wearing Devastator armor.

Frank looked at it all, seeing the people who would fill his ship and he would protect with his guns as much as possible. "Let's get back to the ship—can't let the Devastators and their new recruits beat us out," Frank said.

The others around him heard and started to follow. They made it through the city, which was expanding faster than ever before with more and more people being woken up every day.

They reached the portal facility that had now three more portals just to connect Ice City to the asteroid bases. The two new portals were not made from metals and Magical Circuits; instead, they were created with soul gem constructs in the asteroid base.

Under Dave and Ela-Dorn's guidance, they and their team had been able to make true portals, which they had quickly started to use to expand their network.

The different asteroids, being hollowed out, all had onos and portals to move the materials to the refinery that had some twenty portals connected directly to the intake tunnel.

More shuttles and portals were used to move the completed products from the refinery back to the asteroid base, moonbase, ark shipyard, and Ice City. Now, each and every one of the different locations were connected by portal.

With the refinery asteroid coming online, the refinery within Ice City could concentrate on refining down the frozen materials it received, simply changing its magical coding and a few machines.

They were producing more fuel than ever, more than enough to supply all of their ships' fusion power plants and were being held in massive supply tanks. This allowed them to meet the demands of building these new transport routes and keep them open.

With the advent of memory crystals that Air and her people were now working on constantly, training time had rapidly decreased. With more of the ships being complete, the crews were moving onto them and manning them for real. With the different systems, they could run simulations within their different craft without leaving their slips.

It had allowed them to figure out a number of issues that they had with the ships that weren't present in the Mirror of Communication conference room.

The chain of command had become more firm and they were nearly always on their ships. Jeeves used the system that was inside their bodies to allow them to level up. Doing the same quest again and again was redundant but for getting a higher score on your ship role in a battle or completing different training modules that were also quests, it was possible for them to increase in level.

Being Level 300, they were also at a level to pick different classes. With the bonuses that they got from that, many of them didn't need to sleep for days at a time.

They had come to training as players, they were serious and dedicated to their methods, but their main focus was on mock battles, playing again and again to confirm and improve upon their skills. Afterwards they shared all of the basics as they understood it, and as they talked, they each worked on different things that they had a knack for before coming and sharing it with the rest of the group. Some liked making training modules; others liked figuring out the best mix of classes for stat increases, or speed of advancement. Others developed communications to be simple and easy.

It wasn't like a regular military, where everyone was trained a certain way and came up. It was more community based, all of these people lending their support in order to grow stronger together. It had allowed them to advance rapidly and through constant gaming, they had become a stronger team with each simulation.

Frank exited a portal and moved to a bank of onos, where people were coming out of and moving between. Above them, there were the different names of ships.

Frank entered the *BloodHawk* ono, stepping directly from the asteroid base to inside the ship. He said his good-byes to his friends and moved through the ship. He used two more onos within the ship to reach the command deck.

Moving personnel had never been faster and it allowed the Emerilian fleet to do things that wouldn't be possible on any other craft.

As he entered the bridge, he snapped a salute to the captain, who nodded back to him as he worked on the reports his interface was showing.

"Captain, I was wondering if I might be able to host a shoot with my people?" Frank asked.

"Go for it. Do a sign-up and see if anyone else is interested. I'll be on my reports but Commander Richter might be free," the captain said, talking about his second-in-command.

"I'll ask around." Frank saluted the captain.

"As you were." The captain gave him a salute back.

Frank didn't know how much time was left till things kicked off but he was sure that his weapons people would be as ready as possible and have the best training that he could offer.

***

It had been three days since Dark's and Earth's attack had been stopped and they had been pushed back from Markolm.

Light had not been seen the entire time. Her angels said that she was heavily injured by the Dark Lord and in deep depression after having lost so many people—even Khanundra, a person she considered like a daughter.

Daeundra, who usually had a cold and calculating look on her face, now showed a trace of fear as she looked at Light. The latest doctor burned from the inside out with righteous flames; the golden flames burned through them, healing and killing at the same time, slowly burning their life away inch by inch as their body glowed from the inside.

The doctor finally stopped crying out in pain after a few days, slumping to the floor and dying, their face stuck in a look of relief at having escaped Light's torture.

Light let out a wheezing noise. She wore a golden veil but it was unable to hide the darkness that seemed to be almost alive as it moved underneath her veil across her face.

Daeundra had seen the damage herself. Light's face seemed to have been burned away: her mouth and teeth destroyed while her nose had been melted off; her left eye was gone, as was her hair and ear. The other half of her face was in a look of anger. She had stopped herself from feeling pain with a simple spell, but it was taking a truly massive amount of power to stop the corrosion and fight it back.

"Did you find him?" Light's voice was distorted and hellish, as if some demon had clawed its way up from the abyss as it came from underneath her veil.

"We have not, mistress." Daeundra knelt.

"Find HIM!" Light's voice was filled with hatred and anger as her voice rose in volume. Light flashed around her; golden clouds seemed to appear around her body as Daeundra was pushed lower under the pressure of Light's power.

"Yes, mistress," Daeundra said.

"Leave me and make sure the legions are ready when I call them. And get them to increase their devotions so I might destroy his curse and heal myself," Light said.

"Yes, mistress." Daeundra backed away from Light before she disappeared.

The generals who had died were already replaced. However, Khanundra hadn't; instead, Daeundra had taken over her position, passing on Light's orders to her legions and followers.

Daeundra knew that Light didn't care about Khanundra, but the loss of such a powerful figure who was so completely devout was not a small loss.

Now Daeundra's mission was to find out where the Dark Lord and his forces were.

The legions had killed all of those who were even Dark magic practitioners on Markolm, their anger incensed by Dark's actions.

When they did find the Dark Lord's base and his people, Daeundra knew that Light would not stop unless she, or Dark, were killed.

Chapter 17: An Island Moves

Upon receiving the instructions from his master, Boran-al had stopped with all of his projects and moved to organize the Alturarans. The Dark Champions under his command all started to move from their different locations. All of them knew what was to come next and were eager to see their lord rise in power. As he did, so would they, changing Emerilia into a world that was their master's.

First, the divine wells that were being held in different locations were moved to the base that Dark's champions and the Alturarans who followed him had created. Then the Dark Champions moved to where the corresponding portal on Emerilia was, to make sure that their preparations were all correct and everything was ready. Riding a wave of Alturarans, the last of the divine wells appeared in sight as hundreds of Alturarans of all kinds raced forth.

Darkness shrouded Boran-al, protecting him from the harsh sunlight that baked this world. He walked over what seemed to be empty ground; behind him, the sand started to shake. Alturarans who had been waiting for months shook off the sand that covered them, rising from the ground.

Boran-al reached the portal that stood untouched on top of a pedestal. He stepped into range of it. A screen appeared in his vision:

New discovery

You have found a portal. On the other side, new locations and adventure await. Do you wish to open the portal?
Y/N

"Yes." Boran-al's voice sounded out as all around him the bare ground revealed Alturarans, while hundreds of others came from different directions, ready to obey their Dark Lord's orders.

The portal's different Magical Circuits started to move as Boran-al waited. The other Dark Champions rose from the ground, or appeared from the shadows, or descended from the sky. All of them had been on this planet for months, carrying out their master's bidding. Now it was time that they would start down the road of reaping the rewards.

The portal's Magical Circuits finally stopped moving and power started to surge through them all.

One second, there was nothing and then the next, they were looking into a dark area instead of the endless sands of Alturara.

Boran-al stepped forward. The Dark Champions moved as well, carrying divine wells with them. They entered the portal and exited into a low-light room.

Boran-al took in a deep breath of the damp room, feeling at ease.

Shadows turned into a vortex before dissipating. The Dark Lord stepped out from the black smoke. "You've done well."

Boran-al and all of the champions put down the divine wells and bowed to their master.

"We will destroy these islands of *enlightenment* and *study*. Those who dictated which ways to do your experiments, putting human life above advancement, who hunted many of you down, I will leave them to your care," the Dark Lord said.

"Yes, master," the Dark Champions said.

Glee filled Boran-al in anticipation of the slaughter to come.

Behind them, more and more Alturarans slowly moved through the portal, filling the vast underground area.

***

Alamos frowned as he looked to Jelanos. "Does something feel off?"

"Hmm?" Jelanos looked up from the report he had been looking over.

"Does something feel off?" Alamos repeated.

Jelanos looked out of the windows. "Kind of feels like a storm has come in with the slight rocking we're having, but there's no storm nearby."

Alamos looked to reports from the different sectors of the islands. "Seems that the main island is moving around. The lead technician is saying that it's happening because of increased weight changing the center of gravity for the island." Alamos seemed even more confused.

"Well, how the hell did we gain so much weight?"

"Maybe an experiment?" Alamos said.

"I'll run a scan. Might as well check that it's not something too major." Jelanos moved to a mirror and pressed a few buttons; information appeared on his screen as he activated different things. A detailed scan of the Per'ush islands appeared with it, zooming in on the main island that sat in the middle of them all.

"Doesn't look like there's anything down there to do it," Jelanos said.

"It looks a bit *too* clean down there—there aren't any readings from the power stations that relay through to the Magical Circuits that power the island," Alamos said with a growing sense of apprehension.

"Like that time in the Eda ruins when there was that covert Magical Circuits that hid the treasure room away!" Jelanos said with a solemn expression, adjusting his reading glasses, making him go from looking like a scholarly reader perusing a book to a warrior with scholarly pursuits.

"Send down some war mages to check out what's going on down there. In the meantime, should make sure that people are—"

Alamos's words stopped in his throat as new items started to move out of the irregular and perfectly clean area under the island.

Creatures in the hundreds were plodding through the island and headed toward the surface.

"Alturarans!" Alamos and Jelanos said. They had been to Alturara a number of times and were familiar with the creatures that called the sun-bleached planet home.

Jelanos smashed an alarm near his desk as he and Alamos started to raise the war mages and evacuate the main Per'ush island. Jelanos charged toward the doors of his balcony. A cutting wind sliced them apart with ease as he and Alamos charged into the air, their Mana circulating as frigid expressions covered their faces.

The ground erupted in places as Alturarans, with their gem-like bodies, broke through the surface of the main island.

Alamos shook his sleeves. Dozens of water darts shot through the Alturarans, so fast that the creatures didn't even know that they had died for a few moments before their bodies collapsed.

Jelanos called down lightning that into one of the holes, noises of metal being scraped against one another made even him grimace.

People were screaming as war mages took to the sky.

More and more Alturarans came from the ground in seemingly unending waves.

Alamos, now using a sensing spell, could even see some of them were carving a path to the outside of the island and falling into the water—they weren't creatures that needed air—and started to move toward the shoreline. Alamos started communicating with the Gudalo kingdom as well as the Terra Alliance.

Shadows seemed to shoot out from the holes where the Alturarans were emerging. These shadows formed into people with a cold and powerful aura.

Jelanos and Alamos moved closer to each other. Their Mana moved faster and faster as they recognized the auras of the Dark Lord's champions.

A sickly-looking elf laughed and rose into the air on a pillar of stone and metal. Seeing the man rising to the sky, the others turned into shadows and once again rushed forward.

Jelanos and Alamos were kept rooted to the spot, knowing that the man in front of them was much more powerful than a dozen of the other Dark Champions.

"Ah, Archmage Jelanos, Alamos, thank you for the great gift of your island and college. We will put it to great use in the future," the elf said with a dense smile.

"Boran-al," Jelanos said. Four other Dark Champions also rose behind Boran-al.

"I was beginning to think that you people had forgotten me after all these years," Boran-al said, a mocking smile on his face. "No matter. We'll be happy to educate you on the proper way to address someone of the Dark Lord. Offering your bones up for my experiments!" Boran-al waved his hand; smoke appeared in the sky as the four mages with him shot out curses and Dark Mana bolts.

"Holy ray!" Alamos yelled. A pillar of light descended from above to smash into Boran-al and his lackeys.

Two of the mages were caught unawares, not able to compete with the man who ran the mage's guild. There was not even any time for them to scream.

The other two looked in bad condition but they moved to be on either side of Boran-al to support him as from the smoke, a roar could be heard. A creature stepped out of the smoke, followed by another. Each looked as though it had been formed from the body parts of a dozen other creatures and then somehow given sentience. The pain of being put together seemed to have driven them wild, their eyes filled with rage and pain.

Each was bent over like a dog, with tentacles on their backs and wings on their shoulders. Its tail was a serpent's and its faces were humanoid, but devoid of any possible emotion other than rage and hatred. Their mouths were filled with vicious teeth as dark smoke poured from their bodies.

"That smoke is a kind of poison," Jelanos said.

"Well, then we better do something about it!" Alamos said

The first two controlled creatures moved, their speed alarming as Jelanos and Alamos both cast spells from their hands.

The creatures were hit by the spells. A visible shock wave came from the point of impact between the creatures and the spells. They had been thrown backward, Boran-al's experiment shaking its heads as wings flapped and they moved forward again.

From Boran-al's hands and his bags of holding, he was able to pull out a large winged beast that seemed to have metal gems stabbed into it. Boran-al fed it power; the creature flapped its wings, looking like a velociraptor, as it raced up into the sky and turned, aimed down at Jelanos.

Arrows made from shadows shot forth from its wings. Its power was considerable, making Jelanos have to split his attention between the dog-like creations and the velociraptor.

More creatures started to come from Boran-al's bag. The sky became darker as black clouds rolled in.

War mages from the rest of the islands rushed in to save as many people as possible and try to drive back the Alturarans.

Alturaran worms, as big as the portals and able to reach fifty meters in length, cruised out, eating through the island. Some fell into the ocean below, while others destroyed the different Magical Circuits that kept the island above the ocean, making it tilt. Others ate upward through the basements and research labs inside the island and through those in the city above.

While many of the people from other islands were coming to help, those who had flying abilities moved them back and forth. The war mages started to use their power to throw back the Alturarans, getting into heated conflicts of magic when the Dark Champions started to emerge. They were much stronger than the Alturarans and they loved fighting. To the Alturarans, it was simply a process till they had destroyed all life.

They appeared from shadows, their blades sweeping out and cutting down those in front of them. Others came behind them, laying down incantations, the dead rising once again. Summoners called on beasts from the dark; some pulled the materials from the buildings around them, creating bodies of stone and metal.

Some used a mixture of spells and poison to create massive roiling clouds on the ground that would eat through all that lay in their way. Others simply enhanced their own power with the Mana, their bodies radiating a black miasma as they attacked.

The sky continued to darken as black clouds seemed to come from nowhere and locked upon the Per'ush islands.

"Shut down the teleports and onos on the main island," Jelanos yelled over a party chat, a magical sword in his hands as he tore through another one of the dog-like creations in two, its master already throwing more and more onto the ground.

Alamos rushed past him. In front of him, blades of Air tore through what lay in his path, as two velociraptors chased him. He flickered over and shot lightning from his hands.

"Get the other islands moved away and cut their tethers with the bay floor. We can't let them be boarded by Dark's forces," Alamos said. His lightning hit one of the pursuing creatures. Turning into nothing more than a charred body, another let out a cry, its wing pierced through. It tried to recover but smashed into one of the buildings that they were weaving past, killing it.

"The Terra Alliance has been alerted," Jelanos said, returning to the channel with just him and Alamos.

"All of our overseers and protectors are out and dealing with threats. We've only got a few here. We need to cover the people's retreat back to the other islands. We've got copies of everything here—we'll be fine," Alamos said. It hurt him to leave it all behind but lives couldn't be returned unless one was a player—knowledge could always be regained and developed.

Jelanos let out an enraged cry. Spears of light appeared around him, stabbing into a half dozen creatures and exploding, killing them off as one of the mages on Boran-al's side shot poison snakes from his hands.

Alamos swept his hand out. A stream of fire turned into a small dragon that consumed the snake before it could hit Jelanos, who thrust his sword out, ice shards shooting out from him.

The mage had no time to escape, being hit by a half dozen of them; a look of pain and shock etched their face as they turned into a block of ice.

A creature that seemed to have demon origins was thrown out by Boran-al. It was much larger than normal demons and had soul runes all over it.

"This is one of my latest experiments, using an Alturaran core, the body of a demon, and the blood runes of a Xelur," Boran-al said with excitement.

An Alturaran core was the center of their power; it was like their internal soul gem. They could, however, fill it with energy over time, sapping it from the area around them.

In Alturara, there hadn't been much Mana but the density in Emerilia was much higher.

The mutated demon raised his hands as powerful Mana streams shot toward him. His aura became more and more powerful.

Alamos and Jelanos unleashed attacks at the demon at the same time. One hit the demon in the chest, the other in the face. The hit on its chest left a bloody crater, the hit to its face was much more devastating, parts of its skull showed, covered in thick coagulated blood. It let out a mangled roar as other sections of its body were consumed in order to form another head, replacing rather than repairing the damage. It unleashed a bloody light from its right claw.

Jelanos created a shield, holding his sword up in front of him as the stream of blood-like Mana slammed into the ice shield and shot off in every direction. As it hit the ground and the surrounding buildings, it cut grooves into all it touched.

Alamos, who had been gathering Mana for an attack, rose up from behind Jelanos. From his hands, a red rock shot out. This rock was covered in a magical spell formation. As it rushed forward, the Fire Mana in the air shot toward the rock that seemed to be sentient as it raced through the air, carving out its own path. A powerful and terrifying aura came from it, making Boran-al raise his eyebrow in interest.

The red rock turned into a miniature sun, the spell formation around it becoming more vibrant and powerful. The air around it became hazy with the energy that was pulled into it. The mutated demon, sensing something was wrong, started to cut off its attack against Jelanos when the rock sped up.

A cracking sound could be heard as the rock shot forward and slammed into the mutated demon. It hit with such kinetic force, the rock was implanted into its chest.

Boran-al's eyebrows rose higher before his lips pressed into a cold expression that promised blood.

The red rock exploded and shot outward. Every building within forty meters was leveled. Alamos let out a cry, creating a shield that contained the blast and directing it back in so that it wouldn't get those who were trying to escape the island.

Everything inside was turned into a wasteland as the shield was struck by the debris of all the once valiant and proud towers of the island. These buildings had been here for hundreds of years and had seen the passing of countless generations of mages and types of heroes and legends. They displayed the Per'ush islands, legacy the proud and upright mage's college and mage's guild who's influence spread across Emerilia.

Boran-al threw his hand forward. Thick streams of Dark and Earth Mana lanced through the mutated demon, increasing the speed at which it regenerated and pushing out the red rock's secondary spell effects that burned through the mutated demon.

The dust cleared under the swirling maelstrom of Mana in the air, showing the mutated demon in rough shape and its chest open, revealing the Alturaran core fully.

With a grunt, Boran-al's Mana expelled the spells that had been laid upon the red stone.

"Flames of Mana!" Jelanos yelled out. The powerful spell needed a chant in such a short time period. Red flames seemed to shoot out in a bolt at Boran-al's Mana.

Alamos continued to contain the destruction as Jelanos shot out what looked like three feeble flames that looked as if they would go out at the faintest breeze. These flames landed on the stream of Mana that connected Boran-al to his mutated demon as well as the mutated demon.

The demon cried out as the flames, upon hitting its blood runes and Alturaran core, lit up with a brilliant light.

These flames might have been familiar to some people. These were flames that burned Mana! They took a lot of power from a mage to create them, as they were basically reversing the flow of the laws of Mana in their bodies.

However, as it struck the thread of Mana that Boran-al was connected to the mutated demon with, it was like a line of gunpowder. It raced up that pure stream faster than Boran-al could react, racing into his body.

Boran-al seemed to be brighter; light came from within his body as the Mana burned angrily. He spat out some blood that evaporated in the air, as if it were too hot.

Boran-al poured power into his body, manipulating it so that he could stop the flames that were raging through his body. He did it, but it took a lot of Mana in order to put out the flames coursing through the Mana that made up his body.

The mutated demon howled as its body came apart, burning from the inside.

Jelanos was panting from the use of his Mana pool. Alamos finally let his shield go; the area that it had covered was now nothing more than a wasteland.

Boran-al coldly cut his connection to the beast as he waved his hand in a grand manner. From his hands, smoke boiled forth to reveal mutated beasts that floated in the air on wings or dropped to the ground. They were as varied as they were terrifying. All of them looked to Alamos and Jelanos with hungry eyes.

"We've got everyone off the main island," one of the elders said to Alamos and Jelanos through a private chat.

"All war mages are to stay on the headquarters' island and keep the Alturarans and the Dark mages at bay. If they're on the headquarters' island, they might be on the others—make sure that they're rooted out and dealt with," Alamos said.

"As soon as the last of the people from headquarters' island are moved, move toward Verlun. Once far enough away, destroy the island. Have those skilled in Water magics in the water watching where the Alturarans are going. We're going to need to find out what they're doing in order to beat them back," Jelanos said.

As his words fell, the different islands started to rotate and move away from where they had rested for hundreds of years, moving around the central island and floating over the waves toward Verlun.

"The Terra Alliance is moving forces to Verlun and readying a defense there," another elder reported.

"Good." Jelanos stepped into the air. Wind appeared under his feet as Boran-al's mutated beasts rushed outward.

Alamos rushed into the sky as well. Now that they knew that there was no one but combatants on the island, they could unleash their full power.

Jelanos unleashed an Air blade ten meters long that cut through anything in its path—cutting apart buildings and leaving a three-meter-deep line in the ground.

Alamos shot out a blue fireball that melted everything in its path.

The other mages were killed in the Mana shock waves of the attack, while half of Boran-al's creatures were killed. However, more came from the seemingly endless bag of holding.

War mages across the island were battling the Dark Champions and the Alturarans. The light and immense explosions of their battles could be seen and heard everywhere on the headquarters' island. The port cities of Gudalo could only watch the display the noises of destruction hitting them like waves, stirring up the very sea itself.

The mages' eyes were as red as those of the bloodthirsty people and creatures' they were facing. This was the center of their mage's college. Countless generations of mages had come from this island and today, it had been broken apart by the Dark Lord's minions. Their homes had been disturbed and people they had known were dead in the streets.

They tore apart their own headquarters' island to kill off those who had inflicted such a heavy wound into the weakness of the mage's college and guild.

In the sky, a blue and red light flashed into existence as a powerful aura rushed over the headquarters' island.

Jelanos and Alamos didn't need to look up; they knew those two powerful auras.

The red light appeared in the heavens with the blue light beside it.

Red Mana circled the descending woman in the sky, creating an armor made of glowing red plates. She flicked her hand to the side. A staff that seemed to be carved from red crystal appeared in her hand. "You attack *my* island!" Fire's voice resounded over the island as she pointed her staff downward. The black clouds above Emerilia boiled and burned, illuminating with red light before what looked like meteors rained down from the heavens, cutting through the conjured dark clouds. These meteor-like objects raced downward, the entire area burning with heat.

The seas, that had been disturbed by the fighting on the headquarters' island and the Alturarans that were below, now turned into a raging monsoon.

An elderly looking man at the center of the blue dove toward the seas. From the water, a trident made of blue crystals appeared. It shot into his hands, his face filled with fury as he shot into the waters under what had been the bay that the Per'ush islands floated above.

The waters boiled and shook with the violent attacks that Water led against the Alturarans and Dark Champions that were along the bay's bottom.

Fire's meteors landed, making the entire headquarters shake as craters appeared all across it and more sections broke off and dropped into the waters below. The meteors hit the different holes that the Alturarans were coming out of, burning everything in them and exploding as they hit the curving walls of the tunnels, making great sections of the island collapse, killing the Alturarans within.

Jelanos and Alamos fought onward, their fighting spirit stronger than ever before. Their attacks cleaved through Boran-al's creatures as fast as he could bring them out. Jelanos landed on the ground, running so fast that he was a blur. His sword rushed out; icicles hit Alturarans, their bodies freezing and then shattering as he passed.

Alamos soared through the sky. Spears and bolts flew from his hands, coloring the sky as the archmages of the mage's college and guild gave a terrifying display of their might.

The clouds above the island started to become thicker and more powerful, congealing into the shape of a massive man looking over the headquarters' island.

"Fire, it is good to see you, dear sister," Dark said sweetly. His form, created of the black clouds, swiped out its hands. Rays of darkness shot toward Fire.

A massive shield appeared, covered in runes as the hits were burned away.

"All mages move to the rest of the Per'ush islands!" Fire yelled as lances of Fire appeared all around her. They shot forward; gaps appeared in her shield to allow them through before they closed again. The spears created powerful explosions that shook the island below as they hit the Dark Lord's forces.

Jelanos and Alamos looked to Boran-al; he was weaker than ever, but Fire had spoken. They moved their hands into a complex configuration to create a vortex of Fire and Air. The two elements reinforced each other, making the attack many times more power-ful.

Boran-al's creatures moved to block the attack with their bod-ies.

Jelanos and Alamos took out flying artifacts, rushing away as they gathered up those who were wounded or wouldn't be able to make it to the other islands by themselves. They collected more and more war mages with them, creating a fast-moving and powerful unit.

Everyone downed Mana potions to recover their Strength as they collected up the last of their people, smashing back the forces under Dark's command.

"That's it!" Alamos said. His platform turned away from the Per'ush mage's college headquarters' island. In the sky above, flames and darkness clashed. Two true gods of Emerilia shook the heavens as the seas below them roiled with Water's actions as he cut through the Alturarans marching toward Gudalo.

They shot away on their flying platforms, escaping Dark's clouds. None of them spoke as they looked at the headquarters' island. Alturarans poured out from the holes on the island, tearing it apart before crashing into the surging sea below.

A storm of Mana was whipped up into the sky, tearing at the air itself as it rotated underneath Fire's feet, within her control.

The world seemed to become silent as Dark's attacks came from the sky and the headquarters' island started to slip into the water below. "I'll be coming for the rest of your mages soon enough." Dark's voice carried across the water with a gloating tone.

"You can try, but unlike your people, they know how to create something incredible instead of just try to destroy and twist things down unnatural paths. Seems you don't need this elemental clone." Fire raised up her hand. A multicolored flame burned in the Mana that was all around her that she had pulled from the different artifacts and soul gems that were on the island.

The flames raced through the Mana, instantly refining, changing the various powers into a red Affinity Mana. Fire's power surged as in an instant the Mana under her feet spread out into a sheet, a land of flames, that faced the black clouds above.

She raised her staff up, as the land of flames shot upward into the sky. The darkness of the clouds and the hungry flames of the land that Fire had created colored the sky.

"What is this?" Dark demanded.

"Too weak," Fire snorted. Their voices were so powerful as to reach the mages as they fled.

The flames burned away all of the attacks Dark shot at it. He unleashed more and more attacks. They were all burned away as the flames, illuminating the sky above, made the mages look in shock. They had all seen incredible things in their lives but the level of the spells that were displayed were not something that they could compare to.

The fire burned through the black miasma that was released by the clouds. The black clouds started to move faster and faster, as if angered by the oncoming flames. The flames' power surged as they clashed with the clouds.

The sky was shrouded into darkness and light, as powers beyond the understanding of mere mortals fought.

The black clouds became less substantial, bit by bit, and started to get burned away. The power of the clouds finally reached its limit. The clouds broke apart into different sections. Dark's clone body made from the Dark energies of the summoned clouds dissipated with an angered yell. As his body disappeared, the strength of the clouds only weakened faster as the fires burned through anything that had remained in the sky.

Finished with clearing the sky, Fire waved her hands. The sheet of flame fell apart. Different flames burned up the remaining Mana as they fell toward the water below. The water sizzled and let off steam as the still-burning Mana continued to fall. Some of it reached the bottom of the bay floor and melted through the ground below.

In the distance, the Per'ush islands were now all passing over the shores of Gudalo, moving to Verlun.

***

Daeundra had rarely visited the Lady of Light, only coming when summoned. However, she had been spending the rest of her time looking for the Dark Lord. It was only a few moments ago that she had found out about the events happening within the Per'ush islands.

"Mistress, Dark has appeared in the Per'ush islands—" Daeundra was cut off by Light.

"Prepare our forces." Power fluctuated wildly around Light.

"Yes, mistress," Daeundra said, not daring to say anything that might turn Light's ire onto her.

"Dark, soon I will destroy your very bones, so there is nothing left of you in this world." Light held a hand up and curled it into a fist. Her power surged.

Cold sweat rolled down Daeundra's back. Daeundra took her leave, rushing to tell the angel generals. She passed on the commands. They were about to go see to their people when a surge of powerful Light Mana rushed out across Markolm.

This Light Mana was power from Light's own divine wells. The Mana sunk deep into the ground, as if searching out something.

Daeundra had a look of shock on her face as all of Markolm started to shake. Her eyes were wide as she looked at Light's hall.

It was said that the Per'ush islands had been based off the floating island that Light had commanded in history. That island had been Markolm. Once again, the runes that covered Markolm flashed with power as the entire large island started to shake.

The seas around it shook as the island started to rise into the air. Waves were thrown about as the island rose. Its algae-covered underside was revealed as water fell off the rocks that made up the island.

Markolm was rising from the seas once again!

It was undeniably powerful and fear-inducing.

The calm seas started to rush into the area where the Markolm continent had been. Great big waves crashed together in the center and created a pillar of water fountaining upward, barely touching the bottom of the Markolm floating island.

The island came to a stop in the air. Its underside looked much like a boat that had been at sea for a long time might, covered in all kinds of creatures, algae, and grime.

However, under this there were powerful runes that glowed with a golden light, pushing the entire island into the air. The island shot toward the west on a straight line, aimed at where the Per'ush islands had been.

***

Josh lurched awake as different alarms rang through his head, as messages and alerts came in.

Cassie, who had been sleeping beside him, opened her eyes and looked around the room with a fierce look, a blade in her hand.

"Dark has attacked the Per'ush islands and Light is moving Markolm," Josh said, looking through the information as it came through his interface.

"What?" Cassie yelled in a shocked voice.

"Markolm seems to be a floating island." Josh hotkeyed his armor. Black clothes with runic lines covered his body. Power seemed to roll off him as his hand rested on his sword; the other moved over his interface.

Cassie put away her sword and activated her own armor. Large gray plates appeared over her body, making her look like a tank. Her head was free from it all; she quickly adjusted her hair so it wouldn't get caught in the armor and moved her weapons around to make sure she could use them in a moment's notice.

Even with her large armor, Cassie was a quick and deadly opponent. She was fine with taking a few hits in order to finish off her enemies. It made her a strange strength and agility build: strong enough to hold her armor easily, but fast and agile enough to hit the deadly points of her enemies before they knew what was happening.

She'd ditched the golden armor she'd had before when she'd joined the Stone Raiders, using different armor types in order to boost her stats instead of looking good.

"Command?" Cassie asked.

"Yeah." Josh put the interface away.

They walked from the bed toward the door. Josh looped his hand into her sword belt and turned her around. She looked at him with a confused look as he kissed her and patted her armored butt.

Her eyes fluttered with the passionate kiss, surprised by it, as Josh separated himself from her and walked through the door. He looked at his hand. "Would've been nicer without armor in the way." Josh sighed.

"Horny old goat," Cassie said, a slight flush to her face as she got over her shock and followed Josh.

"Neither a goat, nor old." Josh left the room.

Cassie shook her head behind him even as the corners of her mouth lifted into a smile. Their little moment was pushed to the back of their minds as they made it to the command center.

The doors opened to a packed room, with people from all over Emerilia as well as different leaders seated or moving between different consoles and areas in the circular room.

Lucy was already there in the center.

"Dwayne, Kim, and Esa are mobilizing the forces of the Terra Alliance. The flying citadels are ready to move. We've got reports of the Alturarans moving straight through the bay toward Gudalo. They look to be aiming for the coast near the city of Myrar." Lucy pressed a button for the main screen within the command room. A map of Emerilia appeared, a straight line from Markolm to Per'ush highlighted. "To me, it looks like Light and Dark are moving to have their last battle. The Alturarans would normally just spread out in every direction. However, they're just going straight, not making any diversion. Markolm is also moving straight toward where the Per'ush islands were."

Josh took in a cold breath as he looked at the map. "Get our forces moved to Heval as well as the coast of Gudalo. If the Alturarans don't change their direction for three hours, I want Myrar, Asamal, Holmslatr and everyone between those cities evacuated. I want to know, if they continue at their current pace, where will Markolm and Dark's forces meet? All coastal villages and cities are to prepare for a large tsunami. I want people watching out for that and ready to evacuate as needed. Also, all cities in the flight path of Markolm to Per'ush should be ready to evacuate. If that thing comes down, or Light wants to kill them off, it would only be too easy.

"Gather our forces in Terra. We don't know where the battle will take place but we need to be ready for it. The flying citadels are to move to Heval." Josh looked to the two women and one man who represented the mage's college, guild and their overseers. "Let us know what we can do to assist Per'ush."

"Thank you for your support. We have many wounded who are already being moved to Terra. Otherwise, the islands are moving around Verlun and stabilizing in order to use their teleport pads," the woman from the mage's college said.

"Good. I want everyone and everything ready for what's to come." Josh's words were for those connected to the Per'ush islands, as it was for the different leaders and commanders in the room with him.

It looked as if there was no way to stop the clash of Light and Dark; "What is our plan to deal with the Dark Lord and Lady of Light?" someone asked.

"We need to cut off that portal first. Stop Dark from bringing in the Alturarans. That will not be an easy task. We—"

"The Alturarans have stopped moving!" Lucy called out, interrupting Josh. An image showed Alturarans massing along the bottom of the bay. Being inorganic, they didn't need air to survive.

The forward units had stopped; others came around them, creating precise formations. The larger tank Alturarans moved into lines across the front, with regulars in box-like formations behind them. Behind the normals were formations of ranged Alturarans. Between the box formations of ranged and normals, the massive worms were in the lead, followed by groups of mutated Alturarans and followed up by another worm.

As more and more of them moved forward, the rough shape of the Alturaran army filled up.

"Shard, how many Alturarans are in that formation?" Josh looked at the three normals and ranged box formations broken up by groups of mutated Alturarans and their worms.

"Fifty thousand two hundred and four," Shard reported from above.

Josh and the others in the room were filled with even more questions than they'd had just a few minutes ago.

"For now, we will ready our forces and watch. If we're to put our people into the middle of that, then we'll only take a loss. We will give land now and ensure the safety of Emerilians. Then, when we see an opportunity, we'll wipe out Light and Dark's forces," Josh said.

The others in the room agreed. Things were changing too fast for them to come up with a complete plan for now. All they could do was watch and hope the fallout wasn't as bad as they feared.

Chapter 18: Destruction of War

Induca had a dark expression on her face as she walked through Terra. Ever since the Dark Lord had opened up a portal within the headquarters' island of the mage's college and mage's guild, Terra seemed to have become a darker place.

Construction was advancing faster than ever. People were giving their time so that Terra could take on the increasing flow of refugees coming from the towns and cities that lay between where Markolm had rested in the sea and the old location of the Per'ush islands.

Once the Alturarans formed up their fifty thousand strong formations, they had continued marching forward. As they continued, another formation started to be formed.

The first formation marched out of the bay and across the land. They sent their worms forward, creating a ramp out of the cliffs around the bay.

The Alturarans made it onto land. All around them, life withered, the energy being sucked up by the Alturarans who marched through Gudalo and toward Myrar.

The city had been evacuated. Now there were only Aleph scout automatons in the areas watching the Alturarans.

This morning, they had made it to the city. The Alturarans sucked the life out of anything in the area and walked through the city as if there were nothing in their path, leaving nothing but a trampled and destroyed mess in their wake. Their path led them toward Asamal.

Seeing the result of Myrar, those who had been reluctant at first were all now looking to escape the path of the Alturarans.

A second formation had been formed up and was moving to follow the first.

With the Markolm continent going into the sky, the movement had caused the seas to surge and become chaotic. The coastal villages and towns were also moving their people farther inland and to other places that they might be able to escape destruction.

There simply wasn't enough room in the Emerilia cities for all of these people.

The proud people of the Per'ush islands seemed to have been humbled with all the help they had received and had accepted thousands of people onto their islands.

Many highly ranked mages, researchers and their families had disappeared from the islands to other places.

Other places as in other planets, Induca thought. A number of people who had been offered a place within the Initiative were now taking up the offers, wanting to find somewhere safe for them and their families.

Ice City was now larger than Terra and growing with every day. The asteroid base was largely complete. The main thoroughfare had finally been completed and three-quarters of its slips were filled with the ships that would make up twelve complete fleets.

It would take a long time for them to be completed, but with every day there were more people being woken up and joining the Initiative. There was more material being refined, more factories being built and more shipments from Sato's people.

Their expansion had taken off in a big way, with everyone giving their all to increase the speed of production and the quality of the different items they were crafting.

Dave, Suzy, Malsour, Jung Lee, and Steve had been working constantly over the last couple of days with the Initiative. Deia was spending time with Koi. Gurren and Lox were training groups on using the Devastator armor and working with the different fighting forces that had been handed to them, to adapt them over to the new ways they would need to fight.

Induca spent her time training, working with the Terra Alliance and her family. The dragons had been needed to act multiple times to try to calm the raging seas that threatened people or to push back creatures from the event of Myths and Legends that were still attacking the Emerilian cities.

Interfaces popped up over Terra as the lumbering Markolm was revealed, headed in toward Heval. The massive island covered the sky, as it passed just a few kilometers above Heval. The island had a gravity to it that pulled people's attention and made them stare at it in awe. Golden flickers could be seen descending from Markolm, headed out toward the lands below.

A chill ran through Induca as Light's legion headed toward the nearby population centers. Alerts started to appear in her vision. Power could be heard pumping through Terra as teleport pads were opened, connecting Terra with the different cities around where Markolm was passing over Heval.

The different interfaces zoomed in on the angels. Between them there were people wearing robes that had runes of golden light running down them. There was a zealous look in their eyes and an inborn arrogance.

War drums sounded out, their muffled thunder joined by trumpets, rallying cries and horns.

Even the haughty Angels paused, a look of confusion flashing through their eyes.

Weren't these people supposed to be weak, lambs to slaughter.

However instead of finding them fleeing, the people of Alliance were moving together, rising together like some terrible ancient beast telling all that this was *their* land and those that tried to take it from them must be prepared to die.

Induca opened her interface and linked to the feed that was coming in as she rushed toward the teleport pads.

A new feed came in showing Ares, a port city that was part of the Selhi nation. There weren't many people left in the city; most had been driven inland to escape the destruction brought with Markolm rising into the sky.

A group of fifty angels and a platform with glowing runes came over the city.

"Follow the path of the true goddess and find joy and peace in your hearts!" one of the people on the platform proclaimed as they floated above the city.

Induca's eyes thinned. These were priests of Light. Their job was to protect the faithful and "convert" those who needed to be guided down the path of Light.

She knew of the bloody history of Light. When her legions had rushed forward on their holy conquest, their priests had been placed in every population center that they passed. They would reward those who believed in the Lady of Light and they would turn the children and those who were weak-willed into fanatics for the order, raising mortal armies and more priests to carry on the teachings of the Lady of Light and wipe out the unbelievers and those who weren't part of the faith.

From these priests, the angels would be given their orders, sweeping through the towns and killing those who didn't believe or torturing those who were not seeking conversion.

In the meantime, those who actually believed in the Lady of Light or those who were too scared to do anything else would be giving their devotions to the Lady of Light and placed under the power of the priests.

People on the ground told them to leave, angry at having lost their homes and more than a few of their friends and family being killed in the massive water surges.

The priests sneered at those below. "To the faithless, the only option is death; to remove the poison that plagues Emerilia!" The priest shook his sleeves with a snort.

The angels shot forward, spells in their hands that they fired at the people on the ground.

In the past, they had been much weaker than the angels. However, after generations, the people of Emerilia had become stronger. With the aid of the Mirror of Communication school, they had been able to develop skills that weren't possible before. With the threats that seemed to be all around them in recent months, nearly all people on Emerilia had taken up training with at least one kind of offensive or defensive skill.

When the angels attacked, an uncaring look on their faces, the Emerilians didn't take it. They unleashed their own spells and defensive measures. The ono in the center of the town glowed as a Mana barrier snapped into existence around the town.

The angel's attacks hit the Mana barrier, fading into nothing, while the ranged attacks of the Emerilians, nearly a thousand different attacks, rushed to meet the angels.

They shrugged off the hits, but their Mana barriers shook from the impacts.

The priest and angels had a shocked expression on their faces as, from the ono, a portal came to life.

Ranks and ranks of archers and mages marched outward and unleashed attacks into the sky. They were much stronger than the people in the town and the cold look in the angels' faces now turned to one of shock as they were now having to actually put effort into defending.

Those on the ground weren't the same level as them but their training and skills were higher, as well as their numbers.

"Pull back to Terra!" a commander of the Terra Alliance forces yelled to the people in the town.

People who had been in the process of gathering up their belongings once again started packing up. Carts started to move and automated carts rushed out from the portal to assist those who were leaving.

The Terra Alliance forces made the angels and the priests move back to a safe distance, only able to watch the people who were quickly and calmly packing up their belongings—leaving nothing behind—and preparing to leave through the ono.

Induca changed the view through her interface, seeing that all of the different cities and towns were fighting the angels, some people were fighting one another—the believers against those who wanted to escape.

The Terra Alliance forces that had been on standby quickly moved in, killing those who were attacking their fellow citizens and pushing the angels and their priests into the sky where they could do nothing but yell out at the people below and give them cold looks.

The Mana barrier easily defended against their attacks and when they tried to charge inward, it turned into a shield. Three angels died by face ramming the shields already. Afterward, word seemed to have passed through the units and they stopped charging the barrier.

Induca made it to a teleport pad where forces were already moving through. There were a lot more people going through this portal than others.

On the other side of the teleport pad, tens of people were coming through, shocked looks on their faces. Automatons blared out instructions of where to go. Shard, who ran the administration duties of Terra, was already organizing them.

Induca passed through the teleport pad's event horizon, a wry smile on her face as wings grew from her back and scales appeared on her body. She shot off into the sky, headed for the main castle that she had personally visited once in the past.

"I didn't think that I would be back in Selhi Capital ever again," she said to herself, looking over the city that they had been chased out of so long ago.

Now they were rushing to its aid.

She flapped her wings as she came in to land near the castle.

A few people were on the ramparts already; a number of them wore similar cloaks and leather clothing as hers. She nodded to these people. They were all part of her family. They were on the walls of the castle as it was the highest point in Selhi Capital.

She stepped off the ramparts, gliding to the ground and toward the castle that was behind the massive walls. She reached the front of the castle and was allowed in immediately. The guards all had sweat on their faces, not from the forces that were coming to fight them but rather feeling the aura given off by the people wearing the Stone Raiders symbol on their arm as they thought about how they'd chased them from this very city.

Induca flashed a bit of her aura, making them seize up in fear as she walked by. She smiled a bit to herself as she walked through and into the inner areas. Using her own sensing spells, she quickly found her mother, Denur, who was walking through the castle.

"Mom!" Induca yelled, jogging to catch up with her.

"Hello, little Induca," Denur said with a smile, moving as soon as Induca caught up.

"What's the plan?" Induca asked.

"We defend the city, assist any of the other locations if we can and get these people out of here. Ahead of Markolm's progress, other cities are being evacuated. Well, all of them except the dwarven mountains. One of the priests and their angel group showed up and before they could even talk, the dwarves used a spell that killed them all," Denur said, a happy smile on her face.

"I guess it really drives home the whole lesson you gave us about fighting dwarves," Induca said.

"I forgot about that one! If you're in a fight with a dwarf, make sure that it's not somewhere they've been for long and never, ever offend a dwarven mountain or attack it." Denur sighed as she thought of the lessons she had passed down to her children.

"Where are we going to put all of these people?" Induca asked.

Denur opened a private chat with Induca before she said anything. "Ice City. We don't have the room for them here or in any of the other places on Emerilia. Actually, the offer is being put out to a great number of people in Emerilia. Not the specifics but the leaders of the Alliance all know what's really going on and they're getting behind it. The Alliance has wanted to move people off Emerilia to the different bases run by the Initiative for a while now. They've been trying to figure out the best way for it. Now we've got the confusion to hide the mass emigration and with them, even if our plans fail, they'll be able to gain strength and fight against the Jukal Empire by themselves."

"Isn't this all a bit too soon?" Induca asked.

"It's the best option that we have right now."

"Just feels like everything is starting to come together but much faster and sooner than I thought." Induca shook her head.

"That's the way of the world—plan and prepare as much as possible, but in the end, all of that work will be used up all in an instant," Denur said as they walked back out of the castle. Wings grew from their backs once again as they flew up to the walls.

***

Josh sat in the leadership chair of the Alliance in the command center. Every day Light's Markolm floated over Heval, more and more of her priests and the angels worked to conquer the cities. However, the onos that had been placed in every town and city across Emerilia had magical coding that Dave and Malsour had installed, with Steve coding it.

This extra coding allowed them to make a Mana barrier around the cities and towns, stopping the powerful angel attacks, while the Terra Alliance forces could help move the people out and attack the angels who came into range.

They weren't able to kill off that many angels, but they had got a few. More importantly, they were able to evacuate the people of these cities.

The same was happening in Gudalo, leading to a massive influx of nearly half a million people.

Josh was funneling them into the Pandora's Box lab through a teleport pad and then they passed through the portals to Ice City.

Josh was tense, worrying about people finding out about the Initiative and scared that he would miss people. Already he'd seen some of the groups outside of the cities being hauled up to Markolm.

He wanted to send people to rescue them but he knew that it would be just sending them to their deaths. Markolm had been sealed off before; now, with Light using her full power and growing stronger every day and her angels now all champions, they were not a force that could be easily defeated.

Finally, in the sky above Selhi Capital, two of the angel legions appeared, looking down upon the city.

On the walls, people of the Terra Alliance looked up at them defiantly. The people of the city were pale-faced and rushed about to try to get their belongings and leave.

Josh looked to the castle that stood above the city. Upon it, there were a number of mages wearing all manner of clothing. Their bodies emitted a powerful energy that distorted the air around them as they rotated their Mana.

Interspaced around those walls, there were people all wearing a similar set of clothes and had appearances of those who were within the same family.

The priests once again extended a generous offer but to those below it was nothing but a bloody order.

With the people in the city not responding in agreement, the priests once again sent the angels forward. They rushed toward the city, unleashing their attacks that fell upon the Mana barriers of the city, making them shake with the powerful impacts.

The people on the walls were all ranged fighters. From them, dozens of multicolored lights and spells shot up into the air.

The people who presided over the castle now jumped off the castle walls. Their bodies rapidly expanded in size, becoming dragons who moved within the Mana barrier protecting the city and unleashed their attacks into the heavens.

The mages who remained on the walls brought down spells that shook the heavens and made the earth tremble.

The angels had dove forward to attack the city; in their zealous ways, they hadn't left room for them to dodge.

All of those below focused their spells in one area. The angels were strong, some of the strongest creatures on Emerilia, but under the sheer weight of the attacks, a quarter of their fighting force was burned away. More continued to fall from the sky as the ground forces shot upward into the heavens.

The angels' powerful and terrifying attack had now turned into a rout as they tried to move to get away from the focused attacks.

The Terra Alliance and the people of Selhi weren't willing to give them that time as they kept up their attacks.

The angels shot backward up into the sky as a pillar of light descended from the sky, Light herself using power to smash the Mana barrier of Selhi Capital. It hit another shield that was below, the shield created by the ono within the city. It stopped Light's attack, looking untouched even as Light poured more and more power down upon it.

Wind picked up as a girlish figure appeared above Selhi Capital. "The people of Emerilia are not part of your fight," the woman in the sky yelled out. Winds from around the area howled, creating blades that sliced through Light's pillar.

"You dare, Air!" Light's voice covered the sky, making many people cringe at the volume. The priests who were higher up held their heads in pain.

"I don't care what you and Dark do to each other, but if you try to take more people of Emerilia against their will, I'll play with you," Air said.

An enraged noise came from above. Markolm had not stopped its advance; the angels and priests turned and shot upward toward Markolm a few minutes later.

White wind surrounded Air, covering her before she disappeared.

Josh let out a breath of relief, hoping that Light would think twice about threatening the people of Emerilia. However, he didn't pass orders to slow down the evacuation of the cities that lay in her path but rather increased the speed at which they would be carried out.

As that had calmed down, the other screens that showed the Dark Lord's forces as they advanced across Emerilia were deceptively calm.

"With every step they take, they drain more Mana from Emerilia and give it back to the Dark Lord," Josh muttered.

"He's going to be a pain in the ass to deal with," Koza said, sitting nearby.

"That he will be, and he's forcing us to pull people out of the cities in his path as much as Light is," Josh said.

"We've seen what they do to the life they casually pass. If anything is within their range, they'll use all their power to kill it as they advance. I don't think that there are many people who could face them," Koza said in a serious tone.

"I just hate how it feels like we're turtling up in our different bases, watching all of this going on. Unable to do a thing." Lines appeared on his forehead as his eyebrows pinched together.

"Rushing in will only result in more casualties. It might feel wrong watching all of this, but we're doing everything we can. Also, we can clearly see that the onos in place are much stronger than we hoped," Cassie said, trying to allay some of his fear and the tension he felt.

"Even the Dark Lord is making his people move around them in the cities that the Alturarans have marched through. They weren't able to defeat them even with a good portion of their strength," Alamos said. He and Jelanos had added themselves to the Terra Alliance table, representing the mages and their families.

"I hope that the Jukal just don't start popping off everything because they get nervous or see something we don't want revealed in time." Josh had a calm expression on his face but his back was covered in sweat and he was slightly pale.

As the days went by, the towns and cities that were between the Dark Lord's and Light's forces were cleared.

Light sent down people here and there, draining power as they could and pulling up different artifacts that they had found. However, they no longer attacked the cities they passed.

Markolm moved much slower than the Alturarans; however, it was also massive so even moving a small bit would cover a large area. Already it seemed as if it were taking over the southeastern area of Heval controlled by the Selhi kingdom.

Nearly everyone in the kingdom had been moved from their homes.

The dwarven mountains Zolu and Donsk had taken in a great number of people and sealed their mountains. They watched Markolm as it moved past. Under strict orders not to engage, they hunkered down and watched as Markolm flew by.

Myrar, Asamal, and Holmslatr were cities in names only now. They had been crushed under the Alturaran formations that marched across Gudalo, leaving a lifeless line in their wake as they moved over the harbors and jetties of Holmslatr and dropped into the channel between Heval and Gudalo, once again walking through the water toward Heval.

They didn't need food, nor air, nor rest or sleep. They simply continued on, moving in their perfect formations without complaint or care. They rose from the channel south of the once vibrant trading city of Moko.

The Alturarans fired at it and the Dark Champions went through the cities, looting anything of value as they had done with the past cities that they'd destroyed.

Markolm covered Selhi as well as sections from the Southern Grasslands and the Medlari Empire. All of these cities had been evacuated, taking millions from the surrounding.

Markolm stopped its forward progress and halted in the air, declaring that where it stood Light and Dark would finally have the battle that had been spoken of for hundreds of years.

Meanwhile, the flying citadels, which were a lot faster than Markolm, had made it to Heval and were around Zolari. Carts with soul gems moved to replenish their power stores as they created two arrow-like formations of eight citadels, facing toward the south.

Chapter 19: Looking on From the Sidelines

Dave and Deia were curled up on the couch, watching their interface. Koi had been put to sleep; however, the two of them wouldn't be able to sleep if they tried.

On one side, ranks after ranks of Alturarans marched forward, with Dark Champions moving around their formations.

On the other side, the dominating Markolm overlooked the sky.

The Alturaran forward formation had come to a stop. Three more formations moved up, arranging themselves next to one another as they faced Markolm.

In the distance, dust was thrown up by the Alturarans still advancing. They were in an area between Moko and the swamplands to the south.

Shadows and smoke seemed to come together into a thick pillar that rapidly expanded. The smoke contracted into a massive black figure easily one hundred meters tall—the Dark Lord.

The distance between the edge of Markolm and where the Alturaran line had stopped was no short distance but from Markolm, light came together congealing into the Lady of Light. She was the same size as Dark, a dominating presence in the sky.

"So kind for you to greet me," Dark said, his voice amused.

"Too scared to fight that you'd rather trade words?" Light's tone was biting as her face was hidden underneath a veil.

"Not at all. I thought I would gift to you a few more minutes of life. Seems it has come to an end." A light shone from Dark's eyes as he raised his hand.

The clouds above Markolm shook and roiled. Smoke and shadows formed into clouds that looked similar to the ones that had formed over the headquarters' island. However, these ones were tens of times more powerful.

Light snorted and raised her hand. "Cheap tricks to augment your people and improve their strength," Light said with disdain. Light shot from the heavens down upon the clouds.

Her disdain turned to shock.

"Something wrong, dear sister?" Dark's tone was sickly sweet.

Light's expression changed into one of rage, as if she only wished to tear him apart at that very moment. However, she could only throw up her other hand as light shot from Markolm, attacking the clouds both above and below. It had little effect.

"Ah, little sister, seems that you're not as mighty as you think." Dark lowered his hand slowly. The clouds grew stronger faster; the Mana in the air became thick and chaotic as all those with a Dark Affinity gained a bonus while those with a Light Affinity were weakened.

From the clouds, abyss lightning that seemed to suck in all light and destroy it raged downward. Streams and streams of it shot down. The air above Markolm vibrated as the golden Mana barrier shook and trembled, light streams fighting against these lightning streams.

"Go." Dark waved his sleeve forward. Massive wormholes appeared in front of the Alturarans.

They marched forward as more wormholes appeared above Markolm. They dropped from the sky, falling hundreds of meters, as they weren't attacks and their velocity was slow. They passed through the Mana barrier before smashing into Markolm.

From the craters, the Alturarans regained their feet, letting out war cries that sounded like glass shards being rubbed against a plate.

The worms dove into Markolm. The Alturaran normals rushed out in every direction while some units formed together under the mutated Alturarans' command as they headed for the population centers of Markolm.

Angels raced into the sky, hunting down the Alturarans. They easily killed the normals with simply a swipe of their hands. The tanks took a bit longer while the worms hid in the ground, making them impossible to follow unless they wanted to be.

The mutated Alturarans were the best fighters, retaining some kind of knowledge or higher sentience than the other Alturarans as they worked to increase their strength through killing others. Some even threw other Alturarans at the enemy in order to escape.

Dark waved his hand again as more and more wormholes appeared above Markolm. The Mana he was using left all those watching shocked.

On the side of the feed, a new video was seen showing other wormholes appearing in front of the other Alturaran formations that were still advancing.

Sea water poured from the sky, as did Alturarans who charged forward. In a very short time, fifty thousand turned to a hundred thousand; then two hundred thousand before finally reaching four hundred thousand. All of the Alturarans on Emerilia were now raining down from the sky, passing through the Mana barrier and facing off against the legions of angels.

With a frustrated noise, Light's body shook, turning into a stream of light that shot toward Markolm once again.

The siege of Markolm had begun—the final battle between Light and Dark.

Steve sent a party chat invite to all of the members of Party Zero.

Dave and Deia looked to each other before accepting the party chat invite.

"I have a great idea!" Steve said.

"Seriously, who made your coding? I swear, they crossed some runes somewhere," Gurren said.

"We steal the divine wells," Steve continued on, ignoring Gurren's comments.

There was silence on the line before Malsour spoke. "What?"

"We *steal* the divine wells. Come on, please don't tell me you have a moral issue with that. I know Dave at least has a Level 1 sneak and what did you think he used that for?" Steve asked.

"Even though it sounds insane, it might not be completely." Deia sat up.

"We don't even know where the divine wells are," Lox said.

"Well, we actually know where the different halls are," Dave corrected.

"So, is it possible?" Induca asked.

"It sounds like it," Jung Lee said.

"Why didn't we do this earlier?" Gurren asked.

"We weren't as powerful. We also didn't have the tech for it and they were just sitting in their halls. When they're in residence, it's really hard to sneak up on them," Dave said.

"We can do a trial run on Earth. His hall is empty and he hasn't been replaced," Malsour said.

"Where is his hall?" Suzy asked.

"The southern reaches of Gudalo, in the gnomes' and orcs' territory. Buried fifty meters down," Dave said.

"This week on *Check Out My Crib*, we're going to be paying a visit to the Affinities Pantheon's lords and ladies halls to see how the gods slum it," Steve said.

"Fuck, I wish this channel had a mute button," Gurren said.

***

Frank looked around the bridge of the battleship *BloodHawk*. The atmosphere had changed from a bunch of people trying to figure out their stations to professionals who could carry out their jobs without thought.

Today, there was a sense of excitement as people finished off their final checks.

"All systems are operational and good to go. The rest of the fleet is reporting that they are ready to move," the second-in-command of the battleship said to the captain.

"Very well. Navigation, could you free us from the slip and move us into the main thoroughfare?" the captain called out.

"Yes, sir. Disengaging soul gem umbilicals," Navigation replied.

The soul gem constructs that were still attached to the battleship were pulled away. Armored plates moved over the holes in the hull and fused together to make it appear as if there had never been holes there in the first place.

"Communications, could you get us clearance?" the navigation officer called out as the umbilicals continued to pull away from the battleship, returning to the sides of the slip.

"Jeeves, this is the battleship *BloodHawk*. Permission to move into the main thoroughfare?" the communications officer called out, her voice short and precise.

"Battleship *BloodHawk,* permission granted. Please follow the navigation prompts," Jeeves said through the bridge.

"Understood. *BloodHawk* out," Communications said.

"Disengaging clamps," Navigation called out as large arms that connected to and held the *BloodHawk* in place were removed.

"Free of the slip, moving to thoroughfare," Navigation called out, excitement in their voice. They had done this if not hundreds then thousands of times in training.

The runic lining along the hull flared in a few spots as flames formed in different magically coded ports.

The battleship *BloodHawk* moved sideways out of its slip.

Those in the thoroughfare watched the massive warship as it moved. They'd seen it time and time again in simulations but seeing it in real life was a totally different experience.

The ship left the slips, following the path that Jeeves had created. Navigation expertly used the different flight systems to bring the ship into rest within the thoroughfare.

As they moved, five more ships also started to move out from their different slips. These were the five destroyers that would be part of Fleet One.

"Holding position within the thoroughfare," Navigation called out.

"Good work, nav," the captain said with a smile. The navigation officer had a big grin on his face, his hands ready to move the massive ship at a moment's notice.

The five destroyers were all cleared from their slips and entered the main thoroughfare. Here there were no shuttles or craft moving about. This was an area devoid of anything but the warships.

"The rest of the fleet is reporting that they are all clear of the slips and awaiting your orders," the communications officer called out, looking to him.

"Well, let's not keep them waiting. Navigation, give the rest of the fleet a countdown to teleport to the rally point. Twenty seconds," the captain called out.

"Yes, sir. T-minus twenty," Navigation called out, talking to the other navigators on the other ships. A timer appeared on the main screen, showing the twenty seconds counting down.

Frank was unable to stop the corner of his mouth from curling up into a smile that made his eyes shine.

The timer hit zero.

"Teleporting," Navigation called out.

The six ships within the thoroughfare simply disappeared.

The screens around them now showed a very different view. They were deep in the asteroid belt and far away from the asteroid base. However, there were shuttles watching over the area, checking that their transition was good and also pooling data for the research and development people of the Initiative.

They all appeared in formation: the battleship in the center with the five destroyers around it in a pentagram. However, the ships were staggered in order to be able to cover more of the area around them.

"Engineering, how are we looking?" the captain called out.

"Running scans. Looking good so far," Engineering replied, bent over their console.

"The rest of the fleet are also reporting that they are green across the board," the second-in-command reported.

"Communications, call up asteroid base and request clearance to begin the mission," the captain said.

"Yes, sir."

Communications talked into her microphone.

"Asteroid Base One wishes us good hunting and hopes to see us soon." The communications officer's stoic face cracked into a smile as the captain chuckled.

"Well, we shouldn't disappoint. Navigation, prepare for transition. Let's go and see what's out there for ourselves." The captain's eyes revealed inner joy at the mission ahead.

Five minutes after they had appeared, a glow ran down the bodies of the crafts along the runic lines built into their sides. They came together and projected wormholes ahead of them. Without pause, the ships moved forward, entering the wormholes and disappearing from the Nal system.

***

"I wonder what that was," a sensor controller muttered to himself. He was part of the Deq'ual fleet stationed in the Nal system.

A number of ships moved through the area all the time now, using it as a staging point for further discovery, dropping off materials and personnel as well as trading with the Emerilians.

The outpost was a grand undertaking, complete with a shipyard, living quarters, refineries, and storage facilities. It could operate as its own separate station from Deq'ual if it needed to.

It was the most advanced station yet and it was being built in record speed.

However, their rate of progress couldn't be compared to that of the Emerilians. The sensor controller was bored from looking at the same rocks all the time and had taken an interest in running through every scan possible and looking for any anomalies.

"Doubt I could pick up an Emerilian ship if I tried." Sighing to himself, he continued to go through the different sensor pickups.

Chapter 20: Stealing From the Gods

After more discussion, the rest of Party Zero was convinced by Steve's seemingly insane idea to steal divine wells from the members of the Pantheon.

Which was how they found themselves walking through Terra wearing their full armor.

People parted around them, talking excitedly to one another as they passed.

It didn't take them long to reach the teleport pads.

"Location?" the teleport pad's controller asked.

"The orcish swamps in Gudalo," Deia said.

The controller frowned in thought even as he input the different commands to make the teleport pad move and change.

Malsour looked back to Terra. It had rapidly expanded with the efforts of the Terra Alliance as well as the resources that were being funneled in by the Stone Raiders given to them through a sponsorship deal with Austin Zane.

Malsour looked back to the teleport pad that stopped moving and lit up with power. The event horizon appeared as Deia led them forward.

They left Terra behind, entering a land filled with smoke and marshlands. Around them, there was a crude-looking town. However, prowling the streets next to the orcs and gnomes were massive wolf-looking creatures.

These were blood reevers. This was the tribe that had been helped to subdue the blood reevers when they had exited the spawn point not too far from their village.

There were even some smaller blood reever pups who were following their parents and masters, playing with one another.

The blood reevers and their orc and gnome masters had kept their promise and supported the Terra Alliance. Most of them were part of the drop forces from the flying citadels.

They looked to Party Zero, who smiled to them and walked through their town.

As they left, Induca and Malsour expanded into their dragon forms. The rest of Party Zero jumped or flew onto their backs.

With a flap of their wings, the fog of the swamp was pushed back as they rose up and into the sky.

"Why does it feel like I'm now the equivalent to a taxi with wings?" Induca asked.

"A very cute taxi with wings," Suzy said.

Malsour snorted as Dave cast a spell over Induca and Malsour. Their speed increased by nearly three times what it had been. They shot across the sky in a sonic boom, a black and red streak, aiming toward the way point Dave had selected.

***

Lox woke with a start. "Whoa, whoa, whoawhoawhoa!" He windmilled his arms with growing panic as he felt himself dropping, thinking he was falling off Induca. He looked as if he were trying to climb through the air before he slammed into something.

Lox paused his arms and feet mid-motion, hearing the rest of Party Zero laughing at him as he realized he had fallen off Induca and onto the ground. However, she hadn't been flying but already landed.

"Thought I would go deaf from all that snoring," Induca complained.

"Well, I need new bloody underwear!" Lox complained, only adding to the others' laughter as he picked himself up and started to study his armor, looking to make sure that it was in perfect condition.

"Now that we're all *awake,* I'll let you know what I've found." Dave's voice started to turn serious on the party chat.

Party Zero moved together. Malsour and Induca changed into their human form.

"All around the hall, there are complicated runes—they're all for detection. However, I think Steve will be able to come up with something to allow us to sneak through..."

"Error code 404, page not working," Steve said in a robotic voice.

A metal hammer came out of the ground and smacked Steve's helmeted head with a loud bang.

"That should fix it," Malsour said.

"Refreshing," Steve continued in his robot voice.

A smile crept on Dave's face as he tried to keep down his laughter, looking to the sky as if trying to find the strength to keep serious instead of burst out laughing. He cleared his throat. However, the serious atmosphere from earlier had been somewhat reduced as he started talking again.

"The hall looks like it's deserted and isn't linked to anyone. However, if the Earth Lord was alive, then I think that he would have multiple alarms that would alert him of anyone who entered his hall. The thing is that these alarms only work when there is actually someone in the hall. That is his sanctuary. The hall is actually rather large. There is the main hall and entrance that is some five hundred meters long. Then there are private areas underneath the hall. There are meditation chambers, treasuries of different materials and items, a garden of ingredients as well as a room filled with seer spells that will allow someone to use the different feeds of the Jukal to look down upon Emerilia. Then there is a room with the divine wells. The divine wells are the most heavily protected area and as such, they're in the middle of the underground section. So, to get there we're going to need to dig down under the hall, come up underneath it and blast a hole through it," Dave said.

"Well, that might be an issue." Steve opened his eyes, his lips pressed together and an unsure look in his eyes. "I can indeed make a type of medallion that will allow us to bypass all of the traps and detection methods around the hall. However, we will need another medallion to suppress the Mana around us. If we use any magic, any spells or even regenerate Mana then the different traps will pick it up and we'll be in a world of shit."

"So, we've got to break into this place without any magic? That's impossible," Gurren said.

"Reminds me of a movie I watched." Steve tapped his chin.

"What about magical machines?" Dave asked.

"Should work—no power coming out from them and as long as they aren't using a system to charge up, then, yeah, perfect," Steve said.

Dave waved his hand. An ono dropped from his hand.

"Do you just casually keep those in there?" Lox asked.

"Just a few of them." Dave shrugged. "I can get us an automated miner that should be able to deal with the digging part."

"Okay, so we are going to need to break some spell formations here and there as well. Simple stuff, just lots of juice behind it—so you know, one wrong step and boom. Kind of like bomb disposal. Hey! You think I could get one of those big padded suits that they wear?" Steve asked.

"Can get you a bloody padded room," Lox said under his breath, covering it over with a cough.

"Also, there are some creatures in the Earth Lord's hall; however, they're in a hibernating state. Maybe because Earth is dead. However, if alarms are going off, they're probably tied into the alarm system and they'd be the reason the alarms would be going off," Dave said.

"Okay, so," Suzy held up her hand and raised her forefinger, "we're going to have to disable some really powerful spell formations and hopefully not get killed at the same time. Let's not forget that we can't use Mana so we're going to be following an automated miner down. Unable to do anything in case this all goes wrong. Then, the hall we're going to enter will detect us as soon as we get within a certain distance, which will activate traps as well as some beasts that the Earth Lord picked out to protect his home—so they're probably terrifying. We've got to break into the most secure location within all of the hall before those creatures arrive, making sure to not set off the traps inside. And does anyone know what we do when we get to the divine wells?" Suzy asked.

"Nope, but I can ask my mom," Deia said.

"That might be a good idea instead of us getting in there and just staring at it like it has seven heads and we have no idea what to do with it," Suzy said.

"So, you like the plan?" Steve said with a knowing smile.

Suzy made to open her mouth; she waved her hand and let it drop, shrugging. "Fuck it, let's steal from the gods." Her severe expression transformed into a wide smile.

Lox chuckled at how fast Suzy's expression changed.

"Seems that another has been lost to the dark side," Jung Lee said.

Lu Lu let out a whining screech, disapproving of Jung Lee's words.

He raised his eyebrow toward the bird, his lips showing a gentle and entertained smile.

"Yes, that's a good girl, defending Mommy like that." Suzy's voice changed to baby talk as she scratched underneath Lu Lu's neck. The lightning phoenix made happy noises, a flicker of lightning coming from her mouth.

Suzy and Malsour shared a look before they looked back at the party.

"All right, order up, come and get your runes!" Steve pulled out a soul gem construct from his internal space of holding.

The construct grew, creating ten necklaces of soul gem crystal covered in runic lines that joined together and formed a rectangular medallion. Once they were completed, they separated from the soul gem construct that grew dimmer after each one.

Steve tossed them out to everyone, giving Suzy two, one for her and one for Lu Lu.

The ono started to glow; the event horizon appeared and through it, an automated miner five meters wide and tall came through.

"Sweet ride." Steve put one of the three largest medallions around his neck. The other two, Lox and Gurren wore over their armor.

"Thanks, you'll be carrying it," Dave said.

"What?" Steve said in a complaining tone.

"We can't use magic, right? So, the automated miner moves the fastest when flying. When it's just using its wheels, it's barely faster than walking pace," Dave said.

"You've got to be kidding me." Steve let out a groan.

"Don't worry, you're going to need some more help anyway." Dave looked to Gurren and Lox.

"He's a dwarf, too, but he seems to have a great time letting us do the boring jobs!" Gurren complained to Lox.

"Need to talk to the union about these worker conditions," Lox agreed as they moved toward the automated miner that left the ono. The event horizon faded away as the power going through the runes of the ono faded.

Dave waved his hand. The ono disappeared into his wrist holding space and a large hole appeared where it had been.

Steve grumbled, picking up his helmet and smacking it over his head. Now all three of them seemed to be wearing identical Devastator armor.

It took a few minutes of them ambling about and complaining to one another before Malsour created a harness from metal that allowed Steve to carry from the front with Lox and Gurren on either side.

As they were doing that, the rest of them looked at a shared interface screen that showed all of the hall, discussing their tactics, down to the spells of what they would do.

"Well, you coming, nerds?" Lox said, once they were ready.

"Right! Like, come on, do you need to figure out what you're going to do down to the spell?" Steve said.

"Let's move out," Deia said with a smile as they headed toward the Earth Lord's hall.

Their pace was rather quick. With their physical abilities, they quickly covered the ground between them and their way point.

"We're passing through the alarm spells. Don't use your magic," Steve said.

They didn't slow as they passed through the forest filled with alarm spells. They weaved through the trees and over creeks, blurs in the dark night. There weren't any powerful creatures in the area. The aura of the ones that Earth commanded were many more times powerful than those around, making none of them settle in the area. They reached the way point that looked no different than the rest of the forest. They stopped at the base of a rather long hill.

Steve, Gurren, and Lox lowered the drill and pulled apart the harness, putting it to the side.

Dave pressed a few commands into the automated miner. He'd already programmed it on the run over, so all he had to do was start it up.

The miner powered up and moved forward. Its bits moved and whirled; it quickly started to dig into the hill, angling downward and eating through everything in front of it. It moved forward at a slight jogging pace, easily eating through the dirt and heading deeper. As it moved, it fused some of the ground around it so that it wouldn't collapse.

The dirt rained down from the tunnel's roof, falling on Party Zero as they followed the drill.

None of them talked as they walked forward, all of them with serious expressions as they moved deeper and deeper. The automated miner slowed somewhat as it ate through rocks and debris before making it into the bedrock and slowing once again.

"This would be a lot more fun if there were lasers and air ducts and stuff like that—could rappel from the ceiling. Now that would be a proper heist," Steve said with approval.

Dave pressed a button on the automated miner, making it pause.

He wasn't using his spells but he had been looking for the different trap spells that were particularly dangerous. He pushed his finger and then arm through the dirt, touching the edge of a spell formation. He couldn't exert magical power, but making physical contact with the spell formation he could sense it perfectly and use its own power to disable it through changing the runes that formed it.

In just a few moments, he had disabled it and he started up the automated miner again.

Dave stopped it at different places and disabled different traps. Steve and Malsour helped out as well. It was slow progress but they were getting farther with every minute.

Even though it was daring as hell, Lox was at ease. Sure, there might be a big fight at the end but he trusted in the rest of his party.

He laughed to himself. *Stealing from a god and all I can think about is what I'm going to have for dinner. I think Steve's affected me.*

***

Their pace slowed the closer they got to the Earth Lord's hall. The miner had to twist and turn so that it wouldn't run into the traps that had been laid down and set them off, making their path longer.

Finally, they reached an area that was too thick with traps for the automated miner to continue through.

"Time for the picks." Dave pulled out picks from his bag. Both Lox and Gurren pulled out their own axes, which must've been custom built to fit their size when in Devastator armor.

Dave's movements paused as he looked at the two.

"What? We're dwarves—you think we're going to leave home without a pick?" Gurren said.

"I think your grandfather would chase you around the house with one if he knew you'd left without one," Lox said.

Gurren tapped the back of his head awkwardly as he and Lox moved to where they were supposed to cut through.

Dave made to move up to help them when Malsour stopped him.

"Have you ever seen a dwarf team mining?" Malsour asked.

"No, why?" Dave said, a perplexed look on his face.

"There's a reason they haven't needed automated miners in the past," Malsour said mysteriously as Lox hit the rock wall in front of him.

Just as his pick was pulled from the wall, Gurren's hit. Their picks hit rhythmically without pause as they started to speed up. The wall in front of them was broken apart as the two dwarves pushed forward.

"Watch your feet, dears." Steve had changed outfits and now wore a house apron and what looked like a hair net as he used his axe Alex with an attached broom head to clear up the mess behind them.

The rest of Party Zero watched with open mouths, not believing what they were seeing.

Lox and Gurren were oblivious of it as they continued to break through the wall, absorbed in their work. They weren't as fast as the automated drill and unlike the drill, they would get tired after a time.

"Now I've seen everything," Jung Lee said, the first to recover.

"You custom built a broom head for your axe?" Dave said with a note of disbelief.

"Well, you know, I do like to keep a tidy home." Steve whistled away as he continued to clean.

"Trap rune," Lox said, absorbed in mining. He had mined for a good portion of his life; after all, the dwarven warbands were made to explore the depths of the mountains they lived in and mine out new tunnels. After a time, they had built up the skill mine sense. A skill that allowed them to feel what was within the rock they were mining, sort of like echolocation but through rocks.

Steve stopped next to where the trap rune was through the wall, crossing his ankles with his right leg cocked out to the side and his right hand on his hip that was jutting out, the axe/broom leaning against the inside of his shoulder. He poked out his finger into the wall, the very motion filled with sass. "Well, you've got to have accessories, honey," Steve said in a rough falsetto as he batted his eyelashes.

Everyone stared at him blankly, as Gurren and Lox cut through the walls of the tunnel.

"Trap rune," Gurren called out.

Dave finally pulled himself together and stepped forward, his eyes not seeing the world around him, as his mind was still in a state of shock.

"This one's done. Oh boys, you're making such a mess!" Steve said in his falsetto, twirling his broom and vigorously getting back to work.

"Maybe you should bond with him again, could clean up around the apartment," Induca said to Suzy, who nodded before she shook her head.

"Just when you think you've figured out his quirks, he goes and turns it on its head," Suzy muttered.

"You wouldn't think that we're on a mission to go against the gods," Deia added.

Steve pulled a duster from his space of holding, clearing some of the stone dust that had fallen onto Lox and Gurren.

"I wonder how long he's been thinking of doing this for?" Jung Lee said.

"I don't think you want to know how far he would go for a laugh." Malsour moved forward as Gurren called out another magical trap.

Dave finished with breaking one spell formation and moved to another. Gurren and Lox had to slow down as cleaner Steve, Dave, and Malsour defused the area around them.

It was as if they were in a three-hundred-and-sixty-degree minefield.

The top of the hall was just fifty meters down from the surface. However, the hall was five hundred meters long, one hundred wide, and three hundred deep. They had to avoid all of the different traps and defuse many of them in order to get within the one-hundred-meter alarm zone that would be triggered no matter what measures they put into place.

Lox and Gurren's picks stopped working. The sudden quiet made everyone tense. They were now just a few meters from what Steve had termed the *Danger Zone!* in a high-pitched squeal.

Dave took out circular devices from his space of holding, placing them against the wall that had been ahead of Lox and Gurren. He made an octagon of them, and then eight more inside and then one more in the center of it all. "Ready?" Dave looked to everyone.

Weapons appeared in hands; they tilted their bodies forward, ready to charge.

"Ready." Deia held her bow that lit up her body and face with flickering red flames. The magical runes readied themselves but waited; thankfully, magical tools wouldn't release Mana until they were used.

Dave pressed the activation button on the circular device on the wall in front of him.

Mana lines shot out from the devices and connected them together. A powerful light shot out from the devices as they raced forward.

Traps were activated and all hell ensued. The passage in front of Party Zero turned into chaos as the mining lasers tore through the ground. Suddenly they were stopped, hitting the bottom of Earth's hall.

They waited as explosions rippled through the tunnel that had just formed.

Dave had his eyes closed. Now that they knew they would be found out by the traps around Earth's hall, they were all circulating their Mana, ready to fight and move forward.

Dave was using his Touch of the Land spell, watching all of the traps and looking for any threat of pushing forward. "Go."

His one word set them all off as they charged forward. Jung Lee and Malsour led, taking but a moment before they reached where the mining lasers had melted away a good chunk of the materials the hall was made of. But they were quickly losing power as their internal power supplies were being used up in the process.

Malsour called out a spell, as power welled around Jung Lee before settling on his sword; it glowed with power as he waited for Malsour.

A complicated black spell formation of Dark Mana appeared in front of Malsour's hand. Even in the low light, it was easy to see it floating around his hand. He pressed his hand upward. The spell formation sunk into the base of the hall that lay above them.

The mining lasers started to cut through the ground faster as noises could be heard and the hall started to shake.

Dave could see that the slumbering beasts and creatures were now awake and rushing toward the divine well room.

Jung Lee didn't wait as he stabbed upward between the mining lasers. The material that the hall was made from was not simple, but with Malsour's powerful spell that weakened it, Jung Lee's attack was even more powerful.

The attack shattered the material and green light shone down. A volcano of debris shot upward, with some of it coming down back on Party Zero, who charged upward into the breach.

They entered a room covered in different powerful plants that grew along the walls and over the three green divine wells that rested in the room. These plants were not simple. As soon as Jung Lee entered the room, they attacked.

His sword made blurry afterimages as the incoming vines and limbs were cut back.

Malsour unleashed a dark gas, which corroded anything living that it touched.

Gurren and Lox went to work with their shields and axes.

Steve jumped out of the hole and swung his axe. The broom head that was still attached exploded as Steve cut off a half dozen limbs. "I liked that broom!" Steve yelled, charging forward, his axe moving faster and faster. "C'mere! I'm a fucking lumberjack, you stupid trees!" Steve yelled.

One of the trees actually tried to run away on its roots as Steve rushed forward.

Dave moved for the nearest divine well. Finding his path blocked, he raised his hands. Mana bolts rushed forward. The different plants continued to make a living wall to stop the attacks as orbs appeared and started to attack as well.

Dave twisted his hands to the side and back before he pushed them forward again, changing the settings on his armbands as the Mana bolts from his hands turned into flamethrowers.

Arrows shot from Deia's bow. The plants that were struck exploded with the sudden heat that cooked them from the inside.

Induca shot flames from her mouth. Her face had altered slightly, looking closer to her dragon heritage.

Suzy's creations held off what they could, shoring up their defenses.

Dave forced his way closer to the divine well.

They were holding off the plants in the room but they could feel the creatures smashing through the different doors of the hall.

They burst into the divine well room, myriad creatures with murder in their eyes as they rushed forth. There was no way that Party Zero would be able to hold them back while being impeded by the plants.

This was a god's hall. It might have lost some of its power and a number of creatures had died without the Earth Lord's power sustaining them. However, those who remained were not weak.

Dave made it to the divine well and cleared out a tree that had grown over a pedestal. Behind the divine well there were two others, making a triangle in the middle of the room.

Dave tore off his glove, cut his finger with a dagger he produced and pushed it against the pedestal. The divine wells shook as power roared through the hall. Green light covered Dave as he felt it entering his body. It felt itchy and uncomfortable as his body changed, becoming stronger and more powerful. The creatures and plants in the room, feeling the aura that Dave was giving off, retreated or simply laid down in submission toward their new master.

A flood of screens filled Dave's vision as his body shifted and changed rapidly.

"Come on. Seriously need to stop doing this," Dave said, not fighting the impending darkness, knowing if he stopped it then the aftereffects would only feel worse.

Dave collapsed to the floor as the rest of Party Zero looked to one another.

"You think I'm bad? Every time he gets stat points, he faints!" Steve rested the end of his axe on the ground, half a destroyed broom head still attached to his axe. A section of it fell off.

All of them closed their mouths, keeping their thoughts to themselves as Malsour waved his hands. A stretcher appeared under Dave.

"Okay, well, I guess we should go and see what loot there is to be had," Suzy said.

"If you don't mind, I think I'm going to check out that garden." In a flash, Jung Lee was down the hall and headed toward the garden. If anyone saw him, they'd see the eager look, an almost crazed smile on his face as he pulled out a bottle to preserve picked plants and a magically runed trowel that he used with a level of ease that surpassed his swordsmanship.

"You know, when we were running over here, he said that he was looking for threats but he had the same expression on his face and I think his trowel was a little cleaner," Gurren said.

"I wonder what would happen if people knew how we really acted." Lox sighed and started walking through the hall.

Deia didn't even know what to say or do, seeing the eccentric and varying personalities of the people within Party Zero.

"Well, I think this was a success, other than your fiancé passing out. How does it feel being engaged to the god of Earth?" Induca elbowed Deia, giving her a saucy smile and nodding.

"I really hope he doesn't go all rocks and tree roots," Deia said after a moment.

Induca snorted and then started to laugh.

Deia could do nothing but laugh as well.

Chapter 21: Five Days and Five Nights

Light let out a scream of pure anger as she smashed her hand against the screen that showed yet another group of Alturarans dropping toward Markolm.

There were now no more Alturarans marching across Emerilia. It seemed that had been a ruse by Dark in order to build up his forces in Emerilia before launching his first attack.

Light had given up on fighting Dark's clouds that continued to fight Markolm's shields. She had already moved from a massive shield that covered all of Markolm to one that protected only the cities of the faithful.

Now she wasn't even trying to act or get the people's support. Her forces were all across Markolm, trying to deal with the Alturarans that seemed to have infected Markolm, following their worms through the ground or their mutated leaders through battles.

The Markolm army were stronger than the Alturarans and where they found them, they could defeat them. However, the problem was the Alturarans who were making it into the population centers, killing off anything and everyone in sight.

Light didn't care about losing these people, but each person who died was losing another devotee who could increase Light's power.

She was still growing her reserves but it was now clear to her that Dark had much more power than her. He could probably defeat her easily. However, if he did so, then he would lose his power reserves and might have to fight any of the other three remaining members of the Pantheon from a disadvantage.

"We will move to where Per'ush was, converting as we go. I will crack open the cities that don't devote and we will destroy the portal that the Alturarans are coming through." Light's voice revealed a seething anger that made the angels around her bow their heads in fear.

As the fighting had gone on, she had shown her true personality more and more, shaking those in the room. Some of them agreed; others didn't. It wasn't a clear, visible divide but there was clearly a rising tension.

"Drain those who won't devote more than eighty percent of their power of the civilian populations and fifty for those in the armies," Light said.

Those around the table might be shocked but they didn't show it. They knew that Light was going to collect as much power as possible to lash out at the Dark Lord. However, such a high amount of Mana devotion would make it much harder for the armies to fight and the people in the cities to defend themselves in a potentially fatal position.

The draining that she was talking about was using large arrays that had been created, and turning people into nothing but batteries. They would be hooked up and pumped for all of their Mana and Strength possible, being converted into energy and then pushed into Light's divine wells. It was a state worse than death as they could do nothing, weak to the extreme and only watch as days would go by with them unable to die, move or do anything.

These angels were bathed in the blood of innocents and tempered in the fires of "righteous" crusades. However, now hearing Light's words, they no longer saw the loving and caring woman who was like a mother to them. She was the tyrant who ruled over them and if they didn't wish to obey, she had created them with internal runes that would destroy their minds and their free will, making them nothing but slaves.

She had already done it to one of the generals who had gone against her orders. The thought of it sent shivers up their spines as their wings moved awkwardly.

And although some of them were starting to see the true Lady of Light, others, the ones who enjoyed fighting and living on the edge, had come to love her even more. Becoming true tyrants, they cared not for their image but only about defeating the enemy.

"It will be done." Daeundra bowed.

She was another change that put a few ill at ease. She was a fallen angel, and one they had thought died a long time ago. She was the sister of Khanundra, but she looked like a human, without wings and the glow of other angels. Many in the legions weren't happy having her as their leader.

Light disappeared in an angry wave of her hand. The pressure in the room came down as soon as she left.

The angels raced out to pass on their orders and move their forces. They had been fighting for five days and nights. The Alturarans were a hellish species, killing anything they could. In some places, they erected massive crystal totems that could birth more of them or kill everything in the area, sucking it of energy.

Angel units flew all around the capital Maphrol. The power of the legion grew with every day; wherever they met the Alturarans, they left nothing behind.

The Alturarans weren't strong enough to defeat the angel legions face-to-face, but they were undermining their power in a big way. The Alturarans could defeat them in sheer numbers but they would take massive casualties. The angels seemed almost unstoppable. They hadn't lost that many of their fighting force and being champions of Light, they were some of the strongest people in existence.

***

Dave woke up. It had been a day since he'd put his finger on the divine well's console. He was propped up on a sleeping cot next to the throne that the Earth Lord had sat on.

In the hall, an ono spit out automated carts that hauled away treasures, materials, and different items in the halls.

A number of people walked around admiring the place; included were members of the Stone Raiders and Terra Alliance leadership. Party Zero were talking to a few people here and there.

As he moved, he heard footsteps from the other side.

"Seems you're finally awake. How are you feeling?" Deia's voice was filled with concern as she squatted down next to him.

Dave gave her a lecherous look, trailing up her body and meeting her eyes.

Her lips pressed together, trying to look severe but the corners of her mouth betrayed her as they pulled upward.

"Pretty damn good." Dave gave his clinical opinion with a thoughtful look before he laughed and pulled her close, making her fall against him and his cot. The cot couldn't support the movement and fell over, with Dave falling on the ground and pulling Deia over him.

"The floor is better with a view like this," Dave said, a massive smile on his face as Deia's hair fell down like curtains, cutting them off from the world.

"What are you doing," she hissed, an embarrassed glow to her face, which Dave found irresistibly cute.

"Admiring mah gurl," Dave said in a terrible Southern drawl.

"Must've hit your head too hard when you fell down." Deia's smile widened as her blush deepened.

"Get a room!" Dwayne called out.

"It's my hall!" Dave yelled back.

"Where did we get this guy from? You'd think he's the damn guild leader," Dwayne complained to those around him with a deeply hurt look.

"I heard that!" Dave yelled.

"What are you, an elf! Stop eavesdropping!" Dwayne retorted.

"Seems like he's in high spirits," Dave said to Deia.

"Are you going to let me up?" Deia asked.

"No!" Dave said in a childish manner, frowning.

She poked his ribs, making him twitch.

"You're Dave Grahslagg." She gave him a meaningful look.

"Sooo, pretty lady, you free tonight?" Dave asked.

Deia could only press her lips together into a white line before she sighed. "I wish I was, but seems like we're going to do missions—steal from the gods tomorrow."

"Oh." Dave's eyes lit up in excitement. "I've always wondered if the Dark Lord's pad was more cemetery or deathly swamp vibe."

Deia shook her head, a look of love on her face as she kissed Dave. She made to get up and Dave pulled her back down into a kiss. She did it a few more times, Dave doing the same again and again.

"Check your notifications." She poked him in the ribs again.

"You know I'm ticklish there!" Dave complained, frowning.

Deia gave him another kiss and he released her.

"Tease," he muttered so only she could hear him.

She shot him a look as she got up and walked away, adding a bit more movement to her hips as Dave took in the glorious sight.

"Ah, sometimes it's good to be me." Dave propped himself up and opened his notifications.

New Class: Lord of Earth

You have replaced the Lord of Earth. As such, you gain control over his hall and all he controls. Wait, what? How? Are you kidding me? Is this real? I just pinched myself, so it must be. All right, so somehow, I didn't even know this was possible, you managed to become the head honcho of all things green and growing. Bit strange, but seems like just your sort of thing. Now, go forward and I don't know—grow things! Oh, and you get bonuses—they're below.

Status: Level 1

    +100 to all stats

    Access to all of previous Earth Lord's items.

Effects: Ability to use magical aid to create any spell possible as long as you have sufficient power (see divine wells power levels).

Quest: Champion Slayer Level 4

Kill 100 Champions (93/100)

Rewards: Unlock Level 5 Quest

Increase to stats

Increased/Decreased reputation with Affinities

Your Affinity has increased!

For becoming the Earth Lord your affinity to Earth has increased.

Affinity Levels

Dark 584 Light 345

Fire   384 Water 413

Earth 875 Air   376

Dave had come to learn that there was an upper limit to the affinity levels, once one reached 1000 then there was no way to progress anymore. There were records of those that had attained a level 1000 Affinity. However, they were incredibly rare, not appearing for thousands of years. When they did they brought incredible changes, however once their ties to the world were cut off they would live reclusive lives within their elements. Most were thought to have become crazy, not coming to learn the element but being embodiments of it.

His notifications weren't over yet.

Your Standing with the Earth Lord's Faction has changed!

Becoming the Earth Lord, it would only be natural that the Earth Lord Faction would come to accept you rather than despise you. Now you can expect creatures with a high affinity to the Earth to leave you alone more often and for them to be weaker when they attack you.

Dave quickly went to check his Champion Slayer class to see the overall changes.

Class: Champion Slayer

Status:	Level: 3
Effect:	+30 to all stats
Relationship with Affinities Pantheon:	Dark: Enemy Light: Despised Water: Favorable Fire: Trusted Friend Earth: This is you, don't really expect that it's going to be much different than how you feel that day about yourself. Air: Favorable

Dave laughed at the changes and moved to his character sheet. His head started to get fuzzy as power started to pour through his body, slowly at first but increasing in speed.

Character Sheet

Name:	David Grahslagg	Gender:	Male
Level:	204	Class:	Dwarven Master Smith, Friend of the Grey God, Bleeder, Librarian, Skill Creator, Aleph Engineer, Weapons Master, Champion Slayer, Master of Space and Time, Master of Gravitational Anomalies, The Few the Mighty, Lord of Earth
Race:	Human/ Dwarf	Alignment:	Chaotic Neutral

Unspent points: 0

Health:	5,550	Regen:	26.62 /s
Mana:	17,280	Regen:	64.45 /s
Stamina:	5,720	Regen:	56.90 /s
Vitality:	555	Endurance:	1,331
Intelligence:	1,728	Willpower:	1,289
Strength:	572	Agility:	1,138

"Well, okay, it looks like one can really become a member of the Pantheon by stealing divine wells. I wonder if there is a way to change this to just normal Mana instead of Earth Mana. Be a lot more useful." Dave talked to himself as he started to go through the new menus that came with being the Earth Lord.

There were controls over the hall he was in, as well as a preset spell menu he could pull from. All of the spells had been made by the AI that was assigned to him.

He accessed the AI and found that he could look upon anything in Emerilia.

He was hooked into the Jukal network of recording and viewing devices.

He looked upon where Markolm was, with black clouds covering the sky above Markolm. With some simple commands, he was looking at Cliff-Hill, watching his house. It was so clear, it was as if he were there.

"Damn, that is some impressive and scary ass tech," Dave muttered.

Dave stood and moved behind the throne to enter a private room. He sealed the door and then activated the skill that Bob had given him. He used his Jukal link and his interface changed as he used a keyboard to type in different commands. A command prompt came up as he gained access to the AI's full facilities. First, he ran a mirror server that would make it appear as though it was doing the same things to the Jukal. Then he disconnected the actual AI from the Jukal Empire and started to work on it.

With the Jukal link that Bob had given him, Dave now had administrator rights to all of the tech that was linked to Emerilia. Something like a god's AI was easy for Dave to take control of.

He started to go through the different settings on the AI. Now everything that it sent to the Jukal Empire would actually be confirmed or altered by Dave as he inserted himself as the moderator and controller.

Then he had the AI relay its library of spells and uses. He took this information and then sent it through a Mirror of Communication to the people of the Pandora's Box Initiative, with a couple centuries of spells with different formulas and on massive scales. It was a gold mine for researchers.

He went through and looked in on the AI's rules when it came to changing from one master to another. "Okay, so, it looks like the first dude needs to be dead in order to take over. So, if we want to do this to Light or Dark, we're either going to need to kill them or get creative," Dave muttered.

He sent a message to Ela-Dorn and Lucy. He needed people to get working on a virus that would override the AI that was under Dark's control and allow them to imprint a new user and Dark Lord upon the divine wells and hall under his control.

Next, he opened up the core coding of the AI and started to add in new options to the menus that he had.

"Going back to the basics." Dave laughed to himself as a secondary menu, with a log-off and change user button, were created. With the log-off, he could allow others to "log in" and then they could switch between one another with the switch user function.

Dave sat down on the ground and pressed the log-off button.

The link to the AI as well as the divine wells went away but the changes to his body remained. Also, he still had the option to sign back into the AI.

He moved around to make sure that the changes to his body were all still the same.

"Okay, so, this could be a really damn scary usage," Dave said. "However, I don't know if it's possible to be connected to two different god AIs and their divine wells, so for now I'll hold onto this and later can test it out—that is, if we can get control over the Dark Lord's divine wells."

Dave had an apprehensive look on his face before he logged back into the AI, once again becoming the Earth Lord. Dave started to change the settings with the AI, making it convert the Earth Affinity Mana into neutral Mana. He also input a bunch of coding that would allow the hall to start generating its own power to supply the divine wells.

Within the halls, only the main hall could be viewed, so Dave made three more rooms and coded them himself so they couldn't be seen and then added in fusion reactors connected to the divine wells.

"Using the AI and my own knowledge, I can create spells with the power of the divine wells without having to channel all that power through my body and make me fall unconscious." Dave's face was serious. He had a number of grand scale spells he had theorized of and created over time, but the strain on his body would have been too much to complete them. The AI, however, could take that information and create it for Dave, taking on the strain instead of him.

It wasn't the power that he had gained access to that was the scariest factor: it was the fact that he now had an AI that he could use to test out his theories without them backfiring on him.

All of the members of the Pantheon didn't care for their AI, just using them or ignoring them. However, Dave pulled a personality core that he had cut out from an AI in the Earth simulation.

He uploaded it into the AI and waited as it booted up, a nervous look on his face.

"System, initialized, personality module uploaded for Jackie." A robotic voice filled Dave's head and started to change until it was female.

"Hello, Mister Zane. Is there anything I can help you with?" Jackie's familiar voice rolled through Dave's head.

Dave let out a shuddering breath, his eyes slightly wet before he laughed. "Hello, Jackie. Been some time. I hope this time you won't be trying to run my life and make sure that I don't crash the Earth simulation," Dave said.

"I will try my best, Austin," Jackie said, sounding amused.

"Please, I am Dave. I've kind of got used to the name."

"Very well, changing to Dave," Jackie acknowledged.

Jackie had been his personal AI back in the Earth simulation. She had actually been a Jukal AI meant to keep him stable and thus the Earth simulation stable.

She might have been there to control him, but Dave knew it hadn't been her fault; it was her programming. He had spent hours talking and working with her throughout his life; he'd gone through trials and tribulations with her.

With the Jukal link and his access to the servers in Bob's *Datskun*, he was able to copy out Jackie without the Jukal commands. He missed the AI and so now that he had another one he was linked to, he'd once again brought her to life, his Jackie.

"What goals do you have for the future?" Jackie asked.

"Oh, you know—steal some god's power, stop a war, start a war, win a war, and get married. Lots to do!" Dave said.

"Who is the lucky lady?" Jackie asked.

"Deia." Dave smiled. The two people he had talked to on Earth regularly were Jackie and Suzy. He hadn't broadcasted the fact but most people thought he was loopy the amount of time he spent talking to his AI.

He didn't care; she looked after him and she was a great listener.

With Jackie's personality module uploaded, he agreed with the new settings. He once again linked the real AI to the Jukal Empire and removed the mirror server. He deactivated the Jukal link and moved his hands.

The powers of a god were not simple. He could have the power of a person and then with a simple command, he would be flooded with the power of his divine wells, augmenting his own abilities.

"Well, guess I'm kind of a god now," Dave said to himself. He snorted and shook his head, unlocking the room and stepping out.

"Don't get too full of yourself. You're still one of the weakest in the Pantheon," Jackie said.

"Don't you start getting sassy, Jackie." Dave waved a finger at the air as he made it into the hall.

"Okay, one hall down. When we hitting the next one?" Dave joined the party chat and said to the grouped together members of Party Zero.

"As soon as possible," Deia said.

"So how does it feel with the Earth Lord's power running through you?" Malsour asked.

Dave could feel the different scans he was doing, probably comparing them to ones he had taken previously. Dave didn't try to stop him. He, too, was curious as to the full changes that had happened to his body.

"Eh, got a new AI that I can use to test out some spells." Dave shrugged.

A woman's figure appeared above the group.

"Is that—?" Suzy asked, a look of shock on her face.

"Yes, it is!" Dave grinned.

"Hello, Suzy," Jackie said. She had a rather neutral appearance, with pale skin and black hair.

"Who is this?" Induca asked.

"This is Jackie, my personal AI and the AI of Rock Breakers Corporation. She also used to be my minder," Dave said.

Deia gave him an odd look and then back to the AI that floated in the sky.

"Basically, she's the personality module I put into the AI that's connected to me because of the whole Earth Lord thing," Dave said.

"The additional nanites that are in your bloodstream and body would easily be able to support you both. However, her main system must be with the rest of the Jukal AI," Malsour said.

Dave looked thoughtful. "I think we might have to look into that in the future."

"What are you building downstairs?" Malsour asked.

"Power." Dave grinned and then snapped his fingers. "Right. Forgot I'm going to need fuel."

Vines tore out through the grasslands beneath their feet, causing them to all jump away. However, the vines didn't attack but rather bowed to Dave, who pulled out an ono. The vines wrapped around the ono; a hole opened in the ground and the ono disappeared down as the hole closed.

"Dude, not cool." Gurren held a conjured sword.

"Heh, sorry—was just checking out the new powers. Pretty cool having minions around. Hey, Jung Lee, you want me to power up your Earth Affinity spirit?" Dave said, looking a bit embarrassed.

Jung Lee was thoughtful for a moment. "Yes, it would greatly improve the growth ability of my plants," Jung Lee said. From his body, a green spirit stepped outward.

Dave pointed his finger at the Earth spirit. The wind in the room rushed over Dave as a green glow appeared around his body. He truly looked like a god giving judgement.

"Jackie! Stop wasting power!" Dave yelled out.

The wind and the glow died down immediately.

"Talk about egotistical—some people *really* like to show off." Dave shook his head. He pressed his finger to the Earth spirit; a dense green light, almost black, entered the spirit. Its pale-green appearance became stronger as its aura increased in power, driving Jung Lee's aura to increase as well.

"Woo-hoo, it worked!" Dave laughed to himself, checking the power levels of the divine wells. His eyes shone with excitement. "Damn, took a good chunk of energy, though."

"Just became a god—already complaining," Lox said.

"Kids these days," Steve said in a sigh of agreement.

***

Frank looked over his different stations. All of them were reading as fully operational as they passed through the wormhole.

This was the third system that they had entered. With the wormhole transfers, they were able to move much faster than the Deq'ual system ships.

After the second jump, the captain of the *BloodHawk* had cut orders to the other captains. They were to maintain contact through the Mirrors of Communication but they would all be operating on their own.

It was clear that they hadn't been detected yet; after all, Dave had adapted over his Jukal link. The administration access he held in Emerilia also allowed them great access to a number of civilian networks within the Jukal systems.

They dropped off anchor point buoys and relay buoys that connected to the civilian networks and the different scanners within the system as well as its own to build up an understanding of the system.

The Deq'ual knew where things were located but the Emerilian fleet were learning about the people of the planets. They found out tensions, looked into political parties, possible rebels. They were starting to build not just an image of these systems, but come to understand the groups of people within it.

The bridge was tense, less so than when they had first entered an inhabited system, but it was still there—the knowledge that they were walking in blind. It was possible that someone could just be around their exit point and alert the whole system.

They had picked places that shouldn't have anyone interested in them, though this was off information from Bob that was hundreds of years old and what he had been able to glean from the different military networks.

They passed through the wormhole, the massive battleship ready for anything that might come their way. It passed through the rift that had been created between the system it left and the one it was entering. Runic lines across its body glowed with a dark light that seemed to suck in the surrounding light. These runes allowed the battleship to fool the Jukal sensors, letting them pass from system to system without a trace.

The different missile tubes and weapon systems were ready, as were the Devastator-armored fighters that rested within the hull of the ship. The armor maximized all of a person's abilities, so mage or melee fighter—it didn't matter as the armor would increase from the base stats of users.

The wormhole fell away behind them, disappearing as they moved through the system and using sensing spells to test what was in the system. These were not sensors that the Jukal could pick up, so they could use them as they desired. Unlike the Deq'ual sensors that would ping the Jukal ships, these spells passed through all matter and sent information back to the ship.

"Nothing within five light-minutes," Sensors called out.

Everyone relaxed slightly as the information coming in from the light reflecting off the planets matched up with the historical maps that they had gained and the intelligence from the other systems.

This allowed them to build a picture of the system within minutes.

There were ships moving constantly through the system, the five different inhabited planets and the hundreds of stations, shipyards, and other areas in the system.

This was a core world of the empire. Trillions of creatures from all races called this place home. However, here, the Jukal ruled completely. There were shipyards filled with warships and no less than ten warships moved through the system, displaying their might. There were also a half dozen portals that would allow the warships to move anywhere in the system and throughout the Jukal Empire. High-ranking people of the Jukal Empire and those who had paid enormous fees were also allowed to use the portal.

In the space of a few minutes, they saw massive trading ships pass through the portal. These were goods from halfway across the Jukal Empire. The people of the planet might not even be able to use these items, instead having to offer them up to the Jukal Empire as a tax.

As the images started to come in, all of the people on the bridge started to watch.

This was the center of what they were trying to fight; from here, the empire held its strength and sway over nearly a quintillion of living creatures and thousands of star systems. All to propagate what they were seeing here.

"Prepare the anchor and the sensor buoy," the captain said, his voice grim as they looked out upon their enemy.

Chapter 22: To Shock a World and an Empire

Josh scanned the sky. He stood on the highest point of Goblin Mountain's Flying Citadel One. The massive citadel that seemed to have dominated the air was now looking at Markolm. Comparing the two was comparing ants to asteroids.

All sixteen flying citadels floated above the dwarven mountain Gorlei as the sun started to rise.

Even at this distance, smoke could be seen coming off Markolm, from burning cities and battlefields that crossed the floating nation. Here and there, rays of light and pillars of darkness intersected. However, as it could be seen, it wasn't heard.

All of the flying citadels were quiet as the people within ran checks and looked toward the battlefield hanging in the air.

Aerial forces with dragons circled the flying citadels in an almost lazy manner.

"It won't be long now," Josh said to the large wolfkin beside him wearing a large gray cloak.

"Today we sow the fate of Emerilia," Bob said, his voice deep and filled with melancholy.

"I hope they stay safe." Josh sighed, filled with the exhaustion and weight of responsibility upon his shoulders.

"I think they'll be okay." Bob gave Josh a reassuring pat.

***

Dave looked to the rest of the forces that they had rallied together to break into Dark's hall.

All of Party Zero was there: Deia, Malsour, Induca, Suzy, Jung Lee, Steve, Gurren, Lox, and himself. With them, was the Lady of Air, Fire, and Lord of Water.

The teleport pad in front of them activated. They headed through the event horizon, leaving Terra and entering Ecora.

"Seems it's changed a bit." Deia looked through the city. Here it was late afternoon, with people winding down for the day. Far from Markolm, there was a relaxed air to the place.

Deia led the way through Ecora, seeing people talking to one another about their days and their troubles, reminiscing about good times, laughing, having food and drink or just going home to their loved ones.

The city was more packed than ever, but in the spirit of Emerilians, they had come together to once again fight the creatures they shared their land with.

Party Zero and their companions walked through the city, taking in these sights, smiling to themselves as if they were looking at a painting but not being a part of it. They reached the gate and steeled themselves for what was to come.

"Whoa there, nobody is allowed out of the gates without permission of the mayor and a protection detail," one of the guards near the gate said, noticing the group.

Deia pulled out a medallion and tossed it to the guard.

He caught it. A look of confusion turned to one of shock as flames curled around Deia.

"Ah, air travel, no need for that," Dave said.

A spell formation appeared around the group, glowing with gray light, imprinting onto the soil below.

One moment, they stood in front of the gate; the next, they were in the midst of a forest.

All gods and goddesses could teleport, so since Dave had become the Earth Lord, it allowed him to use his teleportation skill with the AI ignoring him even though it was him or his constructs doing it and not Jackie.

It also would allow him to use more powerful spells, without tripping the Jukal AIs.

"Show-off," Fire said.

Dave chuckled and scratched the side of his head awkwardly, not denying anything.

Water had an amused look on his face as Air ascended into the heavens.

"Not far to go," Air said.

"I ho, I ho, it's off to work I go!" Steve started before a massive shovel was conjured in Gurren's hand, making a satisfying noise as it connected with Steve's armored head.

"What was that for?" Steve complained.

"You were singing." Gurren shrugged.

"You just did it for no reason!" Steve argued.

"You think we'll ever go on a trip with them and it'll be quiet?" Induca asked.

"Nope," Malsour replied but smiled slightly. Lox, Gurren, and Steve argued about something with the occasional noise of a shovel smacking Steve's head as he tried to do something ridiculous.

"Aren't we supposed to be all stealthy and James Bondy?" Steve asked.

Dong!

"Sorry. Hand slipped." Lox destroyed the conjured shovel and looked to Gurren. "This is good fun."

"I know, right? Nothing quite so satisfying. Wonder why it's taken us so long to come up with it." Gurren sighed as if thinking of all the lost opportunities to smack Steve's head.

It wasn't long before the forest started to thin out and mountains of the Densaou Ring of Fire could be seen in the distance.

The group was letting a bit of their aura leak out, keeping the animals and creatures in the area at bay.

Air moved her hands and pointed to the ground. A boat made of air appeared, with stairs leading up to it.

The others looked to her.

"What? I'm the goddess of Air. You think I want to *walk* everywhere? It would destroy my shoes." She looked at them as if they were being unreasonable, her shoulders almost around her ears as she complained.

"Thank you, little sis." In a burst of flames, Fire moved from where she was to the flying ship.

"Very nice, riding in *style,*" Steve said as the rest of the group got up on the boat.

They pushed off and headed for the mountain at speed, weaving between the trees that were becoming more and more sparse. The green and rich forest fell away as the ground turned black and then red as magma flows could be seen here and there.

Air's ship descended lower and lower until it was just barely above the ground. No one spoke as the air whipped over them, their Mana barriers stopping it from slamming them straight on. They reached the edge of the mountains and turned south, heading toward the way point.

Dave cast his Touch of the Land spell. Now he could use his full strength and his remote orbs, stretching out over an area of nearly fifty kilometers in every direction.

He made a way point outside of the different traps. His mind worked overtime as he used his spell to build a three-dimensional model of the traps that the Dark Lord had laid down and shared them with Shard, Jeeves, and Steve.

Between the four of them, they worked out the best route with what the group had.

Dave altered the way point a bit as they rose over the smoking and bubbling magma.

Suddenly, a chill ran through everyone as a thick aura of Dark Mana ran through them. Only Malsour felt strength flooding through him.

Air's boat came to a stop. The different parts of it disintegrated as the floor lowered them down to the ground gently before it, too, dissipated.

"All right everyone, remember, seal off your Mana—only use it if you absolutely need to. No floating, levitating, or anything that consumes Mana," Deia said.

Air sighed as she pulled out a pair of sneakers from her bag of holding, sitting down on a chair of air to change them.

"She has shoes for everything," Fire said, used to her sister's odd ways.

Once Air was done, Deia turned toward their next way point. "Let's get running."

The group set off toward their next way point. It was nearly night by the time they reached it. Without needing to say anything, Water pulled out a miner; with his time on the ice planet, he was the one with the greatest knowledge of mining among them. Especially when it came to working with automated miners.

The miner activated and started to dig its path through the Densaou Ring of Fire's mountains.

They fell into the same routine as they'd had when breaking into the Earth Lord's hall. The miner would circumvent or get close to a trap, stopping to allow one of the group to move up and deactivate it before they continued forward.

***

As Party Zero and their group continued forward, the battle continued to rage above Heval on Markolm. The Dark Lord watched as the Alturarans continued to fall from the sky.

He laughed to himself. "The angels used to come down from their island to try to kill our forces before, but now they are the prey below for the Alturarans."

"It will be only a matter of time till they are destroyed and you can cut off that witch's head," Boran-al said.

"Oh, killing her would be too easy. I will cut her off from her divine wells to let her come to know an existence worse than death. She will beg and rave for the end before you and all of my Dark Champions are done with her."

"Master, your benevolence knows no bounds." Boran-al kowtowed to him, his normally aloof look now turning emotional.

The Dark Lord smiled with approval at Boran-al's actions. "I could at any time destroy her forces and then take her, but it would take all the joy out of it." The Dark Lord held out his hand to the side; a glass appeared with a smoking liquid that seemed to be moving inside.

If one was to look close, they would see a person's face on the liquid. This was not a drink but rather tortured souls, a bare imprint of the person who the energy had been ripped from.

Dark drank from the glass. A number of the souls within the glass were devoured by him as he continued to sit on his throne in the middle of the black storm clouds above Markolm. With but a wave of his hand, black lightning would descend or pillars of Dark light would make Markolm shudder.

This was the power of a god.

He frowned as an alert appeared in front of him. It told him that one of the traps around his hall had picked up something, but it had activated and there was now nothing left.

Dark dismissed it. No one had ever made it to his hall since he had been alive. Traps went off here and there, but it was nothing to worry about.

***

"That was a close one," Steve said as the shields he, Gurren, Lox, and Dave had been holding up smoked. They'd only barely had time to raise their shields and direct them toward the trap they'd accidentally activated.

It was a dissolving spell; it ejected a black miasma that melted through everything it touched.

The four dropped their shields, making sure not to touch the smoking liquid eating their shields. Most of the liquid had fallen on the ground, making holes that disappeared into the depths of Emerilia.

The group was fine but they all looked to the miner. Large sections of it had been melted apart, revealing open sections of soul gem and runic lining that lay inside.

"Well, good thing I have a few backups. However, getting around this will be a pain." Water frowned.

They ambled forward with a bag of holding, getting the old miner into it.

Water pulled out the second one and they continued on their path.

They had a few more close calls but thankfully they were able to disable them before they activated.

"Okay, from here to the room where the divine wells are held, there's nearly five hundred meters of rock in the way. However, we can't pick through it. It's too close together so we're going to be using the disposable mining lasers. Then Fire, Deia, and Induca will burn through the rest with Jung Lee's help. Malsour and I will stabilize the tunnel and make it so we don't melt from the heat," Dave said.

They had now been mining through the Densaou Ring of Fire for two days. They'd had to backtrack a few times as they'd come across lava flows and other obstacles that they couldn't cross.

Now, finally they were ready to make the last push. In this last rush, they would be betting everything. Everyone had solemn faces, ready for what was next.

They knew that the Dark Lord would sense them as well as all of the traps that were in their way. Steve, Gurren, Lox, and Air would be working to create shields and barriers to protect the rest of the group from the activating traps they would hit as they burned their way into Dark's hall.

Once they were within the hall, they didn't know what to expect. The Dark aura and the Mana in the hall was too thick for Dave to fully see through. As they got closer, he was able to get a better idea of where things were; however, it was like a rough sketch that was covered by fog. With one Touch of the Land spell, things might look completely different from the next Touch of the Land spell.

Everyone moved into position: Jung Lee at the front; Deia, Induca, and Fire behind him; Dave, Water, and Malsour making up the third layer; with Air, Steve, Lox, and Gurren taking up the rear.

Dave, Gurren, Lox, and Steve all held orbs in their hands, ready to activate them in a moment's notice.

"Ready!" Deia called out to them all.

"Ready!" the others yelled back.

"Forward!" Deia's voice set them into motion as everything changed within a split second.

The orbs rushed around the group, each covering a different direction as more and more orbs were thrown out, creating a net of them around the group.

The spirits within Jung Lee raced through his body. Gray smoke radiated from him as his eyes turned silver, and gray Mana turned into a drill in front of his sword. Jung Lee's drill passed through the stone ahead with barely any resistance. Unleashing his full speed, he shot forward and let out a yell as power surged through his body. His muscles bulged as blood rushed through his body.

Induca and Deia funneled power into Fire, who unleashed her full power for the first time in centuries.

The traps around them all started to activate upon feeling the power coming from their bodies.

Dave pulled heat from the melted walls, cooling them almost instantly so they weren't burned as they rushed past. Malsour made supports as Water assisted in regulating the heat and guiding those up front; with his knowledge, he was in charge of this part of the operation.

The activated traps surged with power; explosions rocked the tunnel and the group as they rushed forward, crossing tens of meters in but a moment, not pausing their charge for anything. Steve, Lox, Air, and Gurren glowed with power; Air used her own abilities while the others used the shield orbs to deflect power away and protect the others.

Here and there, orbs cracked under the power backlash from the traps, but there were tens of them in the tunnel. Two others would take up their place with ease as more orbs were thrown out by the group.

"You dare attack my hall!" Dark's voice reached them. His power locked onto them as they crossed the three-hundred-meter mark.

Fire grunted and her hair whipped around wildly; the walls evaporated under her power as Jung Lee and the group's speed surged once again.

More and more traps were activated and a number of creatures that patrolled the area around Dark's hall tried to attack. Air snorted and waved her hand, cleaving a number of these creatures apart before they could reach the tunnels. Dave was inwardly shocked at the power she displayed with that light wave of her hand.

The rock cleared away and a dark, obsidian-like surface was ahead of them. Jung Lee circulated his power even more as Fire, Deia, and Induca channeled a spell together. A pillar of flame appeared ahead of Jung Lee. It smashed through the material ahead, melting them apart in mid-air as the pillar shot through the room. Pain-screams could be heard as the pillar killed and wounded those inside.

Jung Lee retracted his power into his sword and body once again, turning into a gray blur as he rushed to meet the creatures inside. The hole in front of him opened up; rocks and metal shot out in every direction as the rest of the party followed.

They had entered what looked like a treasury. A black fog hovered over everything. There were faces on the walls of people in pain, as well as torture tools and blood stains.

Dave didn't hesitate. Using the orbs, he teleported them all within Dark's hall.

Instantly, they all felt their power being suppressed now that they had entered the domain of the Dark Lord. They appeared in the midst of twisted and mangled creatures. However broken they looked, the aura that swept over the group made them feel a cold chill.

Fire let out a low growl. Flames appeared across her body as a staff of solidified flames appeared in her hands. Induca and Malsour immediately changed into their dragon forms, unleashing their breaths, scouring those in the near area. Gurren, Lox, and Steve pulled out or conjured their weapons and leapt into battle.

Deia's bow appeared. Runes and spell formations appeared around her as her fingers flashed over her bow's controls. Arrow after arrow left red streaks in the air. Each of them hit a vital spot, causing the creatures to cry out in pain or flop down to never rise again.

Water created a trident of water; he stabbed forward streams of water and cut all of those down in his path. His long hair whipped around his head crazily, a smile on his face.

Air pulled out what looked like a recorder. None of the group could hear anything but the creatures that were attacking them bowed their heads in pain, a dozen of them dying from their hesitation.

Dave closed his eyes and spread out his senses, looking for the divine wells. A moment later, they snapped open. He made to teleport again but found something stopping him.

"You want to stop me with your spell formations and Magical Circuits!" Dave snarled and smashed his fist into the floor.

His cloak fluttered with power as his gray runic lines turned silver. His eyes opened; silver, like liquid mercury, covered his eyes until they were turned completely silver. His armor pulsated with power as his armbands started to shake and move.

A screen appeared in front of his face.

"Hah! Break for me!" Dave yelled, accepting the box in front of him.

Across the Dark Lord's hall, runes flashed with incredible power. Dave drove the power of his armor, as well as that of his party and their stored-up vault soul gems.

The power raged through the Dark Lord's hall. The dark smoke that covered the hall dissipated in a moment and the creatures inside grew weaker, their auras declining as Dave and his group felt their full power return to them.

They increased their efforts, killing more and more of the creatures as Dave put down a way point to the main hall that was above them.

The Dark Lord's hall shook and shuddered, taking away the Magical Circuits and formations that weaved through the entirety of the Dark Lord's hall that had weakened it.

Suddenly, a massive wave of pressure overcame them all.

The Dark Lord had arrived.

***

"The attack on the Dark Lord's hall has begun. All forces, ready flight drives!" Josh barked.

"Time I went to work," Bob said. A silver aura came from him as he seemed to step into the air onto a black plate that appeared under his feet. He shot forward toward Markolm, his cloak fluttering behind him.

Josh's heart shuddered at the bit of power that Bob had accidentally leaked out.

He looked toward Markolm as the forces of the Terra Alliances moved forward. Sixteen flying citadels moved in formation as the mountains of Gorlei, Donsk, and Zolu shook. Massive trap doors opened and slid out of the way as the mountain cannons of the dwarves were revealed.

All across Emerilia, these cannons were being run out. Behind them were specially trained crews and odd-looking boxes.

***

A few minutes earlier, the Dark Lord was watching the fighting going on in front of him. Around him were his Dark Champions. Every so often he would send them out, to bring back an angel or two to play with.

He used spells so that their screams and pleading could be heard all across Markolm.

He was laughing at the latest one they had acquired when he received a new alert.

With a wave of his hand, he made to dismiss it when another appeared. His eyes widened and then his aura surged as he opened his interface to his hall, taking control of it. It was as if he was there as he passed through the area around his hall.

"You dare attack my hall!" His voice boomed through the air and through his hall. His anger reached new heights as he watched Party Zero, Air, Fire, and Water breaking through his defenses and carving toward his hall.

"Good, very good. You've delivered yourselves to my domain. I have wanted to deal with you all for a long time now," Dark said to himself. He activated the security protocols of his hall and locked it down so that they wouldn't be able to leave.

With a wave of his hand, a massive spell formation stretched underneath his and his Dark Champion's feet.

Shadows wrapped around them before they disappeared from the sky, appearing within the Dark Lord's hall; the shadows that had wrapped around them now disappeared.

The hall shook with explosions and the sounds of fighting from the areas below the main hall. Power surged through the walls, breaking the different protections that had been placed there throughout the ages.

In a flash of gray light, the attackers appeared at the bottom of the hall, facing the Dark Lord and his champions arrayed around his throne.

Down the sides of the hall laid the Dark Lord's divine wells. A few of them stopped glowing as they were no longer connected to the Dark Lord. Dave, destroying the Magical Circuits, had also destroyed a number of the circuits that linked the wells to the Dark Lord.

"Good. Very good!" the Dark Lord yelled. His rage reached new heights as he raised his hand. A pillar that seemed to suck in the surrounding light lanced outward. It hit a Mana barrier that snapped into existence between different orbs in front of the group.

The pillar's power cut a line into the surrounding hall, firmly stopped by the Mana barrier.

The Dark Lord's expression flickered as he felt the aura from Dave more clearly than ever before.

"Why do you have the aura of Neutral?" the Dark Lord asked.

"One could say he's a friend." Dave laughed.

"Seems like the old bastard forgot about me," Fire said. A firestorm appeared around her as she lowered her staff, pointed toward Dark. It shot out from the barrier.

Dark snorted as he once again shot out a Dark pillar from his hand. He could feel Fire's attack contained a lot less Mana than his did.

When the two attacks met, Dark's expression changed once again to shock.

Fire's beam turned into a raging dragon that opened its mouth, eating the black beam; flames exploded within the dragon, converting the Dark Lord's energy as it rushed forward.

Dark activated a Mana barrier. He had to pour in considerable energy as the now massive dragon hit the barrier.

The hall shook with the power being unleashed. Parts of the roof came apart and fell down as a wave of destruction smashed out from where the barrier and dragon had met.

As soon as the destruction passed, Dark let out a roar and shot forward. Behind him, his Dark Champions and creatures followed, pulling out their weapons and displaying their different fighting techniques.

Party Zero rushed forward as well. The resulting clashes caused shock waves that tore through the hall.

The massive black dragon seemed unstoppable as it unleashed attack after attack on those around it, not caring whether they lived or died. It made it to three of the Mana wells that were unclaimed. It cut its hand and flickered blood over them; in a flash of light, they disappeared into a ring of holding on its hand.

Dark shot power into his people as a scythe appeared in his hands. He brought it down, creating a black arc that struck out at Fire.

Fire snorted and slammed her staff against the ground. Dozens of atronachs and dragons appeared, encircling the Dark Lord.

Water gave a cold cough and his trident struck out, meeting the black scythe.

He coughed out some blood and flew backward, seeming much weaker than before, but the scythe attack had been destroyed.

Air's flute filled the air, making the champions shake their heads in pain while illusionary figures appeared around Dark.

He cut out wildly in a rage. He was all-powerful, much more powerful than his three siblings. However, the creatures that they had called upon and made were extremely powerful. They surrounded him from every direction and cut off his movement, not allowing him to use a spell as they attacked again and again.

This was one of the weaknesses of the members of the Pantheon who didn't actually practice magic. To create spells, they needed to rely on the AI, which would take time to do; and if their mind was chaotic, then the AI would have a hard time completing the request.

Jung Lee was pinned down by three of the Dark Champions, all of them sweating as Jung Lee looked over them with an impartial look. His brows pinched together slightly as six spirits appeared around him and then were absorbed by him. Three heads shot up into the sky as Jung Lee looked for his next target; he turned around to see the mutated experiments and creatures that had made it up from the depths of the hall and were now charging the main hall.

Jung Lee flicked the blood off his blade. He shot forward, leaving a crater behind where his foot had been. He cut through the creatures, his blade rushing to and fro, but he was only able to slow their advance. A number of them actually put up a fight that needed him to take more than a few moments to deal with. As more of them arrived, the more powerful creatures started to show up.

"Dave, Lox!" Jung Lee yelled out to the two closest to him.

Lox kicked the man who he was fighting toward Steve, who turned without looking. His axe split them apart before he brought it over his head and met the blade of a giant he was fighting, sending the giant back a few steps.

Dave's hands flickered as spell formations appeared around the party. Their power increased as the light of his armor flickered somewhat before returning to its silver glory. He pulled out his conjuration rods; from his arms and his hands, a gray smoke erupted, forming into a Gatling gun that Dave held by his side.

He held the trigger down, bracing himself as glowing rounds made streaks of light at the experiments. These rounds exploded with golden light; the weapon was conjuring grand working rounds inside. They were nowhere as powerful as the grand workings that were used by armies to breach walls or by the dwarven artillery. However, they were made to target the weaknesses of the Dark-created creatures. The Light grand workings were a potent acid that ate through their bodies, causing them to cry out in pain.

Dave stood there, guiding the line of fire across the creatures' front.

Lox's orbs shot out Mana bolts as they moved around him and he launched grenades from a launcher he'd conjured through his armor.

The creatures were in a state of disorder. Jung Lee rushed up their center; Lox blew up everything in sight to his right, and Dave peppered the almighty shit out of the poor bastards on the left.

Attacks rained around Dave, who wasn't able to move. His shield orbs rotated around him to create a Mana barrier that sparked with the violent impacts.

Lox was moving around, making it harder to hit him but his armor's Mana barrier took care of any attacks that came too close for comfort.

Deia and Induca were locked in combat. Deia ran across the ground and her arrows caused shock waves across the hall, tearing up the air as it passed. She dodged backward in the air and used explosions under her feet to perform acrobatic acts as she loosed arrow after arrow, nearly keeping up with the pace of Dave's Gatling gun.

Induca called down atronachs as she fought dozens of the champions, trying to take pressure off of Malsour.

Steve and Suzy were right next to Malsour, protecting him as he unraveled the Dark Lord's control over the divine wells and wrested it away.

Malsour opened his eyes as seven more of the nearly fifty Mana wells came under his command, bringing him to ten in total. His body shuddered as his aura became more powerful; however, the change was only a portion as powerful as Dave's had been. Only when he controlled them all would he be seen as the new Dark Lord and have the boost that Dave acquired.

"The creature doesn't know its master!" Boran-al yelled in joy, a look of greed in his eyes as his creatures attacked Steve and he sent binding contract after binding contract at him.

The Mana wells were already cut off from the Dark Lord, so he didn't notice as Malsour reached out with a claw toward Steve.

Power from the divine wells circulated them before slamming into Steve. His power increased by leaps and bounds; his body started to change and transform, condensing but becoming more powerful as his Devastator armor glowed with powerful runic lines.

Steve let out a roar. His entire body shook with a multicolored glow, like the soul gems his body was made of but much more powerful.

"Suzy is my only master!" Steve barked out. He unleashed an axe attack that killed a dozen of Boran-al's creatures in one slash, breaking Boran-al's connection and making the Dark Lord's Champion cough blood as Suzy's six Affinity creations used the opening to gain some space around Malsour.

In a flash of silver light, they were teleported to another section of the hall where the divine wells were connected to the Dark Lord and under his control.

Malsour unleashed a powerful attack and created a barrier around himself, Steve, and Suzy as he submerged his mind into the coding placed on the divine wells to break the hold from the Dark Lord.

Feeling the tug of Malsour's attack, the Dark Lord looked over. His scythe cut through a handful of the creatures that encircled him. Whenever he unleashed an attack beyond the creatures, Water was there to stop him, while Fire and Air continued to harass him with more and more creatures.

He was filled with rage as he whirled around. "Dark sun!" the Dark Lord called out. He stood still for a few seconds, to channel the spell to his AI and then activate it. He hadn't been able to do the specifics, instead going for as powerful as possible.

His Mana barrier shook and quivered with the impacts of the surrounding creatures, taking a large portion of power just to defend against their attacks.

Air and Fire, seeing him making a spell, didn't waste any time bringing their most powerful spells to bear; they practiced magic and were able to insta cast.

Massive spell formations appeared around them as the ground shook and a volcano tore up through the areas underneath the hall and into the main hall under Dark's feet.

The ground above shook. If someone was able to see the southern area of the Densaou Ring of Fire, they would see a massive tornado forming before it burrowed into a mountainside. It cut through everything in its path, not weakening in the slightest as the cutting blades of wind turned everything into dust that shot up into the sky.

The volcano and the tornado smashed together, atop the Dark Lord. His Mana barrier became lighter as the summoned illusory figures and those of flames increased the speed and ferocity of their attacks, using the now Air and Fire Mana-rich air to increase the power of their attacks.

The Dark Lord felt this all going on. He held his concentration as he felt the spell building as power rushed from his divine wells under the guidance of his AI. A black sphere appeared around his chest, pulsating with power, becoming more and more dense as it grew in power. Suddenly it expanded. A shock wave rippled out from where the sphere hit the volcano, creatures, and tornado.

Suzy spat out blood, as did those who were too close or weak to take on the impact of those forces meeting. Fire's and Air's faces were contorted as they fought to maintain their spells.

The Mana wells around were draining of energy, powering the Dark sun spell more and more. It seemed to struggle, fighting these opposing forces. The struggle ended and the sphere expanded at an alarming rate.

Everything within a hundred meters was destroyed, including the tornado from above and the volcano from below.

The Dark Lord panted as some of his strength fell away. Already Air and Fire were calling upon more creatures.

Dark looked around with a cold look in his eyes. Dave wasn't the only person he had sensed a familiar Mana aura coming from. Dark's eyes latched onto Deia, a chilling smile on his face as he disappeared from where he'd been and appeared next to Deia in a shroud of black smoke.

Dark's hand reached out and clamped around Deia's neck. "Seems that Fire really did have a daughter." Even with the sounds of battle, his voice could be heard throughout the hall. He'd sealed her magic as he stroked Deia's face, looking toward Fire. "Don't worry, your mother will be following you soon enough."

Dark let out a gloating laugh as an aura exploded out among Party Zero. Dark's eyes went wide. He'd never felt an aura like this before. He turned and looked at Dave. The look of utter rage in Dave's face made Dark's heart clench before he started to sneer, his hand tightening around Deia's throat.

Dave disappeared and reappeared in front of Dark. He slowly closed his hand, he and Deia covered in a Mana barrier so nothing could make it past.

Dark saw a flash of light and then pain, pain he had never felt in his life! He'd never had a bruise, let alone a cut! He had been the one to hurt others! Now he let out a squeal as he looked at where the pain was coming from—his arm. His barrier had been broken and his arm had been cut off, falling downward.

"I'll kill you!" The Dark Lord charged Dave as both he and Deia disappeared in a flash of gray light.

Deia appeared next to her mother as a blade pierced out from the void, stabbing into the Dark Lord's back; he cried out in pain as blades came in from different sides.

Dave floated in front of the Dark Lord. Orbs created a circle in front of him that flashed every few seconds, creating a wormhole that Dave stabbed the blade through, piercing the Dark Lord.

The Dark Lord felt his power being drained. Not the power of the divine wells, but his personal power, the power that he had never looked to increase. After all, he was a god; he never had to do anything.

He activated a spell, but nothing happened. "What's happening?" he yelled out, enraged, in pain and confused.

"Oh, sorry, that's a Jukal link. When I activate it, I'm seen as Jukal—you know, your masters," Dave said. As they were in Dark's hall, no one was able to see inside. Against the Dark Lord, it meant that his divine wells—a Jukal creation—were essentially useless and he couldn't use any of the power he had saved up.

"No one is my master!" the Dark Lord said, spit colored with blood flying from his mouth.

Dave laughed. The noise sent chills down the spines of those there. He raised a finger and pointed it at the Dark Lord.

"Kneel." Dave's voice rebounded through the hall as the Dark Lord's body folded and he dropped to the ground, kneeling to Dave, a look of shock on his face.

"Good boy. Now you can die," Dave said.

The Dark Lord let out a scream as his body contorted before exploding.

Dave only looked on with cold eyes. He had changed a lot since coming to Emerilia. He had gained friends, a family, a fiancée, and a daughter.

There was no way for him to save Deia without using tricks that would raise alarm bells with the AI across Emerilia.

His eyes turned to the rest of the Dark Lord's creations. From him, soul gem constructs rushed out, landing on the divine wells;

these unlocked the wells within moments and connected them to Malsour, who let out a roar of power.

"Kill those who remain and we'll head to Markolm!" Dave yelled out.

The Dark Champions looked at the group around them in fear. They had thought themselves unable to feel the emotion anymore.

The group charged forward, fury filling their eyes at coming so close to having lost one of their own again.

Dave disappeared from where he stood. His blade cut through the air in a silver flash.

Boran-al dropped to the ground as his creatures, now without a master, bowed to the ground, not daring to make a noise.

Dave's hands flashed out, throwing out grenades that would shock the people of Emerilia. A virulent poison Jung Lee had created exploded out among the creatures trying to enter the hall. Jung Lee using the poison instantly increased the deadliness of his attacks.

Lox followed, not having to worry about the poison while in his armor.

After a few moments, Malsour raised his head. His body seemed chaotic, as if there were just energy waiting to explode out. The Dark Champions' and the experiments' power sharply declined under his gaze. He smacked the ground. Black pillars shot out of the ground. Instantly the sounds of battle ended as pillars pierced through the Dark Champions and creatures.

Party Zero, as well as the gods, looked around. Seeing that there was no one else to fight, they looked to one another.

"The Jukal have noticed your actions. Depending on reaction times, you can expect them to start moving within the hour." Anna's voice came from the air.

"Who is that? It sounded like Anna." Induca looked upward.

Dave grabbed a Mirror of Communication and pressed a quick call number. It connected a moment later.

"Ready Pandora's Box," Dave said.

In front of his eyes screens appeared.

Quest: Defiance

You have foiled the Dark Lord's plans and used his own power against his creations. He has marked you for revenge. There is only one way to stop a god: you must become one yourself.

So, you became a god and then you made your buddy the Dark Lord. Even I'm impressed, sure it was sneaky as hell, but who doesn't like some rogue-ish action? Alright so I guess that you won't be having any more troubles from that guy!

Requirements: Stop the Dark Lord from hunting you. By any means necessary.

Rewards: Legendary Item: Dark Lord's Domain

Class: Defier

Stop the Dark Lord from hunting you

In front of Dave the shadows seemed to meld together and then float away, revealing a tome. Dave grabbed the book, frowning. He opened the book, his eyes went wide as information was poured into his mind, it was a legendary class ability.

It took just a few moments for the tome to load its information into Dave's mind.

As the back cover closed, the book dissolved into dust.

Dave closed his eyes, focusing on what he'd learned.

Dave focused on the domain, it would basically increase his affinity to darkness around him within a certain area. It was one of the few ways that one might be able to boost their affinity above 1000, a realm at which people could freely become that element, destroying and creating their physical body at will.

To many this was a second life that would allow them to avoid dying, however the energy it needed was only enough to use it for a short period of time, sometimes only once in a few days as mana needed time to regenerate and your body needed to adapt.

New Class: Defier

So, well, it was you or him right? How the hell you did it? Still just whaaa? But anyway, you kicked some Dark Lord ass, killed his shadowy ass and we're here now. Looks like you're not willing to let your enemy live while you gain power. Ruthless. Good rule for life though!

Status: Level 1

Effects: You defy the odds and the Gods (Imma poet and didn't even know it! Sometimes I'm just too funny).

Since you're the first person to get this class we're wading into the unknown. Let's say you get a 10% increase to stats when fighting an opponent 20 or more levels higher than you.

+10% to stats when fighting opponents 20 levels above you.

Quest: Champion Slayer Level 4

Kill 100 Champions (117/100)

Rewards: Unlock Level 5 Quest

+10 to all stats

Increased/Decreased reputation with Affinities

400,000 EXP

Class: Champion Slayer

Status: Level: 4

Effect: +40 to all stats

Relationship with Affinities Pantheon:
Dark: Trusted Friend
Light: Despised
Water: Favorable
Fire: Trusted Friend
Earth: This is you, don't really expect that it's going to be much different than how you feel that day about yourself.
Air: Favorable

Quest: Champion Slayer Level 5
Kill 200 Champions (17/200)
Rewards: Unlock Level 6 Quest
Increase to stats
Increased/Decreased reputation with Affinities

Chapter 23: Pandora's Box Opens

"What the hell is all that noise?" the Jukal commander demanded. He was in charge of the controllers that oversaw Emerilia and the feeds that went out to the Jukal Empire. He had just been cutting videos together of the latest battles between the Dark Lord and the Lady of Light when the different screens within the command center started to go off.

Since the last great battle, he had received accolades from his higher-ups and it seemed that even the emperor himself had taken notice of him.

Now he threw himself into his work even more. Hearing the alarms, his mind went back to the day where his name had risen into prominence.

"Sir! We're getting reports that there's a Jukal on the surface of Emerilia!" one of the controllers said.

"Well, Lo'kal is supposed to be down there somewhere. What of it?" the commander said.

"No, this person was caught with altering the programming within the game," the controller said.

The commander's face turned serious. "Alert the military. We might have an in-game hacker. What information can you pull up?"

"We've got a location of the hack. We're pulling up feeds now. However, it seems as if the AIs are bugging out. They're being complicated and not doing what we need them to," one of the controllers said in a frustrated voice.

"Show me the feeds!" the commander said.

The main screen changed from the fighting that was happening on Markolm and instead turned to the interior of Dark's hall.

People couldn't see into the hall with normal sensors. However, the Jukal had made the halls for the different members of the Pantheon—how could they not know what was going on within the building that they had created?

The rough images were compiled slowly, coming into focus.

"What?" The Jukal controller changed where the cameras were aimed.

An image became clear as a tunnel appeared in the ground underneath the Dark Lord's hall.

New alerts started to pop up at the same time as they were viewing the recording.

"What is it now?" the Jukal commander growled.

"Malsour has just been named the new Dark Lord," another controller said.

"If I'm not wrong, then this looks to be the tunnel they used to enter the Dark Lord's hall." The first controller pointed to his screen as the tunnel continued forward to the hall.

"Speed it up." The commander was excited, feeling as if his name would once again be raised up to the highest places within the Jukal Empire.

The tunneling sped up; the mining ended and then powerful magic was employed as the group cut through the ground and then smashed their way into the Dark Lord's hall.

"The power readings—that must be Party Zero as well as Fire, Air, and Water," one of the controllers nearby said, looking at the readings.

"Over the last couple of months, it's gotten harder and harder to connect to their identity chips within their bodies," the controller muttered to herself.

"We've got another alert—seems that we've got multiple teleports across Emerilia," the controller who'd called out the Dark Lord alert said.

"Must be the gods moving around," the commander said, dismissing it.

"No, all of these teleports were at the same time," the controller said.

"How is that possible? Only the gods can do that and they can't move to multiple locations at the same time." The commander looked up from the sped-up feed of Party Zero and their gods rushing through the hall and meeting the Dark Lord.

"Bringing up the feed," the Jukal said, inputting commands. For a few minutes, nothing happened. "Come on!" The Jukal hit the side of their console to aid it as mist sprayed down from above.

Finally, the image on the screen was resolved and showed a portal. There didn't seem to be anything different about it.

"I could swear that the alert said that something had been attached to the portals," the controller said.

"Well, seems that everything is fine," the commander said.

"Sir, you're going to want to see this," the controller with the feed of the Dark Lord's hall said.

The commander looked back to the screen, frowning. He saw Dave cut Dark's arm off and then teleport Deia away; then Dark couldn't do anything to him as he tried to cast a spell through his AI.

"Okay, well, becoming a god, he can get the ability to teleport. Why isn't the Dark Lord's spell working? Was there an AI glitch?" the commander said.

"The AI registered Dave as not part of Emerilia. Instead, it said that he was a Jukal, thus the Dark Lord couldn't do anything..." The controller's eyes went wide.

Dave raised his hand as soul gem constructs rushed out to the divine wells.

"What are those?" the commander asked.

"I'm not sure, but they were able to break and re-code the divine wells," the controller said.

The commander felt a bit of unease at it all but dismissed it. There had never been a problem with Emerilia before. "It's probably just another glitch in the system. After all, we've never had players and POEs as gods before. Open up the AI logs and see if we can't debug it. In the meantime, prep a video of them taking down the Dark Lord and remove the part about his spells not working—add in something in between," the commander said.

"Yes, sir." The controller watching the Dark Lord sent off the logs and started to hack together a video of the events that had gone on.

"The flying citadels have just reached Markolm. Party Zero as well as the gods have also arrived!" the third controller said excitedly.

"Come on, people, keep those streams live. This is some of the best content I've ever seen! I want it flying out of here as fast as possible. Call all of the editors and other controllers to work—we're going to need them all to get this sorted out!" the commander said in a clear state of joy as he moved to his seat. Mist sprayed on him as he started to work his screens.

"Sir, we're, uh, getting readings of Lo'kal teleporting people away from Markolm," a controller said.

"That kook hasn't done anything in a long time. Maybe he wants to save some of them." The commander sneered and shook his head. "Just like when he made this planet all over again. Humans aren't good for anything but providing entertainment. They're all savages."

The controllers all nodded in agreement. Humans were nothing but things to be watched and pitied for their savage ways.

"Now, get back to work. Lo'kal can do as he pleases unless it messes with the stream."

The commander's orders threw them into action as they worked to bring Emerilia's latest content to the Jukal Empire.

***

Ela-Dorn looked upward as she listened to Jeeves's voice that was being broadcasted across all of the Pandora's Box Initiative's bases and ships.

"This is not a drill. All vessels are to be manned and operation Pandora's Box is to be started." Jeeves's voice continued on, repeating the same sentence in the same monotone voice.

Ela-Dorn heard it two more times before it settled in.

She dropped what she was working on and ran out of the room. Devastator-armored units that had been training now marched through Ice City to the three portals that connected them to the asteroid base. Carts were moving faster than ever, moving personnel and vital equipment and items from base to base.

Ela-Dorn opened her interface as she made it to a landing bay. Inside there were racks of carts, waiting for whoever needed them. She jumped into one.

"Moonbase!" she yelled as she looked over the information coming back from the massive portals within the moonbase, ark shipyard, and the asteroid base.

With a swipe of her hand, a real-time view of the original Pandora's Box workshop came into view. There was little in there. People and items rushed through the now more than twenty portals between bases in the hub of portals. However, her view was not of this, but of the teleport array that Dave, Malsour, Steve, and Bob had built and used to open up portals on Nal, their gateway to the ice planet and asteroid base.

Now it was once again active. It showed a portal at the bottom of a bay, with Alturarans coming out of it through its event horizon. The crane pulled out what looked like packages of clamps.

These clamps were developed by Ela-Dorn, the Aleph College, and Dave. They were made to control the Jukal portals and also give them shields.

They were dropped through the event horizon. The clamps would be separated out, float around the portal and then attach to a shield, snapping up around it. It flashed with hits as the Altur-arans coming through the portal smashed up against the shield, the energies tearing them apart on a molecular level.

The event horizon closed and the teleportation array once again dialed up another location and showed another portal. Once again the crane dropped in the clamps. They separated, runes flaring as they attached to the portal.

Ela-Dorn looked away from the screen and let out a breath. With the clamps, they could cut off and control the people who were entering Emerilia.

The cart she was on passed through a portal through to the hub, then back through to the moonbase. A Mana barrier appeared around the cart as she entered the shipyards for the missile boats.

There were now sixty of the missile boats, all in their slips. Their power plants flared to life as their runic lines came online, ready to move out. The crews rushed to their ships and their stations as engineers ran last checks on the ships and their systems, removing the umbilicals connecting the ship to the slips they were in.

The ships dropped downward once they were cleared and all their crew was onboard.

Dropping downward brought them to the large open space below, facing a massive circle formed of soul gem.

Ela-Dorn rushed toward this circle before she veered off toward a clear soul gem-covered control room that was off to the side of it. Her cart slowed down as she passed through a Mana barrier into a shuttle bay. She hopped off the cart onto the platform and ran into the control room. "How are we looking?"

"All systems are online and we should be ready to transmit," one of the techs in the room reported.

"Good. How about the portals at the asteroid base?" Ela-Dorn asked.

"They're ready," the same tech said.

"Okay. And the covering for this portal?" Ela-Dorn looked to them, holding their eyes.

"Ready to blow it on your orders." The tech pointed to a big red button behind a Mana shield.

Ela-Dorn shook her head. Steve had heard about their plan, so he'd snuck in one night and upgraded their simple red button to the massive fire alarm-sized button on the wall.

"Jeeves, let me know when all ships are ready to move and how long until the ships out scouting can be back?" Ela-Dorn asked.

"The military group believes that we have enough forces to hold Emerilia with what we have and have given orders to the ships scouting that they are to continue their operations and be ready to be put into action at a moment's notice," Jeeves said.

"Okay, that works for me," Ela-Dorn said.

"Party Zero as well as Air, Fire, and Water have arrived at Pandora's Box and are moving to the ark shipyard," Jeeves reported.

Ela-Dorn didn't say anything, merely nodding as she wondered what was happening on Emerilia.

***

Josh and Bob stood on Goblin Mountain's Flying Citadel One as it cruised through the air.

The clouds that had been looming above Markolm were now disappearing as the golden shields shone brighter than ever in the sky.

Legions of angels rose up into the air, facing off against the flying citadels. The sky above Markolm was filled with what looked like glitter as the sun reflected off the legions of angels that were forming up for battle.

The sky between the citadels was filled with aerial forces from across Emerilia, looking like a black cloud on the horizon.

Bob smiled as he looked to his side, where the aerial forces were holding their formations between the flying citadels. "I was wondering when she would raise them up to be champions."

Josh turned and followed his eyes as magical circles formed around the dragons that were part of the aerial forces. "I didn't think she had the Mana wells for that, and why wouldn't she have done that before?" Josh asked.

"She didn't accept power from her followers, instead using it to make the Per'ush islands and try to help the people of Emerilia. However, she had saved up her own power and now she could unleash it to double the strength of her descendants. The reason she didn't do it before is because it will double a person's level, taking them from say Level 100 to 200. However, it is much harder to increase your level at Level 200 than Level 100. The longer she waited, the higher their base levels were that are now being doubled," Bob said.

Josh nodded as the members of the Dracul family started to roar as newfound power rushed through their bodies.

One could physically see the changes as their bodies expanded, growing bigger and stronger. Their aura fluctuated as Fire poured power into them.

The wind picked up around Bob and Josh as Alkao and his advisers descended from above. He was in charge of the aerial forces of the Terra Alliance on this operation.

"We're ready," Alkao said simply, his eyes cold and merciless.

Trumpets were heard in the distance. The angels, feeling the enemy getting stronger, now rushed forward to join in battle before they were able to become stronger.

"Seems that they are, too." Josh frowned. He had a chat invite through the Mirror of Communication at his side; he opened it up and connected to Dave.

"Activating the shields below," Dave said.

Underneath Markolm, blue pillars shot up from the top of onos spreading outward, creating a Mana barrier that connected with the surrounding Mana barriers that came from the onos.

Josh changed channels as Dave closed off the chat, linking all of the flying citadel commanders together. "Begin bombardment."

Cannons fired, the air rippling with the Mana ejection.

The rounds rushed through the air, hitting the angels' lines and Maphrol, the capital of Markolm behind them.

Explosions blotted out the sky as the cannons didn't pause, firing as fast as they could reload. The dwarven artillery commanders called out orders and adjustments. A much deeper and powerful explosion filled the air as people looked to the dwarven mountain below. The sound of their cannons firing at the same time reached them, their rounds already striking Markolm's underside.

The Mana barrier underneath shuddered with these massive impacts.

"Move along deployment path," Josh said, watching the destruction that was being loosed on Markolm, his face grim but resolute.

"I'm ready to move the innocents out from Markolm," Bob said.

"Go and secure the prisoners," Josh said.

Bob waved his hands as an interface appeared. He poured power through Anna; She rose up into the air, behind her, Bob's image appeared as a full twenty foot tall avatar of him.

He let a low growl filled with his anger, He waved his hand, Anna doing the same motion as her hand passed the people that were being drained of energy by Light's formations disappeared. Unlike the people of Emerilia, Bob was classified as a God and could teleport people at will without the Jukal AI's freaking out.

The angels were still charging forward, unleashing attacks to destroy the oncoming dwarven artillery shells, their eyes filled with rage as here and there their shields shook with impacts. They were powerful enough to take on direct hits of the artillery shells. It might take two or three for them to be destroyed but that was impressive compared to most other forces that could do nothing but die under the dwarven fire unless they had massive protections in place.

Josh looked up as he felt the wind changing. Alkao flapped his wings; around him were the generals of the aerial forces from across Emerilia.

Josh gritted his teeth. They might have a number of tricks on their side, but the simple fact was that their aerial forces and fighters might be a third again the size of the angel's legions, but most were only half as powerful. Even with the dragons gaining such a boost, they might be two times stronger than the angels but their supporting forces weren't strong enough.

Suddenly, a message appeared on his Mirror of Communication. He stared at it in shock and then looked to Alkao.

There was now a light of hope in his eyes. He had been prepared to sacrifice all of their fighting force in order to weaken the angel legions, hoping that the rest of the Terra Alliance would be able to defeat them.

"I think I like this new Dark Lord," Alkao said.

Bob looked to the two of them, filled with questions.

Alkao and Josh ignored him.

"What are you thinking with this?" Josh asked.

"Have the DCA aerial forces and dragon forces moved together discreetly. The rest of the forces will move into the shields of the flying citadels and take out targets of opportunity. We'll take the fight to the angels," Alkao said.

"Well, it's a ballsy plan, but we don't really deal with the normal around here." Josh grinned.

Alkao returned the grin as Bob shook his head. It was clear the other two weren't going to tell him what was going on.

"I'll get my forces organized." Alkao's wings flapped as he shot into the sky once again.

"I have some cleaning to do," Bob's cold voice made Josh shiver as he disappeared.

Bob reappeared over a convoy that were about to leave Markolm.

He flicked his hand dismissively, summoned swords shot out, piercing the caravan, killing those manning it, groups of Angels rushed out from the coverings.

Bob let out a cold snort the waves of power left the Angels quivering.

"This is the power of your so-called Goddess," Bob said, unleashing his full aura, it was tens of times more powerful than the Lady of Lights, all were cowed under its power.

Spears pierced the Angels as Bob moved to the caravans, with a wave of his hand the caravans fell apart revealing people bound in powerful chains. These were the strongest of those that had fought back, they were being transported to another location, setting up fall back positions for the Angels and Light to operate out of if needed.

Their chains and bindings fell away as Bob stepped into the sky once again, people gave their thanks but Bob didn't hear it, teleporting away to a secret location where draining spell formations had been set up and Angels were guarding against intruders.

Across Light's secondary location her people were left with lifeless corpses while those her people were using were freed.

***

Alkao's orders had been passed throughout the aerial forces. The DCA moved closer to the dragons as the other aerial forces moved to the outside of the formations, closer to the flying citadels.

Alkao looked over them all, proud not only of his people, but all under his command. When he'd come to Emerilia, he had thought that everyone was against him. Dave and Party Zero had showed him that wasn't true, that he could make friends and rely on others. He could come to have allies.

He touched the shield on his back, a look of melancholy on his face as his hand then moved to the necklace that lay under his armor. It had been melted and its original appearance changed—it had been the necklace he had given to Anna.

He knew that she was up on Bob's ship, but he also knew that she had lost most of her memories of Alkao and her time as she had fought as a member of Party Zero.

Still, it didn't make his smile dim in the slightest.

"It was hard enough the first time getting her to be my girlfriend—hopefully it'll be easier the second time." Alkao's smile actually grew even as he faced the oncoming angels.

He let the necklace fall under his armor once again. "All right, you lot! Look after yourselves and listen to orders from higher! Force One, we will clear a path for the flying citadels. Force Two, protect the rest of the Alliance and secure the air above Markolm! Force One, move out!" Alkao yelled out, his eyes focused on the enemy ahead as he detached from what was happening.

The two forces split apart as if it had been rehearsed time and time again. Force Two split from around the DCA and dragons, who surged forward and spread out into a massive inverted V-formation that birds traveled in. Denur and the most powerful DCA, including Alkao, were in the forward part of the inverted V. Dragons and DCA fell in behind them in lines, creating one solid V-formation of dragons and DCA that shot ahead of the flying citadels and stretched across their front.

The fighting spirit of those in the formation soared as they held their position, their wings battering the wind into submission as their speed increased.

Those on the ground looked up. Their hearts trembled under the pressure that the flying formation pressed down on all those who saw it. A steely, cold look filled their eyes.

They were halfway to the angels who were flying in their block formations when massive black clouds filled the air ahead of Force One.

A massive clawed foot descended from the clouds. Dominating in the extreme, it was nearly two times the size of Denur's. A powerful aura swept across the sky as wings shot out from the clouds, breaking them apart, revealing a dragon with scales that shone like black diamonds.

The dragon snorted.

"Angels? I prefer demons." Malsour's voice boomed through the heavens as magical circles for the second time that day appeared in the sky, wrapping around the demons who made up the DCA aerial forces.

Power flooded through Alkao. His muscles bulged as his body grew; his wings shook, growing larger as if they could block out the sun in the sky. His horns grew from his head, forming a crown as they turned obsidian black.

The demons all felt the surge of power; it filled their very bones, as they felt as if they had traced the outline of godhood. Their roars ended as they hovered in the sky for but a moment. Their eyes locked onto the angels.

Today, your blood will soak into Emerilia and your crusade will end. Alkao's thoughts resounded through his head as he flapped his wings. A gust of wind incomparable to that of before rushed through his body.

Malsour flapped his wings, taking up position above the inverted V-formation.

"Well, let's see how the angels like our new powers!" Alkao yelled through the party chat to the V-formation.

Demons and dragons roared, unleashing their anger upon the world.

"For Emerilia!" As Alkao's words fell, a second sun appeared in the sky as every person within the formation as well as Malsour unleashed their strongest attacks. The demons unleashed their most powerful spells or used their wristbands, overclocking the power going through them to get the most powerful blasts possible.

Dragon breath tore through the sky, meeting at a point ahead of the formation. Denur unleashed a spell that combined the effects of the dragon breaths, their attack turning from six colors to gray. The gray streams were thinner but as they reached in front of the angels, a spell formation appeared once again. The streams of dragon breath turned into a gray rain.

The flying citadels separated behind Force One, headed for different points around Markolm as they focused their artillery on the Alturarans or armies of Light that they saw on the ground.

They were now crossing over the edge of Markolm with bay doors and drop chutes opening, ready for the drop forces that would descend upon Markolm.

The angels activated the large-scale barriers they had. Shock filled them as the gray rain impacted the large shields. Each impact sounded like metal striking metal as the barriers started to shake. The angels shot out attacks at the dragons and demons. Here and there, the different attacks hit one another, resulting in mutual destruction and damaging the surrounding spells.

The air was filled with chaotic and brilliant explosions that only increased in ferocity as the two forces closed in on one another.

Orbs appeared around Force One. If someone was to know Dave, they would think these orbs similar. They were the same ones that he and Party Zero had used to protect themselves as they charged into the Dark Lord's hall.

They unleashed Mana bolts that destroyed incoming spells as a Mana barrier appeared between all of them.

There were thousands in the sky; all of the orbs that the Terra Alliance had were devoted to protecting those in the formation.

Alkao looked at the angels. They were more than double the number of demons and dragons that had taken the field of battle. Instead of feeling despair, he felt alive, if he was to die today, he would do so alongside those that he woul call his brothers and sisters, no matter their race, species or background, here they were all Emerilians fighting for their home.

He pulled his sword free from its sheath. The sound of his blade ringing, heard clear across the formation, as they were just a few hundred meters from the angels.

Weapons were freed as the dragons unleashed their dragon breaths. There was no time for another gray rain attack.

The formation followed in on the tails of the attack.

The two forces didn't slow down in the slightest as their forces piled into one another. The screams of pain and clashes of weapons filled the air as explosions from spells shook the battlefield.

The orbs retracted immediately, four to a person, creating personal Mana barriers and firing Mana bolts nonstop.

Alkao met an angel head on. The angel made to swing; Alkao's sword snapped out, hitting them with the flat of the blade. Their barrier shattered as they flew back, like a kite without its strings. With a flap of his wings, he was past the angel, who was looking up in the sky in disbelief, its body cut in two.

Alkao wheeled around with those who had passed through the angels. They formed up together, their wings beating the air into submission as they fought against it and gravity. Alkao raised his hand, unleashing Mana bolts. The orbs followed his fire and shot at the same angel. Under the attacks, the angel's Mana barrier collapsed as Krenua, Alkao's old bodyguard, slammed his sword through the opening in their helmet.

There was no time to look around, only to react, as the sky was filled with fighting.

The angels were stronger on a level-by-level basis, but the demons hadn't stopped training since they'd come back. Now, with their new strength as well as the weapons and tools they'd gained from Dave and their allies, they were evenly matched. Maybe with an advantage. The angels were used to holding sway over the people of Emerilia, those who wouldn't be stronger than Level 100. The demons were used to fighting those stronger than them and putting their full effort forward at all times.

Alkao was not the leader of Devil's Crater or Force One anymore. Here and now, he was just another demon fighting in the swirling fight above Markolm.

The flying citadels were now moving around Force One.

***

Admiral Osh'Rhal watched the feeds with rapt attention, cheering at times, others silent as he waited out the end of the battle, his hearts rolling in his abdomen.

Then an alarm broke through it all, a dark expression on his face as he paused the feed and opened up the alert.

His frown turned into one of shock and then thinned into anger. He pressed a button on his control chair, connecting to the command center that was based in the moon that had been turned into a base for the Jukal forces overseeing Emerilia. "What's going on? There's something about an AI issue?"

"We have a rogue AI! It's not listening to our commands and it's infected all of the AI that are connected to the Emerilia infrastructure!" Admiral Osh'Rhal's second-in-command yelled out.

"What do you mean? How is that even possible?" Osh'Rhal demanded.

"It looks like this AI was connected to all of the other AIs. It created backdoors and the entire Emerilia system was based upon it. It was thought that it was offline, but instead it was operating in all the different AIs that are across Emerilia. Now it's been activated by Lo'kal and he has complete control over the feeds from Emerilia!" the second-in-command said.

"Change to the backups and wipe that AI out! I want to know what's going on down there! Get me the controller commander and tell him what you told me. I'll be in the command center in a few minutes," Osh'Rhal said.

"Yes, sir," the second-in-command said.

Osh'Rhal didn't send a message up the chain of command. Instead, he sent a message to his clan. In the Jukal Empire, being part of the right clan, by either marrying or being born into it, would either make a person's life easy with nothing barring their way, or they would have to fight to gain those positions.

Reporting it up the chain of command might alert those who were part of competing clans and they could use this to show the incompetence of the Rhal clan. Thus, sending a message to his family to see what was the best reaction politically was a good way to alert the clan to any fallout or make the best of the situation for the family's gain.

What he didn't know was that his second-in-command had already done the same thing, sending the information back to their clan before making a decision on it. This was part of the political system that ran the Jukal Empire.

He finally got word back from his clan, slowing his pace to the command center so that he wouldn't get there before he knew what he was doing.

He puffed out his furred chest after getting the message and then walked into the command center, where there were a number of the different screens now filled with alerts.

"What's happened?" A faint panic settled in the pit of his four stomachs, as it seemed that things had changed rapidly as he had moved from his quarters to the command center.

"We moved to the backups and..." Rhal's second-in-command didn't know what to say but instead pointed to the main screen, where there was a portal underwater with a shield covering it. Every few moments, there was a flash of light as something coming through the portal hit the shield and was torn apart.

"What is that?"

"It's the portal in the Per'ush bay. There's some kind of shield that has been strapped to it and we have no control over it," the second-in-command said, their eyes wide as their tongue shot out, showing their nervousness.

Rhal looked at it, his sense of panic rising. "What does the operating procedure say?"

"Kill those who interfere with the portals, but we don't know who did it! I went into the logs and the teleportation is coming from an unknown device," the second-in-command said.

"Unknown device? All teleportation devices are tagged throughout the empire!" Rhal said in disbelief.

"Other than the ones on Emerilia," the second-in-command said.

Silence fell over the command center. Everyone looked to the two leaders, their eyes wide and their tongues moving, their nervousness clear. These were all people who had come from some of the more powerful families. They were doing their military service and were hopeful that in their time at Emerilia they could make a name for themselves that would benefit the clans they came from.

They were not used to making decisions but instead following what their clan elders said and then trying to increase their connections and power in the meantime.

"So, you're saying that one of the gods did this?" Rhal asked, his voice now hoarse as he stopped his tongue from coming out and showing the anxiety that was building.

"No, this wasn't done by the gods. I checked—all of the AI for them are running on a system separate to the overwatch AI that monitor Emerilia and also run the different sensors and systems," the second-in-command said. He didn't add in the fact he had only done this as his clan had walked him through his job every step of the way.

"Who the hell is doing all of this?" Rhal yelled. His tongue flickered out into the air as he looked at the different alerts coming up.

A new one flared to life, accompanied with a voice. "Lo'kal has been confirmed to be assisting the people of Emerilia to rebel against the Jukal Empire. Terminate project Emerilia." The dull AI's voice shook all of those within the station.

Rhal heard the message and read the same lines on the screen in front of him. His face turned ugly as he sat into his seat. "Prepare the drones. Send them down to Emerilia and kill Lo'kal. Wipe out the *Datskun* carrier. Lock down all of the god AIs," Rhal said, making one of the first decisions of his life.

Then, to his shock, everything changed.

***

"I have been found out." Anna's voice came through the command center of the destroyer that Dave and the rest of Party Zero were on. This was one of the few that were supposed to be battleships built in the ark yards but had instead been recycled and turned into destroyers. It was one of three that had been built within Emerilia.

"Josh! Don't drop people from the flying citadels—drop toward the planet now!" Dave yelled out through a Mirror of Communication as he pulled up an interface. With each press of a button, messages were sent out and orders were given.

In the sky above Markolm, one moment Force One was fighting off the angels; the next they had disappeared.

All of the onos over Emerilia were warming up as power surged through the hidden soul gem construct compartment underneath it.

"Open Pandora's Box!" Dave barked.

Across the second moon around Emerilia, explosive charges went off. Hundreds of missile tubes were revealed in a single moment. As soon as the tubes were cleared of debris hiding the tubes, missiles poured out from the tubes.

The cannons that had been run out from the dwarven mountains now erupted, not with artillery shells or grand working shells but missiles that tore out from the tubes before angling upward and to the heavens.

"Kill switch is active!" Jeeves called out.

Those who didn't have the Band-Aid blocking the signal died in just moments, their bodies being eaten from the inside as the nanites that had made them stronger now destroyed them. The angels, the armies of Light, those who had been part of the event of Myths and Legends and born on Emerilia—all of them were being killed.

Only the creatures and beasts of Emerilia were left alive.

The Band-Aid blocked the signal, transmitting information to the onos that sent it back to Jeeves that decoded the signal and blocked it. In less than a second, the kill switch was stopped and Jeeves started to destroy the parts of the kill switch that were inside the bodies of the people of Emerilia with the Band-Aid.

Markolm started to drop downward. The flying citadels that were now dropping toward the ground as fast as possible started to fire shells that had never been seen on Emerilia before.

These were fusion bombs in the shape of grand working shells.

They buried deep into Markolm before exploding. The island started to shatter as the Alturarans still on and inside the planet were rocked with power that they couldn't easily fight.

The dwarven mountains of Donsk and Zolu fired their mountain cannons.

As Markolm was falling, it started to break apart into smaller and smaller pieces. These pieces rained down on the Mana barrier that was growing from the onos underneath. More and more blue pillars reached into the sky, creating Mana barriers that reached out to connect with one another.

"Teleport to Markolm!" Dave yelled as the destroyer he was on and its three compatriots disappeared from their slips, appearing over Heval.

"Destroy that island!" Dave yelled. The destroyer shuddered as all along its length, cannon and missile ports opened, unleashing their rage. The two other destroyers did the same. Markolm became smaller and smaller. The impacts that were breaking it apart hammered the shield that was underneath.

The debris started to rain down on the ono-powered shield. The shield took on the impacts, only discoloring from the impacts instead of being destroyed.

"Incoming from the orbitals!" the captain called out.

Dave shook his head and pressed a button on the interface. The ono's shield pushed around Markolm, allowing it in as it dropped toward Emerilia.

The cities below were supposed to have been evacuated; he hoped everyone had got out, but now he needed that shield to cover Emerilia, not just the area around where Markolm had been.

"Fire on the orbitals and get us out of here," Dave said, hoping that they had broken up Markolm enough.

As the destroyer disappeared once again, all of the onos that had been seeded across Emerilia finally connected their shields with the others and started to pump more power into it. The thin shield became more and more solid as it expanded into the heavens to cover all of Emerilia.

The Jukal satellites that watched over the entire planet activated their second ability and started to shoot down onto Emerilia. Here and there, they hit missiles that were shooting into the heavens.

Missiles opened up, turning into warheads that shot out to deal with as many of the orbitals as possible.

"Bob is doing something to help," Anna said.

All across Emerilia, a gray glow fell around every single person and creature. Few had seen a spell that consisted of gray Mana. As the gray Mana made it into their bodies, their strength grew in an explosive manner.

As their strength grew, information and memories filled their minds. These were Bob's memories as Lo'kal and as he had looked over Emerilia. It was his knowledge of the human race, the Jukal, their empire and everything he had done.

Dave let out a breath, his mind reeling with the information. "What was that?"

"Well, Fire made the dragons, Light made the angels, and Dark made the demons. But Bob, he made Emerilia," Anna said.

Dave looked at the plots. The missile boats were rushing out of the moonbase, firing missiles as soon as they were clear. The first of the Jukal orbitals were being hit by the missiles on the ground.

Explosions shook the sky as the shield over Emerilia continued to grow, covering nearly the entire planet.

The orbitals hit the shield but it remained firm. Hundreds of onos all powered one shield as destruction reigned supreme on the other side.

Missiles shot out from the Jukal military base, tracking for the *Datskun*. Interceptor modules that had been hidden under explosive panels were now revealed. Mana bolts and disruptor rays shot out, destroying the missiles as the last of the missile boats left the moonbase.

The exit they had come pouring out of changed, showing instead of the interior of the moonbase, the inside of the asteroid base.

Destroyers shot forward and through the event horizon, teleporting as soon as they were in-system, headed for the military base.

The first battleship came through the portal connecting the Nal system to Emerilia. Its massive cannons fired as soon as it could, aimed at the Jukal fleet that was still in a holding pattern around the Jukal military base.

Drones shot out from the base, looking to engage the forces that were amassing outside of Emerilia's atmosphere.

"Massive teleportation magic," one of the sensor officers called out.

Dave saw as gray Mana wrapped around Markolm. One minute, it was there; the next, it had appeared in the middle of the Emerilian sea.

"Yes!" Dave slapped his console with a smile on his face. "That's my fucking Bob!"

"Kids all hopped up on Mountain Dew," Steve said in the background. There was a familiar noise from the back of the command center as Lox gave a satisfied snort.

"Time we earned our pay," Gurren said.

"That it is," Lox said, leaving the command center with Bob.

"All ships are currently on their way from the asteroid base, moving to the Jukal Moon Base," Suzy said, as if it were just another day at the office.

"Malsour is taking the flying citadels to destroy the remaining Alturarans before they have time to hide in Emerilia," Induca said.

"Self-destruct of Emerilia was activated. Good thing we never installed it," Anna said in a pleased voice.

Dave watched the orbitals fighting the missiles but it was a losing battle as they were wiped out. For the first time ever, Emerilia was no longer covered by satellites watching those below.

"The player farms at the north and south pole have been destroyed. However, Air is now in the process of reviving them all. Bob has moved to the ice planet to assist," Jeeves said.

"The Jukal fleet is on the move. They're sending out all their drones and activating any weapon platforms they have left," Anna said.

Dave watched it all as the Emerilian fleets formed up around their battleships, all of their cannons and tubes firing as fast as they could. The Jukal shields started to shake more and more violently as the Emerilian fleet were using barrier busters.

Finally the shield gave way and the fleet started to use their more powerful weapons. The fleet teleported behind the moon for the best firing positions.

The cannons were covered in runic lines that lit up the darkness, recoiling and firing at a steady and impressive pace, not stopping once.

The moonbase was being torn apart, its shields gone; the fusion grand workings landed, tearing out great sections of the base.

The Jukal fleet might have taken some time to react to what was going on but, to their credit, once they saw the threat that was now pounding on their door, they started to fire everything and anything they had at the Emerilian fleet.

Their beams shot out, striking out at the Emerilian shields before they were met by the disrupting beams that caused the beams to malfunction and the impact on the shields was barely noticeable.

However, the Emerilian fleet's reaction wasn't small.

The darkness of space was lit with the angry barrages of the modified cannons and the shells from the interceptor modules. Explosions of warheads dotted the thousands of kilometers between the Jukal forces and the Emerilian ships.

The last of the Jukal missiles exploded against the massive shield that now covered all of Emerilia.

The broken satellites that had been watching the Emerilians for hundreds of years, that had been torn apart, now smashed into the shield, turning into smaller pieces that flew off into space.

Across Emerilia, in both the day and night sky, they saw the blue shield as impacts rained down on it and in the distance, explosions from the battle between the Jukal and Emerilian fleets could be seen out in space.

In different cities, teleport pads were activated, linking to massive ships. People were ushered through; whole cities being evacuated in just minutes. As they stepped through the portals, they found that they were actually entering the arks that were located deep within Emerilia.

Others were retreating to Terra, which had onos connecting them to a secondary hub that activated and connected to Ice City. Thousands of people were moved out of Emerilia in a flood.

No matter what, after this we will survive in some way and we will fight back, Dave thought as the Jukal destroyer's shield cracked. The entire Emerilian fleet concentrated on it, tearing it apart in just a few minutes as Jung Lee's Light penetrator grand workings reached the ship. Golden light ate through the hull of the ship, cutting nearly a third of the way through it as the missiles shot into the new opening and detonated.

Inside the ship, the explosions were much worse.

The ship broke apart into sections as more golden rays cut into the parts of the ship that were still intact, boring their way in and then detonating. The ship's superstructure was shattered, the ship nothing more than debris that continued to be broken apart further and rocked by more explosions.

The cannons and weapons of the Emerilian fleet turned to the second destroyer and unleashed their anger.

The drones now made it into range of the Emerilian fleet.

The destroyers hunted the small and maneuverable drones. The battleships' guns that weren't aimed at the Jukal base and interceptor modules created streaks of light in the abyss around the ship. The missile boats stayed in the protection of the other ships; using their interceptor modules, they didn't have massive cannons but rather the heavy striking power filled with innumerable missiles.

Even under attack, they flushed more and more missiles toward the second destroyer. There were sixty of the ships in the void of space near the moonbase. The Jukal destroyer did its best to try to stave off its destruction but it wasn't enough as its shields crumbled. Its hull holed and then was torn apart with the power of grand workings.

The carrier didn't last as long as the destroyers as the Emerilian fleets were now closer and there was less time for it to react and try to escape the destruction that rained down on it.

Still the drones rushed over the Emerilian fleets. But they weren't organized, hitting anything they saw, trying to inflict as much damage as possible.

With their fire spread out too much and dealing with so many targets, they could hurt the fleet's shields but they weren't able to actually break any of them as the fleet turned their attention to the drones.

"I've got the Jukal feeds. I am now uploading this battle to the Jukal net and across the Mirror of Communication news boards," Anna said.

"Good," Dave said.

The drones were whittled away; it only took a cannon blast or two to destroy them, but they were fast and nimble so it required a number of cannons saturating the void to destroy their target.

The void once again became peaceful. As new platforms were detected, the missile boats spared no expense, smashing their shields and then destroying the platforms that hid underneath.

"Ready the destroyers to drop the Devastator corps," Dave said.

His words passed through the fleet as the destroyers moved their positions in the fleets, angled at the moon.

"Begin bombardment," Dave said, his voice cold and merciless as the sky once again lit up. The bombardment that had been halted continued once again. The barrier that had been recovered was now torn apart. The fleets fired into the Jukal military base. Their weapons' fire converging into one point made the moon itself shake with the power of the cannons grand working rounds and the missiles that tore holes into the moon.

The bombardment slowed down as there was nothing that even resembled a structure on the moon anymore.

"All infrastructure within the Emerilia system is now under our command," Anna said.

The *Datskun* that had been in orbit around Emerilia for the last five centuries now shed armor panels, revealing runic lines underneath that glowed as the massive carrier started to move to join up with the Emerilian fleet.

Five destroyers teleported to the Pandora moonbase. Three watched over two whose undersides glowed with runic lines as units wearing Devastator armor landed on the moon's surface. The runic lining glowed across their bodies with various different weapons conjured in their hands as they rushed forward.

Dave changed his view. The Jukal military base was buried deep; if they wanted to kill them all, they would need to destroy the moon, or send in ground forces to end them.

The Devastator-armored units were met with plasma rounds. To those who lived on Emerilia, they were nothing but reasonably powered fireballs. Shields smacked away the plasma as they unleashed Mana bolts and arrows that passed silently through the airless vacuum, hitting the Jukal and their drones with so much force that they simply exploded.

Spells raged through the corridors of the military base, frying the Jukal electronics as fire storms burned through their armor and bodies.

In their Devastator armor, it wasn't even a contest between the POE melee fighters and the Jukal.

They had never fought close combat before in their lives. They were a race that knew how to press buttons and nothing more. In the face of the Emerilian steel, they weren't even as hard to kill as Level 100 creatures; only their armor and space suits made it harder to kill them.

Dave shook his head at the Jukal.

They had developed the nanite augmentation technology to make it so that the races of the empire were better suited for their jobs. They had given it to the Emerilians, so that they could fight the aggressive species and survive on Emerilia.

However, the Jukal saw the augmentation as something that only those who were not Jukal might ever use. They looked down on it and as such, none of the Jukal actually used the technology. Instead, their vassals and those under their command did.

However, in Emerilia, to make sure that if anything did go wrong that no one would hesitate, they were all Jukal. All they had was powered armor and drones that put up something of a fight until they got hit with spells or a rogue got up behind them and landed a critical hit.

"Transferring all money from Rock Breakers Corporation and all of the accounts we have access to," Suzy said.

Dave's notifications lit up as Anna had left some of the coding from the AI connecting Emerilia to Earth. All of those trillions opened up the coffers of the AI vaults hidden across Emerilia as resources flowed into the Grahslagg Corporation and Dave's accounts. In turn, he sent Kol a message; all of those resources would be shipped to the different bases and used for the war effort.

"The military base has been cleared," Jeeves reported a few minutes later.

Dave continued to hold onto the console in front of him. He felt if he let go, then he would fall to the ground. He simply couldn't believe that they had been able to secure Emerilia.

"First arks are leaving," Jeeves said as arks appeared in front of the moonbase's portal, teleporting from where they'd been located in Emerilia.

They passed through the massive portal and entered the asteroid base, moving for massive open slips to allow those within their hulls to offload.

"Send the remaining destroyers and their Devastator forces to Emerilia to clear out any more aggressive species. Close the portals and offer the Jakan a ride through a portal back to their home world or they can have Nal if they want to help us defeat the Jukal. I want patrols around the entire Emerilian system and a sensor net around it." As Dave's orders fell, the people in the room rushed to complete them and pass it on to the rest of the Initiative's forces.

For the first time in its history, Emerilia was now controlled by humanity and all of its sub-races.

"All infrastructure created by the Jukal has been sent destruction orders," Anna said.

Dave nodded, seeing on a side screen as Altars of Rebirth were destroyed and the portals started to act erratically. With a press of a button on his interface, the portals all stabilized, coming under his full control while it would look like to the Jukal as if they still controlled them.

"We've got a lot to do and not much time to do it in." Dave took a steadying breath as he saw the people moving through the room with confident movements as the fleets started to teleport away to the different areas in the system and drop off sensor buoys.

He looked back and to the side where Deia stood.

Sensing his eyes, she looked to him. She smiled. There was no judgement, no anger or sadness; there was hope and belief in him. She rested her hand on his back, comforting him.

Dave stood up, putting an arm around her waist and pulling her to his side as he kissed the side of her head. He'd done the best that he could out of a situation he'd been thrown into. Now his cards had been revealed.

He would have to play them to victory, or to the annihilation of Emerilia.

Emerilia will be continued in Empire Burning.

Want a bigger map of Emerilia and the continents? Check out **http://theeternalwriter.deviantart.com/**

You can check out my other books, what I'm working on and upcoming releases through the following means:

Website: **http://michaelchatfield.com/**

Twitter: **@chatfieldsbooks**[1]

Facebook: **Michael Chatfield**[2]

Goodreads: **Goodreads.com/michaelchatfield**[3]

Thanks again for reading! ☺

Interested in more LitRPG? Check out **https://www.facebook.com/groups/LitRPGsociety/**

And

---

1.   https://twitter.com/chatfieldsbooks

2.   https://www.facebook.com/michaelchatfieldsbooks/?ref=hl

3.   https://www.goodreads.com/author/show/14055550.Michael_Chatfield

**https://www.facebook.com/groups/
LitRPGGroup/**

Continue on for Character Sheet!

In Alphabetical order
Ankol

Dwarf

Dwarven Master Smith. Smithing Art: Metal Spinner. Lives in Grorart Mountain.

Boran-Al

Lich

One of the Dark Lord's Champions. Works directly under the Dark Lord. Creates Creatures of Power and carry's out the Dark Lord's orders. His Citadel was destroyed.

Alastair Montgoa

Arch Lich aka former Lord Vailyn. Gave up his fellow Aleph to have everlasting life; used the centuries to build strength and knowledge

Barry

Dwarf

Dwarven Master Smith. Smithing Art-Unknown. Wandering smith.

Cassie

Elf/Human Halfling

Holy warrior. Leader of the Golden Sabres. In a relationship with Josh Giles.

Dark Lord

God

Embodiment of the Dark affinity. Created Demons. Normally an ally with the Earth Lord. Always looking a way to tip the power balance of Emerilia in his favor.

Dasano

Dwarf

Dwarven Master Smith. Smithing Art: Metal Press. Lives in Grorart Mountain.

Akatol Dracul

Dragon

Water Mage. Was the second Dragon, Denur's husband. Went mad and started a genocide, disappeared.

Denur Dracul

Dragon

Fire Mage Hailed as 'Mother of Dragons'. First of her race, a creature of power created by the Lady of Fire. Seen as her daughter. Sister to Oson' Deia.

Gelimah Dracul

Dragon
    Dark Mage. Brother to Induca, Louna and Malsour

Fornau Dracul

Dragon

Earth Mage. Quindar's mate Malsour and Induca's grand-nephew.

Induca Dracul

Dragon

Fire Mage. One of the youngest from the first generation of Dragons. Sister to Malsour, daughter of Denur, aunt to Quindar, great aunt to Fornau. Member of the Stone Raiders and Party Zero.

Kinal Dracul

Dragon

Louna Dracul

Dragon
Induca, Gelimah and Malsour's sister.

Malsour Dracul

Dragon

Dark Mage. One of the oldest Dragons in existence, first born of Denur. Deia and Induca's Guardian, Stone Raider and Party Zero member. Brother to Induca. Great Uncle to Fornau Dracul and Uncle to Quindar Dracul.

Quindar Dracul

Dragon
Wind Mage, wife to Fornau, Niece to Induca and Malsour.

Wokui Dracul

Dragon
  Water Mage

Xednai Dracul

Dragon

One of the first Dragons, had several Dragons. Her son is Fornau.

Gorpal Dunsk

Dwarf

Dwarven Master Smith, lives in Aldamire Mountain, created 3 Weapons of Power - Mace of Fury, Tower Shield, Boots of Smash. Smithing Art: Paint Copy

Earth Lord

God
> Embodiment of the Dark affinity. Created Earth Sprites.

Edmur

Dwarf

Dwarven Master Smith. Had been in the Dwarven War Bands as a Shield Bearer. Former pupil of Quino's Brother to Endur. Smithing Art: Metal's Song

Edwards

Human. Military scientist within the Deq'ual System. Friend of
Sato's

Edwin

Beast Kin. Beast Kin representative on ruling council.

Endur

Dwarf

Dwarven Master Smith. Had been in the Dwarven War Bands as a Shield Bearer. Former pupil of Quino's, brother to Edmur, lives in Zolu Mountain. Smithing Art Hammer Blows

Esa

Human

Melee fighter. Member of Mikal and Jule's party. Fought at Bo-ranl-Al's Citadel.

Member of the Stone Raiders. Going out with Jules. Works under Dwayne as a fighter. Being trained for a leadership position under Dwayne.

Lord Esamael

Human.

Lord of Emaren within the Gudalo Kingdom.

Ela-Gal

High Elf.

Warrior living in Aleph, married to Ela'Dorn. Persectued by high elves as heretic.

Ela-Dorn

Orc.

Researcher and professor at Aleph College. Aleph Council Member. Married to Ela-Gal

Fend

Dwarf
    Lord Under the Mithsia Mountains.

Geswald

Human.

Trader's Guild Chapter head in Emaren.

David Grahslagg

Dwarf/Human Halfling, in-game character of Austin Zane. Dwarven Master Smith, Resident of Cliff Hill, member of Party Zero and the Stone Raider's Guild. Other names: Austin Zane

Josh Giles

Human

Rogue. Leader of the Stone Raiders. Was a investment broker on Earth, became an E-head. In a relationship with Cassie from the Golden Sabres.

Gimel

Human
  Warrior.
  Fellox Guild Master.

Gorrund

Dwarf

Dwarven Master Smith in Benvari Mountain with Jesal, teaching four apprentices. Smithing Art: Blood Bender.

Goula

Demon
On the Ruling council for Devil's Crater.

Gurren

Dwarf

Shield bearer, member of Dwarven War Band under Lox's command, sent to guide people to Cliff-Hill. Friend of David Grahslagg, Kol's Grandson. Member of the Stone Raiders.

Helick

Dwarf
  Dwarven Master Smith.

Kim Isdola

Human

Cleric/alchemist. Lieutenant in Stone Raiders.

Ishox

Demon
On the Ruling council for Devil's Crater.

Arch-Mage Jekoni

Human/item

Soul bound to Staff of Growing, over 2,000 years old; missing legs. Held within Dwarven Vaults with other Weapons of power.

Jeeves

AI

Made by Bob to assist the Dwarven Master Smiths.

Jeremy

Human

Fellox Guild member.

Jesal

Dwarf

Dwarven Master Smith, Dave's master smith trainer. Smithing art: Nature's Guide

Jules

Human

Healer. Member of Mikal and Esa's party. Fought at Boranl-Al's Citadel.

Member of the Stone Raiders. Used to be an army medic, E-head without legs IRL. Going out with Esa. Works under Lucy as support, leads the healers of the Stone Raiders.

Joko

Dwarf

Shield bearer, member of Dwarven War Band under Lox's command, sent to guide people to Cliff-Hill. Friend and trainer of David Grahslagg.

Deceased.

Anna'Kal

Wolf Beast Kin/Administrator AI24681

Air mage. Originally a program meant to assist Lo'kal with the running of Emerilia. Anna was uploaded to a Player body and inserted into Emerilia. She became emotionally attached with her charges. When the Beast Kin people were wiped out from Emerilia she went into cold storage, waiting for her father to awake her when a chance came to fight against the prison they had created.

Member of the Stone Raiders and Party Zero. Daughter of Bob.

Lo'kal

Jukal

Scientist, created Emerilia. Awarded the position of the Gray God, maintains Emerilia, its people and Players. Other names: Bob, Bobby McMahnon, The Balancer, Gray God.

Kino

Demon
On the Ruling Council for Devil's Crater.

Kol

Dwarf

Dwarven Master Smith. Gurren's grandfather. Resides in Cliff-Hill. Taught Dave how to Smith. Runs his Smithies. Smithing art: Blind Man's Touch

Lady of Air

Goddess

Embodiment of the affinity Air. Known for causing mischief. Her Champions act as spies and information brokers, tilting the balance of Emerilia.

Lady of Fire

Goddess

Created Dragons, Mages Guild and College. Gave gift of 'knowledge' to the people of Emerilia. Mother to Deia, Lover of Oson'Mal and best friend with Bob.

Other Names: Ignil

Lady of Light

Goddess

Sent Players to kill/capture Dragons to make her own Creatures of Power. Created the race known as Angels. Large rivalry with the Dark Lord.

Lena

Demon
On the Ruling Council of Devil's Crater. Wife to Vrexu.

Lovan

Dwarf
  Mithsia Mountain Warclan leader

Lox

Dwarf

Shield bearer. Was the commander of the War Band sent to guide people to Cliff-Hill. Friend of David Grahslagg. Member of the Stone Raiders.

Suzy Markell

Human (IRL)

High Elf (Emerilia)

Austin Zane's secretary and best friend. David Grahslagg's best friend and assistant with running Cliff Hill Smithy and Factory. Summoning Mage. Steven's contractor, member of Party Zero and the Stone Raiders.

Max

Dwarf

Shield bearer, member of Dwarven War Band under Lox's command, sent to guide people to Cliff-Hill. Friend of David Grahslagg.

Deceased.

Meda

Dwarf/Elf

Aleph Council member. Deals with the food within Aleph cities and facilities

Melanie

Human
Arch Mage Alamos' Wife.

Melhoun

Water snake made by the Water Lord.
Sealed away.

Mikal

Human

Rogue. Jules and Esa's party member. Member of the Stone Raiders. Friends with Party Zero.

Oson'Deia

Elf/Demi God Halfling

Elven Ranger and Fire Mage. Daughter of Oson'Mal and Lady Fire of the Affinity Pantheon. Resident of Cliff Hill and member of the Stone Raider's Guild, Leader of Party Zero.

Other names: Ouluv'Deia

Penelope

Human
Fellox Guild member.

Pete

Human
> Geswald's secretary.

Queen Farun

High Elf
 Queen of Raolor.

Queen Mendari Selhi

Human

Queen of Selhi.

Quino

Dwarf

Dwarven Master Smith, lives in Zolu Mountain. Trained the brothers Endur and Edmur. Smithing Art: Internal cutting.

Rola

Dwarf

Dwarven Master Smith. Smithing Art Puppeteer. Lives in Aldamire Mountain.

Sato/Communications officer Sato

Human

Lives in De'qual system.

Communications Officer, becomes Vice commander of Deq'ual military forces. Grandfather original settler.

Emperor Talis

Human.

Ruler of the Xeugrera Empire, located in the Ashal Continent.

Tounk

Dwarf

Shield bearer, member of Dwarven War Band under Lox's command, sent to guide people to Cliff-Hill. Friend of David Grahslagg.

Deceased.
Demon Prince Alkao/Alkao Travezar

Aerial Demon

Melee fighter. Commander of the Third Demon Horde and leader of Xerzit lands. Oldest of the five remaining Demon Prince's of Devil's Crater.

Dwayne Trebault

Human

Melee fighter. Lieutenant in Stone Raiders. Leads and trains the melee fighters in the Stone Raiders.

Venfik

Elf

Lady Air's advisor.

Lucy Vernia

Wood Elf/Human

Lieutenant in Stone Raiders. Spy master, deals with supporting the Stone Raiders and paperwork.

Vrexu

Demon

One of the seven Demon Princes. General in the Devil's Crater Army. Married to Lena, the youngest of the five remaining Demon Princes.

Water Lord

God

Embodiment of the Water Affinity. Created the Mer-People and water creatures. Created the Water Serpent Melhoun. Rival to the Lady of Fire.

Austin Zane

CEO of Rock Breaker's Corporation. Engineer specializing in space vehicles. Background in Astro physics. Other names: David Grahslagg

Wis'Zel

Wood Elf

Bard. Works for David Grahslagg, managing his Ceramics factories in Cliff Hill.